STORIES BY ELIZABETH BOWEN

Stories
by
Elizabeth Bowen

NEW YORK: VINTAGE BOOKS

1959

PREFACE

OFTEN, at different times, I thought I should like to select from my own stories—re-read them, as an entire muster, and re-evaluate them as I thus saw them. Intermittently I have been writing short stories for what, now, is more than thirty-six years: no wonder a mass of them has amounted! A selection, I felt, should act as a sort of pointer to those which could be considered the most enduring, the most valid, the most nearly works of art. Those chosen should be those fit to survive—stories on which my reputation, if any, could hope to rest. Also from the first I have had my favourites, dearer, more satisfying to me than others; those, I thought, I should easily single out. The selection (this volume, as I envisaged it) was to have about it an ideality—not that any one story I had written *had* been ideal, but the best should gain, and set one another off, by being no longer crowded by lesser neighbours.

Now it comes to the point, now that I am invited to make my choice and draw up my list, it is not so simple. Choice, for instance, involves judgement; judgement requires a long perspective. Can I stand far enough away from my own work? Also, there cannot but be something alarming about the finality of my own decisions: never shall I be able to appeal against them, for I made them! As I see it, this volume must "represent" my stories—as though on the assumption that those not in it are due to be blown away on the dust of time. What, exactly, do I want to have represented? What, throughout my life, have I been trying to do, and at which points have I come nearest doing it? Have I, since first I sat down to write, had always the same ideas, or have these altered?—my manner has changed, certainly. (This last is a question I have to raise, as I should with regard to the work of another author. But that is not to say that I can reply to it.) Above all, I am confronted by the question of fairness, justice—I must be fair to the writer, not less so because she has been myself; at the same time, I must do right by the public. The writer pleads to be shown at her best only, the public might prefer an "average" view. The fact is, that every short story is an experiment—what one must ask is not only, did it come off, but was it, as an experiment, worth making?

What kind of stories does, or did, Elizabeth Bowen write? This Vintage volume should be the answer. Some idea should be given of the range of subjects, of the technique and its variations, of the imaginative quality, and so on. Misfired pieces, possibly, should go in, alongside those better conceived or more fully realised—as against that, why misuse space when there's not much of it? Stories to be read should be good, as good as they can be: *here* even the best, alas, show cautionary errors to any student of writing who cares to look for them. I have decided to face criticism by offering stories which certainly do invite it, but which also should, in their ways, stand up to it. These eighteen pieces (the earliest written when I was twenty) can claim to be fair examples of themes and treatments. No, to be candid, though I say "fair" examples, these are the most hopeful I can produce. If I had written better stories, they would be here.

Not only—now that I settle down to my task—do I confront problems; I sustain disappointments. A number of "favourites," for instance, have played me false, failing under the test of severe re-reading. I must have cared for them, I can only think, for some subjective or associative reason, long since evaporated. Alternatively, they were (unbeknownst to me) synthetic; not pure in origin, but inspired, rather, by some intellectual fashion or aesthetic caprice—many of them were written some time ago; because they were *of* their day, in their day they pleased me. When I was young—and youth in a writer lasts—I was easily impressed; it appears now that there were moments when I impressed myself! Sad as it is, for whatever cause, several "favourites" have constituted my first discards. What were they but mirages in my memory? I fancied them better than they were.

Equally, I find that I discard stories which reek to me too much of myself, by exhibiting prejudices or sentiments —or, perhaps I should better say, by betraying them. In some, I do not seem to have been enough on guard against self-indulgence, which shows in infatuation with words for their own sakes, a doting upon effects which too much pleased me, or a tendency to revert to the same images. Result: the stories in question seem over-written, and, still worse, limited by *my* personality. I am dead against art's being "self-expression." I see an inherent failure in any story which fails to detach itself from the author's ego— detach itself in the sense that a well-blown soap bubble detaches itself from the bowl of the blower's pipe and spherically takes off into the air as a new, whole, pure, iridescent world. Whereas the ill-blown bubble, as children know, timidly adheres to the bowl's lip, then either bursts or sinks flatly back again.

Total impersonality in story writing is, for me certainly, impossible—so much so that it would be a waste of time to wonder whether it would be desirable. And I doubt, actually, whether for any writer it is either desirable or possible, for this reason: the short story is linked with poetry, and *that,* we know, cannot but bear a signature. The tale without lyricism or passion desiccates into little more than a document. The poet, and in his wake the short story writer, is using his own, unique susceptibility to experience: in a sense, the susceptibility *is* the experience. The susceptibility, equally, *is* the writer, who therefore cannot be absent from what he writes. The short story is at an advantage over the novel, and can claim its nearer kinship to poetry, because it must be more concentrated, can be more visionary, and is not weighed down (as the novel is bound to be) by facts, explanation, or analysis. I do not mean to say that the short story is by any means exempt from the laws of narrative: it must observe them, but on its own terms. Fewer characters, fewer scenes, and above all fewer happenings are necessary; shape and action are framed for simplification. As against that, there are dangers and can be penalties: essentially, at no point in the story must the electrical-imaginative current be found to fail. Novels legitimately have "slack" passages, which serve, like intermissions, to ease off the reader between crisis and crisis. But the short story revolves round one crisis only—one might call it, almost, a crisis in itself. There (ideally) ought to be nothing in such a story which can weaken, detract from, or blur the central, single effect.

This, I recognise, has been one idea I have kept before myself. In short story writing it has been my main aim, and at least as an aim it has been continuous. I state it, though without deluding myself that I have realised it, succeeded in it, in any one story. . . . To return to the matter of the personal, I repeat that one cannot wholly eliminate oneself for a second, and also sufficient, reason: any fiction (and surely poetry, too?) is bound to be transposed autobiography. (True, it may be this at so many removes as to defeat ordinary recognition.) I can, and indeed if I would not I still must, relate any and every story I have written to something that happened to me in my own life. But here I am speaking of happenings in a broad sense—to behold, and react, is where I am concerned a happening; speculations, unaccountable stirs of interest, longings, attractions, apprehensions without knowable cause—these are happenings also. When I re-read a story, I re-live the moment from which it sprang. A scene burned itself into me, a building magnetised me, a mood or season of Nature's penetrated me, history suddenly appeared to me in some tiny act, or a face had begun to haunt me before I glanced at it.

On the whole, places more often than faces have sparked off stories. To be honest, the scenes have been with me before the characters—it could have seemed to me, even, once or twice, as though the former had summoned the latter up. I do not feel, necessarily, that this is wrong: a story must come to life in its *own* order. Also, I re-assert what I said when discussing the art of Katherine Mansfield: I do not feel that the short story can be, or should be, used for the analysis or development of character. The full, full-length portrait is fitter work for the novelist; in the short story, treatment must be dramatic—we are dealing with man, or woman or child, in relation to a particular crisis or mood or moment, and to that only. Though (and as to this, law is stern) the crisis must be one in which such-and-such a character would be likely to be involved, or, still more, likely to precipitate; the mood must be one to which such-and-such a character would be likely to be prone, or still more, to heighten; the moment should essentially be *the* one which would, on the given character, act most strongly. Once a story truly germinates in my mind, the inevitable actors in it take form—and not only this, but they also take hold, to the point of remaining after the tale is told. I give, as examples, four stories in this selection: "The Storm," "Her Table Spread," "Ivy Gripped the Steps," "Mysterious Kôr." Each of these arose out of an intensified, all but spellbound beholding, on my part, of the scene in question—a fountain-filled Italian garden in livid, pre-thundery light; a shabbily fanciful Irish castle overlooking an estuary; an ivy-strangled house in a formerly suave residential avenue; or weird moonlight over bomb-pitted London. Each time I felt: "Yes, this affects me—but it would affect 'X.' more. Under what circumstances; for what reason? And who *is* 'X.'?" In each case, the "X." I pondered upon became the key character in the resultant story. . . . It could seem to me that stories, with their *dramatis personae,* pre-exist, only wait to be come upon! I know I do not invent them; I discover them. Though that does not mean that they are easily told. On me devolves the onus of the narration.

Fantasy . . . another important element. One may of course say that any story (from any pen) is the exercise or working-out of a fantasy—that any author of fiction, to write at all, must have recourse to his or her dreaming faculty. But in Elizabeth Bowen stories, it may be found, fantasy is often present twice over; part as it is of the fabric of the actual plot, or governor of the behaviour of the characters. Looking through this selection I have made, I find fantasy strongly represented. Critics may possibly say too much so? Yet these, I still maintain, are my better stories. If I were a short story writer only, I might well seem to be out of balance. But recall, more than half of my life is under the steadying influence of the novel, with its calmer, stricter, more orthodox demands: into the novel goes such taste as I have for rational behaviour and social portraiture. The short story, as *I* see it to be, allows for what is crazy about humanity: obstinacies, inordinate heroisms, "immortal longings." At no time, even in the novel, do I consider realism to be my forte. Fortunately, however, there are many other writers; taken all-in-all we complement one another—literature is a compost to which we are each contributing what we have. The best that an individual can do is to concentrate on what he or she *can* do, in the course of a burning effort to do it better.

A full and considerable number of years of life, plus more or less continuous care for writing, ought not altogether to go for nothing. I cannot attempt to outline my own development, though I cannot believe there has been none. The fact that this Vintage volume opens with a story about a little girl and closes with a story about a young girl reminds me how recurrent a subject, with me, have been youth and childhood. I cannot say that I see this to be "nostalgia"; for one thing, I now enjoy my own adult state. Rather I perceive how much I rely, in art, on immediacy and purity of sensation; and indubitably the young are unspoiled instruments. Many of the greatest writers of short stories, and poets, died before Time had stolen their freshness from them. I have remained in the world dangerously long: I hope there may still be something I need not forfeit.

ELIZABETH BOWEN

CONTENTS

CONTENTS

Coming Home

ALL the way home from school Rosalind's cheeks burnt, she felt something throbbing in her ears. It was sometimes terrible to live so far away. Before her body had turned the first corner her mind had many times wrenched open their gate, many times rushed up their path through the damp smells of the garden, waving the essay-book, and seen Darlingest coming to the window. Nothing like this had ever happened before to either her or Darlingest; it was the supreme moment that all these years they had been approaching, of which those dim, improbable future years would be spent in retrospect.

Rosalind's essay had been read aloud and everybody had praised it. Everybody had been there, the big girls sitting along the sides of the room had turned and looked at her, raising their eyebrows and smiling. For an infinity of time the room had held nothing but the rising and falling of Miss Wilfred's beautiful voice doing the service of Rosalind's brain. When the voice dropped to silence and the room was once more unbearably crowded, Rosalind had looked at the clock and seen that her essay had taken four and a half minutes to read. She found that her mouth was dry and her eyes ached from staring at a small fixed spot in the heart of whirling circles, and her knotted hands were damp and trembling. Somebody behind her gently poked the small of her back. Everybody in the room was thinking about Rosalind; she felt their admiration and attention lapping up against her in small waves. A long way off somebody spoke her name repeatedly, she stood up stupidly and everybody laughed. Miss Wilfred was trying to pass her back the red exercise-book. Rosalind sat down again thinking to herself how dazed she was, dazed with glory. She was beginning already to feel about for words for Darlingest.

She had understood some time ago that nothing became real for her until she had had time to live it over again. An actual occurrence was nothing but the blankness of a shock, then the knowledge that something had happened; afterwards one could creep back and look into one's mind and find new things in it, clear and solid. It was like waiting outside the hen-house till the hen came off the nest and then going in to look for the egg. She would not touch this egg until she was with Darlingest, then they would go and look for it together. Suddenly and vividly this afternoon would be real for her. "I won't think about it yet," she said, "for fear I'd spoil it."

The houses grew scarcer and the roads greener, and Rosalind relaxed a little; she was nearly home. She looked at the syringa-bushes by the gate, and it was as if a cold wing had brushed against her. Supposing Darlingest were out . . . ?

She slowed down her running steps to a walk. From here she would be able to call to Darlingest. But if she didn't answer there would be still a tortuous hope; she might be at the back of the house. She decided to pretend it didn't matter, one way or the other; she had done this before, and it rather took the wind out of Somebody's sails, she felt. She hitched up her essay-book under her arm, approached the gate, turned carefully to shut it, and walked slowly up the path looking carefully down at her feet, not up at all at the drawing-room window. Darlingest would think she was playing a game. Why didn't she hear her tapping on the glass with her thimble?

As soon as she entered the hall she knew that the house was empty. Clocks ticked very loudly; upstairs and downstairs the doors were a little open, letting through pale strips of light. Only the kitchen door was shut, down the end of the passage, and she could hear Emma moving about behind it. There was a spectral shimmer of light in the white panelling. On the table was a bowl of primroses; Darlingest must have put them there that morning. The hall was chilly; she could not think why the primroses gave her such a feeling of horror, then she remembered the wreath of primroses, and the scent of it, lying on the raw new earth of that grave. . . . The pair of grey gloves were gone from the bowl of visiting-cards. Darlingest had spent the morning doing those deathly primroses, and then taken up her grey gloves and gone out, at the end of the afternoon, just when she knew her little girl would be coming in. A quarter-past four. It was unforgivable of Darlingest: she had been a mother for more than twelve years, the mother exclusively of Rosalind, and still, it seemed, she knew no better than to do a thing like that. Other people's mothers had terrible little babies: they ran quickly in and out to go to them, or they had smoky husbands who came in and sat, with big feet. There was something distracted about other people's mothers. But Darlingest, so exclusively one's own. . . .

Darlingest could never have really believed in her. She could never have really believed that Rosalind would do anything wonderful at school, or she would have been more careful to be in to hear about it. Rosalind flung herself into the drawing-room; it was honey-coloured and lovely in the pale spring light, another little clock was ticking in the corner, there were more bowls of primroses and black-eyed, lowering anemones. The tarnished mirror on the wall distorted and reproved her angry face in its mild mauveness. Tea was spread on the table by the window, tea for two that the two might never . . . Her work and an open book lay on the tumbled cushions of the window-seat. All the afternoon she had sat there waiting and working, and now—poor little Darlingest, perhaps she had gone out because she was lonely.

People who went out sometimes never came back again. Here she was, being angry with Darlingest, and all the

time . . . Well, she had drawn on those grey gloves and
gone out wandering along the roads, vague and beautiful,
because she was lonely, and then?

Ask Emma? No, she wouldn't; fancy having to ask
her!

"Yes, your mother'll be in soon, Miss Rosie. Now run
and get your things off, there's a good girl—" Oh no, intolerable.

The whole house was full of the scent and horror of the
primroses. Rosalind dropped the exercise-book on the
floor, looked at it, hesitated, and putting her hands over
her mouth, went upstairs, choking back her sobs. She
heard the handle of the kitchen door turn; Emma was
coming out. O God! Now she was on the floor by Darlingest's bed, with the branches swaying and brushing outside the window, smothering her face in the eiderdown,
smelling and tasting the wet satin. Down in the hall she
heard Emma call her, mutter something, and slam back
into the kitchen.

How could she ever have left Darlingest? She might
have known, she might have known. The sense of in-
security had been growing on her year by year. A person might be part of you, almost part of your body, and
yet once you went away from them they might utterly
cease to be. That sea of horror ebbing and flowing round
the edges of the world, whose tides were charted in the
newspapers, might sweep out a long wave over them and
they would be gone. There was no security. Safety and
happiness were a game that grown-up people played with
children to keep them from understanding, possibly to
keep themselves from thinking. But they did think, that
was what made grown-up people—queer. Anything
might happen, there was no security. And now Darlingest—

This was her dressing-table, with the long beads straggling over it, the little coloured glass barrels and bottles
had bright flames in the centre. In front of the looking-
glass, filmed faintly over with a cloud of powder, Darlingest had put her hat on—for the last time. Supposing
all that had ever been reflected in it were imprisoned

somewhere in the back of a looking-glass. The blue hat with the drooping brim was hanging over the corner of a chair. Rosalind had never been kind about that blue hat, she didn't think it was becoming. And Darlingest had loved it so. She must have gone out wearing the brown one; Rosalind went over to the wardrobe and stood on tip-toe to look on the top shelf. Yes, the brown hat was gone. She would never see Darlingest again, in the brown hat, coming down the road to meet her and not seeing her because she was thinking about something else. Peau d'Espagne crept faintly from among the folds of the dresses; the blue, the gold, the soft furred edges of the tea-gown dripping out of the wardrobe. She heard herself making a high, whining noise at the back of her throat, like a puppy, felt her swollen face distorted by another paroxysm.

"I can't bear it, I can't bear it. What have I done? I did love her, I did so awfully love her.

"Perhaps she was all right when I came in; coming home smiling. Then I stopped loving her, I hated her and was angry. And it happened. She was crossing a road and something happened to her. I was angry and she died. I killed her.

"I don't know that she's dead. I'd better get used to believing it, it will hurt less afterwards. Supposing she does come back this time; it's only for a little. I shall never be able to keep her; now I've found out about this I shall never be happy. Life's nothing but waiting for awfulness to happen and trying to think about something else.

"If she could come back just this once—Darlingest."

Emma came half-way upstairs; Rosalind flattened herself behind the door.

"Will you begin your tea, Miss Rosie?"

"No. Where's mother?"

"I didn't hear her go out. I have the kettle boiling—will I make your tea?"

"No. *No.*"

Rosalind slammed the door on the angry mutterings, and heard with a sense of desolation Emma go downstairs. The silver clock by Darlingest's bed ticked; it was five o'clock. They had tea at a quarter-past four; Darlingest was never, never late. When they came to tell her about *It*, men would come, and they would tell Emma, and Emma would come up with a frightened, triumphant face and tell her.

She saw the grey-gloved hands spread out in the dust.

A sound at the gate. "I can't bear it, I can't bear it. Oh, save me, God!"

Steps on the gravel.

Darlingest.

She was at the window, pressing her speechless lips together.

Darlingest came slowly up the path with the long ends of her veil, untied, hanging over her shoulders. A paper parcel was pressed between her arm and her side. She paused, stood smiling down at the daffodils. Then she looked up with a start at the windows, as though she heard somebody calling. Rosalind drew back into the room.

She heard her mother's footsteps cross the stone floor of the hall, hesitate at the door of the drawing-room, and come over to the foot of the stairs. The voice was calling "Lindie! Lindie, duckie!" She was coming upstairs.

Rosalind leaned the weight of her body against the dressing-table and dabbed her face with the big powder-puff; the powder clung in paste to her wet lashes and in patches over her nose and cheeks. She was not happy, she was not relieved, she felt no particular feeling about Darlingest, did not even want to see her. Something had slackened down inside her, leaving her a little sick.

"Oh, you're *there*," said Darlingest from outside, hearing her movements. "Where did, where were—?"

She was standing in the doorway. Nothing had been for the last time, after all. She had come back. One could never explain to her how wrong she had been. She was holding out her arms; something drew one towards them.

"But, my little *Clown*," said Darlingest, wiping off the powder. "But, oh—" She scanned the glazed, blurred face. "Tell me why," she said.

"You were late."

"Yes, it was horrid of me; did you mind? . . . But that was silly, Rosalind, I can't be always in."

"But you're my mother."

Darlingest was amused; little trickles of laughter and gratification ran out of her. "You weren't *frightened*, Silly Billy." Her tone changed to distress. "Oh, Rosalind, don't be cross."

"I'm not," said Rosalind coldly.

"Then come—"

"I was wanting my tea."

"Rosalind, *don't* be—"

Rosalind walked past her to the door. She was hurting Darlingest, beautifully hurting her. She would never tell her about that essay. Everybody would be talking about it, and when Darlingest heard and asked her about it she would say: "Oh, that? I didn't think you'd be interested." That would hurt. She went down into the drawing-room, past the primroses. The grey gloves were back on the table. This was the mauve and golden room that Darlingest had come back to, from under the Shadow of Death, expecting to find her little daughter. . . . They would have sat together on the window-seat while Rosalind read the essay aloud, leaning their heads closer together as the room grew darker.

That was all spoilt.

Poor Darlingest, up there alone in the bedroom, puzzled, hurt, disappointed, taking off her hat. She hadn't known she was going to be hurt like this when she stood out there on the gravel, smiling at the daffodils. The red essay-book lay spread open on the carpet. There was the paper bag she had been carrying, lying on a table by the door; macaroons, all squashy from being carried the wrong way, disgorging, through a tear in the paper, a little trickle of crumbs.

The pathos of the forgotten macaroons, the silent pain! Rosalind ran upstairs to the bedroom.

Darlingest did not hear her; she had forgotten. She was standing in the middle of the room with her face turned towards the window, looking at something a long way away, smiling and singing to herself and rolling up her veil.

The Storm

"*DON'T* come near me," she said, turning sharply. "I hate you! Why do you keep on following me about?"

He said, "Well, we've got to go down in the same tram."

"I'll walk."

"Not with those heels. You couldn't."

"If you had any decency, you would."

"I don't care for walking those long distances down hill. It shakes me up. Besides, I feel another blister coming."

He stooped to feel one foot, and the crimson of his face deepened.

"O-oh!" she shuddered, pressing her handbag with both hands to her bosom, and grimacing up at the sky.

He peered over the parapet. "Hush," he said, "there are people on the terrace just below us, listening."

"Danish women," she said scornfully, looking over at the three flat hats, but she dropped into silence, shifting away from him as he leant forward and spread his elbows out on the parapet with a prolonged "Phew!" They were high up on the terrace of a Villa; dizzily high.

The air was warm and tense, stretched so taut that it quivered. Breathing had become an affair of consciousness, and movement they both felt to be impossible. Behind the terrace, the doorways of the Villa grew solid with darkness, the high façade loomed. Colour faded everywhere, the hills grew livid; forms assumed a menacing distinctness, blade-like against the architecture of the clouds.

Immeasurably below them, the trees were clotted together in the unnatural dusk. Steps from the terrace descended in a series of inexorable zig-zags. If one went down the steps into the depths of the garden, one might never come up again.

"I can't bear the noise of the fountains," she said angrily. "Why doesn't somebody stop them?—they get louder and louder."

He did not answer.

"What makes them like that, all of a sudden? Look at that pale strip, along the horizon. That's the sun shining over Rome." She thought of the streets and the houses and the bright, safe trams. "Why didn't we stay in Rome— *Rupert?*"

His squared shoulders looked broader than ever, but did not inspire confidence.

"I don't know why we ever came up here," she continued miserably.

"Well, you wanted to come . . ."

"Now you're going to be sulky. Oh, I can't think why we ever came to Italy at all!"

As he did not answer, she dragged herself a little further away from him down the terrace, trailing her gloved hand along the parapet. She could not bear to look down at the view any longer, nor dared she face the blind-eyed Villa behind her, so she stood with eyes shut, increasingly afraid. She knew that they were caught up here, impenetrably surrounded, on the nakedness of the heights. She was still at times, irrationally, afraid of God. Like other outlaws, it was probable that He had taken to the hills, and she had never cared to venture far into the country of outlaws. He had hung once about certain elemental passages in her life, and had been brought down upon her, sometimes, by Rupert. Here in Italy, in the churches or out in the sunshine, she had been feeling recently a complete security. And now here was Italy turning luridly upon her the whites of its eyes. She felt that she had been led up here and betrayed.

With a succession of uncertain impetuses she had reached the corner of the terrace, where the whole world fell away from under the Villa. The murmur of the Danish women's voices faded here, and she was less troubled by the insistence of the fountains. The darkening skies contracted and the balustrade and the wall of the house looked ash-pale, brittle, and impermanent. She longed to return to the village, and meditated how she would slip away through the chain of empty rooms, defying the echoes, across the courtyard and out into the street. From here, she could see the houses toppling up the hill, the awnings of the cafés colourless and undefined by shadow, the steep street empty in the dusk. Life, however dormant, lay accessible behind her. She reassured herself that she was on a peninsula rather than an island. She craved the comfortableness of strange voices, the impersonality of casual contacts, the touch of hands that would be nothing but human. She wanted an abstraction of humanity. The further proximity of Rupert had become intolerable; he was a bundle of potentialities and grievances; inextinguishably Rupert. She already fatigued herself sufficiently, and was fatigued by herself, without the superimposition of Rupert.

Round the corner, she discovered that the terrace went no further. It was swallowed up into the darkness of an archway, diminishing from sight in an ascent of steps. One could enter the house here, by a doorway to her left; the dark room within was attentive, the mustiness of it stole out on to the terrace and hung here, even on the edge of this illimitable space. Other smells crept up from below, and hung too, unable to disperse themselves, thickening the close air: sultriness from the blossoming trees below, a dank breath from water, and decay, faint and very sickly, from, perhaps, the small dead body of some animal under those impenetrable branches.

Here was a way of escape open to her: she could pass down the long chain of rooms, link on link of frescoed emptiness with garlands duskier in the dusk, with little bald, square windows, lashless eyes, staring out on to the darkening sky. She could regain the courtyard and the village without retracing her steps along the terrace, and bewilder Rupert, and defeat the beleaguering forces of God.

She could not do it; she was too much afraid of the dark rooms and the echoes. She put up her hands to her forehead because her head ached.

After the young woman in orange had passed her, she wondered dully where she had been going, whither she hurried so. Her urgency had cut like a knife through the opaque twilight, and her dress had been curiously brilliant in the drained-out colourlessness of the evening. The chief impression of her passing had been a rustling and a rushing sound, and though she had not passed in an imponderable moment there had been an effect of speed about her forehead and blown-back hair. She left a coolness of displaced air, like the single gesture of a fan. She had taken form out of the darkness of the stairway, simultaneously emerging and descending. At its foot there had been a sort of hesitancy—a gesture of return; then she had rushed forward with an impetus that made her almost luminous. She had vanished round the corner of the terrace, one could not say how long ago. Rupert would feel the wind of her movement, she might brush against him as she passed.

Rupert's wife went slowly to the corner of the terrace, leaned her hand against the blunted angle of the wall, and looking down the long perspective saw that it was empty. Rupert was gone and the other—she could not remember what other she had come to find.

Then she felt the wall of the Villa tilt for a moment over towards her as she cried, "Oh, Rupert, Rupert, I have seen a ghost!"

Rupert had remained leaning forward on his elbows till the sound of her angry breathing from above him died away and the rustle of her dress diminished. The least sound twanged on the taut air. He turned his head with an imperceptible slowness to watch her down the terrace;

she stooped badly and her head poked forward under that feathered hat. The contemptuous nonchalance of her trailed hand irritated him: she was not a person to have brought to Italy. Then the back of his eyes pricked as he remembered how ineffectual they both were, how they neither of them knew what they wanted, how suspiciously they watched one another, jealous of a gleam of certainty. Their journeyings were a forlorn hope, they never found what they had come to seek, nor even knew what they had come for. He bent down again to feel the blister on his foot, and when he raised his eyes she had turned the corner of the terrace. Round the corner, she would find nothing that interested her, and soon she would come slowly back again to tell him how there had been nothing, and to reproach him with Italy, and with the noise of the fountains. Although the whole afternoon he had been determined that she should not evade him, and had kept close on her heels, because she had been somehow eluding him in her displeasure, he now decided to evade *her*, to escape utterly, to walk through the village without her and be found sitting waiting for her in the tram. He would have liked, indeed, to follow the steep curves of that road down on to the Campagna, if it had not been for the blister on his foot.

Furtively, with a quick resolution he darted away across the terrace into the Villa, through air that impeded his movements as in a dream. The sound of his footsteps, suddenly intensified by the constricting walls, rose up startlingly around him. Softly!—she might hear him, even from the end of the terrace! To his left and right, opposite one another, doorways showed him empty doorways in diminishing perspective, and the nakedness of floors. In the windless dusk the painted garlands swayed, it seemed, a little on the walls. From some pin's-head vanishing point, where beyond the long perspective the ultimate blank wall had faded into darkness, steps began. "Hullo!" said Rupert nervously.

The shutter slammed. Black darkness drowned the room and the house shivered. "Hell!" screamed Rupert.

He did not know that there was a wind; indeed, it had
been more than negative, that windlessness. He ran to the
next room, and, pressing back the shutters against the
embrasure of the window (they shook a little under his
hands), saw the tops of the three cypresses that rose above
the terrace making wild gestures against the sky.

The taut clouds, he knew, would never stand this buf-
feting. Why, the very slamming of that shutter must have
ripped through them like a bullet. In flight before an im-
minent Something that he did not dare to imagine, he determined to go further into the Villa and find the passage
and the steps up to the courtyard. He could not go on like
this for ever, from one to another of these infinite rooms—
they were too like one another. Each, too, might crash
again at any moment into darkness, and Rupert did not
like the dark. So he took the exit that a little door offered
him, low in the centre wall, and found himself in a half-
familiar obscurity, like that of his own dining-room at
home. It sounded small, and something facing him, as it
were a sideboard, he understood to be an altar. He
guessed, too, rather than perceived, a tall cross up above
it on the wall. This meant something, anyhow. "This is
the chapel," said Rupert.

He enjoyed patronage, and had at all times adjusted to
their (he believed) mutual satisfaction his relations with
his Maker. An Agency had made arrangements for his passage across Life, at the price of moderate concessions on
the part of Rupert, and to its divine supervision Rupert
trustfully consigned himself. God was everywhere, making
arrangements, even as a Cook's official met him on every
platform when he travelled. Rupert remained sublimely
passive; he was not a fussy man. So this was a chapel—he
sat down in it to wait.

He did not realize whom he was disturbing till they
slipped away behind some curtains into an opaquer darkness. Their rosaries tinkled swinging from their fingers as
they passed him; their gowns, drawing together, relieved
the floor of its blackness as they rose from their knees silently, even faintly revealing the pattern of the tiles. Six

faces, incredibly long, turned towards him—no, not faces, wimples; they were nuns. "Oh, pardon me," said Rupert, as they passed out quietly.

Now that the shadows fell into order behind them, he found, his eyes growing accustomed, that the place was not after all impenetrably dusky. Three shafts lighted it, striking down from the level of the courtyard; under one of them, even, candlesticks faintly glimmered. In the front of the Villa, in those rooms he had come from, a shutter slammed again, then quickly another; there was a long rushing, scudding sound that died away round the corner in a whistle. Rupert felt that it was good for him to be here.

The Danish ladies were also alarmed. This was not Italy as they had been led to expect her, nor, indeed, as she had hitherto displayed herself to them. Deep within them, the Teutonic decencies were outraged by this exposure. They turned their eyes from the livid hills and gasped a little beneath the pressure of the sky. Above, the peevish Englishwoman had finished quarrelling with her husband; he leaned over the parapet, looking down on them, and they wondered if he were going to speak. They were tired of taking photographs of one another beside the fountains, and for this, also, it was now too dark. They wearied of poking their umbrellas up the mouths of the dolphins to intercept the spouting of the water. The exhalations and the darkness of the trees rose toward them like smoke. They wished to return to the village and buy postcards and drink chocolate in a café. "Let us go up," they said. And when they were not yet half-way to the first of the many angles of the ascending stairs the stoutest of them sat down suddenly and said, "I cannot." Later, the others succumbed and sat down also, mopping their faces; having taken off their hats that the perspiration might not injure the linings. The youngest, who, still consistent, felt justified in demanding a certain consistency of Nature, said that she did not see why it should be so hot and yet so black. "Thunder," said the stout one, and the others looked at her incredulously for a moment, then agreed.

They all stared up at the sky, inquisitorially, and one of them, by twisting her neck for a moment, was able to observe that the Englishman had vanished from the upper terrace.

One does not speak much while contemplating a too great expanse of country under the imminence of a storm. They sat close together, so that their mackintoshes creaked in contact; each one enclosed within herself, aloof, chaste, inviolable to emotion. It was sitting thus that they heard the Englishwoman scream.

There was excitement in the scream, they thought pleasurable excitement. They turned their heads, and one of them conjectured that she had picked up a bracelet on the terrace. By the prolonged sustenance of her highest note, it might even have been a diamond bracelet.

"She is calling her husband."

"The man Rupert."

"He has gone in."

They supposed that when she had finished screaming she would go in too, taking whatever she had found, and look for him in the Villa. But no, she came down the steps with her hands shaking; they heard the little loose coins jingling in her handbag. Her hat was pushed back from her forehead; she looked very white, not hot at all.

"I have seen a woman, a woman in yellow. She went round the corner and vanished. Did she come past you? She was a ghost."

They listened very carefully, looked at one another, and assured her in their careful English that they had seen no woman. She herself was the only lady whom they had encountered in the gardens of the Villa.

"Not a lady," she cried, pushing her hat back further from her forehead, "a ghost, a ghost!"

They agreed that the gardens might be full of ghosts, and that many things were possible. Meanwhile, was Madame seeking her husband? He had gone back into the Villa. Did not Madame feel that it was likely to rain? While they hung expectantly upon the silence of Madame the trees below them were sucked sideways with a roar. Pale gashes curled forward, slit and dissipated themselves like waves where the wind flung forward whole branches. Little eddies of sound sucked and whirled down in the shadows. Above it all, there was a high whistling.

The pillar of a fountain, solid as marble, swerved, bent like a bow, and flung a cloud of fine spray into their faces.

"The wind has come," said the youngest lady, tucking away strands of hair behind her ears and putting on her hat. The Englishwoman stampeded like a horse: she cried, "My husband!" and went wildly up the steps again with an agility which surprised them, her skirts shrieking in the wind.

The wind caught the Villa full in the face, one stinging challenge like the lash of a gauntlet. Elegant, rococo, with an air of balance delicately perilous, it yet struck down deep into the rock, deep as a fortress. It braced itself, and now the assailing forces of the wind came singing between the pillars of the parapet. Row on row, the windows looked unflinchingly out into the sky, though here and there the swinging-to of a shutter was like the nervous and involuntary flicker of an eyelid. The attack begun, the clouds brought up their artillery; lightning, splitting the sky, shimmered across the flagstones of the terrace. The honey-coloured façade, soaked and languorous with sunshine, stood up, naked, sensitive as flesh, to the stinging onslaught of the rain that beat against the windows with a faint, fine, infinitesimal clatter.

Deep in the heart of the house, the man Rupert was sitting in the lower chapel. The light coming down from the shafts was darkened, the candlesticks no longer gleamed. Little rapiers of windy draught came whistling and stabbing at him, the curtains twitched audibly, then faintly and more continuously rustled. The chapel suffered Rupert, but did nothing to entice him. He remembered with an immeasurable nostalgia their bedroom at the hotel, warm, crude, actual; the patterned tapestry of the sofa, the painted ceiling, his wife's garments, straggling, be-ribboned, the thermos flask with the coffee that they had forgotten today. He remembered the talk in the lounge.

"Going to the Forum?" "No, we've done the Forum . . ." "they give good coffee and milk here, but the butter is execrable . . ." "a postcard of the Dying Gaul," "Gladiator," "We must do St. Peter's—yes, yes, yes. . . ."

Rupert watched the darkness where the curtains were, and wondered if the nuns were coming back. Faintly envisaged, and thus more faintly desirable, was his smoking-room at home, full of the books he had never finished. Perhaps he had been sometimes too arbitrary in his refusals of hospitality—from books, places, people. He had been always hurrying on to a rendezvous, afraid lest he should miss God and the expedition thus proceed without him. He had hurried his wife along with him, reluctant and suspicious, looking back over his shoulder at the destruction of her cities, trailing after him with slack steps.

She had trailed away from him down the terrace, and he was surprised to find that now he was wanting her. This darkness, potentially, this frightening darkness, made him protective; something passive and weak was wanting, to come and cower against him. A dog, even, or one of the children that they might have had; but better than all, his wife. Failing this, he was at a loss—even, he admitted, frightened. The great thing, he knew, was to stop thinking about oneself. He veered full round towards his wife, mentally and emotionally. She was a listless creature, but now she would be tense, horribly at bay and afraid, propped against a doorpost, clutching at it. She was a coward, he knew; his heart swelled with delight and desire as he felt what a coward she was. She had never been on the side of the angels; he had never been able to explain to her about God. She could not understand that she was being catered for.

Rupert's wife, having taken shelter, stood in one of the front rooms by the window, breathing hard and flinching away from the lightning. She heard the Danes enter, and pressing herself back against the wall listened while they hesitated for a moment and turned, unconsciously, away from her; making their way through the chain of rooms in the direction of the village. Watching them, she observed something duck-like about their recessive backs. Rupert, she guessed, was somewhere near at hand, but might very possibly be inaccessible to her. She was now feeling very definitely in contest with an opposing will, and the storm slanting and flaring beyond the windows, darkness rolling up on darkness, set her tingling with the exultation of a definite encounter. The house enclosed her greedily; it impeded her, and yet it was an ally.

She also had it in her to project herself, to stamp on time her ineffaceable image. She had an urgency which made her timeless, like the woman on the terrace; which made her step clear of the dimensions. She had simply, as she now knew, beheld herself in a mirror as that other went past her; and stepped back, shaken, from her own reality. That was it: she was overcharged. She was too much for herself, and terribly in need of Rupert. He was a slight, dependent thing, and infinitely pitiable, trotting hard and a little hopelessly at the heel of his gigantic Somebody. She ached now with the consciousness of her own sufficiency for him, her potency to crowd out even God.

Crowd out? There was nobody there to oppose her. Up here in the hills she had parleyed, and made an alliance. Rupert had been sold to her; by a treachery of God, which would be inconceivable to him, delivered up utterly into her hands. She sought for and eventually found him, squatting on one of the stools by the altar, low and toad-like, and her own shadow darkened his white face upturned towards her as she stood in the square dull greyness of the open door. They contemplated one another's outlines speechlessly; self-sufficient, travelled, wary, and mutually pitiful.

Then: "Rupert," she cried, "where were you? I've been looking for you, looking for you everywhere!"

"I was waiting here. I knew if I went wandering about we would miss each other. I thought it would be better to wait here till you came to me—I didn't know where you had gone. This place, you know, is part of a convent. It is full of nuns."

"*Nuns?*" she said incredulously. She would not believe him, and when, feeling his way over to the corner of their exit, he drew back the curtain, he found that there was nothing behind it but stone: it was a blocked-up archway.

"Well?" came her voice with a smile in it. It was beautiful to her that Rupert had been making himself nuns.

"They *seemed* to me to be nuns," he faltered, "and they went away here where the curtain is. . . . A kind of archway. . . . But they may only have been shadows, black and white ones. You know, the wind was so terrible that I couldn't hear anything, and I couldn't see or think properly either. It was rather fine, I thought, to think of good women still living in this house and coming here and praying. It—it was a Testimony," he concluded huskily. "It seemed to me extraordinarily fine."

"Extraordinarily fine," her voice echoed, soft and kindly. "But, Rupert, I was afraid and lonely. I wanted you. I was alone."

"Afraid!" he cried gladly, clambering to his feet and making his way toward her tall shadowiness. His hand stretched out and touched hers and withdrew timidly: he did not often caress her. "I ought to have been with you . . . Darling . . ." he said rustily.

"I'm all right now. But let's go, Rupert, let's go up to the village together, and soon we can go down in the tram." They heard thunder, a dull sound, low and enveloping, and the room behind her shimmered with two or three flashes. They thought the house trembled.

"Not yet: stay here," said Rupert.

"Does this make you feel religious?" she asked, shutting the door behind her.

"Well, God's everywhere."

They stood together by the musty canopy of the altar, shoulder to shoulder. His arm crept round her waist and lightly encircled her. "Poor darling!" he whispered, "poor dear!" She leaned toward him in the dark, her feathers brushed his cheek.

"You're very strong," she said.

"I think when one believes in an ultimate Rightness . . ."

"Yes . . ."

She was beginning to understand, he thought. He was beginning to be able to win her over. God with him, she was learning to cling to him. And she ran her hands over his tweed shoulders, stroking them, sighing ineffably, knowing that he was delivered up utterly into her hands.

The Tommy Crans

HERBERT'S feet, from dangling so long in the tram, had died of cold in his boots; he stamped the couple of coffins on blue-and-buff mosaic. In the Tommy Crans' cloak-room the pegs were too high—Uncle Archer cocked H.M.S. *Terrible* for him over a checked ulster. Tommy Cran—aslant meanwhile, in the doorway—was an enormous presence. "Come on, now, come!" he exclaimed, and roared with impatience. You would have said he was also arriving at the Tommy Crans' Christmas party, of which one could not bear to miss a moment.

Now into the hall Mrs. Tommy Cran came swimming from elsewhere, dividing with curved little strokes the festive air—hyacinths and gunpowder. Her sleeves, in a thousand ruffles, fled from her elbows. She gained Uncle Archer's lapels and, bobbing, floated from this attachment. Uncle Archer, verifying the mistletoe, loudly kissed her face of delicate pink sugar. "Ha!" yelled Tommy, drawing an unseen dagger. Herbert laughed with embarrassment.

"Only think, Nancy let off all the crackers before tea! She's quite wild, but there are more behind the piano. Ah, is this little Herbert? Herbert . . ."

"Very well, thank you," said Herbert, and shook hands defensively. This was his first Christmas Day without any father; the news went before him. He had seen his mother

off, very brave with the holly wreath, in the cemetery
tram. She and father were spending Christmas afternoon
together.

Mrs. Tommy Cran stooped to him, bright with a tear-
glitter, then with a strong upward sweep, like an angel's,
bore him to gaiety. "*Fancy* Nancy!" He fancied Nancy.
So by now they would all be wearing the paper caps.
Flinging back a white door, she raced Herbert elsewhere.

The room where they all sat seemed to be made of
glass, it collected the whole daylight; the candles were
still waiting. Over the garden, day still hung like a pink
flag; over the trees like frozen feathers, the enchanted icy
lake, the lawn. The table was in the window. As Herbert
was brought in a clock struck four; the laughing heads all
turned in a silence brief as a breath's intake. The great
many gentlemen and the rejoicing ladies leaned apart; he
and Nancy looked at each other gravely.

He saw Nancy, crowned and serious because she was a
queen. Advanced by some urgent pushing, he made his
way round the table and sat down beside her, podgily.

She said: "How d'you do? Did you see our lake? It is
all frozen. Did you ever see our lake before?"

"I never came here."

"Did you see our two swans?"

She was so beautiful, rolling her ringlets, round with
light, on her lacy shoulders, that he said rather shortly:
"I shouldn't have thought your lake was large enough for
two swans."

"It is, indeed," said Nancy; "it goes round the island.
It's large enough for a boat."

They were waiting, around the Christmas cake, for tea
to be brought in. Mrs. Tommy Cran shook out the ribbons of her guitar and began to sing again. Very quietly,
for a secret, he and Nancy crept to the window; she
showed how the lake wound; he could guess how, in summer, her boat would go pushing among the lily-leaves.
She showed him their boat-house, rusty red from a lamp
inside, solid. "We had a lamp put there for the poor cold
swans." (And the swans were asleep beside it.) "How old
are you, Herbert?"

"Eight."

"Oh, I'm nine. Do you play brigands?"

"I could," said Herbert.

"Oh, I don't; I'd hate to. But I know some boys who do. Did you have many presents? Uncle Ponto brought me a train; it's more suitable for a boy, really. I could give it to you, perhaps."

"How many uncles—?" began Herbert.

"Ten pretence and none really. I'm adopted, because mummy and daddy have no children. I think that's better fun, don't you?"

"Yes," replied Herbert, after consideration; "anybody could be born."

All the time, Nancy had not ceased to look at him seriously and impersonally. They were both tired already by this afternoon of boisterous grown-up society; they would have liked to be quiet, and though she was loved by ten magic uncles and wore a pearl locket, and he was fat, with spectacles, and felt deformed a little from everybody's knowing about his father, they felt at ease in each other's company.

"Nancy, cut the cake!" exclaimed Mrs. Tommy, and they all clapped their hands for Nancy's attention. So the coloured candles were lit, the garden went dark with loneliness and was immediately curtained out. Two of the uncles put rugs on and bounded about the room like bears and lions; the other faces drew out a crimson band round the silver teapot. Mrs. Tommy could not bear to put down the guitar, so the teapot fell into the hands of a fuzzy lady with several husbands who cried "Ah, don't, now!" and had to keep brushing gentlemen's hands from her waist. And all the others leaned on each other's shoulders and laughed with gladness because they had been asked to the Tommy Crans'; a dozen times everyone died of laughter and rose again, redder ghosts. Teacups whizzed down a chain of hands. Now Nancy, standing up very straight to cut the cake, was like a doll stitched upright into its box, apt, if you should cut the string at the back, to pitch right forward and break its delicate fingers.

"Oh dear," she sighed, as the knife skidded over the

icing. But nobody heard but Herbert. For someone, seeing her white frock over that palace of cake, proposed "The health of the bride." And an Uncle Joseph, tipping the tea about in his cup, stared and stared with juicy eyes. But nobody saw but Herbert.

"After tea," she whispered, "we'll go and stand on the lake." And after tea they did, while the others played hide and seek. Herbert, once looking back through a window, saw uncles chasing the laughing aunts. It was not cold on the lake. Nancy said: "I never believed in fairies—did you either?" She told him she had been given a white muff and was going to be an organist, with an organ of her own. She was going up to Belfast next month to dance for charity. She said she would not give him the train after all; she would give him something really her own, a pink glass greyhound that was an ornament.

When Uncle Archer and Herbert left to walk to the tram terminus, the party was at its brightest. They were singing "Hark, the herald" around the drawing-room piano: Nancy sat on her Uncle Joseph's knee, more than politely.

Uncle Archer did not want to go home either. "That was a nice little girl," he said. "Eh?"

Herbert nodded. His uncle, glad that the little chap hadn't had, after all, such a dismal Christmas, pursued heartily: "Kiss her?" Herbert looked quite blank. To tell the truth, this had never occurred to him.

He kissed Nancy later; his death, even, was indirectly caused by his loss of her; but their interchanges were never passionate, and he never knew her better than when they had been standing out on the lake, beyond the cheerful windows. Herbert's mother did not know Uncle Archer's merry friends: she had always loved to live quietly, and, as her need for comfort decreased, she and Herbert saw less, or at least as little as ever of Uncle Archer. So that for years Herbert was not taken again across Dublin to the house with the lake. Once he saw Nancy carry her white muff into a shop, but he stood rooted and did not run after her. Once he saw Mrs. Tommy Cran out in Stephen's Green throwing lollipops to the ducks: but he did not approach; there was nothing to say. He was sent to school, where he painfully learnt to be natural with boys: his sight got no better; they said he must wear glasses all his life. Years later, however, when Herbert was thirteen, the Crans gave a dancing-party and did not forget him. He danced once with Nancy; she was silenter now, but she said: "Why did you never come back again?" He could not explain; he trod on her toes and danced heavily on. A Chinese lantern blazed up, and in the confusion he lost her. That evening he saw Mrs. Tommy in tears in the conservatory. Nancy clung, pressing her head, with its drooping pink ribbons, to Mrs. Cran's shoulder; pressing, perhaps, the shoulder against the head. Soon it was all right again and Mrs. Tommy led off in "Sir Roger," but Nancy was like a ghost who presently vanished. A week afterwards he had a letter: "Please meet me to tea at Mitchell's; I want your advice specially."

She was distracted: she had come in to Dublin to sell her gold wrist-watch. The Tommy Crans had lost all their money—it wasn't fair to expect them to keep it; they were generous and gay. Nancy had to think hard what must they all do. Herbert went round with her from jeweller to jeweller: these all laughed and paid her nothing but compliments. Her face, with those delicate lovely eyebrows, grew tragic under the fur cap; it rained continuously; she and Herbert looked with incredulity into the grown-up faces: they wondered how one could penetrate far into life without despair. At last a man on the quays gave her eight-and-six for the watch. Herbert, meanwhile, had spent eight shillings of his pocket-money on their cab —and, even so, her darling feet were sodden. They were surprised to see, from the window, Tommy Cran jump from an outside car and run joyfully into the Shelbourne. It turned out he had raised some more money from somewhere—as he deserved.

So he sold the house with the lake and moved to an ornamental castle by Dublin Bay. In spite of the grey scene, the transitory light from the sea, the terrace here was gay with urns of geraniums, magnificent with a descent of steps—scrolls and whorls of balustrade, all the grandeur of stucco. Here the band played for their after-noon parties, and here, when they were twenty and twenty-one, Herbert asked Nancy to marry him.

A pug harnessed with bells ran jingling about the ter-race. "Oh, I don't know, Herbert; I don't know."

"Do you think you don't love me?"

"I don't know whom I love. Everything would have to be different. Herbert, I don't see how we are ever to live; we seem to know everything. Surely there should be something for us we don't know?" She shut her eyes; they kissed seriously and searchingly. In his arm her body felt soft and voluminous; he could not touch her because of a great fur coat. The coat had been a surprise from Tommy Cran, who loved to give presents on delightful occasions —for now they were off to the Riviera. They were sailing in four days; Nancy and Mrs. Tommy had still all their shopping to do, all his money to spend—he loved them both to be elegant. There was that last party to give be-fore leaving home. Mrs. Tommy could hardly leave the telephone; crossing London, they were to give yet another party, at the Euston Hotel.

"And how could I leave them?" she asked. "They're my business."

"Because they are not quite your parents?"

"Oh, no," she said, eyes reproachful for the misunder-standing he had put up, she knew, only from bitterness. "They would be my affair whoever I was. Don't you see, they're like that."

The Tommy Crans returned from the Riviera subdued, and gave no more parties than they could avoid. They hung sun-yellow curtains, in imitation of the Midi, in all the castle windows, and fortified themselves against de-spair. They warned their friends they were ruined; they honestly were—and there were heartfelt evenings of con-solation. After such evenings Mrs. Tommy, awaking heavily, whimpered in Nancy's arms, and Tommy ap-proached silence. They had the highest opinion of Nancy, and were restored by her confidence. She knew they would be all right; she assured them they were the best, the happiest people: they were popular—look how Life came back again and again to beg their pardon. And, just to show them, she accepted Jeremy Neath and his thousands. So the world could see she was lucky; the world saw the Tommy Crans and their daughter had all the luck. To Herbert she explained nothing. She expected everything of him, on behalf of the Tommy Crans.

The two Crans were distracted by her apotheosis from the incident of their ruin. They had seen her queen of a perpetual Christmas party for six months before they themselves came down magnificently, like an empire. Then Nancy came to fetch them over to England, where her husband had found a small appointment for Tommy, excuse for a pension. But Tommy would not want that long; he had a scheme already, a stunner, a certainty; you just wrote to a hundred people and put in half a crown. That last night he ran about with the leaflets, up and down the uncarpeted castle stairs that were his no longer. He offered to let Herbert in on it; he would yet see Herbert a rich man.

Herbert and Nancy walked after dark on the terrace: she looked ill, tired; she was going to have a baby.

"When I asked you to marry me," he said, "you never answered. You've never answered yet."

She said: "There was no answer. We could never have loved each other and we shall always love each other. We are related."

Herbert, a heavy un-young young man, walked, past desperation, beside her. He did not want peace, but a sword. He returned again and again to the unique moment of her strangeness to him before, as a child, she had spoken. Before, bewildered by all the laughter, he had realised she also was silent.

"You never played games," he said, "or believed in fairies, or anything. I'd have played any game your way; I'd have been good at them. You let them pull all the crackers before tea: now I'd have loved those crackers. That day we met at Mitchell's to sell your watch, you wouldn't have sugar cakes, though I wanted to comfort you. You never asked me out to go round the island in your boat; I'd have died to do that. I never even saw your swans awake. You hold back everything from me and expect me to understand. Why should I understand? In the name of God, what game are we playing?"

"But you do understand?"

"Oh, God," he cried in revulsion. "I don't want to! And now you're going to have a stranger child."

Her sad voice in the dark said: "You said then, 'Anybody could be born!' Herbert, you and I have nothing to do with children—this must be a child like them."

As they turned back to face the window, her smile and voice were tender, but not for him. In the brightly lit stripped room the Tommy Crans walked about together, like lovers in their freedom from one another. They talked of the fortune to be made, the child to be born. Tommy flung his chest out and moved his arms freely in air he did not possess; here and there, pink leaflets fluttered into the dark. The Tommy Crans would go on for ever and be continued; their seed should never fail.

Her Table Spread

ALBAN had few opinions on the subject of marriage; his attitude to women was negative, but in particular he was not attracted to Miss Cuffe. Coming down early for dinner, red satin dress cut low, she attacked the silence with loud laughter before he had spoken. He recollected having heard that she was abnormal—at twenty-five, of statuesque development, still detained in childhood. The two other ladies, in beaded satins, made entrances of a surprising formality. It occurred to him, his presence must constitute an occasion: they certainly sparkled. Old Mr. Rossiter, uncle to Mrs. Treye, came last, more sourly. They sat for some time without the addition of lamplight. Dinner was not announced; the ladies, by remaining on guard, seemed to deprecate any question of its appearance. No sound came from other parts of the Castle.

Miss Cuffe was an heiress to whom the Castle belonged and whose guests they all were. But she carefully followed the movements of her aunt, Mrs. Treye; her ox-eyes moved from face to face in happy submission rather than expectancy. She was continually preoccupied with attempts at gravity, as though holding down her skirts in a high wind. Mrs. Treye and Miss Carbin combined to cover her excitement; still, their looks frequently stole from the company to the windows, of which there were too many. He received a strong impression someone outside was waiting to come in. At last, with a sigh, they got up: dinner had been announced.

The Castle was built on high ground, commanding the estuary; a steep hill, with trees, continued above it. On fine days the view was remarkable, of almost Italian brilliance, with that constant reflection up from the water that even now prolonged the too-long day. Now, in continuous evening rain, the winding wooded line of the further shore could be seen and, nearer the windows, a smothered island with the stump of a watch-tower. Where the Castle stood, a higher tower had answered the island's. Later a keep, then wings, had been added; now the fine peaceful residence had French windows opening on to the terrace. Invasions from the water would henceforth be social, perhaps amorous. On the slope down from the terrace, trees began again; almost, but not quite, concealing the destroyer. Alban, who knew nothing, had not yet looked down.

It was Mr. Rossiter who first spoke of the destroyer—Alban meanwhile glancing along the table; the preparations had been stupendous. The destroyer had come to-day. The ladies all turned to Alban: the beads on their bosoms sparkled. So this was what they had here, under their trees. Engulfed by their pleasure, from now on he disappeared personally. Mr. Rossiter, rising a note, continued. The estuary, it appeared, was deep, with a channel buoyed up it. By a term of the Treaty, English ships were permitted to anchor in these waters.

"But they've been afraid of the rain!" chimed in Valeria Cuffe.

"Hush," said her aunt, "that's silly. Sailors would be accustomed to getting wet."

But, Miss Carbin reported, that spring there *had* already been one destroyer. Two of the officers had been seen dancing at the hotel at the head of the estuary.

"So," said Alban, "you are quite in the world." He adjusted his glasses in her direction.

Miss Carbin—blonde, not forty, and an attachment of Mrs. Treye's—shook her head despondently. "We were all away at Easter. Wasn't it curious they should have come then? The sailors walked in the demesne but never touched the daffodils."

"As though I should have cared!" exclaimed Valeria passionately.

"Morale too good," stated Mr. Rossiter.

"But next evening," continued Miss Carbin, "the officers did not go to the hotel. They climbed up here through the trees to the terrace—you see, they had no idea. Friends of ours were staying here at the Castle, and they apologised. Our friends invited them in to supper. . . ."

"Did they accept?"

The three ladies said in a breath: "Yes, they came."

Valeria added urgently, "So don't you *think*—?"

"So to-night we have a destroyer to greet you," Mrs. Treye said quickly to Alban. "It is quite an event; the country people are coming down from the mountains. These waters are very lonely; the steamers have given up since the bad times; there is hardly a pleasure-boat. The weather this year has driven visitors right away."

"You are beautifully remote."

"Yes," agreed Miss Carbin. "Do you know much about the Navy? Do you think, for instance, that this is likely to be the same destroyer?"

"*Will they remember?*" Valeria's bust was almost on the table. But with a rustle Mrs. Treye pressed Valeria's toe. For the dining-room also looked out across the estuary, and the great girl had not once taken her eyes from the window. Perhaps it was unfortunate that Mr. Alban should have coincided with the destroyer. Perhaps it was unfortunate for Mr. Alban too.

For he saw now he was less than half the feast; unappeased, the party sat looking through him, all grouped at an end of the table—to the other, chairs had been pulled up. Dinner was being served very slowly. Candles —possible to see from the water—were lit now; some wet peonies glistened. Outside, day still lingered hopefully. The bushes over the edge of the terrace were like heads —you could have sworn sometimes you saw them mounting, swaying in manly talk. Once, wound up in the rain, a bird whistled, seeming hardly a bird.

"Perhaps since then they have been to Greece, or Malta?"

"That would be the Mediterranean fleet," said Mr. Rossiter.

They were sorry to think of anything out in the rain to-night.

"The decks must be streaming," said Miss Carbin.

Then Valeria, exclaiming, "Please excuse me!" pushed her chair in and ran from the room.

"She is impulsive," explained Mrs. Treye. "Have *you* been to Malta, Mr. Alban?"

In the drawing-room, empty of Valeria, the standard lamps had been lit. Through their ballet-skirt shades, rose and lemon, they gave out a deep, welcoming light. Alban, at the ladies' invitation, undraped the piano. He played, but they could see he was not pleased. It was obvious he had always been a civilian, and when he had taken his place on the piano-stool—which he twirled round three times, rather fussily—his dinner-jacket wrinkled across the shoulders. It was sad they should feel so indifferent, for he came from London. Mendelssohn was exasperating to them—they opened all four windows to let the music downhill. They preferred not to draw the curtains; the air, though damp, being pleasant to-night, they said.

The piano was damp, but Alban played almost all his heart out. He played out the indignation of years his mild manner concealed. He had failed to love; nobody did anything about this; partners at dinner gave him less than half their attention. He knew some spring had dried up at the root of the world. He was fixed in the dark rain, by an indifferent shore. He played badly, but they were unmusical. Old Mr. Rossiter, who was not what he seemed, went back to the dining-room to talk to the parlourmaid.

Valeria, glittering vastly, appeared in a window.

"Come *in!*" her aunt cried in indignation. She would die of a chill, childless, in fact unwedded; the Castle would have to be sold and where would they all be?

But—"Lights down there!" Valeria shouted above the music.

They had to run out for a moment, laughing and holding cushions over their bare shoulders. Alban left the piano: they looked boldly down from the terrace. Indeed, there they were: two lights like arc-lamps, blurred by rain and drawn down deep in reflection into the steady water. There were, too, ever so many portholes, all lit up.

"Perhaps they are playing bridge," said Miss Carbin.

"Now I wonder if Uncle Robert ought to have called," said Mrs. Treye. "Perhaps we have seemed remiss—one calls on a regiment."

"Patrick could row him out to-morrow."

"He hates the water." She sighed. "Perhaps they will be gone."

"Let's go for a row now—let's go for a row with a lantern," besought Valeria, jumping and pulling her aunt's elbow. They produced such indignation she disappeared again—wet satin skirts and all—into the bushes. The ladies could do no more: Alban suggested the rain might spot their dresses.

"They must lose a great deal, playing cards throughout an evening for high stakes," Miss Carbin said with concern as they all sat down again.

"Yet, if you come to think of it, somebody must win."

But the naval officers who so joyfully supped at Easter had been, Miss Carbin knew, a Mr. Graves and a Mr. Garrett: *they* would certainly lose. "At all events, it is better than dancing at the hotel; there would be nobody of their type."

"There is nobody there at all."

"I expect they are best where they are. . . . Mr. Alban, a Viennese waltz?"

He played while the ladies whispered, waving the waltz time a little distractedly. Mr. Rossiter, coming back, momentously stood: they turned in hope: even the waltz halted. But he brought no news. "You should call Valeria in. You can't tell who may be round the place. She's not fit to be out to-night."

"Perhaps she's not out."

"She is," said Mr. Rossiter crossly. "I just saw her racing past the window with a lantern."

Valeria's mind was made up: she was a princess. Not for nothing had she had the dining-room silver polished and all set out. She would pace around in red satin that swished behind, while Mr. Alban kept on playing a loud waltz. They would be dazed at all she had to offer—also her two new statues and the leopard-skin from the auction.

When he and she were married (she inclined a little to Mr. Garrett) they would invite all the Navy up the estuary and give them tea. Her estuary would be filled up, like a regatta, with loud excited battleships tooting to one another and flags flying. The terrace would be covered with grateful sailors, leaving room for the band. She would keep the peacocks her aunt did not allow. His friends would be surprised to notice that Mr. Garrett had meanwhile become an admiral, all gold. He would lead the other admirals into the castle and say, while they wiped their feet respectfully: "These are my wife's statues; she has given them to me. One is Mars, one is Mercury. We have a Venus, but she is not dressed. And wait till I show you our silver and gold plates . . ." The Navy would be unable to tear itself away.

She had been excited for some weeks at the idea of marrying Mr. Alban, but now the lovely appearance of the destroyer put him out of her mind. He would not have done; he was not handsome. But she could keep him to play the piano on quiet afternoons.

Her friends had told her Mr. Garrett was quite a Viking. She was so very familiar with his appearance that she felt sometimes they had already been married for years —though still, sometimes, he could not realise his good luck. She still had to remind him the island was hers too. . . . To-night, Aunt and darling Miss Carbin had so fallen in with her plans, putting on their satins and decorating the drawing-room, that the dinner became a betrothal feast. There was some little hitch about the arrival of Mr. Garrett—she had heard that gentlemen sometimes could not tie their ties. And now he was late and would be dis-

couraged. So she must now go half-way down to the
water and wave a lantern.

But she put her two hands over the lantern, then
smothered it in her dress. She had a panic. Supposing
she should prefer Mr. Graves?

She had heard Mr. Graves was stocky, but very merry;
when he came to supper at Easter he slid in the gallery.
He would teach her to dance, and take her to Naples and
Paris. . . . Oh, dear, oh, dear, then they must fight for
her; that was all there was to it. . . . She let the lantern
out of her skirts and waved. Her fine arm with bangles
went up and down, up and down, with the staggering
light; the trees one by one jumped up from the dark, like
savages.

Inconceivably, the destroyer took no notice.

Undisturbed by oars, the rain stood up from the waters;
not a light rose to peer, and the gramophone, though it
remained very faint, did not cease or alter.

In mackintoshes, Mr. Rossiter and Alban meanwhile
made their way to the boat-house, Alban did not know
why. "If that goes on," said Mr. Rossiter, nodding towards
Valeria's lantern, "they'll fire one of their guns at us."

"Oh, no. Why?" said Alban. He buttoned up, however,
the collar of his mackintosh.

"Nervous as cats. It's high time that girl was married.
She's a nice girl in many ways, too."

"Couldn't we get the lantern away from her?" They
stepped on a paved causeway and heard the water nibble
the rocks.

"She'd scream the place down. She's of age now, you
see."

"But if—"

"Oh, she won't do that; I was having a bit of fun with
you." Chuckling equably, Mrs. Treye's uncle unlocked
and pulled open the boat-house door. A bat whistled out.

"Why are we here?"

"She might come for the boat; she's a fine oar," said
Mr. Rossiter wisely. The place was familiar to him; he lit
an oil-lamp and, sitting down on a trestle with a staunch
air of having done what he could, reached a bottle of
whisky out of the boat. He motioned the bottle to Alban.

"It's a wild night," he said. "Ah, well, we don't have these destroyers every day."

"That seems fortunate."

"Well, it is and it isn't." Restoring the bottle to the vertical, Mr. Rossiter continued: "It's a pity you don't want a wife. You'd be the better for a wife, d'you see, a young fellow like you. She's got a nice character; she's a girl you could shape. She's got a nice income." The bat returned from the rain and knocked round the lamp. Lowering the bottle frequently, Mr. Rossiter talked to Alban (whose attitude remained negative) of women in general and the parlourmaid in particular. . . .

"Bat!" Alban squealed irrepressibly, and with his hand to his ear—where he still felt it—fled from the boathouse. Mr. Rossiter's conversation continued. Alban's pumps squelched as he ran; he skidded along the causeway and baulked at the upward steps. His soul squelched equally: he had been warned; he had been warned. He had heard they were all mad; he had erred out of headiness and curiosity. A degree of terror was agreeable to his vanity: by express wish he had occupied haunted rooms. Now he had no other pumps in this country, no idea where to buy them, and a ducal visit ahead. Also, wandering as it were among the apples and amphoras of an art school, he had blundered into the life room: woman revolved gravely.

"Hell," he said to the steps, mounting, his mind blank to the outcome.

He was nerved for the jumping lantern, but half-way up to the Castle darkness was once more absolute. Her lantern had gone out; he could orientate himself—in spite of himself—by her sobbing. Absolute desperation. He pulled up so short that, for balance, he had to cling to a creaking tree.

"Hi!" she croaked. Then: "You *are* there! I hear you!"

"Miss Cuffe—"

"How too bad you are! I never heard you rowing. I thought you were never coming—"

"Quietly, my dear girl."

"Come up quickly. I haven't even seen you. Come up to the windows—"

"Miss Cuffe——"

"Don't you remember the way?" As sure but not so noiseless as a cat in the dark, Valeria hurried to him.

"Mr. Garrett—" she panted. "I'm Miss Cuffe. Where have you been? I've destroyed my beautiful red dress and they've eaten up your dinner. But we're still waiting. Don't be afraid; you'll soon be there now. I'm Miss Cuffe; this is my Castle—"

"Listen, it's I, Mr. Alban—"

"Ssh, ssh, Mr. Alban: *Mr. Garrett has landed.*"

Her cry, his voice, some breath of the joyful intelligence, brought the others on to the terrace, blind with lamplight.

"Valeria?"

"Mr. Garrett has landed!"

Mrs. Treye said to Miss Carbin under her breath, "Mr. Garrett has come."

Miss Carbin, half weeping with agitation, replied, "We must go in." But uncertain who was to speak next, or how to speak, they remained leaning over the darkness. Behind, through the windows, lamps spread great skirts of light, and Mars and Mercury, unable to contain themselves, stooped from their pedestals. The dumb keyboard shone like a ballroom floor.

Alban, looking up, saw their arms and shoulders under the bright rain. Close by, Valeria's fingers creaked on her warm wet satin. She laughed like a princess, magnificently justified. Their unseen faces were all three lovely, and, in the silence after the laughter, such a strong tenderness reached him that, standing there in full manhood, he was for a moment not exiled. For the moment, without moving or speaking, he stood, in the dark, in a flame, as though all three said: "My darling . . ."

Perhaps it was best for them all that early, when next day first lightened the rain, the destroyer steamed out— below the extinguished Castle where Valeria lay with her arms wide, past the boat-house where Mr. Rossiter lay insensible and the bat hung masked in its wings— down the estuary into the open sea.

The Disinherited

AUTUMN had set in early. While the days were still
glowing, the woods took on from a distance a yellow,
unreal sheen, like a reflection from metal; their fretted
outlines hardened against the blond open hills that the
vibrations of summer no longer disturbed. In the early
mornings, dew spread a bright white bloom between long
indigo shadows; the afternoon air quickened, but after
sunset mists diluted the moon. This first phase of autumn
was lovely; decay first made itself felt as an extreme sweetness: with just such a touch of delicious morbidity a lover
might contemplate the idea of death.

Later the rain came, and there were drenching mono-
tone days; the leaves, rotting uncoloured, slid down
through the rain. Mid-autumn set in mild, immobile, and
nerveless; the days had unclear margins, mists webbed the
gardens all day, the sun slanting slowly through them to
touch the brown pear-trees and pale yellow currant-
leaves, here and there a marigold or a sodden rose. There
was no wind, and the woods stood heavily tense; against
their darkness, in the toneless November evenings, the
oaks were still yellow and shed a frightening glare. Everything rotted slowly. The dark, rain-swollen rivers flowed
fast between bleaching sedges, with leaves caught on the
current. After the rain, an unlit grey sky bound the earth,

and pools threaded the grass and lay unglittering inside the brittle reeds. Now and then the skies were disturbed by a high-up swift rustling sigh: the summer birds flying south. The shredded last leaves still clung to the trees, as though they would not fall: eternity seemed to have set in at late autumn. Some way into November, a wind sprang up at nights.

Marianne Harvey was not aware of the autumn to which her friend Davina was becoming a prey. Since August, Marianne had been cheerfully busy, without a moment for any kind of reflection; the Harveys were nesting over again, after twelve years of marriage, making a new home. But all those weeks Davina Archworth had been idle with a melancholy and hollow idleness, with all day to kick the wet leaf-drifts and watch the birds go.

The Harveys had left London and come up to live on the new building estate, in a freshly built white rough-cast house with a touch of priggishness in its architecture. The estate, on a hill dominating from some distance a university city, was exclusive; lots here could only be purchased on the distinct condition that houses of a fixed value were to be put up. You undertook not to keep chickens, put up a frame garage, or hang out clothes. Into the tone of this niceness the Harveys easily fell. Few houses had gone up so far; those there were stood apart, like Englishmen not yet acquainted, washed by clear upland air and each in its acre of wiry grass that had lost its nature, being no longer meadow and not yet lawn. Half-made roads, like the first knowing cuts of a scalpel, mapped the flank of the hill out, up to the concrete water-tower upon its crest. No buses approached, and there were and would be no shops.

At the foot of this genteel hill, at the river level, the old village frowsted inside its ring of elm-trees, mouldy and snug. Its lichened barn-roofs were yellow, and from the church spire the weathercock now and then shot out one sharp gold ray; from the tower there came up, climbing the hill on Sundays, ponderous chimes. A clot of thin smoke hung melting in watery river light over the roofs

of the village; after sunset a few dark lights outlined the
three-cornered green. A wide pitch-black by-pass road
with white kerbs swept south round the foot of the hill,
cutting off the old village from the new building estate.
On the far flank of the village the stretching brick-red
tentacles of the city made their advance over water-
meadows tufted with lines of willow; far off, the brittle
city spires pricked at the skyline. The small, shallow river
on which the village was built ran into another, grand
one: a beetle-green gasometer stood at this point, and
there was a steel bridge over which London expresses
rumbled and rang. Sometimes a swan, disturbed, sailed
up the backwater.

It enraged Davina that the new estate (no affair of her
own, as she had not been asked to live there) should not
have any shops. Naturally aristocratic, she loathed refine-
ment. She especially liked little shops to be just a minute away from wherever she might be living, shops that
are cheesy and mixed and stay open on Sundays, where
you buy cigarettes, peppermints, shoelaces, picture papers, sardines, purgative pills, and writing compendiums
with pictures on the outside. She liked chatting late across
counters in the dark lamplight and charming unauthorised
people into selling her stamps. She had that kind of restless feeling for Marianne that makes one critical; she
therefore despised Marianne's habit of shopping by telephone, which put her, she thought, out of touch with
reality. The whole new estate with its rawness, its air at
once hygienic and intellectual, revolted Davina. All the
same, she was up there constantly, dropping in at all times
of the day to see Marianne Harvey. Attraction, propin-
quity, and, on Davina's part, idleness fostered this funny
alliance.

Davina had come to live in the old village with and on
her aunt—or, strictly, her uncle's widow—Mrs. Walsing-
ham Archworth. Her existence was temporary; though
she had few prospects she was, or had been till lately,
hoping for better times. Her aunt's house had been the
manor, and Mrs. Archworth, though she had by now disposed of all other property, still looked on herself as pa-

troness of the village. Her house, backed by an ilex and
flanked by lines of clipped hollies, had a high, narrow
face, with dark inanimate windows, and looked like the
frontispiece to a ghost-story. Inside, however, it was
kindly, crimson, and stuffy. Its front windows looked
down a lawn, through wrought-iron gates, on to the village green, where the lime-trees shed their leaves early.
. . . Davina could not enjoy living here, on her aunt;
mortification and dullness ravaged her. But, at twenty-
nine, she had no more money of any kind; she had run
through her capital; love-affairs and her other expensive
habits had ruined her. To earn was out of the question:
she had no idea what to do. In an agony of impatience,
she waited about indefinitely. Something that should have
occurred—she was not sure what—had not occurred yet,
and became every day more unlikely. She remained,
angry, immobile, regretting that circumstances over which
she had had really, at one time, every control, should have
driven her into exploiting her aunt's affection.

This was too easy. In looks as well as in temperament
Davina resembled her dead uncle, who, melancholy and
dashing, had hung up his hat in this house with a gracious
despondent gesture and had been loved to distraction by
his dull, pink wife throughout the years of their marriage,
in return for which he had given her scarcely a smile.
Davina herself had, further, just that touch of the sombre romantic about her that appeals to all other women,
even to relatives. She was adored by her aunt, now a
puffy, huffy, formal, bewildered, charmless elderly widow.
Davina was tall, with a head set strikingly on a dark-ivory
neck; her springy dark hair, shortish, was tucked back
behind her ears. Her features, well cut, were perhaps
rather pronounced, but her sombreness and her unwilling smile could be enchanting. She could command that
remarkable immobility possible only to nervously restless
people, when only her dark eyes' intent and striking glitter betrayed the tension behind. She moved well, with
an independent and colt-like carriage; her manner was,
for a young woman's, decided, a shade overbearing, in-
timidating to lovers whom her appearance beguiled. Had

she had sphere, space, ease of mind, she might have been generous, active, and even noble; emotion need only have played a small part in her life. She was a woman born to make herself felt.

As things were, hurt pride distorted her memories; an inflamed sense of self isolated her; miscarried projects darkened her whole view. Her thoughts were almost all angry. "If I had money—" she said again and again. She walked miles a day, clicking her third left-hand finger angrily on her thumb, pacing the fields with a long nervy mannish stride. In this countryside she was a stranger; in the mild academic city she cared to know nobody. Friends, it appeared, had forgotten her. Indoors she smoked, kicked the fire up, tore the plots from crime novels, and switched the wireless scornfully on and off.

Mrs. Archworth was sorry to see the hill she had known all her life, and sometimes walked with her husband, cut up for building plots. For several months this had made her huffy, distressed. She had to admit, however, that times were changing, and after some searchings of heart she decided to call on the newcomers. So her heavy Daimler ploughed uphill one afternoon through the mud of the half-made roads, swerving past rubble and bouncing her on the springs. Alas, the new houses were draughty, with sweating plaster, and she returned with a chill: it was unfortunate that she had found anybody at home. Marianne, for her part, had been gratified by Mrs. Archworth's visit, for she took her to be county. It was in returning the call that Marianne had met Davina for the first time; she was shown by the parlourmaid into a morning-room dense with smoke and loud with the wireless, from which Davina, glowering, found no way to escape.

Six days after that, on the ridge of the hill by the water-tower, they met again. Marianne, hatless, was exercising two dogs. Her thick honey-fair hair, ruffling away from her forehead, glinted in afternoon sunshine that fell on the unspoilt country beyond the hill. Rivery twists of mist lay along the river below. This was the first phase of autumn, the air agitating and sweet. When Marianne saw Davina she blushed with pleasure and shyness. They walked on the skyline, between the brambles that still gave out a morningish smell of dew: Marianne invited Davina back to her house for tea. . . . She was house-proud, and led this new friend with a touch of emotion up the path to the porch, across the ambitious raw garden. Davina, however, looked neither to right nor left: indoors, she did give one glance of surprise rather than pleasure round the Harvey living room, artfully pale and bare, where through steel-framed windows blue-pink afternoon light flooded the walls and waxy expanse of floor. It all looked to Davina nullish, with, here and there, the stigmata of intellectual good taste. The hearth was bare, but steam heating drew out sweat from the plaster while, to Davina's senses, devitalising and parching the air. Ranged round the cold brick hearth, three low chairs with sailcloth cushions invited a confidence everything else forbade. A clock ticked, but the room had no pulse.

"My husband's not here," said Marianne, looking uncertain. Davina simply said "Oh." They sat down to tea.

"I am fifteen years younger than Matthew," Marianne said later, apropos of something else.

Matthew had lately retired from the Civil Service owing to ill health. However, he felt better now. At the same time his aunt had died, leaving Matthew more money, so he had decided to live where he liked, and to build. Sentiment had drawn him back to the scene of his happiest years, Marianne having agreed that it would be interesting to live near a university. He was honorary secretary to a society here; in addition to this, he had some philanthropic work in connection with which he was quite often away. He was a member of the senior common-room of his college, and dined in hall three times a term. Once or twice a week the Harveys would dine early and motor into the city to attend the meetings of learned societies or soirées given by the Art Club. Life here was full of interest, Marianne said. Moreover, Matthew and Marianne were happy in each other's affection. After twelve years of marriage his wife still charmed him with her serenity, mild good spirits, and love of home. And she had more than this: he took pride in that touch of the farouche about her beauty; she was big-limbed, wide-browed, and looked like a diffident goddess, but her eyebrows turned up to her temples like impatient wings and her alive hair in honey-dark ringlets fell every way. Her fairness and uncertain manner made her seem still quite young: in his friends here she stirred up a dusty sentiment. All this was dear to Matthew, who craved little more than refreshment: he was not a passionate man. Living closely, since they came back here, with the ghost of his own adolescence, raising the old evocations from the same poetry— out of one book slipped a grass-blade twenty-five years old, from another a pressed fritillary—taking the same river-walks, he saw how his friends grew greyer, how their sentiments creaked, and, with dismay for himself, dreaded to desiccate. He clung to his wife's over-freshness, her touch of the vine-leaf. . . . Cautious, well-read, tolerant, and inclined to be prosy, Matthew had fluffy pepper-and-salt hair thinning away from the temples, a rather too constant kind smile, and a nose veined at the bridge; he wore shell-rimmed spectacles with gold hook-on side-pieces, a Norfolk jacket of antique cut, and grey flannel trousers that always bulged at the knee. He and Marianne had two sons, Edwin and Luke; Luke had just joined Edwin at a preparatory school. When the boys came back for their first Christmas in the new home they would be taken for walks by their father, who would describe his youth here and make them familiar with the antiquities of the city.

Davina had never learned how a poor relation behaves. She exacted, grumbled, and ordered the servants around, walked mud into carpets, and stayed in bed overtime, rang bells all day long, and, till recently took out the car when she chose. Her aunt's maids admired Davina's lordly habit of being unfair: their own mistress, with her affronted, muddled, and rather tippeting manner, they had well in control. . . . From the first, however, there had been trouble with the chauffeur.

Prothero, the chauffeur, lived in the coachman's room

above what had been the stables, up a built-in staircase
at the end of the yard. His window faced the Manor back-
bedroom windows. He had been with Mrs. Archworth
four months, a few weeks more than Davina, having been
engaged after good old Robinson died. He had come with
a first-rate character; none of his former employers could
write too highly of him. He was forbiddingly faultless, a
careful driver; he did not grumble, make love to the
maids, or expect beer. Mrs. Archworth could never be
certain why she did not like him better, or why his proximity while he was tucking her into the car, his way of
receiving orders, even the set of his shoulders and back
of his ears as he drove, should fill her with a resentful uneasiness. There was something unlikely about him, and
she mistrusted the odd. Between his flat peaked blue cap
and his blue collar his face was always shadowless, abstract, null: a face remembered as being unmemorable.
The only look he gave you was level and unmoving.
Though she got all she paid for, she could not feel he was
hers. Her cook was "my cook," but he remained "the
chauffeur." His manner had not that alacrity to which she
was accustomed; always on the polite side of surly, he was
at the same time unsmiling and taciturn. Here, however,
he was, and she dreaded change as in some way an ally
of death. . . . So that she liked to think his oddness was
simply his surname; such an unusual name for a chauffeur,
everyone said.

But one point against Prothero Mrs. Archworth *could*
fix: he burnt light too late. Her own nights were often
disturbed by a windy form of dyspepsia; her long bedroom extended the depth of the house, and it was annoy-
ing to see, through the blind of her back window,
Prothero's light still burning, behind the screen of the ilex,
till one or two o'clock. It became her nervous habit to
court the annoyance, to wake again and again to see if
this were still so. Mrs. Archworth would lie rigid with anger and speculation. Finally, one morning, flushing with
apprehension, she protested against this use of her electricity. Prothero bowed. That night, at ten o'clock, he

flicked off his hanging light with sardonic promptness: a dimmer glow succeeded: he sat up by candlelight. She had to suppose, with an obscure sense of frustration, the candles might be his own. Night after night, as she still peered through the ilex, not a shadow moved on his blind. She suspected him, all the same, of bringing in women—but the yard gates were bolted and there was never a sound from the dog.

His life at the edge of this household of women remained inscrutable. But one thing they could all see: he could not do with Davina. She would take out the car when it pleased her, without a word to Prothero; she brought it in always dirty and sometimes late. Then one night she had found the gates bolted against her; two days after that he had locked the garage. Davina went, stormy, for Prothero. No one knew what occurred, but after that she no longer took out the car. No word from either side reached Mrs. Archworth direct. During this friction between her niece and her chauffeur she behaved like a terrified ostrich. After that week, things had quieted down for a bit.

One night in early November, Prothero, in reply to a whistle repeated on a rising note and each time with less caution, opened his door at the head of the built-in staircase and came half way down, cigarette in his mouth. The stairs creaked as he padded, and came to a stop silently. Davina stood in the arch at the foot of the staircase, with Marianne Harvey behind her out in the yard. Their figures were silhouetted against a patch of yard lamplight. Both the young women were hatless and wore heavy overcoats. Against the night sky, clotted and dense, the papery ilex shivered; night wind, with a sinister flitter of dead leaves, raced round the yard, whose cobbles dappled away into leathery bat's-wing darkness beyond the lamp.

The two stood looking up; the staircase creaked again, and Prothero still said nothing. Davina advanced with a nervous swaggering movement and put one foot on the stairs. She began: "Look here—"

He said uncivilly: "Well?"

She dug her hands into her pockets. "I want some more money," she said with a casual air.

He shifted his cigarette. "What," he said, "*now?* To-night?"

"Naturally," said Davina, with some impatience. Outside the archway Mrs. Harvey stepped back and glanced uneasily round her into the dark, as though she did not care at all for her company. An unseen smile hung in the dark of the stairs; Prothero let his cigarette drop and ground it out with his heel. "For heaven's sake," she said, "*hurry*"; and shifted her foot. The deliberate and endless silence was painful to Marianne. "Right," he said. "Come on up."

He turned back into his room, and Davina, with automatic swiftness and energy, went springing upstairs after him. His door stayed ajar; vibrations of heat from the stove came down through the arch to the horrified Marianne. Looking up at the dark sky, she fought for a feeling of everybody's nonentity. The clock in the church tower, not far away, struck nine: before the last stroke finished Davina was down again. She caught Marianne by the elbow and ran her across the yard. They paused by the lamp a minute; Davina held a crackling note close up to Marianne's face. "That is that," she said.

Wincing away from the note, with its smell of delinquency, Marianne, not for the first time, wished herself safe at home. But the wish was the merest moment's frightened retraction and not sincere: Marianne's heart was set on this evening's pleasure, this fantastic setting-out. In these weeks of knowing Davina her faculty for disapproval seemed to be all used up. She was under a spell. She blamed herself, and knew Davina despised her, for being too shy or too sly to ask Matthew for money before he started for London, where he would stay to-night.

She said faintly, "Oh, how you *could* . . ."

Her friend looked satirical. She had seen Marianne's recoil from the servant's money. On the subject of class, she knew, Marianne felt as awkwardly and obscurely as

people do about sex. Marianne said: "But why not go to
your aunt?"

"You have no idea of what's impossible and what's not!
It would make *me* sick to ask Matthew— However, that's
your affair. Now, for God's sake, my good girl, don't waste
any more time!"

Marianne's brain hummed with frightening anticipation. Leaving the yard, they crept like a couple of cats
round the unlit flank of the house, between the wall and
the spiny flutter of hollies. Round at the front, an inch-
wide slit of bright light fell on Davina's smile: secrecy
quickened their breath as they stopped a minute to look
in between the drawing-room curtains at Davina's aunt
at bridge with three of her neighbours. In the dense red-
shaded lamplight sealed in by the pane the two ladies'
lace jabots, the two gentlemen's shirt-fronts, stood out like
tombstones: the intent quartette, the glazed cabinets and
woolly white rugs, all looked embedded in something
transparent, solid and hot, like clarified red wax. Not a
sound came through the pane. The two turned and crept
away down the dark lawn.

Outside the gates, Marianne's coupé had been run up
on to the rough grass of the green, with its lights out. Its
air was lurking and crookish. They got in, and Marianne
ran the car bumpily off the grass and away down a lane
between blank end-walls of cottages, on to the by-pass
road. Marianne's heart went up as they slid clear of the
walls that had stared amazed in her headlights: the sweeping black irresistible river of road sucked at her will like
a current; their speed heightened; with a swing of lights
they swept south. Davina eyed the speedometer. "Hurry,"
she said.

Marianne had a flicker of spirit. "If you bully me, I'll
go home."

"Let me *drive*—"

"No."

"Oh, very well, Mrs. Harvey."

"This is a good beginning," said Marianne, sore.

"Left!" said Davina sharply, and held to the lights of

the dashboard, as they approached a cross-roads, a vague little pencilled map. After some minutes she said: "If it makes you feel any better, he's not a chauffeur; he's a crook."

"Don't be silly," said Marianne. An impassable wall of good humour divides any lady from fact. But she could not resist saying, "Besides, how do you know?"

"I know he knows I know. He's lying low here. I've seen his photograph somewhere—something once happened."

"You get ideas in your head from reading those frightful books."

"But things do happen, you know," said Davina calmly. Sliding down in her seat and eyeing the flying darkness, she fingered the note in her pocket with cautious pleasure, like someone hugging a thought. Meanwhile Marianne thought of a smart little Jewish girl she used to go to tea with when she was nine years old and living at Dulwich. That little girl had declared there was a dead baby strapped up in a trunk in her family's cistern loft. After tea in the frightening Gothic house, they had crept up to the door, but Marianne would not go in, hearing with horror the cistern inside gurgle. But later her mother told her the little Jewish girl was not a lady, and ever since then Marianne had thought of the extraordinary with contempt. Pressing her chin down in the folds of her muffler, she made up her mind to ask no more about Prothero.

Prothero's pound note was soon changed, for Marianne had not filled up the car and they had to pull up for petrol: she ran the car into the bay of a filling station. While the man unlocked the pump, Marianne got out a minute, restlessly, from the car. Behind them, the last lights of streets were strung along the horizon; the thin glow above a provincial city hung on the sky. Marianne felt her face turned for ever to the unknown. But flight was life to Davina, with nothing to leave behind.

A friend's unknown friends are dæmons or demigods with frightful attributes. Marianne's heart sank at the thought of the meeting ahead. The night air was uncalm-

ing and anxious: no moon but a rolling hurry of clouds:
a circle of rotting flower-stalks outside the petrol station
shivered under their headlights in the dark wind.

They drove on.

A glittering Neon sign like wolves' eyes read: OPEN
ALL NIGHT, at which thought a dry weariness pervaded
the brain. "We shan't be staying *all* night," said Davina
easily. Here they were, and they tore up the pencilled
map and scattered the scraps on the wind.

The road-house stood at the cross-roads, its row of
Christmas-card windows shedding a fictitious glow. Four
wide black roads had been levelled into the hill, and met
in a kind of circus inside the clay banks of the cutting.
The road-house stood high up; to the porch you mounted
some steps up the high embankment; a car park was
scooped out fifty yards further on. The wind moaned
cheerlessly over the down behind, but the scene had a
hard air of late night merriment, like a fixed grin. . . . In
the porch, Marianne pulled off a gauntlet to tuck back a
strand of hair; Davina whipped out her lipstick and gave
herself new, bright lips. "We were once rather in love."

But inside there was no one. A long row of swinging
lanterns bobbed in their own horrid light as they pushed
open the door. The lounge was empty and bald as the inside of a bandbox, glazed with synthetic panelling. The
chairs were askew, empty, with flattened cushions; ashtrays sent up a cold fume; the place wore an air of sudden, sheepish vacuity, as though a large party had just
got up and gone out. The barman leaned, yawning, just
inside the bar shutter. When they came in, he took no
notice. Davina's friends had not come.

Davina, who had sauntered in with a smile on her fine
reddened lips, dropped the smile and looked round her,
utterly at a loss.

"Perhaps we are early," said Marianne.

"No."

"Perhaps they are late?"

"They can't be later than us."

"Perhaps they've given us up?"

"They know I am always late——" Davina broke off, crossed the room, and angrily questioned the barman. No, no one had asked for her; no one had waited; no one had telephoned. Sitting down by the shutter, she snapped out an order for bitter. "I can't drink beer," said Marianne, as it was brought.

"You'd better," Davina said with a hollow look.

Marianne fingered her glass. "This seems a funny place to be meeting anyone in . . ."

"Well, we're not, you see. Does that make it all right?"

A clock struck ten; someone bumped down the bar shutter and locked it. The barman came for their glasses. So that was that.

After some time Marianne said: "You know, we can't wait all night."

"I don't see why not."

Lighting a cigarette, Davina said no more. An uneasy silence set in. Marianne, watching her friend's lips pulling at the cigarette, the once bold dark eyes that now crept to the door then dropped quickly to cover their mortification, felt pity go through her heart with a shameful pang. She also was mortified, and could have easily wept. She only half knew now all she had hoped of to-night. Girlish delicious expectancy went sour inside her. She was tragically sold. She had been, from the first, imposed on by something about Davina—her dashingness, curtness, and air of experience. In these last weeks, Marianne's consciousness had been extended deliciously, painfully. A segment of bright unknown world had fallen across her path, where it shed prisms. Only she knew what formless excitement had racked her lately.

But where was To-night?

Seeing Davina sitting, so much at a loss, with "Forgotten" pasted across her, too proud to look up, Marianne felt the world contract again. In the next room, someone put a wailing blues on the gramophone. Marianne wished she were home, with her feet on the hot pipes and the cat on her stomach. Out here, draughts raced round the floor.

Davina shot up and said: "I shall telephone!"

.   .   .   .

They drove on again. "I'll tell you one thing," Davina was saying. "Somebody's double-crossed me. Unless Oliver's lying—and I don't think he'd be lying—I ought to have got his message at aunt's to-day."

"Plans are changed?" quavered Marianne.

"Yes, don't you *see*—" said Davina. Her spirits, however, were up. She sat smiling and silent, looking along the headlights. Things had changed for the better. They had swung east at the cross-roads, always further from home. After more miles of flying hypnotic night, Davina said it ought to be anywhere now. "Any time now, on your right. . . ." On their right, they crept in between two Palladian lodges, unlit and staring, the wide gates standing apart. Beech-trunks raced past their lights and a sleek wettish avenue spattered under the tires: three more gates were hooked back.

The immense façade of the house rushed glaring on to their headlamps: between high white-shuttered windows pilasters soared out of sight above an unlit fanlight like patterns of black ice. Reaching across Marianne, Davina touched the horn, which sent up that face of coldness its peevish cry. The cry repeated—"They can't even *hear!*" she groaned. But then the fanlight amazingly sprang into light, the hall door burst open on a perspective of pillars, and, with so much thrusting and force that this seemed a muffled riot, dark people shot out, surrounded the car, and pulled open both doors at once. Marianne ducked in a sweep of night air. Davina, peering, said: "Oliver?"

"I've g-got this all to myself!" exclaimed an excitable voice.

"Where's Thingummy?"

"O-o-oh, be never turned up."

"So he's not here," said a woman.

"I am furious," said Davina.

"That's too bad," said Oliver, pulling Davina out of the car with a glass in his other hand. "Never mind, you're here now."

"It was too bad," agreed someone. "However, here we all are."

They trooped back into the hall. A stout, speechless man who had pulled Marianne through the other door of the car looked at her in the light, closely, to see what he had got. He seemed satisfied. Indoors, the immense cold hall, all chequered pavement and pillars, wore an air of outrage, ravished by steps and voices. One door stood open, and light peered in at the glacial sheeted outlines of furniture and a chandelier that hung in a bag like a cheese and glittered inside the muslin. A chill came from the hearthstones; the house was masterless. Along a pathway of drugget over the marble, at a quick muffled shuffle as though conducting a funeral secretly, the revellers passed down the hall to a door at the far end. They shot through with a rush, each unwilling to be the last, and shut the door defiantly on the echoing house.

"Outside there gives you the creeps," said the only woman who spoke. Davina's friend Oliver, dishevelled, fair, aquiline, and unnaturally tall, turned and shook hands with Marianne. "I didn't see you," he said. "I'm so glad you came. I hope you had no trouble; I went down just now and opened the gates myself. Do you know if the sheep got out? They are grazing sheep; things are not what they used to be."

Smoke and human stuffiness thickened the air of this room with its dead undertone of chill on which a snapping wood fire had little effect. It was a high, shabby, gilt-and-white octagonal ante-room, the naked shutters of three windows fortified by iron bars. Bottles crowded a top-heavy ornate table under the chandelier; panels of tarnished mirror kept multiplying the company, and on a red marble column a Psyche balanced with one hand over a breast. Oliver said: "I brought her in here for company: I always liked the girl." On a settee, pulled across the hearth at an angle, an enormous congested old lady slept with her feet apart, letting out stertorous breaths. Her wool coatee was pinned over the heaving ledge of her bust with a paste brooch in the form of a sailing-ship, and at each breath this winked out a knowing ray. Her hands, chapped and knouty, lay in the trough of her lap.

Half under her skirts a black pair of kitchen bellows lay
on the marble fire-kerb. There was not much more furniture in the room.

"That is Mrs. Bennington, who takes care of me. She's
so nice," said Oliver. He rinsed a glass out at a syphon and
brought Davina a drink. "It's a nice house, too," he said,
"till you get used to it."

"It's all right once one's got here. Why not suggest
this first?"

"You see, I thought there'd be Thingummy."

"Well, you certainly muddled things," said Davina with
less rancour, her nose inside her glass. When he and she
had been younger, handsome, high-spirited, and still with
something to spend, they had been in love, and expected
to marry one day. Their May had been blighted. Now,
each immobile from poverty, each frozen into their set-
tings like leaves in the dull ice of different puddles, they
seldom met. They had the dregs of tenderness left for
each other, but, each time they met, less to say. It was
best to meet in a crowd, as they met to-night. To-night
the crowd was not large, but things might have been
worse.

Oliver shook the dregs from another glass and absently
rinsed it, meanwhile looking at Marianne. He said to
Davina: "Will she enjoy herself?"

"She has a deadly life. Her standard is not high."

"She looks most beautifully shy," Oliver said wistfully.

Marianne felt very shy. The more the room settled
down, the more strongly she felt she had no place here.
She stood with a hand on the mantelpiece, looking blindly
about with her wide-apart troubled eyes. The stout man
who had her in charge snatched the glass Oliver had been
so vaguely holding, filled it, and brought it to Marianne.
"Now you'll feel better," he said. His name was Purdon.
Marianne could not explain that she did not like whisky.
The smell of spirits repelled and interested her; her nostrils quivered; she drank. "*That's* better," said Purdon,
and bustled up with a chair. Marianne sat down blinking
and holding her glass. As though she had been a refugee,

her coming in had seemed to constitute some kind of emergency.

"Where are we?" she said.

"Ah, *that's* just the fun," said Purdon. "Where we've no call to be!"

"As much call as anyone else," said the platinum blonde oldish girl, Miriam. She knelt by the kerb and, pulling the bellows from under Mrs. Bennington's skirts, began to puff at the fire. She coaxed the flames up knowingly; firelight flapped on her face and up Marianne's knees. An un-English man in a crimson high-necked pullover reached his drink from the floor and resettled himself on the settee, one arm around Mrs. Bennington, with an air of content. These were all the people there really were in the room. The party resumed its tenor, illicit but not defiant. A low-spirited intimacy, an innocent kind of complicity, made itself felt. Little seemed worth saying, everything understood. What was said strayed up like bubbles from depths of interiority. They had the flat, wise air of a party of bandit children with their bravado put off, gathering in a cellar.

Marianne looked into her glass; where had all that gone? Her dilated eyes swam round the smoky gilt-and-white room with its tarnished reaches of mirror. She met Oliver's look that was like something swimming desperately on a heaving tide of light. Her throat pricked and she pulled at the scarf she still wore. She exclaimed to the fat man: "This is nicer than where we were!"

"More homey?" he said nicely. She let him unwind her scarf and drape it about the Psyche. "That poor girl," he said, "gives me the shivers."

"It feels homey all right to me," said Miriam, withdrawing her head from the grate. She wiped bellows-black from her fingers on to her black velvet skirt and went on: "Which may throw some light on my pedigree, now that I come to think."

No one knew who her father was; he might have been almost anyone. Owing her unkind and scandalous mother no duty, Miriam was always glad to air this uncertainty:

it gave her a feeling of space and sometimes, to her mind, a slightly divine quality. She was herself a shady and bitter very good-hearted girl whom everyone liked and nobody seemed to want.

All Oliver's friends were like this. He was, like Davina, an enemy of society, having been led to expect what he did not get. His father had sold himself up and Oliver had had from him little but bad advice. Oliver despised the rich and disliked the poor and drank to the bloody extinction of the middle classes. He wished to call no man brother, and disbelieved with ferocity in himself. The old order left him stranded, the new offered him no place. He lived as he could, and thought well of Davina for settling herself on her aunt. His own relations had, under the suavity of their aspect, a mean kind of canniness, and were not to be imposed upon: they did what they could by imposing him on their friends. Perverse bad manners and clumsiness disqualified Oliver for the profession of being a guest, by which otherwise he might have victualled and housed himself. He had once or twice, on his uncle's recommendation, catalogued country-house libraries; his work was impatient, showy, and incorrect, but no one had said so so far, for fear of offending his uncle. He was an ungracious beggar, and, handicapped by a stammer, uncertain health, and excitable sensibility, an embarrassment to himself. With his height and fairness he was, in an overcast kind of a way, magnificent-looking: a broken-spirited Viking. He was capable of fantastically disinterested affections. Not having been born for nothing into a privileged class, he was, like Davina, entirely unscrupulous.

Lord Thingummy—so Oliver called him, and it is good enough for the purposes of this tale—possessed a fine, mouldy, unreadable library. Inflated, one night at his club, by intellectual pride, he had let himself be persuaded by Oliver's uncle as to the existence, down at his house in the country, of possible unknown treasures in calf and vellum, and induced to hire Oliver to explore and catalogue these. For this he gave Oliver twenty pounds and his victuals.

Lord Thingummy had been disposed to join Oliver for a few days in the country; but yesterday he had wired to put off. The very thought of the place had been too damp for him. His caretaker, Mrs. Bennington, was put in charge of Oliver, with instructions not to make him too comfortable, for one had heard of Oliver as a dilatory chap. . . . Lord Thingummy was thus, to-night, the party's unconscious host.

The man on the settee in a crimson pullover was a White Russian with little stake in the future. To-night he was on a holiday; as a rule he lived rather drearily with a woman of means who had a feeling for Russians, in a maisonette just off Addison Road. Miriam was a girl he and Oliver knew. The stout man, Purdon, was a dentist who had won five thousand pounds in an Irish Sweep and shut up his surgery till this should all be spent: he regretted nothing. To-morrow he went back to work. He was over-flowing with friendliness and had bought the drinks for to-night.

Thingummy, said Oliver, was so damned mean he had had the heating turned off and taken the key of the cellar. The library, where he had said he had no doubt Oliver would be happy browsing about, smelt of must. "He had the n-nerve," said Oliver, "to send me down here to live on chops in this ice-house. May his soul rot like his books!"

Purdon explained to Marianne by what a remarkable stroke of luck they all came to be here. When she understood, she had only one thought: she was agonised—the angry earl would appear. Her brain stopped like a clock; she had met few peers. She said unsteadily: "I must be going home."

"Rats," said Purdon. Nobody else heard.

Davina and Oliver pulled cushions on to the parquet and sat with their shoulders against a corner of the settee. She said: "How is the catalogue?"

"Getting on fast; I'm so anxious to get away."

"Where shall you go next?"

"How should I know?"

"You might come and stay with my aunt."

"That would depend," he said. "I must have a look at her first."

Miriam tittered: "He's put in the names of the stuck-on books on the doors."

"He's as likely to read those as any others," said Oliver.

Marianne trembled and stood up, eyeing her empty glass. She thought: "Where am I?" put down her glass, and began to finger her way along the mantelpiece's swags and medallions. She thought the marble throbbed. In despair, she sat carefully down again, gripping the scrolled gold chair-arms. Looking across for Davina, she met Oliver's eyes once more. He immediately got up and came to her side. "I've forgotten your name," he said.

"Marianne," she said. "But I've got to be going home."

He exclaimed in distress: "Aren't you happy?"

She hesitated. "I feel lost."

"Why do you say that?" said Oliver miserably.

Her uncertain look turned away from him to the fire; he saw her cheeks burn and her trembling, obstinate grip on the arms of the chair. Feeling unutterably misspent and guilty, he turned and said to Davina: "Don't let her go!"

"She's worn out," said Davina, "naturally." Mortification came flooding back to her; she plucked angrily at a carnation she had taken from one of her aunt's vases and stuck in her buttonhole. "That place was awful," she said. "*You* simply thought, 'No doubt they'll turn up here somehow.' Message? I got no message. You seem to expect one to know where you are by instinct! People like you waste one's life!"

"Your aunt ought to be on the telephone."

"You just hate trouble," she said.

"Well, don't make it," said Oliver.

"Please don't quarrel," said the Russian. Their angry dialogue took place across the room. Through some seconds of silence Mrs. Bennington wheezed.

"I took the message," said Miriam, "I, in my little fly— I mean, in my little car: I took the message. Purdon and I drove up to your aunt's house on the way from buying the drink. We snooped around the front lawn and just felt we couldn't face it, so we went round to the back and you still weren't there. They said you weren't anywhere. So we left word with a man who was polishing up a Daimler—"

"That is so," said Purdon. "We left word with the chauffeur."

"We left word very particularly," said Miriam. "*Don't* come where we said, we said, come straight to Thingummy's, here, because he's not here, so we can be. We even drew you a map," said Miriam earnestly.

Davina pulled the carnation to pieces. "I'd like to believe you," she said, "but I got no message."

"Then somebody double-crossed you," said Miriam.

By half past ten Mrs. Archworth's evening was over. The parlourmaid let out the retired Indian Civilian and his wife and the retired admiral, who pattered away round the green, with its dim lamps, to their cottages past the church. In the drawing-room the parrakeet, disturbed by the sudden silence, fidgeted under its red baize cover. Mrs. Archworth turned two of the lamps out and stooped for a good night chat with the Pekinese. The parlourmaid came in to take out the tray of glasses.

"Shall I shut up, madam?" she said.

"Not till Miss Davina is in. She is dining at Mrs. Harvey's; she won't be late. No doubt they will see her home. You must leave the door on the latch and come down later to bolt it."

Kissing the Pekinese between the eyeballs, Mrs. Archworth handed it over regretfully to the parlourmaid; she picked up her lozenge-box, her patience cards, and a paper-knife, and, with her usual air of unfocused indignation—for she seldom expected to sleep—went up to bed. The parlourmaid followed her up with a glass of hot water. Shaking her nightly powder into the glass and watching the water cloud, the aunt awaited, on the stretch and uneasy, Davina's step on the gravel. Outside two red rings of lamplight the darkness showed flat and empty; her thoughts groped around in it ignorantly, like tentacles, asking what everybody was doing, where everybody might be. She did not regret, however, that she was not on the telephone. Her axiom had been always: People can come to see one, or else people can write.

At ten o'clock to the minute Prothero lit four candles stuck into bottles and with satiric promptness flicked out the hanging light. So that Mrs. Archworth, peering out later through her back window-curtains, found his blind pallid. His room, a manservant's, with match-boarded ceiling, glazed cotton blind and fibre matting, was bare; the furniture showed by candlelight mean outlines on the whitewash. The man had no belongings; the place seemed to be to let. His chauffeur's tunic hung huddled against the back of the door. The stove through its mica front shed a dull red glow on the matting. The wind had dropped; inside its walls and high locked gates the yard down there was as still and deep as a well. Not a draught stirred those thin sheets of close-written paper shuffled over his table. Reaching the four candles closer to his left elbow, he went on writing again.

His hand with the twitching pen went rushing from line to line at a fever-high pace. He did not once pause. The pen rushed the hand along under some terrific compulsion, as though something, not thought, vital, were being drained out of him through the point of the pen. Words sprang to their places with deadly complicity, knowing each other too well. . . . Once or twice when a clinker fell in the stove, or the outside staircase unaccountably creaked as though a foot were upon it, he looked up, the tyrannic pen staggered, he looked round the room with its immutable fixtures as though he were a ghost—

"—*grave to the N.N.E. of the church tower in the sunk bit by the wall. No stone yet as it's too soon, the earth is too soft, but a wire wreath frame left with some stalks of some sort of flowers, they were quite dead. Last month you must have got soaked through to what was your heart, rain comes hard on a grave with the earth not set yet. So now you must do without company. I went once.*

"*You said once you thought you should like to die in a ward, for company. As much as you thought, you thought that. Well I was there. But you never thought much of that. Whatever you did want it wasn't that, whatever you did want you didn't seem to be getting. I never did know what you did want and I don't think you did. What you did get you didn't want, that was me. But you got what you didn't want. You got that and now I don't want any more.*

"*I don't want you any more because I don't want any more. I don't want more of all that so I don't want you or see you. I don't see your eyes that you thought as much as you thought I should not forget. If you could think now you could not think how much I never want you and how much I forget. I don't go back to the bungalow. If you could see you could see how much I forget that time. You could see I don't see the picture of dogs' heads and the pink dotted curtain flapping or standing still or the moth bumping round the whole time or the magazine with the girl's face by your feet on the bed. You tried with eyes to say I should always see them but you were wrong. They are in a list, I can say them but I can't see them.*

"*The bungalow is shut up, the papers call it a love nest but what you got there does no good to that kind of place. No woman would go there now and no one but a fool woman would have gone there in the first place. You said that yourself first thing when I came, it was no good, it was mouldy, the trees drip on the roof and over the edge of the roof, that made green smears, the press was musty inside where you hung your dress and it was you said the sheets had a musty smell. If you wanted to be by the river you should have been by the river and not a field off, and then that might not have been such a lonely place. For all I know no one goes there and as I do not see it it may not be there, for all I know.*

"*Now I don't want all that any more, now I don't want, I get on fine here with no more ants in my brain. The old woman's all right. She gets what she wants. I shut her into the hearse, it is like a hearse, with her rug and her dog*

*and we go bumping along. My ears stick out like you said
under my cap and the buttons have crests, a fist with a
knife, and I click my heels when she talks. I give satisfaction here if you know what that means but you do not
know what that means. She gets her money's worth.*

"I always was what I am, now I am what I always was,
what you said that time. Flunkey. I like what I am, a free
man. Up here I'm as snug as a monk with a stove with two
hours' fuel, no pictures, no pictures of dogs. The bed
squeaks when I turn so I lie still like you lie, only it's
broader, with your arms down at your sides. My stairs are
my stairs and no one comes up, if I did want they would
come. I have that money you had, that was my money
you had, a bad debt after all I did. The girl owes me seven
pound ten six, so I buy the kisses now. All the fun's in the
deal now I know what I don't want.

"They say when you've done what I've done you go
back. But that's not true. I went once where you are to
be sure you are there, but I don't go where we were that
last time. I don't act any way they would think I would
act. I act my own way now, only I act that way because
it is my way. If I don't know what I will do, how can they
know what I will do? I act now before I think, and I don't
think after I act. I act how I like. You always knew what
I would do, so I always had to do that. Now no one knows,
I don't know, I act.

"Love was just having to act in the one way. There was
just one way we could go, like both being in a tram. We
acted the way we had to. Slippings-off just us two and
fake names and quarrels and all that fun. They all go that
same way. Where the tram didn't take the points, where
the bump was, was your way with that money you had.
You had all the money. The clink in your gold chain bag
that you always watched and always kept by your hand
and the wallet you brought out when the bills came, smiling because it was you had the money to spend but not
liking to spend your money and smiling at me that knowing way and pushing the notes back that we didn't want
yet. You could pay for the fancies you had with all that
money you had. Our bed smelt of all your money. I was

*a fool then to love you the way I did, I gave more than
you paid for, you saw I was a fool and that you paid for a
fool. You were not the big business man's daughter for
nothing, Anita, and not the great big business man's wife.*

"No one saw so no one knew, we met first of all in the
train so no one knew we had met, we didn't write letters,
you were very smart that way, you were very sly. I saw
you were no good. Your husband was a strict man. For
some time we tricked your husband all over the place in
a hurry, then you said there was no time, we had to have
more time, we had to have some place. What with being
so plotty, so damned smart, so careful no one would see
us who would remember, a different place every time—
that was not value, you thought. You had to have more
time, you said. What did you have to have more time
for? You'd torn me up by that time, in that first month,
what more did you want? You went off and leased that
bungalow in a fake name. By that time I was poison to
you, and you were to me. It rained that first day that was
the last time, when you told me I had to come there. I
left my car in the garage outside the town up the river
and then I walked down in the rain to where you were.
I felt like lead, the wind bent the trees back on the hill
on the far side, the rain hit the river, it was all dark grey
like a photograph. No one was out, I didn't meet anyone.
I felt like a stone. When I came round the trees I saw that
was the place and I hated the place with trees dripping
on the roof and streaks on the white gate. It looked a hole
for a toad. When I came up the path a window blew open,
a pink dotted curtain blew out in the wet. Your arm came
out after the curtain and shut the window so I knew you
were in there waiting. The trees up there lashed about.
You had seen me, of course. Then, at that time, I couldn't
see any way out. There was no air in the house. Though
the place was alone with nobody going by you drew the
pink curtain as soon as I came in. The whole time the
windows rattled, the rain got lashed down by the trees
on our roof.

"At sunset the wind stopped and then the rain stopped,
I got up and opened the window. There was a yellow

*light near the river, it was hot because it was July, now
the wind had stopped, and then everything steamed. The
steam made everything hot, moths came out and bumped
on the windows as it was getting darker, musty
smells came out of the walls of the room where we were.
We were done in by then. You began crying and I went
off to open a can of corned beef to eat. I shut the door but
you opened it, you went on talking at me while I was
opening the can and that note came in your voice like the
needle skidding on the inside of a record when the record
is done. When I didn't answer you came into the kitchen
the way you were and asked for a cigarette. I said I hadn't
a cigarette, I'd been looking for yours. Then you said what
you said. So I went out and walked.*

*"I walked along by the river and didn't meet anyone,
I thought I wouldn't go back but my hat was there and
you had to have some answer to what you had said. I saw
you had me bought up. A motor salesman who didn't do
big business and didn't have money and started to have
tastes he didn't have money for. A war gentleman after
the war, you'd have liked me then in the war. I could see
how things were. A man with the sort of face everybody
forgot, that you said you mostly forgot. I walked some
time by the same bit of the river, I didn't go far...*

*"When I came back you had lit the lamp by the bed
and lay smoking and reading a magazine with a girl's face
on the front, you knew I would come back. I came and
stood the other side of the lamp to wait till you had finished your magazine story. You stretched your arms past
your head and yawned and arched up your back, then
you smiled the way you smiled and said you'd been nervous. You said how much you liked company, like you
had always said. But when I didn't say anything but
just waited, without noticing you, you turned over slowly
as though you were so comfortable and slid your hand
slowly between your cheek and the pillow and said that
again slowly. You said that again. You said what you
meant. You said what you'd said before. I saw a red mist
where your face was, just a mist on the pillow. I took the
pillow and smothered you.*

"The moth bumped about the whole time I leaned on the pillow, then flew into the curtain. The picture of dogs' heads was over the bed and the magazine stayed by your feet on the bed, when you didn't move any more it was still there. Your eyes were looking at me when I lifted the pillow. I took the note-case out of your gold handbag and took your pearls off the table and took your rings and I left the lamp by you to burn out. I left finger-prints, I suppose. I took no trouble. I had taken trouble enough. I banked on no one knowing I knew you. I rubbed your face powder off the mirror with my elbow and had a good look, I thought at least I'd remember my own face. I went out leaving the door on the latch. You stayed there, that was all you knew. You stayed alone.

"I took the gold bag that you always kept by your hand and dropped it in the river along the bank. Clouds came up again but everything was quite quiet, it was dark then. Walking away for always from where you were I didn't feel like me yet. Two swans went by but I didn't meet anyone by the river. It was past ten, I came to the town with the garage, I passed the cinema then, they were all coming out. I joined in with them all and walked to the garage along with some people, we all took our cars out. I drove south towards Newhaven, and pulled up the car by a wood and slept for a bit, then I drove on. I put up the car at Newhaven when it was light and crossed by the day boat the way it had been arranged. I was crossing to France that day on the firm's business anyhow. In Paris I sold your pearls and two of your rings, I kept the third I liked best. I was at Le Mans when I saw they'd found you, then the firm sent me on to Lyons and I saw your face in the papers, you were the bungalow crime, the French papers had you in because you were young and pretty and it looked like a man. It seemed funny to think I knew you when I saw you in those papers. Your husband covered our tracks, he thought more of being so strict than of hanging anybody, he was just like you always said. He said you'd taken the bungalow for yourself for a rest cure and he had been going to join you. That didn't help the police so they fixed robbery for the motive and pulled *in a tramp but the finger-prints didn't fit, then they went after a deserter from Aldershot, they're not so sharp as they say. For all everyone knew I might not have been born.*

"This seemed odd to me, when I knew for the first time I had been born and knew who I was now. I felt grand those weeks and fit to lift a ton weight with nothing to lift but pennies. I felt so grand I didn't know what to do. I was all alone. I didn't get thick with anybody for fear of talking when there was only the one thing I wanted to tell anybody. My head stayed very good and I saw the sense of things I never had seen the sense of. Everything got simple. So I began to like life and want a run for my money, else what was the good of being the way I was? So I wasn't taxing my good luck any more, I thought I would stage a get-out and start new, the chance came when the firm sent me to Marseilles. Mutts disappear there every day.

"A man came along there that was what I wanted, a drunk, Prothero, a chauffeur who'd been sacked from a villa near Antibes, he'd drunk all his money in Marseilles, he was so tight he sold me his passport for two hundred francs and threw in his references for fifty more. His face fitted mine all right. I said if he'd meet me again I'd give him the fifty francs that I hadn't on me the first time: he turned up blind again. I walked him down by the quays where there weren't so many lamps and then nudged him over into the harbour, he wasn't giving a damn for what happened next anyhow, so that was all right by him, he sank like a stone. I went back to his place and checked out his luggage, I left mine where it was in my hotel. The hotel people reported me missing, they found my papers and passport along with my luggage and wrote back to the firm. I wasn't just then owing the firm anything, so they didn't worry, they concluded I'd been one more of those fool English who get themselves done in in the pleasure quarter and aren't heard of again. The French police poked round but they get sick of the English. I hadn't any family to make trouble, nobody cared so everyone let things drop. My photograph was in the French papers and in the English papers, and it must have been *funny for people to think they had known me. No one remembered my face. No one went into mourning, no one felt that way. After a bit I came back to England and began to put Prothero's references into action. I was anxious to lie low, so applied here. The old woman considered herself lucky. So I got on without you, you see. You lie expecting me back, I don't come back.*

"You never considered yourself lucky. You considered you'd saddled yourself with a fool but you had to have me, I was a fool to love you that way, you were quite right. We are quit of each other, if that was what you wanted you got what you wanted, it was what I wanted, perhaps all the time we were wanting the same thing, and now I've got that I don't want anything more. You thought I had to have you, as much as you thought you thought that. You thought that when you said what you said then, and you thought that under the pillow. When I took the pillow off that was in your eyes. Well, unthink that. If I thought you thought that still, if I thought you lay thinking that where you are now, I'd break right through, I'd tear anything down to get at you and tear the thought out, I'd tear up the sunk earth. Yes, it makes me mad to see you don't see that I don't see you or want you, that you don't see when these stairs creak outside that I don't think 'Here she is,' that I lie as still as you lie with my bed not creaking any more than your sunk earth and don't think, 'She was here once.' If I were to write, 'I love you, I cannot bear this, I want you, come back'—you might be tricked. You might come back to see me see you, then you would see me not see you, you would unthink the thought you thought under the pillow, as much as you thought. Yes, look, if I tricked you this way, you'd come back, you could not not come back, you could never resist that. Yes, so look, I'll trick you I'll write loud, like a scream would be if anyone was in the dark with nothing (but I am not in the dark) I'll write so loud you will hear though you can't hear, Anita—"

The pen charged in his hand. Dragging his hand down to the foot of the paper, in staggering charging characters it wrote—"*Anita, I love you Anita, Anita, where are you?*

*I didn't mean that, that was not me, I didn't, I can't bear
you away. I see your eyes on my pillow, I can't lie alone,
I cannot get through the night, come back, where are you,
I won't hurt you, come back, come back, come back—"*

Prothero dropped the pen as though it were burning.
He watched it, frightfully animate, roll to the edge of the
table and over the edge. He stared at his right hand and
spread out the fingers slowly; they reasserted his will.
Shutting his eyes, he screwed round full to the light of
the four candles a blank-lidded square fair face clammy
with sweat. His hands meanwhile groped over the table,
gathering up by feel the close-written sheets. Rising, an
automatic and mindless movement, he flung open the lid
of the stove with a pothook and thrust the papers in,
heard for a minute the hot red roar of the stove, then
dropped the lid on the roar.

So his nights succeeded each other. At the back of the
Manor House, through the ilex, a light was still burning
in Mrs. Archworth's room. Downstairs, behind the red
kitchen blind, a sleepy, indignant maid sat up for Davina.
The village clock struck midnight with rolling strokes.

The wreathed gilt clock above Marianne's head struck
midnight with brittle chimes, at which the air quivered
like something stretched too tight. The chandelier glittering high up exhausted itself on the smoke, light losing
quality as the evening wore on, and a sluggish chill crept
over the party's wearied over-acute senses like a miasma.
With drifts of cigarette-ash in the lap of her black velvet
skirt, Miriam sat talking introspectively to nobody in particular; she did not drink any more. The Russian played
cat's cradle with a bit of gold cord from a chocolate-box.
Purdon sat on a highish chair with his legs crossed, yawning at the chandelier. Mrs. Bennington slept on.

"You see, I'm that way," went on Miriam. "I don't believe in anything. I don't belive anything really exists,
you see."

The Russian slipped the gold cord off the tips of his
fingers and, frowning with concentration, started over
again. "But look here," said Purdon, "if you're not going

to believe in anything, you have to have something not to believe *in*."

"*I* don't have to," said Miriam. "I can believe in nothing. I always could; I was always funny that way."

"Do you believe in progress?" said the Russian.

"Everything's talk," said Miriam, "and what does all that come to? I see through it."

"I don't, either," said the Russian.

"And look at all this fuss all the time. Every time you pick up a paper there's a fuss about something. What I want to know is, what are they getting at? Have you any idea?" she said to Davina.

"No," said Davina.

"I daresay you've never thought; I daresay you're right, too. What do *you* do?"

"Nothing," replied Davina. "I can't."

"Oh, well," said Miriam kindly, "perhaps you've got money?"

"No, not now."

"Dear me," said Miriam, "none of us have any luck. If you'd had a hundred pounds I'd have taken you into partnership. I'm looking round for a partner. Or, strictly, I'm looking round for a hundred pounds, but I wouldn't mind a partner; it would be company. Have you heard about me?"

"No. What?"

"I keep a tea-and-cake parlour called The Cat and Kettle. If you like cakes it's all right, but it puts you off them. It's not far from here, at Warring—on the river, you know. I've got check blinds and an inglenook and olde-oak beams and a cat; it's nice till you get used to it. I do Devonshire Teas at one and six and Dainty Teas *à la carte*. I lose on the Devonshires, mostly; you've no idea how much a person can eat to spite you. Still, it's a draw, and you've got to consider that. I wouldn't mind so much if it weren't for the black-beetles; I always think they try and run up my legs. My cat eats them, but you should see how they multiply; however, don't tell me a cat's not faithful. I bake the stuff myself; I'm a real home girl, I am; there's plenty of use for a gas-oven without putting one's head in it, as I always tell the girls. Every now and then my hand goes right out; I don't mind telling you, you could knock a man down with some of my gingerbread. But people would eat a boot if it was home made. They like getting caraways into their teeth and spitting out burnt currants; it feels like the old home. I've had customers drive thirty miles to see the dear old black kettle sit on the hob and kid themselves I made the tea out of it. Neurotic, that's what they are. I get mostly courting couples; the girls like it; there's something about that kettle that brings a man to the point. He mashes my comb honey about and goes soppy about his mother; it makes you sick. You'd think it would make a girl sick, but a girl goes through worse than that, as I always say. However, no times like the old times— Look in next time you're passing," she said to Davina.

"I never am," said Davina. "I haven't got a car."

"Well, you won't miss much," said Miriam without rancour. "It's a hole of a place where I am. Dishwater fogs all the winter and a slow motion High Street with no one about all day but the dear vicar. In summer it's like the inside of a hot pipe and you can't hear yourself think. Cars in a screaming jam all down the street, and punts jammed down the river till you couldn't drown a kitten between, and couples tie up all night, with ukuleles and portables, to the bank under my yard wall. You never know what goes on. It wouldn't be *your* cup of tea."

"You know," said Purdon to Miriam, "you ought really to marry me."

"Yes," sighed the Russian, "that's what I always say." He put his head down on Mrs. Bennington's shoulder and dropped the twist of gold cord despondently into her lap.

All this time, Oliver had been standing above Marianne, leaning against the mantelpiece. He had said nothing since the clock struck, but now he turned and said eagerly to Marianne: "Come for a turn."

The fire had "caught" and danced fluttering up, throwing pink light on the kerb: Marianne sat so close that a faint smell of wool scorching came from her skirt. She fixed her eyes on the smiling, familiar flames and felt more herself. Once or twice with a sleepy unconscious movement she leaned her forehead against the cold marble upright of the mantelpiece. Remotely she had heard midnight strike on the gilt clock. All the time she was aware with some apprehension of Oliver standing silently tall above her, like a tree that might fall. When he did speak, she looked away from him round the room with her frightened eyes: everything seemed to vacillate. The table toppling with bottles seemed to be balancing anxiously, splaying its gilt claw feet out on the parquet like an animal on the ice.

"Won't you come?" said Oliver.

"It's so late. It's so cold."

"We will walk round the house."

He opened the door; she rose and, unwinding her scarf from the Psyche, walked through the door ahead of him in a dream. The others said nothing. Like children in a large temple the two walked through the hall and up the bare white stone staircase, ascending to meet themselves in a darkish mirror at the head of the first flight. Here the staircase divided and rose in two sweeps like antlers against the high wall that was hung each side of the mirror with pastoral tapestries. From the head of each flight ran a gallery, waxy and dark. The house's great vacant height and resounding unlit perspectives weighed upon Marianne. As they went from room to room she heard Oliver's fingers tap in the dark on the wall for the light switch, then Italianate ceilings and sheeted icebergs of furniture sprang into cold existence. "Think of living here!" she said.

"Where *do* you live?"

She began to explain. But she was held up by something ardent and curious in his manner, the impatience with which, shaking his lock of fair hair back, he stared through her outline, not seeming to listen. What she was saying trailed off into unimportance. To-night and his presence tightened their hold on her spirit; the everyday became cloudy and meaningless and, like a tapestry, full

of arrested movement. At the tapestry she looked down
—for they had come back to the gallery. She stood fixing
her eyes on the subfusc temples on hills and the nymphs
trailing dead garlands, inanimate in brown gloom.

"Shan't I see you again, then?"

She did not know what to say.

"You tell me you're married," Oliver said accusingly.

Coming in to-night with Davina, quite unexplained, she
had seemed to him as disconnected from fact as an angel
or goddess. Her lost face, mild wild air, and, once or twice
as they groped through the dark house, her anxious touch
on his arm, had set up in him a violent solicitude. Now,
outraged by what she had only begun to tell him, he exclaimed excitedly: "Damn the natural affections!"

"Oh, you mustn't say that!"

"They are a ramp," said Oliver. One angry hand on
her elbow, he wheeled her right-about to face a pair of
heavily moulded doors. He flung one of these open on a
resounding void, announcing: "The grand saloon." They
went in. He flicked at a half-dozen switches but no light
came. "The bulbs are all gone; he's as poor as a rat," said
Oliver.

Reflections from outside touched the glass fronts of
cabinets; a white path of canvas drugget led off into the
dark. The room sounded enormous. He pulled the sheet
from a sofa and they sat down; behind them the door
swung to with a heavy click and Marianne caught a
breath. Oliver swooped on her two hands in the dark and
kissed the side of her cheek as she leaned wildly away.

"This isn't the way to behave—"

"It's how I behave!" he said with a touch of hysteria.

"I'd rather go home."

"I've been missing you all my life!"

"We can't meet again now!"

"For God's sake don't play-act!" said he.

Excitement with Oliver took its most crippling form.
Her wrists encircled in his tyrannic clutch, Marianne
heard his hurried breathing check and gather into a sob.
A tear, then another, splashed on the back of her hand.

Speechless, he let go her hands to dash the tears from his face. In the large unknown room a ring of autumnal silence, sealike and desolate in its unbounded nature, bore in on Marianne their distance from everything fixed.

"What's the matter?" she said.

"You're the last straw."

"Haven't you got any home?"

"Damn, damn," said Oliver at a fresh burst of tears. Fumbling and trembling, she thrust her cambric handkerchief into his hand. She put her arm round him, his head slid on to her shoulder, the sofa shook with a sob and he swore again.

"Why do you keep saying that?"

"This is not how I feel," he said angrily.

"What can I do?"

Davina and Paul, the Russian, left the restless anteroom a few minutes later; they went for a turn, too, and wandered about the mansion, upstairs and down, knocking ash off their cigarettes. It was very cold; Davina stopped in the hall to put on her overcoat. They could see from lights on upstairs that the other two must be somewhere, and were uncertain whether to join them or not. They opened and shut doors without much curiosity. They sat down on a chest in the gallery, and Paul said how much mistaken Miriam was, not marrying Purdon, not believing in anything. Then he said he thought the end of the world would soon come.

"No doubt it's high time," said Davina. "But don't let's talk of it."

"Who is your friend?"

"Marianne? She has a dull life. But look here, Paul: about me—I never know what to do."

"Wait for something to happen."

"I hate having no power. To-night, for instance, I'm furious with someone."

Not understanding, he looked at her sympathetically, got up and opened one of the grand saloon doors. They stood on the threshold and stared in at the dark. He said: "The lights are not working."

"Never mind, it's only a room." They both turned away. "All the same, we ought to find Oliver. It's high time Mrs. Bennington went to bed."

Next morning, pale milky sunshine flooded the façade of Lord Thingummy's house. In a bedroom behind the parapet Mrs. Bennington, fully dressed under the eider-down, lay breathing spirituously. The solitary housemaid, having risen at nine, opened the shutters all over the house, and long shafts of misty sunshine slid through the rooms. Patiently stooping, she picked up the cigarette-ends stamped out on the floors. In the grand saloon she sheeted up again an unsheeted sofa and picked up a lady's handkerchief and a striped woollen scarf. Down-stairs, in the ante-room, the gilt clock had stopped at ten minutes to four: the hearth was white with cold wood-ash. The housemaid flung up a window and let out on to the morning the stale, cold fumes that hung like lead in the air. She sniffed each of the bottles and swept up some broken glass: a cigarette had burnt out in the trough of a brocade cushion. Fine dust lay everywhere; the sleepy housemaid bumped vaguely round with her broom, swirling the dust up and letting it settle again.

The housemaid's steps in the hollow house, her violence with the shutters and the knock of her broom, woke Oliver up. He woke saying "She's gone," and lay sprawled rigidly sideways across his bed with his eyes shut, unwilling to wake, while thoughts of his own ignobility raced through his brain. . . . The grass of the park rolled fawn-pale to the horizon in the veiled sunshine; the lake stretched bright white against a brown belt of trees, fringed with papery pale windless reeds. A swan slowly turned on the lake and a man on horseback rode along the bare skyline: nothing else moved. The outdoor world lay reflected in the dark glass of Oliver's mind as he lay, with his eyes shut, sideways across his bed; he groaned at the still morning scene as though he stood at his win-dow. For himself he could see no reason. He had, unwill-ing, deluded her with his tears: one cannot weep all the time. He longed to see himself otherwise, like any other man, with a sound and passionate core. He thought of the grand saloon with alarm and pity, as though she lay dead in there. Opening his eyes a moment on the accusing daylight, he rolled over to reach for his first cigarette. . . . He never finished Lord Thingummy's catalogue.

A thin veil of river-mist lay on the Archworth garden. Davina woke late, looked at the unclear trees, and thought: "At least we are honest." Getting up, she found she had circles under her eyes: one did not grow any younger. She thought with relief of last night's pleasure, because it was over, because it had been so slight. She and her friends had come to the same sad age when one can change no longer, and only become more oneself. They could enthrall and bluff each other no longer—but still, to meet is to meet. They had made some kind of a hearth, and its warmth remained. Oliver with his dispirited Viking air, at once gallant and craven, and Paul with his placid and disenchanted smile, were renewed in her heart; she pictured Miriam on her high heels stepping over the beetles this morning and Purdon re-opening his surgery with a sigh. Combing back her springy dark hair and making up her mouth with pomegranate lipstick—alas! for no one—Davina thought of them kindly, regretting their premature autumn. "We are not so bad," she thought.

She went to her aunt's room.

Mrs. Archworth sat propped up in bed in a hug-me-tight trimmed with marabout. Beside the hot bedroom fire the Pekinese snored and dribbled. As Davina tapped on the door and came in smartly, resentment fought with affection on her aunt's face: "I was a little anxious—" Mrs. Archworth began.

"But just you wait till you hear—"

Mrs. Archworth could not resist that flashing dark look. Poor plain pompous fussy old woman, no one else was at pains to fascinate her these days. She shifted her feet in bed, making room for Davina to sit, and patted the eiderdown with an uncertain smile. Davina explained with more than usual vividness how, Marianne's car having broken down, on a drive after dinner, outside unknown gates, the two had been for some hours the guests of Lord Thingummy.

"He would be kindness itself," said her aunt. "I once danced with him. And we dined there once, I remember, not long after your uncle and I were married. I am glad you should be making friends in the neighbourhood. This house, Davina, I'd like you to understand, is to be yours when I die."

Davina said, startled: "That's very good of you."

Her aunt, with a wry and oddly dignified smile, said: "My dear, *I* shall not need it."

Marianne drove to meet Matthew at the 12.33 from London. The down platform was crowded, and for a moment or two of uncertain feeling she thought he had missed the train. Then he came ambling her way with light on his spectacles. His overcoat flapped and he carried a small despatch-case. "How is my girl?" he said, as they made their way through the barrier.

She was disorientated; she did not know. At home, she had not renewed the water in the bowls of chrysanthemums; it was a greenish colour, and stank faintly. The dogs, not yet exercised, fawned rather pointedly on the returning pair. The cat ran to meet them with its tail straight up; turned for no reason and ran away again. Mild unclear morning light filled the new white house with its evenly heated rooms. Matthew Harvey never kissed in a station, so half way across the hall he put down his despatch-case, closed the door to the kitchen, and kissed his wife. Colour rushed up her face, but he did not see.

He returned a book to the shelf and looked through a pile of letters. Meanwhile Marianne's look trailed wearily round the living-room, as though it were she who were just back from a journey and could still find no place to rest.

"I think," said Matthew, "I must get my glasses changed."

"Changed?" said Marianne, starting.

"My glasses, yes," said Matthew, leaning back in his chair and looking at her with affection. Then he stooped to pick up an end of white cotton from a hand-woven rug. He rolled this into a cocoon and flicked it into the fire. "A bit of white cotton," he said, "but I picked it up."

She stood with her back to him, looking out of the window, and said: "The weathercock's pointing the other way."

"The wind must have changed," he said pleasantly.

She looked downhill, over the raw garden terraces, at the tops of the village trees with, in their heart, the glinting veering gold bird. Over the Archworths' chimneys a whorl of white smoke immobilised. Far off, across the flat water-meadows, the creeping red streets waited: beyond, a crowd of pale spires pricked the stooping grey sky. The world reflected itself in the vacant glass of her mind. Her hands, on which tears had fallen, vaguely clenched and unclenched in the pockets of her tweed coat.

"It is good to be back," observed Matthew.

She did not reply.

"What's the matter?" he said. "You're not quite yourself."

"Perhaps I have got a slight chill."

Davina looked over the net blind of Mrs. Archworth's window, down into the yard. There was no one about in the yard, least of all Prothero. Biting her lip, she stared down at the white cobbles, the cement incline to the garage, the drifted leaves. A flush of angry intention appeared on her cheekbones. "What's that?" exclaimed Mrs. Archworth, struck by her rigid attitude. But the bedroom door had shut sharply: Davina was gone.

Inside its kennel, the foolish yard dog stirred with a rustle, dragging its chain in the straw; the pigeons rose wheeling on noisy wings. Davina slid back the garage door on its rollers, but found only the Daimler's wide polished back. The cook looked out of the back door and said that if it was Prothero anyone wanted, he had gone out.

"Why should he do that?"

"I couldn't tell you, I'm sure, miss. We're so independent, we are."

Davina swung round and went out through the yard gate, down the lane to the village. Her tremendous anger made the village spread round the green, with its porches, dark little shop-fronts and stooping gables, look like a stage scene, a scene set for to-day. The raggy grass of the green was shredded with dead lime-leaves, a smell of wood-smoke hung in the still air. Her look darted round the green; she had only one thought: "He's gone." That thought was bitter.

But Prothero came out of the grocer's opposite, with a felt hat pulled down over his forehead and a packet of candles under his arm. He stood in the shop door, not seeing Davina. Then, with his swinging, leisurely, damned independent stride, he started back round the green to the house again. Davina cut back before him to the mouth of the lane. She waited; they came face to face and Prothero pulled up patiently.

"Well?" said he.

"What about that message?"

"What about that money?"

"That's no way to talk—whoever you are."

"It was good enough for you last night—whoever I am."

She said contemptuously: "I was in a hurry."

"Oh, come," said he, "we had quite a pleasant chat."

His light eyes and her dark eyes met implacably. Davina, driving her hands down into her pockets, said: "They gave you a message for me. What became of it?"

"If your friends want to leave messages, they should go to the front door, not hang round the yard like tinkers. I'm not here to take messages; I am a busy man."

"You'll be dismissed for this. You forget yourself."

"I should like to," he said, smiling without pleasure. "But what would your aunt say to our little bill? I wouldn't upset her now you've feathered your nest so nicely. Besides, we should miss each other, I daresay."

"That's blackmail," she said. "You're a crook, aren't you?"

"I got even with someone."

"That was grand," she said bitterly.

"Yes, I'm right on top of the world." He looked up at the weathercock.

"You must be mad," she said, looking at him intently. "Else why spoil my evening? Why make an enemy of me? Suppose I gave you away?"

"You wouldn't do that if you could. For one thing, you haven't the guts, and it wouldn't get you anywhere. Spoil your evening?" He looked at her incuriously. "How you do set your heart on things!"

"A monkey trick," she said scornfully. "Oh, you're a great man!"

"Mmn. I do what I want. And I take what I want, I don't hang about for it. I wonder it doesn't sicken a girl like you, hanging about here, waiting. You'd better get out. I'm through. Don't keep coming after my money; it's not my money you want. I know your sort. Well, I'm through with all that. I'm buying, not selling, these days. You keep your place, Miss Archworth, and I'll keep mine. You can't have it both ways. Good day."

Nodding, he walked away from her down the lane. She followed him, at a distance, through the yard gates. He was mad, in plain terms—her own. She watched him, with fascination, cross the yard to his staircase. It was true she had, in some strange fashion, fed her own pride by the hasty sale of her kisses, feeling set free of herself each time those anonymous lips without pleasure had claimed her own, or those unseeing abstract cold eyes lit on her face. She went to the archway and called up the hollow staircase: "Who *are* you?"

"My own man," he said, and shut his door vigorously. Flakes of plaster slid from the staircase wall, and the steps creaked into silence after his tread. Davina felt in her pocket but found no cigarette. She called: "I'm going," and turned back to the house.

In the drawing-room, she filled up her case from the cigarette-box put out last night for the admiral and the Indian Civilian. The parrakeet wobbled on its perch; upstairs, she heard her aunt beginning to move about; she

leaned on the mantelpiece thinking about Prothero: free
men do not boast. . . . She decided to walk up, now, at
once, to the Harveys, to tell Marianne she was going away,
would be quite gone in a week. But Matthew would be at
home.

Davina walked up the hill, but not to the Harveys;
straight up between the ruts of the half-made road;
then she struck out across the grass to the water-tower.
Along the brambly skyline she walked rapidly, clicking
her finger against her thumb and thinking: "If I had
money . . ."

She saw that events led nowhere, crisis was an illusion,
and that passions of momentary violent reality were struck
off like sparks from the spirit, only to die. One could
precipitate nothing. One is empowered to live fully: occasion does not offer. The whole panorama of life seemed
spread out under this hill: between the brambles, hit-
ting an old tin can with her stick idly, Davina stood still to
stare. . . . Downhill from the tower the gentlemanly new
houses reflected the autumn daylight in steel-framed windows. As the sky sharpened with clouds and over the
landscape the morning darkened, the skyline spires went
leaden, the gasometer and the far-off curve of the river
took on a wary glint. An almost inaudible hum of wind
rising began below in the trees.

Davina decided to throw off her dashing character and
ask her aunt for the money to repay Prothero. Two men
came uphill her way, stopped and debated: they were sur-
veyors coming to peg out a new road.

The Easter Egg Party

THEIR object was to restore her childhood to her. They were simple and zealous women, of an integrity rooted in flawless sentiment; they bowed to nothing but their own noble ideas, and flinched from nothing but abandoning these. They issued the invitation on an impulse but awaited the answer with no drop in morale. They did not shrink from facts, for they attended committees for the good of the world—most facts, however, got to West Wallows a little bit watered down: such things did happen, but not to people one knew. So that when their eye was drawn—they were unmarried sisters, with everything in common, and had, in regard to some things, one eye between them—when their eye was drawn by a once-quite-familiar name to an obscure paragraph in their daily paper, their hearts (or their heart) stopped. The case was given in outline, with unusual reticence. When they saw what had either happened or nearly happened—they were not quite clear which—to the little girl of a friend they had known as a little girl, shyness and horror drove a wedge between them; they became two people whose looks could not quite meet. Across the breakfast table of their large cottage, in the half-acre of garden already gladey and glittering with the first greens of spring, they failed to discuss the matter. After a day of solitary side-by-

side reflection it came up with them in its happier prac-
tical aspect: "Could one *do* anything, now? . . . Is there
any way one could help?"

Eunice and Isabelle Evers were both just over fifty:
their unperplexed lives showed in their faces, lined only
by humour, and in their frank high foreheads. They were
amazons in homespuns, amazons without a touch of
deprivation or pathos; their lives had been one long vigor-
ous walk. Like successful nuns, they both had a slightly
married air. An unusual number of people in Gloucester-
shire knew and respected them, and they cut ice in the
village of West Wallows. They thought the world of
children, of any children; and children, in consequence,
thought the world of them: they were past mistresses at
blowing that bubble world that is blown for children by
children-loving grownups—perhaps, also, the dearest of
their own pleasures lay there. If they had any fantasies,
these centred round ponies and bread-and-jam on the
beach, and they still received intimations of immortality.

Therefore, any unspeakable thing happening to any
child was more upsetting to them than if they had been
mothers. It was against their natures to judge Dorothea
(the friend they had known as a little girl) in any way. All
the same, across what line, into what world had she wandered in these years since her marriage, since they had
lost sight of her, that her little girl should be exposed to
such things as this? Dorothea's marriage had failed. Must
one own she failed as a mother? They knew, vaguely,
Dorothea was 'on the stage'—though one never saw
her name on the programme of any play.

Dorothea's answer to their invitation took so long in
coming that they had begun to fear she was out of reach.
But when she did answer, Dorothea accepted with alacrity. She said that it really was truly sweet of them, and
she only hoped they would find Hermione good. "She's
really as good as gold, but she's always rather reserved.
I am sure it might do her good to be away from me for a
bit; you see, I am really very upset these days. I suppose
that's only natural; my nerves have always been awful,
and now *this* coming, on top of everything else. It's nearly

killed me, of course. I suppose one will get over it. Well, it really is dear of you; you always were such dears. *Oh*, how far away all those happy days seem now! . . . I will send Hermione down on April 12th. Yes, I think she's fond of animals; at all events you could try. Of course she's never had any, poor little soul."

So they began to prepare for Hermione.

West Wallows was more than a village: it was a neighbourhood. From the wide street branched roads that led past the white gates of many homes. The rector was tactful and energetic, the squire unusually cultivated; there were a number of moderate-sized dwellings—some antique, some quite recently built. Inexpensive sociability, liberal politics, shapely antique family furniture, 'interests,' enlightened charity set the note of the place. No one was very rich; nobody was eccentric, and, though few people hunted, nobody wrote letters against blood sports. The local families harmonized with the pleasant retired people who had settled here. Probably few neighbourhoods in England have such a nice atmosphere as West Wallows. In the holidays all the children had a jolly time. . . . The Easter holidays were in progress now, and this created a slight predicament: how much should Hermione be with other children?

The Misses Evers decided to wait and see.

They decided to wait for grace and see what line things took. They hinted at nothing to anyone. In the week before Hermione came, the tortoiseshell cat Barbara was persuaded to wean her two patchy kittens, who learned to lap prettily from an Umbrian saucer. The honeysuckle up the south front of the cottage unfolded the last of its green shoots, and in the garden and in the strip of orchard the other side of the brook daffodils blew their trumpets.

The first afternoon was windy. Every time a sucker of honeysuckle swung loose and tapped the window Hermione jumped. This was the only sign she gave of having grown-up nerves. She was not quite a pretty child; her face was a long plump oval; her large dark-grey eyes were set rather close together, which gave her an urgent air. Her naturally curly dark hair had grown too long for a bob and swung just clear of her shoulders. She sat in the dark glass dome of her own inside world, just too composedly eating bread and honey. Now and then she glanced, with mysterious satisfaction, at the bangles on one or the other of her wrists.

"This is honey from our own bees, Hermione."

"Goodness."

"It tastes quite different from other honey, we think."

"Yes; Mummy said you kept bees. Do you keep doves too?"

Eunice glanced at the white forms that whirled rather frighteningly over the wind-teased garden. "Those are the next-door pigeons; they kept on flying over, so we have the fun of them."

"The next-door cat in London keeps getting into our larder. I do hate cats."

"Oh, but you must like Barbara—and she's got two kittens."

"Cats always do that, don't they?"

After tea Eunice took her up to what was to be her room, the spare-room over the porch, snug as a ship's cabin and frilly with sprigged stuff. She showed her the sampler worked by another little girl of eleven, just a hundred years ago, and some framed photographs of Italy. "That's Assisi, where St. Francis lived."

"Goodness," said Hermione, biting her thumb vaguely. She looked through the loops of dotted muslin curtain at the tops of the apple trees. "It's just like on a calendar," she said. She sat on the bed, with her tongue feeling round one cheek, while Eunice unpacked her two suit-cases for her. "Oh, what pretty clothes and things," said Eunice deprecatingly. "But I don't think you'll have a chance to wear most of them here. You'll want to wear old clothes and simply tumble about."

"I haven't got any old clothes. Mummy gives them away."

In her tweed skirt, with her knotted oak walking-stick, lifting her forehead to the sweet spring air Isabelle, next morning, swung down the village street, and Hermione walked beside her, changing step now and then with a queer little dancing hop. In her raspberry-woolen dress, her turned-up hat with the Donald Duck clip and her long, white, carefully pulled-up socks, the child looked like a stage child half-way through a tour: nothing would tone her down. Isabelle pointed out the village pond with its white ducks, the saddle-back church tower, the Beacon on the top of the steep green nursery-rhyme hill, the quaint old sign of the Spotted Cow, which made all children laugh—Hermione did not smile. A street is a street, and the point of a street is, people: looking boldly up, she challenged whoever passed with her dusky, gelatinous dark-grey eyes. It was their attention she wanted; she collected attention like twists of silver paper or small white pebbles. Her search for attention was so arduous that she gave less than half her mind to whatever Isabelle said. Whenever Isabelle turned into a shop, Hermione would ferret along the counter. In the chemist's she said she would like to buy that green celluloid box to keep her toothbrush in.

"Have you brought your pocket-money?" said Isabelle brightly.

"Oh—but I haven't any."

"Then I'm afraid the green box will have to wait," said Isabelle still more brightly, with an inspiring smile. She did not approve of buying hearts with small gifts: besides, one must teach Hermione not to 'hint.' Hermione gave the green box a last look, the first fully human look she had spent on anything since she came to West Wallows. She slowly dragged her eyes from it and followed Isabelle out of the chemist's shop.

"This afternoon," said Isabelle, "we'll go primrosing."

"I think those lambs are pretty," said Hermione, suddenly pointing over a wall. "I should like a pet lamb of my own; I should call it Percy."

"Well, perhaps you can make a friend of one of these lambs. If you go every day very quietly into the field—"

"But I want it to be my own; I want to call it Percy."

"Well, let's call 'Percy,' and see which of them comes

. . . Percy, Percy, Percy!" called Isabelle, leaning over the wall. None of the lambs took any notice: one of the sheep gave her a long, reproving look. Hermione, meanwhile, had frigidly walked away.

Eunice and Isabelle took it in turns to what they called take Hermione out of herself. They did not confess how unnerved they sometimes were by their sense of intense attention being focused on nothing. They took her in to see the neighbour who kept the pigeons; Eunice taught her to climb the safe apple trees; Isabelle took her out in a pair of bloomers and dared her to jump the brook. Hermione jumped in and was pulled out patient and very wet. They borrowed a donkey for her, and the run of a paddock, but she fell off the donkey three times. This child stayed alone the whole time and yet was never alone; their benevolent spying on her, down the orchard or through windows, always showed them the same thing—Hermione twirling round her silver bangles at some unseen person, or else tossing her hair. They took her primrosing three times; then they took her bird's-nesting in the Hall grounds. In the great hollow beech hedges, in the dense ivy, the secret nests excited her: she stood up on tiptoes; her cheeks flamed. But all this waned when she might not touch the eggs. She could not understand why. The glossy blues, the faint greens, the waxy buff-pinks, the freckles seemed to her to be for nothing: while the sisters, breathless, held apart the branches she now looked only glumly into the nests. When they found a brood of fledglings she ran six yards back and said: "Ugh! Fancy leaving eggs just for *that!*"

"But they're alive, dear. Next spring they'll be singing away, like all the birds we hear now, or laying eggs of their own."

"Well, I don't see why."

The sisters bound each other to silence with quick glances.

Hermione said: "I'd sooner have sugar eggs."

It was from this rather baffling afternoon that the idea of the Easter egg party arose.

Hermione ought now, they felt, if ever, to be fit for younger society. Perhaps she might find friends—how they doubted this! At all events, one must see. And since she was to meet children, why should she not meet all the West Wallows children at once? About a quite large party there should be something kind and ambiguous: if she failed to hit it off with Maisie or Emmeline, she might hit it off with Harriet or Joanna. (The fact was, they felt, in a way they rather dreaded to face, that in a large party she would stand out less.) The Misses Evers were well known for their juvenile parties, but up to now these had always been held at Christmas, when guessing games could be played, or at Midsummer, when they got permission for their young guests to help to make someone's hay. An Easter party was quite a new idea and looked like running them in for more expense—they did not jib at this, but they dreaded the ostentation. Isabelle bicycled into Market Chopping and bought three dozen sweet eggs— a little reduced in price, as Easter was just over. Some were chocolate, wrapped in brilliant metallic paper; some were marzipan, with the most naturalistic freckles; some were cardboard, containing very small toys. That same afternoon, Eunice, at her bureau, wrote out invitations to the fourteen young guests, ranging in age from fourteen down to six. As she addressed each envelope she would pause, to give Hermione, entrancedly doing nothing on the sofa beside her, a biography of each possible child.

The afternoon of the party was, happily, very fine. From three o'clock on the garden gate clicked incessantly: unaccompanied by grown-ups the guests in their coloured jerseys or very clean blouses came up the path—to be mustered by Eunice and Isabelle on the patch of lawn by the sundial. They were already tanned or freckled by the spring sun, and all wore an air of stolid elation. "Now, finding *ought* to be keeping," said Isabelle, "but we think that if any one of you people finds more than three, he or she might hand the rest back, to go at the end to some other person who may not have been so clever."

Eunice put in: "And we shall be giving a prize: this

Easter rabbit" (she held up a china ornament) "to whoever hands in most eggs by the end of the afternoon."

Isabelle took up: "They are hidden about the garden
and in the orchard the other side of the stream. To make
things just a little easier we have tied a piece of pink wool
somewhere near every place where an egg is. And whoever finds each egg must untie the pink wool, please, or
it will be so difficult. Now, are we all here? Oh, no: we
are still waiting for Poppy. The moment she's here I'm going to blow this whistle, then—off with you all! At five
o'clock I shall blow the whistle for tea."

At this moment the late-comer bolted in at the gate,
whereupon Isabelle blew the whistle piercingly. The children—the boys were small, the girls larger-sized, some of
them quite lumpy—glanced at each other, tittered and
moved off. For some distance they stayed in compact for-
mation, like explorers advancing in dangerous territory;
though all the time their sharp eyes were glancing left
and right. Then, in the glittering sunshine of the garden,
shreds of pink wool began to be discerned. One by one
children bounded off from the others, glancing jealously
round to see that no one was on their tracks.

Hermione had lagged a little behind the party that
moved off. She had been introduced to all the children by
name, but after the how-d'you-do's no one had spoken
to her. She had secured by the wrist the only other child
that tagged behind the party, a small, dumb little boy:
she gripped this child by the wrist as though he were not
human—he appeared in some way to give her countenance.
From the beginning she had been difficult: she had been
reluctant to come down from her room at all: from the
lawn below Eunice had called and waved; Hermione had
answered but not come. Ghostly just inside her shut window, or like a paper figure pasted against the glass, she
had watched strange children invade the garden she knew.
She had gone on like a kitten that somehow gets up a tree,
panics, and cannot be got down again—till Eunice ran up
to dislodge her with some well-chosen words. But alas,
once one had got her on to the lawn, her up-a-tree air only
became more noticeable. She shook hands with a rigid

arm, on which all the bracelets jumped. She looked straight at everyone, but from a moody height: what was evident was not just fear or shyness but a desperate, cut-off haughtiness. In her eyes existed a world of alien experience. The jolly tallish girls with their chubbed hair, the straddling little boys with their bare knees, apt to frown at the grass between their sandshoes, rebounded from that imperious stare. Either she cared too much or she did not care a fig for them—and in either case they did not know how to meet her.

Sloping south to the brook, the garden was made devious by swastika hedges: it was all grots and plots. Japanese plums caught light in their ethereal petals; flowering currants sent out their sweet, hot smell. The waving shreds of pink wool made round themselves centres of magnetic attraction, in which children hummed and jostled, like the bees round the currants. The garden, the orchard became tense with the search: now and then yelps of triumph struck their silence like sharp bells. By the end of a half-hour everyone seemed to have found at least one egg. Children met to compare their spoils, then pounced jealously off again.

Only Hermione and the doomed little boy that she would not let go of had not yet found an egg. She sometimes shifted her grip on his hot wrist. In her haze of self-consciousness, weighted by that deep-down preoccupation, she moved too slowly, dragging the little boy. Once or twice she did see pink wool, but when she got to the spot it was always being untied by the child who had found the egg. Disgraced by their failure, she and the little boy said not a word to each other; they moved about in a silence of deepening animosity. Now they stood on the bridge, between the garden and orchard: Hermione looked from one shore to the other with eyes that held incredulity and despair. She had not found *any* egg.

Without warning the little boy went rigid all over, braced himself against the rail of the bridge, threw open his cave of a mouth and yelled: "Oh, *Mais-see*, I wanner go with you!"

A girl bustling contentedly through the orchard, three

bright eggs shining on the palm of her hand, stopped and
lifted her nose like a mother dog. Then she approached
the bridge. "I say," she said to Hermione, "would you
mind letting my little brother go? He'd like to look by
himself."

"He and I are looking together."

"Oh. How many have you each found?"

"Somebody else always finds the ones we are looking
for."

"Good gracious," said Maisie, "then haven't you found
any? Someone says that Harriet's got six, and everyone
else here has found at least two. Do you mean to say poor
Simon hasn't got *any*? . . . Never mind, Simon; come
and look with me. *We'll* soon find some."

"I don't see why he should. Why should I be the only
person left who hasn't got any egg?"

"Well, I can't help that, can I? You'd better look more
properly . . . Come along, Simon."

Hermione let him go.

When she found herself quite alone on the bridge she
shaded her eyes (because the sun was descending) to
peer at the round white object under one apple tree. It
was a Panama hat, last seen on the girl Harriet: now it sat
on the grass. As though something inside her answered a
magnet, Hermione left the bridge and ran to that apple
tree. The general search had ebbed back to the garden:
in the orchard no one shouted; no one swished through the
long grass—the place was deserted suddenly. Hermione
knelt down, cautiously raised the hat, and saw the clutch
of six supernatural eggs—two gold, one red, one silver
and two blue. They lay tilted together in their nest in the
grass. Trembling with satisfaction, she regarded them
steadily. Then she made a pouch of her skirt and gathered the eggs up into it. Clumsily, cautiously rising, she
made off at a trot for a hedge that cut off the orchard from
Church Lane.

She was not missed till the five o'clock whistle sounded
and the children trooped in through the french window
for tea. Then Eunice and Isabelle combined to pass the
contretemps over as smoothly as possible. While Eunice

poured out, and kept the chatter going, Isabelle, with
the whistle, slipped out for a thorough look. Sadly, sadly,
she saw some trampled daffodils—the nicer the set of children, the larger their feet. When she got to the end of the
orchard she saw the gap forced through the hedge, and
her heart sank.

The big scandal only broke at the end of teatime, when
Eunice began to check up the eggs found. Throughout
tea the outraged Harriet had not suffered in silence: there
had been a good deal of mumbling at her end of the table,
but Eunice did not know what the matter was. When the
loss came out Eunice put two and two together with dis-
heartening rapidity—so did everyone else. Speaking looks
were cast by the West Wallows children at the place
where Hermione did not sit. There was nothing for it but
to present the china rabbit to Harriet with as much haste,
and still as much pomp, as possible and to suggest we
should now all play prisoners' base on the lawn.

Seven strokes from the church clock fell on the sad,
clear evening. The Easter egg party guests had been sent
home an hour ago; the sisters had returned from their
desperate search up and down the village, in the fields, in
the near woods. Something made Eunice go up to Hermione's room—there *was* Hermione, sitting on the bed.
She must have slipped back while nobody was about. In
the deep dusk she was sitting across the bed, legs stuck
out and back stuck to the wall, in the attitude in which
one props up a doll. She was, presumably, waiting: the
moment the door opened, she said, without looking up:
"I want to go home now."

"But Hermione—"

"Mummy said I needn't stay if I didn't like it. She said
I could come straight home."

"Dear, this isn't because you think *we* are . . . upset
about anything?"

"I can't help *what* you are," said Hermione, quite dis-
passionate. "Couldn't you get some other girl to stay with
you? There's nothing for me to do here; I mean, I can't
do anything. And all those girls were awful to me to-day;
nobody cared if I found an egg or not. That girl Maisie

wouldn't let me play with her brother. No one has ever been so awful to me as they all were; they took all the eggs, and I never found even one. And you never let me talk, all the time, and you never let me touch anything. You keep on making me take an interest in things, and you never take the slightest interest in me. Mummy said you were interested in me, but now I don't believe her. I feel just as if I was dead, and I do want to go home. Oh, and I took those six old eggs."

"Well, hush now, dear: we're all tired. Hop into bed, like a good girl, and I'll bring you some biscuits and milk. Would you like me to bring up one of the kittens, too?"

"No, thank you; your kittens scratch. Well, can I go home to-morrow?"

"We'll see about that to-morrow."

Eunice sighed and went downstairs. She filled a beaker with milk and put out a plate of biscuits, then she looked into the parlour for a word with Isabelle. The lamps were lit, but the curtains were not drawn yet: outside there was a dark twitter of birds. Isabelle, reading the look on her sister's face, came round the table, saying: "Oh, Eunice . . ."

"I know," Eunice said. "It apparently can't be helped. Her mind's set now on going home. I wonder whether she'd better . . ."

"Eunice, that's not like you!" cried Isabelle, with a burst of their old heroic energy.

"I know," said Eunice, putting down the biscuits. Absently, she began to sip the milk. "But you see, this is really not like anything else. There are times when being like one's self, however much one's self, does not seem much help. Well, there it is, Isabelle. We've always known life was difficult, but I must confess, till to-day I'd never really believed it. I don't see quite where we failed: she *is* a child, after all."

"I suppose, once a child has been the centre of things . . ."

"Oh, look—I'm drinking this milk. It really was for Hermione."

Hermione left next day: perhaps it was for the best.

They never speak of her to the children at West Wallows, and the West Wallows children do not ask about her. The sisters seldom speak of her even between themselves; she has left a sort of scar, like a flattened grave, in their hearts. It rained the day she left, but cleared up again at sunset. When Isabelle, in her gum-boots, walking in the orchard, found the six Easter eggs under the original apple tree, the chocolate under the paper had gone to a pulp, and the gold and colours of the paper had run.

No. 16

TO APPROACH Medusa Terrace by its east corner, on a first visit to the Maximilian Bewdons, was to fancy oneself, for an unnerving minute, the victim of a hoax. Maximilian's only visitors, nowadays, were of the type least able to bear this—idealistic, friendless, new from the provinces: accordingly, unaware of the slump in him. One can make for oneself a pretty picture of the distinguished writer's St. John's Wood home—jasmine outside, *objets d'art* within. Maximilian had not, in fact, been distinguished for fifteen years. But the last circle from the splash he had once made faded slowly—and meanwhile he was able to make a living. The masks on Medusa Terrace had lost their features; the pilasters crumbled; front doors were boarded up.

The differing fortunes of St. John's Wood house property give that uphill landscape a dreamlike inconsistency. To walk there is to have a crazy architectural film, with no music, reeled past. Every corner brings you to something out of the scheme—even without a touch of fever on you (and Jane Oates had more than a touch of fever) some starts of taste or fancy look like catastrophes. Pale tan brick blocks of flats, compressed cities, soar up over studios all trellis and vine. There are gashes and pitted gardens where villas have been torn down. Criss-cross go roads of dun silent stucco, frosted glass porches, grills. A perspective gallops downhill all jade-and-whiteness and bird-song—but you may turn off into a by-street as mean, faded and airless as any in Pimlico. Dotted among the bosky gothic love-nests are vita-glassed mansions, avid for sun and money, still on the agent's lists. Here, a once bewitching villa, now scabrous, awaits the knacker for some obscure shame—next door, its twin is all paintpots and whistling workmen, being dolled up again. The straight roads string all this on an old plan. The stranger feels abnormally keyed up; he finds himself in a sort of nightmare of whim.

Jane Oates' troubled sensations *were* heightened by fever: she had a temperature, had only got up this morning and should have been still in bed. But to-day—now—she was to meet Maximilian Bewdon for the first time: she would not have failed if she'd had to come from the tomb. Not only influenza but hero worship made her pulses race. His letter, with the invitation to lunch, had been brought to her the first day she was ill, and her thought then had been: I must go if I die. So images had swum through her drowsy days and made her delirious nights ecstatic. Here she was, on her way to Medusa Terrace—too eager, she had got off the bus too soon. Her feet were lead, her spine ached, her head sang, glassily clear.

The thaw had left London glistening, supine, sunny. From gardens the snow, swept up into mounds, had not gone yet. Jane had come on on buses from Battersea Park; she was not a Londoner; she had not been up here before. Everything, in this maze of trees and doorways as she walked towards Maximilian, gave her its message or mystery. The sun still hurt her still rather weak eyes. She had the stolid, untroubled beauty of a mature country girl, and a touch of old-fashioned style.

In the autumn, about three months ago, Jane's book had been published. It was a naïve book, but sufficiently disconcerting, and *new*—too new to go far unless it should happen to catch some important eye. She had no friends (in London), no one to make a splash. So the publisher gave the book an agreeable format, a vermilion cover with a chalky surface, gave one or two luncheons for Jane (at which she could not speak) and hoped for a *success d'estime*. Maximilian, reviewing for an obscure paper, had not only "done" the book but had made a feature of it. The publisher shrugged when he got the cutting and saw Maximilian's name. But Jane's cup was full. She got the column by heart and, for days, sang a Magnificat. That *he* should have written this—and that he should have written *this*. Her liberation into this sudden book could have been all: but now she was truly crowned. She wrote Maximilian a humble letter, confessing the hero worship of years. Since she was seventeen (she was now thirty) she had hardly missed a word Maximilian signed. She was deeply feeling; she lived alone in the country. She was a true enough artist to have false taste—for the ignorant artist, like the savage, is attracted by what is glittering: by the time he learns what is what, some virtue is gone already.

Maximilian Bewdon, after about a week, had replied to Jane's letter: they started to correspond. Though her book was prose she wrote poems also, she told him, but she was shy of those. She learned that he was married; he asked her if she were married; she answered that she had never been in love. Before Christmas, she was able to write and tell him she was coming to London, to share a flat for three months with a friend who lived in Battersea Park. When she got to Battersea Park, already ill, she got his letter, bidding her bring the poems to lunch.

So here they were, in a folder under her arm. She was not nervous; fever floated her or distilled her out of herself. But when she turned the corner into Medusa Terrace, Jane Oates stopped—like everyone else. She instinctively put her hand up, then took her hand from her eyes to see the same thing again—that north-facing terrace of cracked stucco, dank in its own shadow, semi-ruinous, hollow, full of sealed-up echoes. Doors nailed up, windows boarded or stony with grime. In the gardens, the snow was trodden black. The place so much expected an instant doom, one felt unsafe standing near it.

"*Am* I—? Or, *could* he have—?"

Jane looked up at the numbers stuck on the broken fanlights. Still at the 1's and 2's—he had said, No. 16. Plung-

ing into the shadow with a shiver—she had kept to the
sunny sides of the streets—she walked the length of the
façade. At the end she dared look up: the last house *was*
No. 16. Through less dusty panes she saw curtains like
orange ghosts. A shaft of sun struck through from a back
window, through a bunch of balloons hung in an arch.
This one end house was tacked, living, to the hulk of the
terrace. She turned up the steps and rang.

When she had rung twice, a lady came to the door,
knocking back a strand of grey hair from her eyes. She
eyed Jane and eyed the folder of poems. "Oh dear—I
hope you are not Miss Oates?"

"I—"

"Oh dear. I had wired to put you off: you did not seem
to be on the telephone. My husband has been ill for several days; he's just up, but not fit to see anyone. He only
remembered this morning that you were coming, or I
should have—I *am* sorry. Oh dear."

At these words Jane, in her feverish weakness,
sweated: she saw sweat and a flush break out on the lady's
forehead, and Mrs. Bewdon put up a hand and said:
"We've had influenza." "I've had it too." "It seems to be
everywhere." "I'm sorry I didn't get your telegram: I
started early, it was a long way—"

"Nancy," said a voice from inside a room, "let Miss
Oates come in."

So Jane, unable to say anything further, was let into
the shabby decent hall—an oak chest with letters stamped
for posting, prints hung on the paper seamed with damp,
a humid smell of broth. She turned through a door to face
Maximilian, who stood in the archway, underneath the
bunch of coloured balloons. She heard the roar of two
antique gasfires, one in the dark front room, one in the
sunny back, and saw Maximilian's figure crucified on the
sunshine in an extravagance of apology. "What must you
think?" he said. She stood blind, the sun in her eyes, and
could not think anything. There was a moment's silence,
while Jane shifted the folder, pressing it with the thumb
of her woollen glove. Then he said: "Thank you for missing the telegram."

"But I must go."

"No, you mustn't go. There *is* lunch." He reached out
—the act seemed vague and belated like an act in a dream
—and shook Jane's hot dry hand in his hotter and drier
hand. "Now you're here," he said.

"But you're ill."

"Still, I'm here," he said, with an obstinate frown. They
sat down beside each other on the sofa, and she saw his
exposed-looking forehead, the spectacles through which
he sent, obliquely, a look at once baited and fiery, the
short hands wasting their force in uneasy fleeting nervous
touches on things. Maximilian looked about fifty; he
looked frustrated and spent. His hair, weak as fur, flowed
back and he wore a little moustache. He said, with an accusing smile: "You thought I had gone."

"Yes, I did, when I first came to the Terrace."

"That's what they all think—that lets them out, don't
you see. They take one look and go home. 'He'd gone,'
they say to the others. Lots don't start at all. 'We don't
know where he is now. They've pulled down where he
once was. There's no tracing him—' "

"How *can* you?" Jane said gently. Maximilian repeated:
"It lets them out. That's my tact."

Jane, looking apprehensively round at the room, said:
"But some day, I suppose, it *will* happen?"

"Oh, we'll be pulled down all right," said Maximilian, pressing his forehead.

"If the idea upsets you—"

Mrs. Bewdon, laying the front room table, said: "The
idea does not upset my husband at all. When we move, he
will miss it. We are let keep this house on from week to
week: when the men come, they'll begin at the other end.
They work fast, I daresay, and it will be so noisy. So *then*
we shall have to think—"

"I am so sorry," said Jane.

"I shan't be sorry," said Mrs. Bewdon. "That will be
something settled." She bent to straighten a fork. "But he
—I—we cannot bear to decide . . ."

Her husband said: "One decides quickly enough when
there is any question of desire."

"It's so long since the last of our neighbours left: they

expected something to happen, but nothing has, as you see. At the same time, it's still a shock to find *nobody* else. It is not as though this house stood by itself. When we cannot sleep, or when we are at all ill. . . . For instance, since my husband has been ill he keeps hearing the piano next door. 'Go in,' he said to me yesterday, 'and tell her how much I like her playing. Ask her to go on playing—' Yes, you *did*, Maximilian, but No. 15 is empty; it's nailed up; there is a crack under the balcony."

She looked through the arch at her husband, laughing, not altogether kindly.

"The house suits me," he said. "Are we going to have no lunch?" Mrs. Bewdon picked up her tray and floundered out of the room.

.   .   .   .

A slight steam came from the dishes. Jane Oates could taste nothing: she scalded her mouth with the broth, and the fish pie lay on her tongue like wadding. The Bewdons put up an even less good show. She no longer heard what was said, or heard if anything *was* said: before the end of lunch she had to stop and rest her brow on her hands. Maximilian poured himself out a glass of water. The sun wheeled off the face of the extinct terrace opposite: reflections no longer entered the north room. Someone left the table, and when Jane raised her forehead Maximilian said, "Nancy has gone to make the coffee."

"Oh, it will be too hot."

Maximilian agreed: "This is the worst time of day."

She looked: behind his and her figures she saw bookshelves, in the flat fading light. She looked up, at the cracks across the ceiling and at the bunch of balloons— air must have escaped from them, for they were already flaccid like old grapes. "Why are those balloons there?"

"A man peddled them up and down the terrace, so I had to buy them all."

"That was kind."

"He held me responsible." Maximilian hitched one elbow over the back of his chair; he turned away from Jane with a quick, rather frenzied movement.

"Mr. Bewdon, I ought not to make you talk."

"We shan't meet again like this—for the first time. We shan't meet again when we don't know what we are saying."

Birds and waterfalls sounded in Jane's head, so that when Mrs. Bewdon brought in the tray of coffee and poured out, talking, Jane sat not listening but smiling. "Maximilian, you're not drinking your coffee. It's no use to sit twisting round from the light. Miss Oates will excuse you: you must go and lie down."

"Miss Oates must stay with me, to read her poems."

"Well, you may read, Miss Oates, but *he* must not say anything. When he goes to sleep, creep away, if you don't mind. I'm going up to lie down in my own room. It will do me good."

.   .   .   .

Maximilian went through the arch and lay down on the sofa in the back room: Mrs. Bewdon tucked a rug over his feet, and soon the gas fire drew a scorched smell from the rug. For some time one heard Mrs. Bewdon walking about upstairs; then a spring cracked in her bed as *she* lay down. Maximilian crossed his hands over his eyes; Jane undid the folder of poems and sat on a low chair, one elbow on the typewriting table so that she could prop her cheek on her hand. The wintry sun no longer afflicted them; it sent rays obliquely across the garden, through the boughs of a tree. Jane did not know she knew her poems by heart, but now she heard herself speak them as though she had been hypnotised. It frightened her not to know what was coming next—and she felt something mounting up round her in the dusk, was again frightened, did not know where it came from. Whenever she stopped, the outdoor silence pressed as close as suspense: you had the sensation of a great instrument out there in London, unstruck.

Jane kept her eyes down as though she were reading, but when she paused she looked towards Maximilian—at his face pitched up unkindly by the end of the sofa, and at his eye-bandage of knotted hands. All at once he said: "Stop."

She broke off a line.

"You're so beautiful."

"But your hands are over your eyes."

"I remember you coming in and standing there in the sun. So ill, when I am so ill. You might be a lovely neighbour. You played the piano yesterday."

"I was ill yesterday."

"Then you did play the piano—Come over here, Jane."

Jane dropped the poems and knelt by the sofa. Maximilian uncovered his eyes—after a moment he caught at her two wrists and held them so that her fingers were pressed to his temples. "Fever and pain," he said. "You make me hear the piano. What do you hear?"

"A waterfall in my head." She felt her pulse jumping inside his grip and said: "We are making each other iller." He had shut his eyes; she looked at his face and said: "I wish I had cool hands."

"If you had cool hands you would go away. I shall lose you when you are well." Pressing her fingers close to his temples he said: "All this will be gone—where we are— not a rack left. There'll be no 'here' left—how can you come back?" Then he let go her wrists roughly. "But I don't want you to come again."

"Why?"

"You'd soon see why."

"But my poems . . ."

"Take them away. Burn them. You'll only lose your way."

"Are you lost?"

"Yes, I'm lost. You don't understand yet. We only know when we're ill—the piano inside my head, the waterfall inside yours. My image of you, that neighbourly image. Eternity is inside us—it's a secret that we must never, never, never try to betray. Look where just *time* has brought me; look at where it's left me. When you make friends, don't talk about me."

"You praised my book," she said wildly starting up.

"I've got to live. How could I write, in a paper, 'She should have burned her hands off before she wrote'?"

"Are we not to believe in each other?"

"Come back here; put your head beside me." Maximilian rolled his head sideways on the end of the sofa, and, sitting back on her heels on the ground beside him, Jane laid her head where he had made room. Maximilian's voice went drowsy; his eyes closed. "You sweet neighbour," he said. "You sweet distempered friend."

"But Shakespeare . . ."

"Go to sleep, Jane, never mind, go to sleep."

Mrs. Bewdon woke and came down to make tea. She fumbled her way to the kitchen, where she put on the kettle, then into the back room, where she turned the light on and saw Jane and Bewdon asleep with their foreheads together: he lying, she kneeling twisted beside the sofa. They looked like a suicide pact. The room smelled of the scorching of Bewdon's rug. Mrs. Bewdon, when she had drawn the curtains, stooped and gave Jane's shoulder a light pat. "Teatime," she said.

Jane opened her eyes, and Mrs. Bewdon gave her a hand up. Maximilian went on breathing stertorously.

"I ought to go."

"Oh, I should have something hot first. You don't look really fit to be out at all. He'll sleep on," she said, without a glance at the sofa, "so you can slip away just when you like."

The two women, at tea in the front room, talked low, so as not to wake Maximilian. They did not want to wake him for their peace sake. Jane learned, from the way Mrs. Bewdon spoke of her husband, that she felt a dogged loyal unsmiling unloving pity for him. Mrs. Bewdon's demoralised manner seemed to come from her opinion that she did not live with a real man. She must have married during some delusion of youth.

Mrs. Bewdon's kindness to Jane was profoundly chagrining. Mrs. Bewdon said: "It's been kind of you to have come. Such a long way—I hope it has been worth while. I'm sorry my husband was not more himself, but you know what influenza is. He's always interested in young writers, though I'm afraid he's inclined to discourage them. He likes to say to them 'Don't write.'"

"Do they mind?"

"They think it is just his fun," said Mrs. Bewdon, looking round for the sugar. "Or else they think he is jealous. But he does really take an interest in them. He's disappointed they don't come back."

Jane tried to feel sorry for the sleeping man. She still felt herself closely bound to him—he had done no more than hold her wrists, but she was a girl who had never been touched. Now, the indifference in Mrs. Bewdon's voice, and her half-understanding, brought everything low. He has lost me, too, she thought. I shall be unhappy when I am well again.

"Oh, must you be going?" said Mrs. Bewdon. "Perhaps you are right, though: your eyes look rather ill. Shall I ring up a taxi?"

"No thank you; I can't afford one."

"Don't forget your poems," said Mrs. Bewdon, running back for the folder, "I expect they are good." Jane heard Bewdon, the other side of the archway, turn over and exclaim something in his sleep—one of those sleeping protests. Running quickly away from his helplessness, she followed Mrs. Bewdon into the hall. The hall door, opened by Mrs. Bewdon, showed cracked steps dropping into the dark. "You must walk past some day," said Mrs. Bewdon, "and see if we are still here."

The terrace gave out a hundred hollow echoes and, as the door shut, just perceptibly shook. The lamplight picked out its sad face. Not a step but Jane's on the pavement; not a note from the piano. They stared at Jane when she got into the bus. . . . On the Battersea Park hall table she found the telegram: she pushed away her poems behind her bureau but took the telegram to her cold bed. Through the night, she kept starting up, switching her lamp on: she re-read *"Should not see anyone."* In the dark again she heard Bewdon's voice saying "Sleep . . ." Her pillow sounded hollow with notes and knockings, notes and knockings you hear in condemned rooms.

Reduced

THE Carburys' two little girls, Penny and Claudia, went upstairs again with their governess, Miss Rice, as soon as lunch was over; their steps could be heard retreating along the pitch-pine gallery round the hall. The visitors were disappointed—Mrs. Laurie liked children and Frank Peele had been hoping to see more of the governess. Rain drummed on the hall skylight; still smoking their host Godwin Carbury's rather musty cigarettes, the grown-ups allowed themselves to be driven into the library. Here no chair invited you, the uninviting books must have been bought in lots and looked gummed in the shelves. It could have been a pretty September day; the plum-tree leaves in the tilting orchards round were bright yellow, but for days the Forest of Dene had been clouded and sodden.

Mrs. Laurie, who was vivacious and had married at nineteen, and Mrs. Carbury, who was muddled and dim, had been friends years ago in India when they were both young girls. They had kept in touch, Mrs. Carbury having no other vivacious friend, life having taught Mrs. Laurie that there was no knowing when anybody devoted might not come in useful—besides, she had always been sorry for Mima.

Mima's life had been unrewarding. She returned flatly

from India after her friend's wedding and it had not been till she was twenty-seven or -eight that she met Godwin Carbury, who at forty was looking round for a wife. He had the reputation of being the most unpopular man in his part of the country, and that reputation followed him up to London. He was careful, savagely careful, about money and not careful enough about seeing this was not known. Added to this, he had a dour self-importance. It was understood that economy kept him single as long as his mother had lived to keep house at Pendlethwaite. Possibly Mima saw something in him that no one else saw; she was anxious to "settle" suitably, and not herself accustomed to being liked. At all events, they married, and had had after some years these two thin, remote little girls. They had few neighbours at Pendlethwaite and Godwin's peculiarities cut them off more and more from anybody there was. Whatever misgivings she had, Mima pandered to him blindly. On her own account she had just a little money, so once or twice a year she came up to London, gazed into shop windows, met Mrs. Laurie (now widowed) and bought reduced coats and shoes for the little girls. She had begun lately to talk of giving up London; the girls' education would be a heavy expense, she said.

It surprised Mrs. Laurie to find herself at Pendlethwaite, but she had been at a loose end, with nowhere to go for a week. So she thought, "Try the Carburys," and had written to Mima. She was a shiftless woman, maintaining herself by the exercise of a good deal of charm: she could say daring things without sounding impertinent, and determined to get a little fun out of Godwin—apart from this, she did not expect very much.

Pendlethwaite was not a lovable house. Built about 1880 of unpleasing maroon brick, it creaked inside with pitch-pine; its church-like windows peered narrowly at the smiling landscape round; its grounds darkened a valley with belts of laurel and stiff, damp-looking clumps of un-indigenous firs. The house looked dedicated to a perpetual January: sunnier seasons beat back from its walls. The bloomy red plums and mellow apples bending the boughs this month were pagan company for it. Indoors, there was no electricity; panels absorbed the lamplight; before October, no fires were lit till night. It had not even the insidious charm of decay, for Godwin had great ideas of keeping things up: the laurels were kept clipped, the thrifty meals served formally . . . Mrs. Laurie had been diverted to find that she had a fellow guest, but this did not see her far. Frank Peele, just back on leave from Siam, was Mima's second cousin. He must have asked himself here because he had to be somewhere; she thought he was not a man you would scramble to entertain. At about thirty, he was a haggard schoolboy—shambling, facetious, huffy, forlorn, melancholic, with perhaps (she feared most of all) a romantic soul. She supposed Mima must enjoy being even sorrier for him than she need be for herself. . . . Entertaining on this scale must be a plunge for the Carburys. Mrs. Laurie could almost hear Godwin saying to Mima: "Well then, in for a penny, in for a pound." He went through with his duties as host with glum correctness. "But if one stayed a day too long he'd cut off supplies." As it was, his rigid economies hit you everywhere.

The one startling un-economy was the governess. Mrs. Laurie, though unhappily childless, knew an expensive governess when she saw one. Miss Rice's technique was perfect. Her first appearance, at lunch, took Nella's breath away with its unobtrusiveness. Penny and Claudia—their dark eyes set close in, tucking their long fair hair back behind their shoulders primly—clearly revolved round her. "Those two little mice adore her," thought Mrs. Laurie, recalling the composed retreat after lunch: three people going back to a world of their own. But the adoration was kept within nice bounds. "How does Mima *keep* the woman in this mausoleum? She might be anywhere. Mima can't be such a fool as I thought. . . . I must find out."

In the library, she lost no time in doing this. In the bow window, Frank Peele with his hands in his pockets stood looking out unexpectedly at the rain; Mima poured out thin coffee; Godwin glumly handed the cups round. Mrs. Laurie said affably, "So you got a governess? Last time we met, you were busy looking for one."

"Yes, oh yes. We did," Mima said in her flustered way.

"Miss Rice came in May," said Godwin firmly.

"She seems a great success. . . ."

Frank Peele grunted.

"When she first came in," went on Mrs. Laurie, "I felt certain I'd seen her somewhere. I wonder where she was before? She's startlingly good-looking, but in such a tactful way. Hag-ridden—but that's the life, I suppose."

"She appears content with us," said Godwin, handing the sugar to Mrs. Laurie bitterly. "Mima, what are your plans for this afternoon?" His wife looked blank.

"Our guests should be entertained."

"It struck me," said Frank, wheeling round, "as one of the few faces I had not seen before."

"Really?" said Godwin.

Mima touched the coffee-tray clumsily; everything on it skidded. Did she not want Cousin Frank to fall for the governess? The nicest women like having unattached men around. "She must be full of brains," said Mrs. Laurie vaguely.

"She teaches wonderfully; she's got the children on so. They seem to be learning everything."

"Can we have them all down after tea to play Up Jenkin or something?"

"They do preparation then," said Godwin repressively. ("Set," thought his guest, "on getting his money's worth.") Mima's eyes, oddly overwrought in her pink creased face, stole to meet her husband's. "Frank," Godwin continued, "I could show you those maps now." Clearly, any discussion of Miss Rice was closed.

"Not to-day, thanks," said Frank, "I've got a crick in my neck." Godwin, after one more forbidding look at Mima, left them, shutting the door reprovingly. Frank loafed along the bookshelves, pulled out *Monasteries of the Levant*, and folded himself in a chair with an air of resigned discomfort. A man with a book is practically not present. Mrs. Laurie whipped out her *petit point,* and the two women, pulling their chairs together zestfully, settled down for a talk. Rain streamed down the windows, paper rustled inside the cold grate.

Mima saw so few friends that talk went to her head like wine. Evenly sing-song, the women's voices began rising and falling. After half an hour, Frank's book slipped on to his knee; his head rolled back, jaw dropping; he let out a sharp snore. "Really . . ." exclaimed Mima, stopping the talk to titter. "A tropical habit," said Mrs. Laurie. This was better than Frank with a book, they were quite alone. She hopped back to her topic.

"Mima, what's Godwin got up his sleeve about Miss Rice?"

"Miss Rice?—nothing," Mima said, overacting.

"His one wicked extravagance?"

"No," faltered Mima. "That's just the point—she's not."

"A bargain? You amaze me. Can she be at all fishy?"

"My dear Nella—she's good with the children, isn't she?" Mima fixed her friend with such oddly imploring eyes that Mrs. Laurie, startled, put down her work: "She's made princesses of them," she said extravagantly. "How wise you have been, Mima!"

"You do really think so? Godwin and I wanted the best we could get, you see: he has such ideas for Penny and Claudia."

"It does him credit," said Mrs. Laurie warmly.

"I suppose so—" blurted out Mima—then, looking wretched, put her hand to her cheek. "I've never quite liked—I mean if she—I can't help wondering—"

"Why did Godwin snap me up when I said I thought I knew her face?"

"We'd hoped no one would think that," said Mima surprisingly. "As a rule, you see, almost nobody comes here, and in every other way she seemed quite ideal: she is. In the ordinary way, we never could have afforded her. It did seem such an opportunity. You see, we could not offer a high salary."

"That would narrow things down . . ."

"It did. All the ones I had interviewed were so vulgar and pushing, besides seeming to know nothing at all. The agency woman said, 'For that, what can you expect?' I was in despair."

"Oh? So then—?"

"I came round more and more to Godwin's idea. As he said, it was practically a charity. It did seem unfair that the thing should count against her. When she had paid for her defence she hadn't a penny, and no other future, of course. And she was acquitted."

"What on earth do you mean?"

Looking thoroughly frightened, Mima caught herself up. "Oh dear," she said, "and I swore never to speak of it. Nella, will you swear to let this go no farther? It's such a relief to tell you: it's on my mind the whole time. You see, Godwin had followed all the evidence carefully. The witnesses gave her such magnificent testimonials, almost all her former employers were called. Even the Prosecution didn't make out she wasn't a good *governess*. And after all, she was cleared. (If only they'd found who'd done it. . . .)"

"Begin at the beginning."

"Well. . . . Do you ever read murder trials?"

"Hardly ever miss one."

"Do you remember that Sir Max Rant dying suddenly?"

"Mima—she's not *Henrietta Post?*"

"Sssh—sssh," whispered Mima, glancing Frank's way cautiously. Then she nodded at Nella with frightened important eyes.

Mrs. Laurie stared, galvanised, at her hostess. Then: "She's lucky to be alive," she said. "It was touch and go."

"He was a dreadful old man, apparently. At the very worst, they said nothing against her *morals*."

"No wonder she's haunted-looking. That was an appalling ordeal. . . . But, after that, how on earth—?"

"Godwin got me to write to her three weeks after the trial, offering her a new life and twenty-five pounds a year. . . ."

"Godwin is on the spot! Well, they're your children, not mine—*Henrietta Post!*"

Immovably, without batting a closed eyelid, Frank said, "Who is Henrietta Post?"

II

"Miss Rice's hands are cold again," said Penny.

Claudia went on painting a moment longer, then, balancing her brush on the glass jar of paint-water, which gave out a prussic smell and had a red sediment, looked intently across the table at Penny, who stood by Miss Rice's chair, chafing her right hand. Their governess, with her book propped on the table, her pale cheek on her left hand, read on, smiling unnoticingly. Once she withdrew her hand from Penny's to turn over a page.

"Whatever will she do in winter?" said Claudia.

"There'll be fires then."

"This fire never burns much." They shared the same desperate thought: "Suppose our darling should leave us?"

This afternoon, the black chill of the grate focused your fancy as firelight might have done. The schoolroom had a faded sea-blue wallpaper cut into by pitch-pine presses and two doors: not a colour warmed it; the high windows looked into a rain-blurred hill. Miss Rice had put nothing of her own on the mantelpiece, along which marched a file of plasticene animals modelled by the little girls. About the room were products of other hobbies good governesses encourage children to have—on the windowsill a nursery-garden in pots: pink-cheeked "Bubbles" and "Cherry Ripe" looked queerly down at the bleak room where these three people were living as best they could.

Miss Rice put away the book and with it her happy forgetful smile—the book had been *Emma*. "Have you stopped painting?" she said.

She had given them for their subject a Greek temple. Claudia's temple had a sunset behind it, Penny had filled in the columns with Mediterranean blue. Miss Rice came round and looked. "A sunset like that would make reflections on white stone, Claudia. Penny, on such a fine day there would be shadows." They saw. She always thought of something they had not thought of: they wrinkled up their foreheads in ecstatic despair. "Penny, if you are stopping, wash that blue off your paint-brush."

"Are paints poison?"

"Sometimes. Well, are you cold, too?"

They would admit nothing that could distress her.

"Then push the table back and get the skipping-ropes out."

The little girls were alike, though there were two years between them, as though they could not decide to part in any particular. There was not much difference in size, as though Penny had waited for Claudia. Their voices were pitched on the same persuasive note; when their vehement dark eyes met they seemed to consult. What they thought of being alive their parents would never know; their characters were like batteries storing something up. Before Miss Rice was here, the doctor's sister had come in every morning to give them lessons. They had known before how to read and write, so all they had learnt from the doctor's sister was what everyone else knew: just why their house was avoided, how bitterly father was laughed at and mother pitied because of him. They learnt that it was wretched to be themselves. They marked the contempt with which every morning she bicycled up their evenue, and how insolently she ate what there was at lunch. Her raspy finger-tips, the pearls screwed tight in her fleshy ears, her horse-sense, all seemed part of her power to mortify them. She was the world and they prayed she might die, but she married. After that they waited, in armour. Then came Miss Rice.

"If you want to keep warm you must hurry," said Miss Rice.

Claudia unwound the skipping-ropes and they took one each: they stood with their arms out, gripping the handles eagerly. "One, two, three—go!" The ropes zip-zipped on the oilcloth. Penny stumbled at fifty-six, but Claudia kept in and skipped seventy-eight: her toes bounced and bounced, her hair flopped, her eyes started out of her head. At last the rope caught her toe. "That's the record," said Miss Rice, "but Penny may beat it next time." Both breathless they knelt on the hearthrug, life tingling up through them from their toes to their cheeks.

"If *you* skipped," said Claudia, "you might skip a hundred."

"The rope is too short," said Miss Rice.

"What else used you to do—dance?"

"Yes, once."

They had never seen anyone dancing except in pictures of ballrooms; they preferred to imagine Miss Rice not on the crook of an arm but floating alone around a floor, with her ageless shining white face, unfrivolous as an angel. At this happy moment, near her and warm from skipping, they felt on the edge of the story she did not tell. . . . But *she* looked down at the skipping-ropes on the floor. "Better put those away," she said. Except when she was reading she never stayed quiet long: something they could feel creep up behind her chair would make her speaking eyes go suddenly cold and dark as the grate. Against this their love was powerless. This dreadful expectation seemed wrong in their darling—mother without her worries would not be anyone, father was there to stare and bite his moustache, but she seemed to them born to inherit light. . . . Feeling their enemy here now the children, helpless, got up to put the skipping-ropes back in the press.

"Someone's coming!" said Penny. They heard the baize door at the far end of their passage swing to behind somebody, then a man's step. A knuckle rapped the door once, unconfidently: Miss Rice and the children waited. "Come in," she said.

Frank Peele peered round the door. "Oh?" he said. "May I come in? Sorry, I was exploring. Looking for secret passages. Exercise before tea." Miss Rice smiled composedly. "So here you all are," he went on. He looked at the table. "Painting?"

"Yes."

"What a day!" he said to Miss Rice humbly. "Very cheery up here, though. You believe in fresh air?" Then he saw that both windows were bolted: what he felt were the draughts. Miss Rice had moved to the table where she had been reading; Frank dropped into the wicker chair with a creak. The children shut their paint-boxes up. "Must be getting on tea time," remarked Frank.

"Are you hungry, Cousin Frank?" said Claudia gently. Frank looked relieved at hearing someone say something. "I don't deserve tea; I slept like a log in the library. Your mother and Mrs. Laurie complain I snored." He looked round the schoolroom wistfully, like a dog. "They were talking nineteen to the dozen. When I dropped off they were well away about India; when I came to it was one Henrietta Post."

Penny laughed. "Who's Henrietta Post?" she said.

"Don't ask me," said Frank. "Miss Rice, who's Henrietta Post?"

Miss Rice pondered while the clock ticked several seconds and a cart rattled off into silence behind the wet orchards. The children turned to see how she took Frank's joke. She looked twice at him with steady considering dark eyes. "Surely you know?" she said at last.

"I don't know a soul," said Frank, "I've been in Siam."

"But you get the papers there, don't you?"

"She's a celebrity, is she?"

"She was accused of murder," said Miss Rice, as though giving a history lesson, "tried last spring, acquitted, but never properly cleared. So she disappeared, hoping to be forgotten."

"Good God," exclaimed Frank. "Where would a woman go to, after a show like that?"

"She is fortunate to be anywhere."

"Stop: it's coming back!" Frank said, delighted to have a topic. "Wasn't she that governess? The old swine whose house she was in had been making up to her, so when someone did him in they tried to fix it on her. I remember I thought at the time—"

Miss Rice's marked unresponse reminded Frank where he was. Chidden, he stopped awkwardly, with a glance at the children. *They* sat stone-still, clasped hands thrust down between their knees; you could not possibly tell what was going on in their heads, which were both turned intently away from their governess. Frank kicked himself. But for the life of him he couldn't stop blurting out: "She was very good-looking, wasn't she?"

"You never saw any photographs?"

"Out where I am I only get *The Times*, you see. No pretty pictures in it."

"I see."

Frank went on violently: "I know I thought at the time what a shocking unfair thing to happen to any woman!" . . . Miss Rice with her cold smile looked thoughtfully into the grate as though there were a fire burning there: she said nothing more. Her charges' agonised tension became startling. Frank hummed and beat a nonplussed tattoo on his knee. They were waiting to see the last of him. Whatever brick one had dropped, they were all very odd up here. . . .

This wet autumn evening closed in so early that the children had to stop work and wait for the lamp to come; when Mrs. Carbury looked in they were all in the dark. "Why, whatever are you doing?" she said nervously. "Where's Miss Rice? Why doesn't she ring for the lamp?"

"It never comes any sooner."

"Father wouldn't like you wasting your time like this. Where is Miss Rice?"

"In her room," Penny said, so indifferently that there seemed to be something foolish about the fuss. At this point a band of light appeared in the passage; the housemaid brought in the lamp and Mima saw her daughters facing each other like images across the table of lesson books, their unchildish eyes dark in the sudden lamplight. She sat down, acting calm while the housemaid was in the room; all the same, her manner made the girl so jumpy that she went away again without drawing down the blinds. Mrs. Carbury sat eyeing the other door; the children's bedroom opened off the schoolroom and Miss Rice's room was beyond, connecting with theirs. Her relief at not finding the governess was tremendous: all the same, she felt she was being defied.

"Does she always leave you to do preparation alone?"

"She's tired," said Claudia. "Cousin Frank was up here."

"Oh? . . . Well, tell her I want to speak to her. Then you can leave your lessons, just for this evening, and go downstairs; Mrs. Laurie says she will play games with you."

The children looked at their books without stirring, and Mima for the first time felt mutiny in the air. . . . Mima had had to brace herself to come in; twice already since tea she had started up to the schoolroom, then turned back before the baize door to that wing. Ever since her revelation to Mrs. Laurie she had been in a fearful state: the way Mrs. Laurie took it brought her own most persistent throttling fears to the top: "Henrietta Post. . . . Well, they're your children, not mine." What Nella said was what anybody who knew would say. Mima had shrunk back from the schoolroom door, feeling: "No, I really cannot face her." Then she had been forced to think: "But that is the woman my children are with the whole time. . . ." Once she had gone as far as Godwin's study to tell him he must agree to send Miss Rice away to-morrow, but the way he had looked up at her settled that. "Nothing has changed since I agreed to engage her." Mima knew too well that her husband found her a fool. "I will give her notice first, then tell Godwin. It won't be so bad with Nella in the house here. Nella will back me up. *But when Godwin hears I've told Nella?* . . . He said before she came to stay: 'Suppose your friend is inquisitive?' . . . What are they doing up there? What does she say to them? What goes on the whole time? My own children are strangers; they don't like being downstairs now. *What was it the prosecution said about influence?*"

Mima raised her voice. "Run along now at once, children: Mrs. Laurie is waiting."

"We would much rather not, mother."

"Then you're very ungrateful. Besides, I have got something to say to Miss Rice—Penny and Claudia, don't look at each other like that! It's rude to look at each other when mother speaks!"

"Miss Rice is tired," repeated Claudia gently.

"If you give us the message," said Penny, "we'll tell her."

"No, I want to talk to Miss Rice," said Mima, her voice unnatural.

"Do you, mother?" said Penny. "You don't generally."

The wicker chair Mima sat in creaked convulsively. "When we're alone again you may learn to make your mother happy. You may understand mother then and not be unkind to her. To-morrow, Miss Rice will be going away, children."

Penny and Claudia looked at the chair their mother now sat in, then up at *Emma* left on the edge of the mantelpiece. Claudia looked at their row of young plants in the windowsill, sharp in the lamplight against the rain-lashed dark outside, Penny at the wrinkled rug where that afternoon they had knelt at their darling's feet. Then their gentle vehement dark eyes, meeting, paused to consult again. They said in their quiet voices: "Then we will go too."

Look at All Those Roses

LOU exclaimed at that glimpse of a house in a sheath of startling flowers. She twisted round, to look back, in the open car, till the next corner had cut it out of sight. To reach the corner, it struck her, Edward accelerated, as though he were jealous of the rosy house—a house with gables, flat-fronted, whose dark windows stared with no expression through the flowers. The garden, with its silent burning gaiety, stayed in both their minds like an apparition.

One of those conflicts between two silent moods had set up, with Lou and Edward, during that endless drive. Also, there is a point when an afternoon oppresses one with fatigue and a feeling of unreality. Relentless, pointless, unwinding summer country made nerves ache at the back of both their eyes. This was a late June Monday; they were doubling back to London through Suffolk by-roads, on the return from a week-end. Edward, who detested the main roads, had traced out their curious route before starting, and Lou now sat beside him with the map on her knees. They had to be back by eight, for Edward, who was a writer, to finish and post an article: apart from this, time was no object with them. They looked forward with no particular pleasure to London and unlocking the stuffy flat, taking in the milk, finding bills in the letter-box.

In fact, they looked forward to nothing with particular pleasure. They were going home for the purely negative reason that there was nowhere else they could as cheaply go. The week-end had not been amusing, but at least it had been "away." Now they could foresee life for weeks ahead—until someone else invited them—the typewriter, the cocktail-shaker, the telephone, runs in the car out of London to nowhere special. Love when Edward got a cheque in the post, quarrels about people on the way home from parties—and Lou's anxiety always eating them. This future weighed on them like a dull burden. . . . So they had been glad to extend to-day.

But under a vacant sky, not sunny but full of diffused glare, the drive had begun to last too long: they felt bound up in the tired impotence of a dream. The stretches of horizon were stupefying. The road bent round wedges of cornfield, blocky elms dark with summer: for these last ten miles the countryside looked abandoned; they passed dropping gates, rusty cattle-troughs and the thistly, tussocky, stale grass of neglected farms. There was nobody on the roads; perhaps there was nobody anywhere. . . . In the heart of all this, the roses looked all the odder.

"They were extraordinary," she said (when the first corner was turned) in her tired little dogmatic voice.

"All the more," he agreed, "when all the rest of the country looks something lived in by poor whites."

"I wish we lived *there*," she said. "It really looked like somewhere."

"It wouldn't if we did."

Edward spoke with some tartness. He had found he had reason to dread week-ends away: they unsettled Lou and started up these fantasies. Himself, he had no illusions about life in the country: life without people was absolutely impossible. What would he and she do with nobody to talk to but each other? Already, they had not spoken for two hours. Lou saw life in terms of ideal moments. She found few ideal moments in their flat.

He went on: "You know you can't stand earwigs. And we should spend our lives on the telephone."

"About the earwigs?"

"No. About ourselves."

Lou's smart little monkey face became dolorous. She never risked displeasing Edward too far, but she was just opening her mouth to risk one further remark when Edward jumped and frowned. A ghastly knocking had started. It seemed to come from everywhere, and at the same time to be a special attack on them. Then it had to be traced to the car's vitals: it jarred up Lou through the soles of her feet. Edward slowed to a crawl and stopped. He and she confronted each other with that completely dramatic lack of expression they kept for occasions when the car went wrong. They tried crawling on again, a few tentative yards: the knocking took up again with still greater fury.

"Sounds to me like a big end gone."

"Oh my goodness" she said.

All the same, she was truly glad to get out of the car. She stretched and stood waiting on the grass roadside while Edward made faces into the bonnet. Soon he flung round to ask what she would suggest doing: to his surprise (and annoyance) she had a plan ready. She would walk back to that house and ask if they had a telephone. If they had not, she would ask for a bicycle and bicycle to the place where the nearest garage was.

Edward snatched the map, but could not find where they were. Where they were seemed to be highly improbable. "I expect you," Lou said, "would rather stay with the car." "No, I wouldn't," said Edward, "anybody can have it. . . . You like to be sure where I am, don't you?" he added. He locked their few odd things up in the boot of the car with the suitcases, and they set off in silence. It was about a mile.

There stood the house, waiting. Why should a house wait? Most pretty scenes have something passive about them, but this looked like a trap baited with beauty, set ready to spring. It stood back from the road. Lou put her hand on the gate and, with a touch of bravado, the two filed up the paved path to the door. Each side of the path, hundreds of standard roses bloomed, overcharged with colour, as though this were their one hour. Crimson, coral, blue-pink, lemon and cold white, they disturbed with fragrance the dead air. In this spell-bound afternoon, with no shadows, the roses glared at the strangers, frighteningly bright. The face of the house was plastered with tea-roses: waxy cream when they opened but with vermilion buds.

The blistered door was propped open with a bizarre object, a lump of quartz. Indoors was the dark cold-looking hall. When they had come to the door they found no bell or knocker: they could not think what to do. "We had better cough," Lou said. So they stood there coughing, till a door at the end of the hall opened and a lady or woman looked out—they were not sure which. "Oh?" she said, with no expression at all.

"We couldn't find your bell."

"There they are," she said, pointing to two Swiss cowbells that hung on loops of string by the door she had just come out of. Having put this right, she continued to look at them, and out through the door past them, wiping her powerful-looking hands vaguely against the sides of her blue overall. They could hardly see themselves as intruders when their intrusion made so little effect. The occupying inner life of this person was not for an instant suspended by their presence. She was a shabby amazon of a woman, with a sculptural clearness about the face. She must have lost contact with the outer world completely: there was now nothing to "place" her by. It is outside attachments—hopes, claims, curiosities, desires, little touches of greed—that put a label on one to help strangers. As it was, they could not tell if she were rich or poor, stupid or clever, a spinster or a wife. She seemed prepared, not anxious, for them to speak. Lou, standing close beside Edward, gave him a dig in a rib. So Edward explained to the lady how they found themselves, and asked if she had a telephone or a bicycle.

She said she was sorry to say she had neither. Her maid had a bicycle, but had ridden home on it. "Would you like some tea?" she said. "I am just boiling the kettle. Then perhaps you can think of something to do." This lack of grip of the crisis made Edward decide the woman

must be a moron: annoyance contused his face. But Lou,
who wanted tea and was attracted by calmness, was entirely won. She looked at Edward placatingly.

"Thank you," he said. "But I must do something at
once. We haven't got all night; I've got to be back in London. Can you tell me where I can telephone from? I must
get through to a garage—a good garage."

Unmoved, the lady said: "You'll have to walk to the
village. It's about three miles away." She gave unexpectedly clear directions, then looked at Lou again. "Leave
your wife here," she said. "Then she can have tea."

Edward shrugged; Lou gave a brief undecided sigh.
How much she wanted to stop. But she never liked to be
left. This partly arose from the fact that she was not
Edward's wife: he was married to someone else and his
wife would not divorce him. He might some day go back
to her, if this ever became the way of least resistance. Or
he might, if it were the way of even less resistance, move
on to someone else. Lou was determined neither should
ever happen. She did love Edward, but she also stuck to
him largely out of contentiousness. She quite often asked
herself why she did. It seemed important—she could not
say why. She was determined to be a necessity. Therefore
she seldom let him out of her sight—her idea of love was
adhesiveness. . . . Knowing this well, Edward gave her
a slightly malign smile, said she had far better stay,
turned, and walked down the path without her. Lou, like
a lost cat, went half-way to the door. "Your roses are wonderful . . ." she said, staring out with unhappy eyes.

"Yes, they grow well for us; Josephine likes to see
them." Her hostess added: "My kettle will be boiling.
Won't you wait in there?"

Lou went deeper into the house. She found herself in
a long, low and narrow parlour, with a window at each
end. Before she could turn round, she felt herself being
looked at. A girl of about thirteen lay, flat as a board, in a
wicker invalid carriage. The carriage was pulled out across
the room, so that the girl could command the view from
either window, the flat horizons that bounded either sky.
Lying there with no pillow she had a stretched look. Lou

stood some distance from the foot of the carriage: the dark eyes looked at her down thin cheekbones, intently. The girl had an unresigned, living face; one hand crept on the rug over her breast. Lou felt, here was the nerve and core of the house. . . . The only movement was made by a canary, springing to and fro in its cage.

"Hullo," Lou said, with that deferential smile with which one approached an invalid. When the child did not answer, she went on: "You must wonder who I am?"

"I don't know; I did when you drove past."

"Then our car broke down."

"I know, I wondered whether it might."

Lou laughed and said: "Then you put the evil eye on it."

The child ignored this. She said: "This is not the way to London."

"All the same, that's where we're going."

"You mean, where you were going. . . . Is that your husband who has just gone away?"

"That's Edward: yes. To telephone. He'll be back." Lou, who was wearing a summer suit, smart, now rather crumpled, of honey-yellow linen, felt Josephine look her up and down. "Have you been to a party?" she said, "or are you going to one?"

"We've just been staying away." Lou walked nervously down the room to the front window. From here she saw the same roses Josephine saw: she thought they looked like forced roses, magnetised into being. Magnetised, buds uncurled and petals dropped. Lou began to wake from the dream of the afternoon: her will stirred; she wanted to go; she felt apprehensive, threatened. "I expect you like to lie out of doors, with all those roses?" she said.

"No, not often: I don't care for the sky."

"You just watch through the window?"

"Yes," said the child, impatiently. She added: "What are the parts of London with most traffic?"

"Piccadilly Circus. Trafalgar Square."

"Oh, I would like to see those."

The child's mother's step sounded on the hall flags: she

came in with the tea-tray. "Can I help you?" said Lou, glad of the interim.

"Oh, thank you. Perhaps you'd unfold that table. Put it over here beside Josephine. She's lying down because she hurt her back."

"My back was hurt six years ago," said Josephine. "It was my father's doing."

Her mother was busy lodging the edge of the tray on the edge of the tea-table.

"Awful for him," Lou murmured, helping unstack the cups.

"No, it's not," said Josephine. "He has gone away."

Lou saw why. A man in the wrong cannot live where there is no humanity. There are enormities you can only keep piling up. He had bolted off down that path, as Edward had just done. Men cannot live with sorrow, with women who embrace it. Men will suffer a certain look in animals' eyes, but not in women's eyes. And men dread obstinacy, of love, of grief. You could stay with burning Josephine, not with her mother's patient, exalted face. . . . When her mother had gone again, to fetch the teapot and kettle, Josephine once more fastened her eyes on Lou. "Perhaps your husband will be some time," she said. "You're the first new person I have seen for a year. Perhaps he will lose his way."

"Oh, but then I should have to look for him!"

Josephine gave a fanatical smile. "But when people go away they sometimes quite go," she said. "If they always come back, then what is the good of moving?"

"I don't see the good of moving."

"Then stay here."

"People don't just go where they want; they go where they must."

"Must you go back to London?"

"Oh, I have to, you know."

"Why?"

Lou frowned and smiled in a portentous, grown-up way that meant nothing at all to either herself or Josephine. She felt for her cigarette case and, glumly, found it empty

—Edward had walked away with the packet of cigarettes that he and she had been sharing that afternoon. He also carried any money she had.

"You don't know where he's gone to," Josephine pointed out. "If you had to stay, you would soon get used to it. We don't wonder where my father is."

"What's your mother's name?"

"Mrs. Mather. She'd like you to stay. Nobody comes to see us; they used to, they don't now. So we only see each other. They may be frightened of something—"

Mrs. Mather came back, and Josephine looked out of the other window. This immediate silence marked a conspiracy, in which Lou had no willing part. While Mrs. Mather was putting down the teapot, Lou looked round the room, to make sure it was ordinary. This window-ended parlour was lined with objects that looked honest and worn without having antique grace. A faded room should look homely. But extinct paper and phantom cretonnes gave this a gutted air. Rooms can be whitened and gutted by too-intensive living, as they are by a fire. It was the garden, out there, that focused the senses. Lou indulged for a minute the astounding fancy that Mr. Mather lay at the roses' roots. . . . Josephine said sharply: "I don't want any tea," which made Lou realise that she would have to be fed and did not want to be fed in front of the stranger Lou still was. Mrs. Mather made no comment: she drew two chairs to the table and invited Lou to sit down. "It's rather sultry," she said. "I'm afraid your husband may not enjoy his walk."

"How far did you say it was?"

"Three miles."

Lou, keeping her wrist under the table, glanced down covertly at her watch.

"We are very much out of the way," said Mrs. Mather.

"But perhaps you like that?"

"We are accustomed to quiet," said Mrs. Mather, pouring out tea. "This was a farm, you know. But it was an unlucky farm, so since my husband left I have let the land. Servants seem to find that the place is lonely—country girls are so different now. My present servant is not very clear in her mind, but she works well and does not seem to feel lonely. When she is not working she rides home."

"Far?" said Lou, tensely.

"A good way," said Mrs. Mather, looking out of the window at the horizon.

"Then aren't you rather . . . alone?—I mean, if anything happened."

"Nothing more can happen," said Mrs. Mather. "And there are two of us. When I am working upstairs or am out with the chickens, I wear one of those bells you see in the hall, so Josephine can always hear where I am. And I leave the other bell on Josephine's carriage. When I work in the garden she can see me, of course." She slit the wax-paper top off a jar of jam. "This is my last pot of last year's damson," she said. "Please try some; I shall be making more soon. We have two fine trees."

"You should see mother climb them," said Josephine.

"Aren't you afraid of falling?"

"Why," said Mrs. Mather, advancing a plate of rather rich bread and butter. "I never eat tea, thank you," Lou said, sitting rigid, sipping round her cup of tea like a bird.

"She thinks if she eats she may have to stay here for ever," Josephine said. Her mother, taking no notice, spread jam on her bread and butter and started to eat in a calmly voracious way. Lou kept clinking her spoon against the teacup: every time she did this the canary started and fluttered. Though she knew Edward could not possibly come yet, Lou kept glancing down the garden at the gate. Mrs. Mather, reaching out for more bread and butter, saw, and thought Lou was looking at the roses. "Would you like to take some back to London?" she said.

Josephine's carriage had been wheeled out on the lawn between the rosebeds. She lay with eyes shut and forehead contracted, for overhead hung the dreaded space of the sky. But she had to be near Lou while Lou cut the roses. In a day or two, Lou thought, I should be wearing a bell. What shall I do with these if I ever do go? she thought, as she cut through the strong stems between the thorns and piled the roses on the foot of the carriage. I shall certainly never want to look at roses again. By her wrist watch it was six o'clock—two hours since Edward had started. All round, the country under the white stretched sky was completely silent. She went once to the gate.

"Is there any way from that village?" she said at last. "Any bus to anywhere else? Any taxi one could hire?"

"I don't know," said Josephine.

"When does your servant come back?"

"To-morrow morning. Sometimes our servants never come back at all."

Lou shut the knife and said: "Well, those are enough roses." She supposed she could hear if whoever Edward sent for the car came to tow it away. The car, surely, Edward would not abandon? She went to the gate again. From behind her Josephine said: "Then please wheel me indoors."

"If you like. But I shall stay here."

"Then I will. But please put something over my eyes."

Lou got out her red silk handkerchief and laid this across Josephine's eyes. This made the mouth more revealing: she looked down at the small resolute smile. "If you want to keep on listening," the child said, "you needn't talk to me. Lie down and let's pretend we're both asleep."

Lou lay down on the dry cropped grass alongside the wheels of the carriage: she crossed her hands under her head, shut her eyes and lay stretched, as rigid as Josephine. At first she was so nervous, she thought the lawn vibrated under her spine. Then slowly she relaxed. There is a moment when silence, no longer resisted, rushes into the mind. She let go, inch by inch, of life, that since she was a child she had been clutching so desperately—her obsessions about this and that, her obsession about keeping Edward. How anxiously she had run from place to place, wanting to keep everything inside her own power. I should have stayed still: I shall stay still now, she thought. What I want must come to me: I shall not go after it. People who stay still generate power. Josephine stores herself up, and so what she wants happens, because she knows what she wants. I only think I want things; I only think I want Edward. (He's not coming and I don't care, I don't care.) I feel life myself now. No wonder I've been tired, only half getting what I don't really want. Now I want nothing; I just want a white circle.

The white circle distended inside her eyelids and she looked into it in an ecstasy of indifference. She knew she was looking at nothing—then knew nothing . . .

Josephine's voice, from up in the carriage, woke her. "You were quite asleep."

"Was I?"

"Take the handkerchief off: a motor's coming."

Lou heard the vibration. She got up and uncovered Josephine's eyes. Then she went to the foot of the carriage and got her roses together. She was busy with this, standing with her back to the gate, when she heard the taxi pull up, then Edward's step on the path. The taxi driver sat staring at the roses. "It's all right," Edward shouted, "they're sending out from the garage. They should be here any moment. But what people—God!— Look here, have you been all right?"

"Perfectly, I've been with Josephine."

"Oh, hullo, Josephine," Edward said, with a hasty exercise of his charm. "Well, I've come for this woman. Thank you for keeping her."

"It's quite all right, thank you. . . . Shall you be going now?"

"We must get our stuff out of the car: it will have to be towed to the garage. Then when I've had another talk to the garage people we'll take this taxi on and pick up a train. . . . Come on, Lou, come on! We don't want to miss those people! And we've got to get that stuff out of the car!"

"Is there such a hurry?" she said, putting down the roses.

"Of course, there's a hurry. . . ." He added, to Josephine: "We'll look in on our way to the station, when

I've fixed up all this, to say good-bye to your mother."
He put his hand on Lou's shoulder and punted her ahead
of him down the path. "I'm glad you're all right," he said,
as they got into the taxi. "You're well out of that, my girl.
From what I heard in the village—"

"What, have you been anxious?" said Lou, curiously.

"It's a nervy day," said Edward, with an uneasy laugh,
"and I had to put in an hour in the village emporium,
first waiting for my call, then waiting for this taxi. (And
this is going to cost us a pretty penny.) I got talking,
naturally, one way and another. You've no idea what they
said when they heard where I had parked you. Not a soul
round there will go near the place. I must say—discount-
ing gossip—there's a story there," said Edward. "They
can't fix anything, but . . . Well, you see, it appears that
this Mather woman . . ." Lowering his voice, so as not
to be heard by the driver, Edward began to tell Lou what
he had heard in the village about the abrupt disappear-
ance of Mr. Mather.

A Love Story

MIST lay over the estuary, over the terrace, over the hollows of the gummy sub-tropical garden of the hotel. Now and then a soft sucking sigh came from the water, as though someone were turning over in his sleep. At the head of the steps down to the boathouse, a patch of hydrangeas still flowered and rotted, though it was December. It was now six o'clock, dark—chinks of light from the hotel lay yellow and blurred on the density. The mist's muffling silence could be everywhere felt. Light from the double glass doors fell down the damp steps. At the head of the steps the cast-iron standard lamps were unlit.

Inside the double glass doors, the lounge with its high curtained bow windows was empty. Brilliantly hotly lit by electric light, it looked like a stage on which there has been a hitch. Light blared on the *vieux rose* curtains and on the ocean of carpet with its jazz design. The armchairs and settees with their taut stuffing had an air of brutal, resilient strength. Brass ashtrays without a segment of ash stood on small tables dotted over the lounge. A glass screen kept the lounge from any draughts from the door; a glass screen protected the lounge from the stairs. But there was nothing to dread: the heating was on, only a smell of tinder-dry turkey carpet, ivory paint, polish and radiators came downstairs from the empty floors above. In the immense tiled fireplace a fire burned with a visible silent roar.

From a cabinet came a voice announcing the six o'clock war news. In the middle of this, three berries fell from a vase of holly and pattered noisily into a brass tray. The temperate voice of the announcer paused for a moment, half-way through a disaster, as though disturbed by the noise. A spurt of gas from a coal sent a whicker up through the fire. The unheard news came to an end.

Two women came up the steps and pushed in at the glass doors. Their hair was sticky from the damp of the mist. The girl steered her mother round the screen to the fire, then went across and turned off the wireless. The mother unbuttoned her leather coat and threw it back from her handsome full chest. Keyed up by the sudden electric light, her manner was swaggering and excitable. She looked with contempt at the wireless cabinet and said: "I don't care what I hear—now!"

"Do shut up, mother. Do sit down."

"Do stop being so nervous of me, Teresa. Whatever do you think I'm going to do?"

Teresa took off her trenchcoat and slung it over a chair, then crossed the lounge with her loose cross walk, in her slacks. "I know what you want," she said flatly, ringing the bell. She sat down in an armchair by the fire and stuck her young slender jaw out and crossed her legs. Her mother stayed standing up, with her shoulders braced back; she kept pushing her hair back from her forehead with her long plump fine-wristed ringed hand. "I daresay you're right to be so nervous," she said. "I don't know myself what I'll do, from minute to minute. Why did I have to come here—can you tell me that? Why was this the only thing I could do? Do you know when I was last here—who I was with?"

"I suppose I know," said Teresa, defensively. "You know you don't want me to understand you, mother, so I'm not trying to."

"It's a terrible thing to say," said Mrs. Massey, "but it would be better if this had happened to you. I'd rather see you suffer than have no feelings. You're not like a woman, Teresa. And he was your age, not my age."

"Is that so?" Teresa said, in a voice too lifeless for irony.

Mrs. Massey looked angrily round the lounge and said: "They've changed the chairs round, since." She pointed to an empty space on the carpet and said: "*That* was where he sat. . . . There isn't even his chair."

Teresa looked pointedly off down the corridor. "Michael's coming," she said. A boy in a white cotton coat, with a dark vivid Kerry face, beamed at them through the glass screen, then came round the screen for orders. "Good evening, Michael," said Teresa.

"Good evening, miss. Good evening to you, ma'am."

"It's not a good evening for me, I'm afraid, Michael."

Michael lowered his eyes. "I'm sorry to hear that," he said, in a trembling and feeling voice. "It's a long time since we saw you."

"Does it seem so—?" Mrs. Massey began wildly. But Teresa put up her hand and in a curt, raised voice ordered her mother's drink. . . . "But I wanted a double," objected Mrs. Massey, when Michael had gone.

"You know you had that at home," said Teresa, "and more than once." More coldly, she added: "And how fed up Teddy used to get."

Frank and Linda, their fingers loosely linked, came downstairs on their way to their private sitting-room. They glanced vacantly through the screen and turned left down the corridor. "We missed the news again," she said, as he shut the door. "We always seem to run late." "We can't help that, darling," he said. Their fire had been made up while they were upstairs. She gave it an unnecessary kick with her heel, and said: "Did you see those two making a scene in the lounge?"

"I sort of did see the girl," Frank said. "Which was the other?"

"I thought they looked like locals in for a drink. Or I daresay they came round here to make a scene. I do think the Irish are exhibitionists."

"Well, we can't help that, darling, can we," said Frank, ringing the bell. He sat down in a chair and said: "Oh, my God . . ." Linda dropping into the chair opposite. "Well, really . . ." Frank said. "However, I feel fine. I don't care what time it is."

Up in a sitting-room on the first floor, the Perry-Duntons' two dogs slept in front of the fire, bellies taut to the heat. Legs rigid, they lay in running attitudes, like stuffed dogs knocked over on to their sides. On the sofa pulled up opposite the fire was Clifford—feet braced against one end, backbone against the other, knees up, typewriter in the pit of his stomach, chin tucked down into his chest. With elbows in to his ribs in a trussed position, he now and then made a cramped dash at the keys. When the keys stopped, he stayed frowning at them. Sheet after sheet, completed without conviction, fluttered on to the hearthrug between the dogs.

Polly Perry-Dunton's armchair was pushed up so that one arm made telepathic contact with Clifford's sofa. Curled up childishly in the cushions, she held a Penguin volume a little above her face. She kept the stiff Penguin open by means of an anxious pressure from her thumb. She read like someone told to pose with a book, and seemed unable to read without holding her breath.

Crackles came now and then from the *Daily Sketch* that Clifford had folded under his feet. Light blazed on their two heads from a marble bowl near the ceiling. The top of the mantelpiece was stacked with Penguins; the other armchair was stacked with American magazines. Polly's portable wireless in its shagreen cover stood silent on the floor by her chair. An art photograph of Clifford and Polly, profiles just overlapping like heads on a coin, was propped on the whatnot and kept from slipping by Polly's toy panda from Fortnum's.

Clifford reached out his right hand, apparently vaguely: Polly uncoiled like a spring from the armchair, knelt on the hearthrug and lit him a cigarette. Cigarette pressed tightly between his lips, Clifford turned back to frown at the keys again. She sat back on her heels to adore his

frown, his curls, his fresh skin—then she locked her arms
tightly around his neck. The impulsive light little-girlish-
ness of the movement let him still say nothing, not even
turn his head.

She said into his cheek: "May Polly say one thing?"

"Mm-mm."

"I've left my pussy gloves in the car."

"Mm-mm. . . . You don't want them, do you?"

"No, not indoors. I wouldn't want gloves indoors. But
let's remember to-morrow. . . . Look, you crumpled one
sheet right up. Did you mean to?"

"I meant to."

Polly reverently uncrumpled the sheet. "Pity," she said.
"It's beautifully typed. Do you mean you're *not* going to
say all that?"

"No. I'm trying to think of something else."

"I should think most people could never think of so
much that they were even not going to say."

Clifford waited a minute, then he unfastened Polly's
arms from his neck with as little emotion as a woman un-
doing a boa. He then typed five or six lines in a sort of
rush. She returned with a glutted sigh to her chair,
thumbed her book, held her breath and thought of her
pussy gloves.

Clifford's voice to Polly was always the same: resigna-
tion or irony kept it on one note. The two of them had
been over here on honeymoon when the war began; here
they still were, because of the war. Some days he went
out with his gun along the foot of the mountain, some days
they ran the motor-boat in and out of white inlets or to an
island, some days they went out in Polly's big car. When
they had run the car back into the lock-up they would
walk back, her hand creeping inside his, down the tarmac
curve to the hotel between walls of evergreen. At this
hour, the tarmac gleamed wet-white in the lasting luminous Irish dusk. From this hour, claustrophobia resumed
its sway. Polly hardly reached up to Clifford's shoulders;
she walked beside him with her little skip-and-jump. She
felt that his being so tall, she so little, cancelled out their
adverse difference in age. She was thirty-two, he twenty-

four. Her trim little sexless figure, her kilted skirts, socks and little-girl snooded hair that flopped forward so softly could make her look fourteen. Without the ring of technicians who got her up she could have easily looked faded and sluttish, like a little girl in Woolworth's wilting behind the goods. But she had a childish hard will, and by day she never looked old.

She grew up when she was asleep. Then, a map of unwilling adult awareness—lines, tensions and hollows—appeared in her exposed face. Harsh sleep froze her liquidity; her features assembled themselves and became austere. An expression of watching wrote itself on the lids of her shut eyes. The dread she denied all day came out while she slept and stood in the door. The flittering of a palm tree, the bump of a moored boat as the tide rose, the collapse of a last coal in their grate went straight to the nerves upright under her sleep. She slept tenaciously, late into the daylight—but Clifford never looked at her long.

Her rape of Clifford—with his animal muteness, nonchalance, mystery and the charm of the obstination of his wish to write—had been the climax of Polly's first real wish. Her will had detected the flaw in his will that made the bid possible. Her father had bought him for her. Till they met, her wealth and her years of styleless backgroundless dullness had atrophied Polly. The impulse with which she first put her arms round Clifford's neck and told him never to leave her had been, however, unforced and pure. Rain—a little rain, not much—fell on her small parched nature at Clifford's tentative kiss. There had seemed no threat to Polly in Clifford's nature till the war came, with its masculine threat. Their sequestration now, here, remained outwardly simple: Clifford handled no money, Polly drew all the cheques.

They stayed on here where they were hidden and easy —any move might end in some fatal way. The Perry-Duntons knew almost nothing of the hotel. They had meals served in their suite, and only went down or upstairs or through the lounge on their way outdoors or in. During such appearances, Polly's service-flat temperament sheathed her in passive, moronic unseeingness. Her blindness made everything negative—Clifford saw nothing, either. He walked out or in through the public rooms beside her, tense, persecuted by the idea of notice, with his baited, defensive frown. The hotel had come to return the Perry-Duntons' indifference. The out-of-season skeleton staff of servants served them without interest, acting the automata Polly took them to be. Servants love love and money, but the Perry-Duntons bored the servants, by now. By now even Mrs. Coughlan, the manageress, thought and spoke of them with apathy. The Perry-Duntons deadened the air round them with their static depleting intimacy.

Now, Clifford twitched one more sheet off the machine. Leaning sideways over from the sofa, he, with absorption, began to tickle a dog's belly with an edge of the sheet. The dog bent itself further backward, into a bow. Watchful, Polly judged that this meant a break. She got up and began to tug like a bird at the *Daily Sketch* under Clifford's feet. "What's that there for?" she said. "I don't think I've looked at it yet."

"Sorry," said Clifford, raising his feet.

"But what's it *there* for, Clifford?"

"I was taught not to put my boots up on things—not straight up on things, that is."

"How funny, because you generally do. I wonder what made you just think of that?"

Clifford could not tell her. He swung his feet off the sofa on to the hearthrug between the dogs. Sitting forward on the edge of the sofa, elbows on his wide-apart knees, he dug his heels slowly, without passion, into the rug. He looked slowly down from his hands with their hanging bunches of fingers to the oriental pattern under them. Polly picked up a sheet of typewriting and began to read. "Goodness," she said, after an interval, "I hope you're not going to *throw* this one away! . . . What's the matter?"

"I'm going out for your gloves."

"Oh, but I don't want them."

"I'd like to go out for them, rather. I'd like a stretch."

"*Alone,* Clifford?"

"There's a mist."

"You might get lost. You might walk into the water. Do you really *want* to go out?"

At this, the dogs got up and looked eager. He pushed at them with his feet. "No, stay with Polly," he said. "I won't be long."

"You do promise?" She folded herself away from him in an abandon of puzzled sadness. Clifford kicked the dogs back again and went quietly round the door.

Frank stepped across the corridor to the office to get a stamp for Linda. The plate-glass and mahogany front of the office was framed in tariffs of summer trips, sets of view postcards printed in dark blue and a bill of the working-hours of the Protestant church. The glass hatch was down: Frank put his face against it and looked flirtatiously into the back recess. On an inside ledge, the register was just out of view. Mrs. Coughlan put up the glass hatch, like a lady playing at keeping shop. She received the full blast of Frank's full-blooded charm. "Stamp?" she said. "Oh dear, now Miss Heally knows where they are. To tell you the truth, I'm afraid I don't, and Miss Heally's just upstairs having a little rest. We're very quiet just now. Don't you find it terribly quiet—Major Mull?"

"Mr. Mull," said Frank. "Oh, we love it," he said.

"Still, it's not like the season, is it? Will you be back with us then?"

"Will I not!" said Frank, using his eyes.

"Is the stamp for yourself?"

"Well, it's not: it's for my cousin."

"Ah, yes," said Mrs. Coughlan, not batting an eyelid. "The post went, you know; it went about five minutes. But I tell you what— Were you never in the last war?"—

"I was," said Frank. "But I'm not in this one, thank God."

—"Now Miss Heally thought you had some military rank —I tell you what I could do, I could let you have a stamp I have, if I could trouble you to step this way."

She pressed with her corsets against the door of the

counter, and Frank let her out. She preceded him down
the warm, half-lit, spongy-carpeted corridor to the door
of her sitting-room: from this, she recoiled on to Frank's
toe, at the same time blowing a whisper in at his right ear.
"I won't ask you in here," she said, "if you don't mind.
I've a lady in here who is a little upset." As she spoke, the
door of the sitting-room opened, and then, to Frank's eye,
the snappy form of Teresa appeared, outlined in electric
light. Teresa glowered at Frank, then said: "We'll be going now, Mrs. Coughlan. I think my mother would really
rather be home."

"I would not rather!" exclaimed unseen Mrs. Massey.
"For God's sake, Teresa, let me alone."

"No, don't let me barge in," said Frank, standing firmly
just where he was. Mrs. Coughlan flashed at him the recognition that *he* would be always the gentleman. "Well, if
you'll excuse me," she said, "for just a jiffy, I'll bring the
stamp along to your sitting-room."

Frank went back to Linda. He left their door an inch
open and, while they were waiting, rang for a glass of
port. "What's that for?" said Linda. "I wanted a stamp."
"That's for Mrs. Coughlan. You'll get your stamp to
play with. But of course you know that the post's gone?"
"Then hell, what is the good of a stamp?" "You said you
wanted a stamp, so I'm getting a stamp for you. I love getting you anything that you want." "Then what's the point
of me having written this letter?" "None, darling; I told
you that. Writing letters is just fidgets. Never mind, it will
come in some time when you want a letter to post."

Disengaging herself from Frank's kiss, Linda propped
the letter up on the mantelpiece, on a carton of cigarettes.
While he kissed her again, she looked at it out of one eye.
This made Frank look too. "Oh, *that's* who it's to," he
said. He made faces at it, while Linda, still held pressed to
his chest, giggled contentedly. "I sort of had to," she
said, "or he wouldn't know where I am."

Mrs. Coughlan came in with the stamp. The port was
brought in by Michael and put on the mantelpiece. She
started at it, but after a certain amount of fuss was

induced to lift her glass daintily. "Well, here's to you," she said. "And to you too," she said to Linda. "But isn't this really dreadful, at this hour?"

"Good for the heart," said Frank. "Not that your heart needs it, I'm sure. But your caller sounded to me a bit off."

"Oh, Mrs. Massey's had bad news. She came round here with her daughter, then didn't feel well."

"Was she in the lounge?" said Linda.

"She was first, but it didn't seem fit for her, so Miss Teresa made her come in to me. You don't know who might come into a public room. So I said, to come in to me for a little rest, while I kept an eye on the office while Miss Heally was up. We are all devoted to Mrs. Massey," said Mrs. Coughlan, meeting the eye of Linda just a shade stonily. "I was saying to Miss Heally only this morning, wasn't it too long since we'd seen Teresa or her. They're in and out, as a rule, with the friends Mrs. Massey has staying. They're quite near to here, through the woods, though it's longer if you take the two avenues. They've a sweet place, there, but it's lonely; they've nothing there but the sea."

"Through the woods?" said Linda. "Then, do you mean that pink house?—That's that house *we* want," she said to Frank. Mrs. Coughlan glanced primly midway between the two of them. "Yes, it's a sweet place, Palmlawn," said Mrs. Coughlan. "We often say, she seems quite wedded to it."

Frank said: "Is Teresa the tiger-cat?"

Far too much won by Frank's eye and manner, Mrs. Coughlan had to pause to prop up her loyalties. "Well, her manner's just a weeshy bit short," she said. "And this evening, of course, *she's* upset, too."

"She sounded more fed up."

Mrs. Coughlan, replacing her glass on the mantelpiece, jabbed her mouth with an *eau de nil* handkerchief charged with *Muguet de Coty*. Reassembling herself as manageress, she threw an inventorial glance round their sitting-room. "I hope," she said, "you have everything? Everything comfy? Ring if it isn't, won't you?" "Yes, thanks," said Linda, "we're very cosy in here." Mrs. Coughlan, whose business it was to know how to take everything, knew perfectly well how to take this. "Well, I must be running along. Thank you very much, Major Mull—Mr. Mull—I hope you'll join *me* for a minute or two this evening, unless, of course, you're engaged. . . . Isn't this war shocking?"

"Shocking," said Frank. "I sell cars."

"Very," said Linda. "Why?"

"I can't help thinking," said Mrs. Coughlan, "of poor Mrs. Massey's friend. A flying man. He was often in here, you know."

Fumbling with the slimy lock in the mist, Clifford unlocked the lock-up. He reached into the Alvis, switched the dashboard lights on and got in and sat in the car to look for Polly's gloves. Mist came curdling into the lock-up after him. He put the wrist-length fluffy gloves in one pocket. Then he checked up on the petrol: there were six gallons still. Then he plunged his hand slowly into another of his pockets, touched the pennies, thumbed the two half-crowns. In the dark his body recorded, not for the first time, yet another shock of the recurrent idea. The shock, as always, dulled out. He switched the lights off, folded his arms, slid forward and sat in the dark deflated —completely deflated, a dying pig that has died.

Frank and Linda, intently silently cosy in front of their sitting-room fire in the dark, heard people break into the passage from Mrs. Coughlan's room. At this Frank, with pussy-cat stealth and quickness, raised his face from the top of Linda's head. His clean ears, close to his head, might have been said to prick up. "Damn," said Linda, missing Frank, "something is always happening." The concourse passed their door. "That's Mrs. Massey, that was." Frank at once pressed his hands on Linda's shoulders. But he said: "Should I just have a look-see?" He got up, padded across the room, opened the door an inch and put one eye to the inch.

Mrs. Coughlan had not gone far. She immediately came

back and put her mouth into the inch of door. "Mr. Mull, could I trouble you just a minute?" she said. Frank edged round the door and Linda was left alone.

Mrs. Massey was not equal to the walk back. This— only felt by herself as an additional rush of sorrow—was clear to Teresa, and also to Mrs. Coughlan, as a predicament. There had been talk, before they left Mrs. Coughlan's parlour, of telephoning to the village for a car. Mrs. Massey would not brook the idea. "I won't give trouble," she said. "There's trouble enough already." Magnificent with protest, she now stood trembling and talking loudly and sweeping her hair back at the foot of the stairs. "I should never have come," she said. "But how could I stay where I was? We'll go home now; we'll just go quietly home—Are you gummed there, Teresa? Come home: we've been here quite long enough." She gave Frank a haunted look as Mrs. Coughlan brought him up. "This is Mr. Mull, Mrs. Massey," said Mrs. Coughlan. "Mr. Mull says he'll just get his car out and run you home."

Mrs. Massey said: "I don't know what you all think."

Teresa, taking no notice, put on her trenchcoat and tightly buckled the belt. "That is good of you," she said to Frank slightingly. "Aren't you busy?" "Not in the world," said Frank. "Hold on while I get the car round."

"You needn't do that, thank you: Mother and I can walk as far as the car."

Teresa and Frank, with Mrs. Massey between them, started off down the aisle of carpet to the glass doors. "Aren't the steps dreadfully dark for her!" helped Miss Heally, who was there with the rest—she shot ahead to switch on the outdoor lamps. The three passed down the steps in the blur of a blaze of lights, as though leaving a ball. "Good night now. Safe home, Mrs. Massey dear!" called Miss Heally and Mrs. Coughlan from the top of the steps. Linda, hearing the noise, hearing Frank's step on the gravel, threw a window up and leaned into the mist. She called: "Frank?" He replied, if at all, with a gesture that she could not see: he was busy steering the party. "Left turn," he said, patting at Mrs. Massey's elbow. The mother and daughter wheeled docilely.

"Do you know where we are, at all?"

"Oh, I'm used to all this."

"Do you come from London, then?" Teresa said.

"I've come back from London."

"On leave?" said Teresa quickly.

"No, thank God. I sell cars."

"You won't sell many just now." Teresa's trenchcoat brushed on the evergreens. Majestic and dazed between her escort, Mrs. Massey stumbled along in a shackled way. In the yard, the open doors of the lock-up beside Frank's stuck out clammy into the mist: they almost walked into them. "That lunatic's taken that Alvis out," said Frank. Teresa, in her not encouraging way, said: "Well, you'll be another lunatic, in a minute." Mrs. Massey, ignoring the dialogue, detached herself quietly from Teresa. While Frank and his torch and key were busy over a padlock, Mrs. Massey passed quietly into the open lock-up next door. She bumped her knee on the Alvis and started to climb round it. "It's all right, Teresa, the car's in here," she called back, with quite an approach to her usual gaiety.

Clifford's reflex to the bump on the car was to blaze all his lights on. Inside, his lock-up became one curdled glare; his tail light spread a ruby stain on the mist. He turned his head sharply and stayed with his coinlike profile immobilised against the glaring end-wall. Mrs. Massey came scrambling into view. Clifford put down one window. "I beg your pardon?" he said.

"Better back out a little," said Mrs. Massey. "I can't get in this side while you're in here." Clifford started his engine and backed out. But then he pulled up, got up and got half out of the car. "I'm afraid this is not your car," he said.

"How could it be my car," said Mrs. Massey, "when my car's at home? This is so kind of you—I don't know what you must think. Let me in now, though." Clifford shrank back; she got in and settled herself by him contentedly. "There's my daughter to come," she said, "and a man from the hotel. Just wait, now, and they'll show you the way."

Frank had only just got his lock-up open when Teresa was at his elbow again. "We'll hang on a minute," he said, "and let this other chap out. I'll start up. Be getting your mother in at the back."

"My mother's got into the other car."

"Which car?"

"I don't know. Don't dawdle there—are you mad? Mother might be off anywhere!"

Frank went out to blink. The Alvis, almost silently turning, swept a choked glare through the mist. "Oh, *that* chap," Frank said. "That chap won't eat anyone. Cut along, Teresa—look, he's waiting for you."

"I don't know him."

"Mother knows him by now."

"You're well out of us," said Teresa, standing still bitterly.

"If that's what you think," Frank said, "I'll come along too."

Linda was told of Frank's kindness in volunteering to drive the Masseys home. Mrs. Coughlan was very much pleased and could not praise him enough. He should be back at the hotel in twenty minutes—but Linda knew he would not be. Frank's superabundance of good feeling made Linda pretty cross—his gusto, his sociability, his humane fun, and his conquering bossiness. He liked life, and wherever he was things happened. This evening, first Mrs. Coughlan, now Mrs. Massey . . . Except in bed, one was seldom alone with Frank. Having interfered once more, and got one more kind act in, he would come back like a cat full of rabbit again. Linda felt quite suspended. She wished there were pin tables in this high-class hotel. She rang for a drink and two packs of cards and sat down and laid out a complex patience on the octagonal table below the sitting-room light. She thanked God she was not as young as she had been and no longer fell into desperations or piques. It was not that Frank did not concentrate, but he did not concentrate consecutively.

She looked up once from her patience at her stamped letter, and half thought of tearing it up and writing a warmer one.

Mrs. Coughlan and Miss Heally returned to their sitting-room: opening the piano they began to play a duet.

Polly Perry-Dunton, as well as Linda, heard the piano. Every three minutes Polly looked at her watch. After ten minutes, Polly left her sitting-room and went and lay on her bed in a sort of rigour. She pulled Clifford's pyjamas out from under the pillow and buried her face in them.

The Alvis, dip lights squinting along the row of sticky trees on the left, nosed its way through the mist down the avenue. Mrs. Massey, in absolute quiescence, leaned back by Clifford's shoulder: he drove in silence. Frank, in the back of the car beside Teresa, had noncommittally drawn her arm through his. Teresa did not take her eyes from the back of her mother's head. When the open white gates loomed up, Teresa leaned forward and told Clifford which way to turn. About a mile down the main road Teresa again spoke up. Clifford turned through more gates, and the four of them passed with well-sprung smoothness over the bumps of a peaty wet avenue. An uneasy smell of the sea came up the mist. Rhododendrons lolled and brushed the sides of the car. The left wheels mounted an edge of lawn. Clifford took a sweep and undipped his lights on verandah-posts and the pallid walls of a house.

"Teresa," said Mrs. Massey, "tell them to come in."

Teresa lit the two oil lamps under their dark-pink shades. Mrs. Massey, one hand on her drawing-room mantelpiece, swayed with the noble naturalness of a tree. Her form, above a smoulder of peat fire, was reflected in a mirror between the two dark windows—a mirror that ran from ceiling to floor. The room with its possessions, its air of bravura and slipshod moodiness, its low smoked ceiling, armchairs with sunk seats, cabinets of dull glass began to be seen in the dark light. Clifford's scraggy Nordic figure, and Frank's thick-set springy figure, firmly poised on its heels, were also seen in the mirror, making a crowd.

"Sit down," said Mrs. Massey, "I feel more like standing. I'm afraid I'm restless—I had bad news, you know."

"That is frightfully tough," said Frank.

"I feel bad," said Mrs. Massey, "at not knowing your names. Yes, it's tough to be dead, isn't it? He was about your age," she said to Clifford. "—Teresa dear, are you gummed there? Go and look for the drinks."

Through the shadows in which they were all still standing up, Clifford threw a quick begging look at Frank. Frank had to defer to Clifford's panic, and to Clifford's being unable to speak. "Look, we must be pushing along," Frank reluctantly, firmly said. Clifford bowed his heroic head sharply and took two steps to the door: the nightmare of being wanted was beginning, in this room, to close in round him again.

Mrs. Massey only removed her eyes from Clifford to attend to a cigarette she was lighting over a lamp. Obliterated in shadows round the unglowing fire, Teresa, crouching, puffed at peat with a bellows. "Teresa," said her mother, "do *you* see who he's so like—?"

"—There's no drink left, as you know," said Teresa quickly. "I could make some tea, but they're just off."

Clifford said: "I'm afraid we *are* just off!"

In reply, Mrs. Massey lifted the lamp from its low table to hold it, unsteadily, on a level with Clifford's face. She took a step or two forward, with the lamp. "It's extraordinary," she said, "though you don't know it, that you should be in this house *to-night*. You mustn't mind what I say or do: I'm upset—you're English, too, aren't you? He looks like a hero, doesn't he?" she said appealingly to Frank.

"Now we've all had a look at each other," said Frank firmly, "let me take this out of your way." Taking the wobbling lamp from Mrs. Massey, he put it safely back on its table again.

"I wish I were proud of my country," said Mrs. Massey. "But I'm ashamed of this country, to tell you the truth."

"Oh, come," said Frank. "We have much to be thankful for."

Teresa crashed the bellows into the grate and went out

of the room through the open door. Outside, she pulled
up a chair and stood on it to light the lamp in the hall.
Frank strolled after her and leaned in the door to watch.
He said: "Are you very fed up?" The hanging lamp spun
round, and Teresa's eyes, fixed on the burner, glittered.
"Is it bad?" Frank said. "You don't tell me anything. Did
you love the poor chap?"

"Did I get a chance?"

The chair she stood on wobbled on the uneven flagstones: Frank came and stood close up to steady the chair,
"Come down off that," he said, "like a good girl." Teresa
stepped down off the chair into Frank's arms—but she
stood inside them like steel. He let her go, and watched
her pick up her trenchcoat and walk off down a stone passage to hang it up. There she stayed, as though she were
falling and could fall no farther, with her breast and face
thrust into the hanging coats. Her shoulder-blades
showed through her sweater, and Frank, coming up gently, put his two hands on them. "She'd rather him dead,"
said Teresa into the coats, "she'd rather him dead than
gone from her." She kept moving her shoulders under
Frank's hands.

"Could you cry? Could you have a cry if I took you off
now in that car?"

Teresa, into the coats, said something he could not hear.
"And leave those two?" she said in a louder voice.

Frank had to agree: he looked back at the drawing-
room door.

Mrs. Massey and Clifford, waiting for Frank, now sat
in two armchairs opposite the fire. "I don't understand,"
she said. "How did we come in your car?"

"You got in . . ." he said tentatively.

"And where had you been going?"

"Nowhere; I was looking for my wife's gloves." He
pulled the pussy gloves out of his pocket and showed
them, to show he spoke the truth. Looking intently at the
pussy gloves, Mrs. Massey's eyes for the first time filled
with tears. The access of some new feeling, a feeling with
no context, resculptured her face. In the musty dark of

her drawing-room, the dark round the dull fire, her new face looked alabaster and pure. The outline of her mist-clotted fair hair shook, as though shaken by the unconscious silent force of her tears.

"Aren't they small!" she said. "Is your wife quite a little thing? Are you two very happy, then?"

"Very."

"Take her gloves back safe . . . How English you are."

Frank came in and said they must be pushing along. Teresa did not come in; she was opening the hall door. Out there on the sweep above the lawn and the sea, Clifford's lights were still blazing into the mist. Teresa went out and examined, as much by touch as anything, the wonderful car. An idea of going away forever lifted and moved her heart, like a tide coming in. A whiteness up in the mist showed where there should have been the moon; the sleep-locked sea of the bay sighed. A smell of fern-rot and sea-water and gravel passed by Teresa into the house. Frank came to the hall door and saw her in the mist close to the car. He thought, calmly, of Linda wondering where he was, and wanted to go, and wanted to stay, and conceived how foolish it was, in love, to have to differentiate between women. In love there is no right and wrong, only the wish. However, he left Teresa alone and, going back into the drawing-room, said something further to Clifford about dinner.

Mrs. Massey was just detaching her arms from Clifford's neck. "I had to kiss him," she said. "He'll never understand why." She went slowly ahead of the two men out to the car. "Dinner?" she said. "Is that really what time it is? . . . Teresa?"

But there was no reply.

Up the mist between the formless rhododendrons the Alvis, with Frank and Clifford, crawled back to the main road. "If you thought of turning this car in before leaving this country," Frank said, "you might let me know first? My name's Mull—Mull, Cork always finds me."

"My name is Perry-Dunton," said Clifford, after a pause.

"Yes, I thought it might be."

"Why?" said Clifford, alarmed.

"Caught my eye on the register. You two seem to like it here. And how right you are. Staying on?"

"Well, we're not quite sure of our plans."

"I wish I wasn't—we've only got the week-end. Look, why don't you two drop down for a drink with us after dinner? My cousin would be delighted."

"It is most awfully nice of you, but I don't think—"

"Right-o," said Frank, nodding his head.

Summer Night

AS THE sun set its light slowly melted the landscape, till everything was made of fire and glass. Released from the glare of noon, the haycocks now seemed to float on the aftergrass: their freshness penetrated the air. In the not far distance hills with woods up their flanks lay in light like hills in another world—it would be a pleasure of heaven to stand up there, where no foot ever seemed to have trodden, on the spaces between the woods soft as powder dusted over with gold. Against those hills, the burning red rambler roses in cottage gardens along the roadside looked earthly—they were too near the eye.

The road was in Ireland. The light, the air from the distance, the air of evening rushed transversely through the open sides of the car. The rims of the hood flapped, the hood's metal frame rattled as the tourer, in great bounds of speed, held the road's darkening magnetic centre streak. The big shabby family car was empty but for its small driver—its emptiness seemed to levitate it—on its back seat a coat slithered about, and a dressingcase bumped against the seat. The driver did not relax her excited touch on the wheel: now and then while she drove she turned one wrist over, to bring the watch worn on it into view, and she gave the mileage marked on the yellow signposts a flying, jealous, half-inadvertent look. She was driving parallel with the sunset: the sun slowly went down on her right hand.

The hills flowed round till they lay ahead. Where the road bent for its upward course through the pass she pulled up and lighted a cigarette. With a snatch she untwisted her turban; she shook her hair free and threw the scarf behind her into the back seat. The draught of the pass combed her hair into coarse strands as the car hummed up in second gear. Behind one brilliantly-outlined crest the sun had now quite gone; on the steeps of bracken, in the electric shadow, each frond stood out and climbing goats turned their heads. The car came up on a lorry, to hang on its tail, impatient, checked by turns of the road. At the first stretch the driver smote her palm on the horn and shot past and shot on ahead again.

The small woman drove with her chin up. Her existence was in her hands on the wheel and in the sole of the foot in which she felt, through the sandal, the throbbing pressure of the accelerator. Her face, enlarged by blown-back hair, was as overbearingly blank as the face of a figure-head; her black eyebrows were ruled level, and her eyes, pupils dilated, did little more than reflect the slow burn of daylight along horizons, the luminous shades of the half-dark.

Clear of the pass, approaching the county town, the road widened and straightened between stone walls and burnished showering beech. The walls broke up into gateways and hoardings and the suburbs began. People in modern building estate gardens let the car in a hurry through their unseeing look. The raised foot-paths had margins of grass. White and grey rows of cottages under the pavement level let woodsmoke over their half-doors: women and old men sat outside the doors on boxes, looking down at their knees; here and there a bird sprang in a cage tacked to a wall. Children chasing balls over the roadway shot whooping right and left of the car. The refreshed town, unfolding streets to its centre, at this hour slowly heightened, cooled; streets and stones threw off a grey-pink glare, sultry lasting ghost of the high noon. In this dayless glare the girls in bright dresses, strolling, looked like colour-photography.

Dark behind all the windows: not a light yet. The in-going perspective looked meaning, noble and wide. But everybody was elsewhere—the polished street was empty but cars packed both the kerbs under the trees. What was going on? The big tourer dribbled, slipped with ani-mal nervousness between the static locked cars each side of its way. The driver peered left and right with her face narrow, glanced from her wrist-watch to the clock in the tower, sucked her lip, manœuvred for somewhere to pull in. The A.A. sign of the hotel hung out from under a bal-cony, over the steps. She edged in to where it said *Do Not Park*.

At the end of the hotel hall one electric light from the bar shone through a high-up panel: its yellow sifted on to the dusty dusk and a moth could be seen on the glass pane. At the door end came in street daylight, to fall weakly on prints on the oiled walls, on the magenta an-nouncement-strip of a cinema, on the mahogany bench near the receptionist's office, on the hatstand with two forgotten hats. The woman who had come breathlessly up the steps felt in her face a wall of indifference. The impetuous click of her heeled sandals on the linoleum brought no one to the receptionist's desk, and the drone of two talkers in the bar behind the glass panel seemed, like the light, to be blotted up, word by word. The little woman attacked the desk with her knuckles. "Is there nobody there—I say? Is there nobody *there?*"

"I am, I am. Wait now," said the hotel woman, who came impassively through the door from the bar. She reached up a hand and fumbled the desk light on, and by this with unwondering negligence studied the cus-tomer—the childish, blown little woman with winglike eyebrows and eyes still unfocussed after the long road. The hotel woman, bust on the desk, looked down slowly at the bare legs, the crumple-hemmed linen coat. "Can I do anything for you?" she said, when she had done.

"I want the telephone—want to put through a call!"

"You can of course," said the unmoved hotel woman.

"Why not?" she added after consideration, handing across the keys of the telephone cabinet. The little woman made a slide for the cabinet: with her mouth to the mouthpiece, like a conspirator, she was urgently putting her number through. She came out then and ordered herself a drink.

"Is it long distance?"

"Mm-mm . . . What's on here? What are all those cars?"

"Oh, this evening's the dog racing."

"Is it?"

"Yes, it's the dog racing. We'd a crowd in here, but they're all gone on now."

"I wondered who they were," said the little woman, her eyes on the cabinet, sippeting at her drink.

"Yes, they're at the dog racing. There's a wonderful crowd. But I wouldn't care for it," said the hotel woman, fastidiously puckering up her forehead. "I went the one time, but it didn't fascinate me."

The other forgot to answer. She turned away with her drink, sat down, put the glass beside her on the mahogany bench and began to chafe the calves of her bare legs as though they were stiff or cold. A man clasping sheets of unfurled newspaper pushed his way with his elbow through the door from the bar. "What it says here," he said, shaking the paper with both hands, "is identically what I've been telling you."

"That proves nothing," said the hotel woman. "However, let it out of your hand." She drew the sheets of the paper from him and began to fold them into a wad. Her eyes moved like beetles over a top line. "That's an awful battle . . ."

"What battle?" exclaimed the little woman, stopping rubbing her legs but not looking up.

"An awful air battle. Destroying each other," the woman added, with a stern and yet voluptuous sigh. "Listen, would you like to wait in the lounge?"

"She'd be better there," put in the man who had brought the paper. "Better accommodation." His eyes watered slightly in the electric light. The little woman, sitting upright abruptly, looked defiantly, as though for the first time, at the two watching her from the desk. "Mr. Donovan has great opinions," said the hotel woman. "Will you move yourself out of here?" she asked Mr. Donovan. "This is very confined—*There's* your call, now!"

But the stranger had packed herself into the telephone box like a conjuror's lady preparing to disappear. "*Hullo?*" she was saying. "Hullo! I want to speak to—"

"—You are," the other voice cut in. "All right? Anything wrong?"

Her face flashed all over. "You sound nearer already! I've got to C——."

The easy, calm voice said: "Then you're coming along well."

"Glad, are you?" she said, in a quiver.

"Don't take it too fast," he said. "It's a treacherous light. Be easy, there's a good girl."

"You're a fine impatient man." His end of the line was silent. She went on: "I might stay here and go to the dog racing."

"Oh, is that tonight?" He went on to say equally (having stopped, as she saw it, and shaken the ash off the tip of his cigarette). "No, I shouldn't do that."

"Darling . . ."

"Emma . . . How is the Major?"

"He's all right," she said, rather defensively.

"I see," he said. "Everything quite O.K.?"

"In an hour, I'll be . . . where you live."

"First gate on the left. Don't kill yourself, there's a good girl. Nothing's worth that. Remember we've got the night. By the way, where are you talking?"

"From the hotel." She nursed the receiver up close to her face and made a sound into it. Cutting that off she said: "Well, I'll hang up. I just . . ."

"Right," he said—and hung up.

Robinson, having hung up the receiver, walked back from the hall to the livingroom where his two guests were. He still wore a smile. The deaf woman at the table by the window was pouring herself out another cup of tea. "That will be very cold!" Robinson shouted—but she only replaced the cosy with a mysterious smile. "Let her be," said her brother. "Let her alone!"

The room in this uphill house was still light: through the open window came in a smell of stocks from the flower beds in the lawn. The only darkness lay in a belt of beech trees at the other side of the main road. From the grate, from the coal of an unlit fire came the fume of a cigarette burning itself out. Robinson still could not help smiling: he reclaimed his glass from the mantelpiece and slumped back with it into his leather armchair in one of his loose, heavy, good-natured attitudes. But Justin Cavey, in the armchair opposite, still looked crucified at having the talk torn. "Beastly," he said, "you've a beastly telephone." Though he was in Robinson's house for the first time, his sense of attraction to people was marked, early, by just this intransigeance and this fretfulness.

"It is and it's not," said Robinson. That was that. "Where had we got to?" he amiably asked.

The deaf woman, turning round from the window, gave the two men, or gave the air between them, a penetrating smile. Her brother, with a sort of lurch at his pocket, pulled out a new packet of cigarettes: ignoring Robinson's held-out cigarette case he frowned and split the cellophane with his thumbnail. But, as though his sister had put a hand on his shoulder, his tension could be almost seen to relax. The impersonal, patient look of the thinker appeared in his eyes, behind the spectacles. Justin was a city man, a black-coat, down here (where his sister lived) on holiday. Other summer holidays before this he had travelled in France, Germany, Italy: he disliked the chaotic "scenery" of his own land. He was down here with Queenie this summer only because of the war, which had locked him in: duty seemed to him better than failed pleasure. His father had been a doctor in this place; now his sister lived on in two rooms in the square—for fear Justin should not be comfortable she had taken a room for him at the hotel. His holiday with his sister, his holiday in this underwater, weedy region of memory, his holiday on which, almost every day, he had to pass the doors of their old home, threatened Justin with a pressure he could not bear. He had to share with Queenie, as he shared the dolls' house meals cooked on the oil stove behind her sittingroom screen, the solitary and almost fairy-like world created by her deafness. Her deafness broke down his only defence-talk. He was exposed to the odd immune plumbing looks she was forever passing over his face. He could not deflect the tilted blue of her eyes. The things she said out of nowhere, things with no surface context, were never quite off the mark. She was not all solicitude; she loved to be teasing him.

In her middle-age, Queenie was very pretty: her pointed face had the colouring of an imperceptibly fading pink-and-white sweetpea. This hot summer her artless dresses, with their little lace collars, were mottled over with flowers, mauve and blue. Up the glaring main street she carried a *poult-de-soie* parasol. Her rather dark first-floor rooms faced north, over the square with its grass and lime trees: the crests of great mountains showed above the opposite façades. She would slip in and out on her own errands, as calm as a cat, and Justin, waiting for her at one of her windows, would see her cross the square in the noon sunshine with hands laced over her forehead into a sort of porch. The little town, though strung on a through road, was an outpost under the mountains: in its quick-talking, bitter society she enjoyed, to a degree that surprised Justin, her privileged place. She was woman enough to like to take the man Justin round with her and display him; they went out to afternoon or to evening tea, and in those drawingrooms of tinted lace and intently-staring family photographs, among octagonal tables and painted cushions, Queenie, with her cotton gloves in her lap, well knew how to contribute, while Justin talked, her airy, brilliant, secretive smiling and looking on. For his part, he was man enough to respond to being shown off—besides, he was eased by these breaks in their *tête-à-tête*. Above all, he was glad, for these hours or two of chatter, not to have to face the screen of his own mind, on which the distortion of every one of his images, the war-broken towers of Europe, constantly stood. The immolation of what had been his own intensely had been

made, he could only feel, without any choice of his. In the
heart of the neutral Irishman indirect suffering pulled like
a crooked knife. So he acquiesced to, and devoured, society: among the doctors, the solicitors, the auctioneers,
the bank people of this little town he renewed old ac-
quaintanceships and developed new. He was content to
bloom, for this settled number of weeks—so unlike was
this to his monkish life in the city—in a sort of tenebrous
popularity. He attempted to check his solitary arrogance.
His celibacy and his studentish manner could still, although he was past forty, make him acceptable as a young
man. In the mornings he read late in his hotel bed; he
got up to take his solitary walks; he returned to flick at
his black shoes with Queenie's duster and set off with
Queenie on their tea-table rounds. They had been introduced to Robinson, factory manager, in the hall of the
house of the secretary of the tennis club.

Robinson did not frequent drawingrooms. He had come
here only three years ago, and had at first been taken to
be a bachelor—he was a married man living apart from
his wife. The resentment occasioned by this discovery had
been aggravated by Robinson's not noticing it: he worked
at very high pressure in his factory office, and in his off
times his high-powered car was to be seen streaking too
gaily out of the town. When he was met, his imperturb-
able male personality stood out to the women unpleas-
ingly, and stood out most of all in that married society in
which women aspire to break the male in a man. Husbands
slipped him in for a drink when they were alone, or shut
themselves up with him in the dining-room. Justin had
already sighted him in the hotel bar. When Robinson
showed up, late, at the tennis club, his manner with
women was easy and teasing, but abstract and perfectly
automatic. From this had probably come the legend that
he liked women "only in one way." From the first time
Justin encountered Robinson, he had felt a sort of anxious, disturbed attraction to the big, fair, smiling, off-
hand, cold-minded man. He felt impelled by Robinson's
unmoved physical presence into all sorts of aberrations of
talk and mind; he committed, like someone waving an anx-

ious flag, all sorts of absurdities, as though this type of creature had been a woman; his talk became exaggeratedly cerebral, and he became prone, like a perverse person in love, to expose all his own piques, crotchets and weaknesses. One night in the hotel bar with Robinson he had talked until he burst into tears. Robinson had on him the touch of some foreign sun. The acquaintanceship—it could not be called more—was no more than an accident of this narrowed summer. For Justin it had taken the place of travel. The two men were so far off each other's beat that in a city they would certainly not have met.

Asked to drop in some evening or any evening, the Caveys had tonight taken Robinson at his word. Tonight, the night of the first visit, Justin's high, rather bleak forehead had flushed from the moment he rang the bell. With Queenie behind his shoulder, in muslin, he had flinched confronting the housekeeper. Queenie, like the rest of the town ladies, had done no more till now than go by Robinson's gate.

For her part, Queenie showed herself happy to penetrate into what she had called "the china house." On its knoll over the main road, just outside the town, Bellevue did look like china up on a mantelpiece—it was a compact stucco house with mouldings, recently painted a light blue. From the lawn set with pampas and crescent-shaped flowerbeds the hum of Robinson's motor mower passed in summer over the sleepy town. And when winter denuded the trees round them the polished windows, glass porch and empty conservatory sent out, on mornings of frosty sunshine, a rather mischievous and uncaring flash. The almost sensuous cleanness of his dwelling was reproduced in the person of Robinson—about his ears, jaw, collar and close-clipped nails. The approach the Caveys had walked up showed the broad, decided tyre-prints of his car.

"Where had we got to?" Robinson said again.

"I was saying we should have to find a new form."

"Of course you were," agreed Robinson. "That was it." He nodded over the top of Justin's head.

"A new form for thinking and feeling . . ."

"But one thinks what one happens to think, or feels what one happens to feel. That is as just so happens—I should have thought. One either does or one doesn't?"

"One doesn't!" cried Justin. "That's what I've been getting at. For some time we have neither thought nor felt. Our faculties have slowed down without our knowing—they had stopped without our knowing! We know now. Now that there's enough death to challenge being alive we're facing it that, anyhow, we don't live. We're confronted by the impossibility *of* living—unless we can break through to something else. There's been a stop in our senses and in our faculties that's made everything round us so much dead matter—and dead matter we couldn't even displace. We can no longer express ourselves: what we say doesn't even approximate to reality; it only approximates to what's been said. I say, this war's an awful illumination; it's destroyed our dark; we have to see where we are. Immobilised, God help us, and each so far apart that we can't even try to signal each other. And our currency's worthless—our 'ideas,' so on, so on. We've got to mint a new one. We've got to break through to the new form—it needs genius. We're precipitated, this moment, between genius and death. I tell you, we must have genius to live at all."

"I am certainly dished, then," said Robinson. He got up and looked for Justin's empty glass and took it to the sideboard where the decanters were.

"We have it!" cried Justin, smiting the arm of his chair. "I salute your genius, Robinson, but I mistrust my own."

"That's very nice of you," said Robinson. "I agree with you that this war makes one think. I was in the last, but I don't remember thinking: I suppose possibly one had no time. Of course, these days in business one comes up against this war the whole way through. And to tell you the truth," said Robinson, turning round, "I do like my off times to *be* my off times, because with this and then that they are precious few. So I don't really think as much as I might—though I see how one might always begin. You don't think thinking gets one a bit rattled?"

"I don't think!" said Justin violently.

"Well, you should know," said Robinson, looking at his thumbnail. "I should have thought you did. From the way you talk."

"I couldn't think if I wanted: I've lost my motivation. I taste the dust in the street and I smell the limes in the square and I beat round inside this beastly shell of the past among images that all the more torment me as they lose any sense that they had. As for feeling—"

"You don't think you find it a bit slow here? Mind you, I haven't a word against this place, but it's not a place I'd choose for an off time—"

"—My dear Robinson," Justin said, in a mincing school-masterish tone, "you seem blind to our exquisite sociabilities."

"Pack of old cats," said Robinson amiably.

"You suggest I should get away for a bit of fun?"

"Well, I did mean that."

"I find my own fun," said Justin. "I'm torn, here, by every single pang of annihilation. But that's what I look for; that's what I want completed; that's the whole of what I want to embrace. On the far side of the nothing— my new form. Scrap 'me'; scrap my wretched identity and you'll bring to the open some bud of life. I *not* 'I'— I'd be the world. . . . You're right: what you would call thinking does get me rattled. I only what you call think to excite myself. Take myself away, and I'd *think*. I might see; I might feel purely; I might even love—"

"Fine," agreed Robinson, not quite easy. He paused and seemed to regard what Justin had just said—at the same time, he threw a glance of perceptible calculation at the electric clock on the mantelpiece. Justin halted and said: "You give me too much to drink."

"You feel this war may improve us?" said Robinson.

"What's love like?" Justin said suddenly.

Robinson paused for just less than a second in the act of lighting a cigarette. He uttered a shortish, temporising and for him unnaturally loud laugh.

Queenie felt the vibration and turned round, withdrawing her arm from the windowsill. She had been looking intently, between the clumps of pampas, down the lawn to the road: cyclists and walkers on their way into town kept passing Robinson's open gate. Across the road, above the demesne wall, the dark beeches let through glitters of sky, and the colour and scent of the mown lawn and the flowers seemed, by some increase of evening, lifted up to the senses as though a new current flowed underneath. Queenie saw with joy in her own mind what she could not from her place in the window see—the blue china house, with all its reflecting windows, perched on its knoll in the brilliant, fading air. They are too rare—visions of where we are.

When the shock of the laugh made her turn round, she still saw day in Robinson's picture-frames and on the chromium fingers of the clock. She looked at Robinson's head, dropped back after the laugh on the leather scroll of his chair: her eyes went from him to Justin. "Did you two not hit it off?"

Robinson laughed again, this time much more naturally: he emitted a sound like that from inside a furnace in which something is being consumed. Letting his head fall sideways towards Queenie he seemed to invite her into his mood. "The way things come out is sometimes funny," he said to Justin, "if you know what I mean."

"No, I don't," Justin said stonily.

"I bet your sister does."

"You didn't know what I meant. Anything I may have said about your genius I do absolutely retract."

"Look here, I'm sorry," Robinson said, "I probably took you up all wrong."

"On the contrary: the mistake was mine."

"You know, it's funny about your sister: I never can realise she can't hear. She seems so much one of the party. Would she be fond of children?"

"You mean, why did she not marry?"

"Good God, no—I only had an idea . . ."

Justin went on: "There was some fellow once, but I never heard more of him. You'd have to be very on-coming, I daresay, to make any way with a deaf girl."

"No, I meant my children," said Robinson. He had got up, and he took from his mantelpiece two of the photographs in silver frames. With these he walked down the room to Queenie, who received them with her usual eagerness and immediately turned with them to the light. Justin saw his sister's profile bent forward in study and saw Robinson standing above her leaning against the window frame. When Robinson met an upward look from Queenie he nodded and touched himself on the chest. "I can see that—aren't they very like you?" she said. He pointed to one picture then held up ten fingers, then to the other and held up eight. "The fair little fellow's more like you, the bold one. The dark one has more the look of a girl—but he will grow up manly, I daresay . . ." With this she went back to the photographs: she did not seem anxious to give them up and Robinson made no movement to take them from her—with Queenie the act of looking was always reflective and slow. To Justin the two silhouettes against the window looked wedded and welded by the dark. "They are both against me," Justin thought. "She does not hear with her ears, he does not hear with his mind. No wonder they can communicate."

"It's a wonder," she said, "that you have no little girl."

Robinson went back for another photograph—but, standing still with a doubtful look at Queenie, he passed his hand, as though sadly expunging something, backwards and forwards across the glass. "She's quite right; we did have a girl," he said. "But I don't know how to tell her the kid's dead."

Sixty miles away, the Major was making his last round through the orchards before shutting up the house. By this time the bronze-green orchard dusk was intense; the clumped curves of the fruit were hardly to be distinguished among the leaves. The brilliance of evening, in which he had watched Emma driving away, was now gone from the sky. Now and then in the grass his foot knocked a dropped apple—he would sigh, stoop rather stiffly, pick up the apple, examine it with the pad of his thumb for bruises and slip it, tenderly as though it had been an egg, into a baggy pocket of his tweed coat. This was not a good apple year. There was something stand-ardised, uncomplaining about the Major's movements—you saw a tall, unmilitary-looking man with a stoop and a thinnish drooping moustache. He often wore a slight frown, of doubt or preoccupation. This frown had intensi-fied in the last months.

As he approached the house he heard the wireless talk-ing, and saw one lamp at the distant end of the drawing-room where his aunt sat. At once, the picture broke up—she started, switched off the wireless and ran down the room to the window. You might have thought the room had burst into flames. "Quick!" she cried. "Oh gracious, quick!—I believe it's the telephone."

The telephone was at the other side of the house—be-fore he got there he heard the bell ringing. He put his hands in his pockets to keep the apples from bumping as he legged it rapidly down the corridor. When he un-hooked on his wife's voice he could not help saying hag-gardly: "You all right?"

"Of course. I just thought I'd say goodnight."

"That was nice of you," he said, puzzled. "How is the car running?"

"Like a bird," she said in a singing voice. "How are you all?"

"Well, I was just coming in; Aunt Fran's in the drawing-room listening to something on the wireless, and I made the children turn in half an hour ago."

"You'll go up to them?"

"Yes, I was just going." For a moment they both paused on the line, then he said: "Where have you got to now?"

"I'm at T—— now, at the hotel in the square."

"At T——? Aren't you taking it rather fast?"

"It's a lovely night; it's an empty road."

"Don't be too hard on the car, she—"

"Oh, I know," she said, in the singing voice again. "At C—— I did try to stop, but there was a terrible crowd there: dog racing. So I came on. Darling . . . ?"

"Yes?"

"It's a lovely night, isn't it?"

"Yes, I was really quite sorry to come in. I shall shut up the house now, then go up to the children; then I expect I'll have a word or two with Aunt Fran."

"I see. Well, I'd better be pushing on."

"They'll be sitting up for you, won't they?"

"Surely," said Emma quickly.

"Thank you for ringing up, dear: it was thoughtful of you."

"I was thinking about you."

He did not seem to hear this. "Well, take care of yourself. Have a nice time."

"Good night," she said. But the Major had hung up.

In the drawing-room Aunt Fran had not gone back to the wireless. Beside the evening fire lit for her age she sat rigid, face turned to the door, plucking round and round the rings on her left hand. She wore a foulard dress, net jabot and boned-up collar, of the type ladies wear to dine in private hotels. In the lamplight her waxy features appeared blurred, even effaced. The drawing-room held a crowd of chintz-covered chairs, inlaid tables and wool-worked stools; very little in it was antique, but nothing was strikingly up-to-date. There were cabinets of not rare china, and more blue-and-white plates, in metal clamps, hung in lines up the walls between water-colours. A vase of pink roses arranged by the governess already dropped petals on the piano. In one corner stood a harp with two broken strings—when a door slammed or one made a sudden movement this harp gave out a faint vibration or twang. The silence for miles around this obscure country house seemed to gather inside the folds of the curtains and to dilute the indoor air like a mist. This room Emma liked too little to touch already felt the touch of decay; it threw lifeless reflections into the two mirrors—the walls were green. Aunt Fran's body was stranded here like some object on the bed of a pool that has run dry. The magazine that she had been looking at had slipped from her lap to the black fur rug.

As her nephew appeared in the drawing-room door Aunt Fran fixed him urgently with her eyes. "*Nothing wrong?*"

"No, no—that was Emma."

"What's happened?"

"Nothing. She rang up to say good night."

"But she had said good night," said Aunt Fran in her troubled way. "She said good night to us when she was in the car. You remember, it was nearly night when she left. It seemed late to be starting to go so far. She had the whole afternoon, but she kept putting off, putting off. She seemed to me undecided up to the very last."

The Major turned his back on his aunt and began to unload his pockets, carefully placing the apples, two by two, in a row along the chiffonier. "Still, it's nice for her having this trip," he said.

"There was a time in the afternoon," said Aunt Fran, "when I thought she was going to change her mind. However she's there now—did you say?"

"Almost," he said, "not quite. Will you be all right if I go and shut up the house? And I said I would look in on the girls."

"Suppose the telephone rings?"

"I don't think it will, again. The exchange will be closing, for one thing."

"This afternoon," said Aunt Fran, "it rang four times."

She heard him going from room to room, unfolding and barring the heavy shutters and barring and chaining the front door. She could begin to feel calmer now that the house was a fortress against the wakeful night. "Hi!" she called, "don't forget the window in here"—looking back over her shoulder into the muslin curtains that seemed to crepitate with dark air. So he came back, with his flat unexpectant step. "I'm not cold," she said, "but I don't like dark coming in."

He shuttered the window. "I'll be down in a minute."

"Then we might sit together?"

"Yes, Aunt Fran: certainly."

The children, who had been talking, dropped their voices when they heard their father's step on the stairs. Their two beds creaked as they straightened themselves and lay silent, in social, expectant attitudes. Their room smelled of toothpaste; the white presses blotted slowly into the white walls. The window was open, the blind up, so in here darkness was incomplete—obscured, the sepia picture of the Good Shepherd hung over the mantelpiece. "It's all right," they said, "we are quite awake." So the Major came round and halted between the two beds. "Sit on mine," said Di nonchalantly. "It's my turn to have a person to-night."

"Why did mother ring up?" said Vivie, scrambling up on her pillow.

"Now how on earth did *you* know?"

"We knew by your voice—we couldn't hear what you said. We were only at the top of the stairs. Why did she?"

"To tell me to tell you to be good."

"She's said that," said Vivie, impatient. "What did she say truly?"

"Just good night."

"Oh. Is she there?"

"Where?"

"Where she said she was going to."

"Not quite—nearly."

"Goodness!" Di said; "it seems years since she went." The two children lay cryptic and still. Then Di went on: "Do you know what Aunt Fran said because Mother went away without any stockings?"

"No," said the Major, "and never mind."

"Oh, *I* don't mind," Di said, "I just heard." "And I heard," said Vivie: she could be felt opening her eyes wide, and the Major could just see, on the pillow, an implacable miniature of his wife's face. Di went on: "She's so frightened something will happen."

"Aunt Fran is?"

"She's always frightened of that."

"She is very fond of us all."

"Oh," burst out Vivie, "but Mother likes things to happen. She was whistling all the time she was packing up. Can't *we* have a treat to-morrow?"

"Mother'll be back to-morrow."

"But *can't* we have a treat?"

"We'll see; we'll ask Mother," the Major said.

"Oh yes, but suppose she didn't come back?"

"Look, it's high time you two went to sleep."

"We can't: we've got all sorts of ideas. . . . *You* say something, Daddy. Tell us something. Invent."

"Say what?" said the Major.

"Oh goodness," Vivie said; "*something*. What do you say to Mother?"

He went downstairs to Aunt Fran with their dissatisfied kisses stamped on his cheek. When he had gone Di fanned herself with the top of her sheet. "What makes him so disappointed, do you know?"

"I know, he thinks about the war."

But it was Di who, after the one question, unlocked all over and dropped plumb asleep. It was Vivie who, turning over and over, watched in the sky behind the cross of the window the tingling particles of the white dark, who heard the moth between the two window-sashes, who fancied she heard apples drop in the grass. One arbitrary line only divided this child from the animal: all her senses stood up, wanting to run the night. She swung her legs out of bed and pressed the soles of her feet on the cool floor. She got right up and stepped out of her nightdress and set out to walk the house in her skin. From each room she went into the human order seemed to have lapsed—discovered by sudden light, the chairs and tables seemed set round for a mouse's party on a gigantic scale. She stood for some time outside the drawing-room door and heard the unliving voices of the Major and aunt. She looked through the ajar door to the kitchen and saw a picked bone and a teapot upon the table and a maid lumped mute in a man's arms. She attempted the front door, but did not dare touch the chain: she could not get out of the house. She returned to the school-room, drawing her brows together, and straddled the rocking-horse they had not ridden for years. The furious bumping of the rockers woke the canaries under their cover: they set up a wiry springing in their cage. She dismounted, got out the box of chalks and began to tattoo her chest, belly and thighs with stars and snakes, red, yellow and blue. Then, taking the box of chalks with her, she went to her

mother's room for a look in the long glass—in front of this
she attempted to tattoo her behind. After this she bent
right down and squinted, upside down between her legs,
at the bedroom—the electric light over the dressing-table
poured into the vacantly upturned mirror and on to
Emma's left-behind silver things. The anarchy she felt all
through the house to-night made her, when she had
danced in front of the long glass, climb up to dance on
the big bed. The springs bounced her higher and higher;
chalk-dust flew from her body on to the fleece of the
blankets, on to the two cold pillows that she was tram-
pling out of their place. The bed-castors lunged, under her
springing, over the threadbare pink bridal carpet of
Emma's room.

Attacked by the castors, the chandelier in the drawing-
room tinkled sharply over Aunt Fran's head.

She at once raised her eyes to the ceiling. "Something
has got in," she said calmly—and, rising, made for the
drawing-room door. By reflex, the Major rose to stop her:
he sighed and put his weak whisky down. "Never mind,"
he said, "Aunt Fran. It's probably nothing. I'll go."

Whereupon, his Aunt Fran wheeled round on him with
her elbows up like a bird's wings. Her wax features sprang
into stony prominence. "It's never me, never me, never
me! Whatever *I* see, whatever I hear it's 'nothing,' though
the house might fall down. You keep everything back
from me. No one speaks the truth to me but the man on
the wireless. Always things being said on the telephone,
always things being moved about, always Emma off at
the end of the house singing, always the children hiding
away. I am never told, never told, never told. I get the
one answer, 'nothing.' I am expected to wait here. No one
comes near the drawing-room. I am never allowed to go
and see!"

"If that's how you feel," he said, "do certainly go." He
thought: it's all right, I locked the house.

So it was Aunt Fran's face, with the forehead lowered,
that came by inches round Emma's door. She appeared to
present her forehead as a sort of a buffer, obliquely looked

from below it, did not speak. Her glance, arriving gradually at its object, took in the child and the whole room. Vivie paused on the bed, transfixed, breathless, her legs apart. Her heart thumped; her ears drummed; her cheeks burned. To break up the canny and comprehensive silence she said loudly: "I am all over snakes."

"So this is what . . ." Aunt Fran said. "So this is what . . ."

"I'll get off this bed, if you don't like."

"The bed you were born in," said Aunt Fran.

Vivie did not know what to do; she jumped off the bed saying: "No one told me not to."

"Do you not know what is wicked?" said Aunt Fran—but with no more than estranged curiosity. She approached and began to try to straighten the bed, her unused hands making useless passes over the surface, brushing chalk-dust deeper into the fleece. All of a sudden, Vivie appeared to feel some majestic effluence from her aunt's person: she lagged round the bed to look at the stooping set face, at the mouth held in a curve like a dead smile, at the veins in the downcast eyelids and the backs of the hands. Aunt Fran did not hurry her ceremonial fumbling; she seemed to exalt the moment that was so fully hers. She picked a pillow up by its frill and placed it high on the bolster.

"That's mother's pillow," said Vivie.

"Did you say your prayers to-night?"

"Oh *yes*."

"They didn't defend you. Better say them again. Kneel down and say to Our Lord—"

"In my skin?"

Aunt Fran looked directly at, then away from, Vivie's body, as though for the first time. She drew the eiderdown from the foot of the bed and made a half-blind sweep at Vivie with it, saying: "Wrap up, wrap up."

"Oh, they'll come off—my snakes!" said Vivie, backing away. But Aunt Fran, as though the child were on fire, put into motion an extraordinary strength—she rolled, pressed and pounded Vivie up in the eiderdown until only the prisoner's dark eyes, so like her mother's, were left free to move wildly outside the great sausage, of padded taffeta, pink.

Aunt Fran, embracing the sausage firmly, repeated: "Now say to Our Lord—"

Shutting the door of her own bedroom, Aunt Fran felt her heart beat. The violence of the stranger within her ribs made her sit down on the ottoman—meanwhile, her little clock on the mantelpiece loudly and, it seemed to her, slowly ticked. Her window was shut, but the pressure of night silence made itself felt behind the blind, on the glass.

Round the room, on ledges and brackets, stood the fetiches she travelled through life with. They were mementoes—photos in little warped frames, musty round straw boxes, china kittens, palm crosses, the three Japanese monkeys, *bambini,* a Lincoln Imp, a merrythought pen-wiper, an ivory spinning-wheel from Cologne. From these objects the original virtue had by now almost evaporated. These gifts' givers, known on her lonely journey, were by now faint as their photographs: she no longer knew, now, where anyone was. All the more, her nature clung to these objects that moved with her slowly towards the dark.

Her room, the room of a person tolerated, by now gave off the familiar smell of herself—the smell of the old. A little book wedged the mirror at the angle she liked. When she was into her ripplecloth dressing-gown she brushed and plaited her hair and took out her teeth. She wound her clock and, with hand still trembling a little, lighted her own candle on the commode, then switched off her nephew's electric light. The room contracted round the crocus of flame as she knelt down slowly beside her bed —but while she said the Lord's Prayer she could not help listening, wondering what kept the Major so long downstairs. She never felt free to pray till she had heard the last door shut, till she could relax her watch on the house. She never could pray until they were *all* prostrate

—loaned for at least some hours to innocence, sealed by the darkness over their lids.

To-night she could not attempt to lift up her heart. She could, however, abase herself, and she abased herself for them all. The evil of the moment down in the drawing-room, the moment when she had cried "It is never me!" clung like a smell to her, so closely that she had been eager to get her clothes off, and did not like, even now, to put her hands to her face.

Who shall be their judge? Not I.

The blood of the world is poisoned, feels Aunt Fran, with her forehead over the eiderdown. Not a pure drop comes out at any prick—yes, even the heroes shed black blood. The solitary watcher retreats step by step from his post—who shall stem the black tide coming in? There are no more children: the children are born knowing. The shadow rises up the cathedral tower, up the side of the pure hill. There is not even the past: our memories share with us the infected zone; not a memory does not lead up to this. Each moment is everywhere, it holds the war in its crystal; there is no elsewhere, no other place. Not a benediction falls on this apart house of the Major; the enemy is within it, creeping about. Each heart here falls to the enemy.

So this is what goes on . . .

Emma flying away—and not saying why, or where. And to wrap the burning child up did not put out the fire. You cannot look at the sky without seeing the shadow, the men destroying each other. What is the matter to-night —is there a battle? This is a threatened night.

Aunt Fran sags on her elbows; her knees push desperately in the woolly rug. She cannot even repent; she is capable of no act; she is undone. She gets up and eats a biscuit, and looks at the little painting of Mont Blanc on the little easel beside her clock. She still does not hear the Major come up to bed.

Queenie understood that the third child, the girl, was dead: she gave back the photograph rather quickly, as though unbearable sadness emanated from it. Justin, how-

ever, came down the room and looked at the photograph
over Robinson's shoulder—at the rather vulgar, frank,
blonde little face. He found it hard to believe that a child
of Robinson's should have chosen the part of death. He
then went back to the table and picked up, with a jerky
effrontery, the photographs of the two little boys. "Do
they never come here?" he said. "You have plenty of room
for them."

"I daresay they will; I mean to fix up something. Just
now they're at Greystones," Robinson said—he then
looked quite openly at the clock.

"With their mother?" Justin said, in a harsh, impertinent voice.

"Yes, with my wife."

"So you keep up the two establishments?"

Even Robinson glanced at Justin with some surprise.
"If you call it that," he said indifferently. "I rather landed
myself with this place, really—as a matter of fact, when I
moved in it looked as though things might work out dif-
ferently. First I stopped where you are, at the hotel, but
I do like to have a place of my own. One feels freer, for
one thing."

"There's a lot in that," said Justin, with an oblique
smile. "Our local ladies think you keep a Bluebeard's castle up here."

"What, corpses?" Robinson said, surprised.

"Oh yes, they think you're the devil."

"Who, me?" replied Robinson, busy replacing photographs on the mantelpiece. "That's really very funny: I'd
no idea. I suppose they may think I've been pretty slack
—but I'm no good at teafights, as a matter of fact. But I
can't see what else can be eating them. What ought I to
do, then? Throw a party here? I will if your sister'll come
and pour out tea—but I don't think I've really got enough
chairs . . . I hope," he added, looking at Queenie, "*she*
doesn't think it's not all above board here?"

"You're forgetting again: she misses the talk, poor girl."

"She doesn't look very worried."

"I daresay she's seldom been happier. She's built up

quite a romance about this house. She has a world to herself—I could envy her."

Robinson contrived to give the impression that he did
not wish to have Queenie discussed—partly because he
owned her, he understood her, partly because he wished
to discuss nothing: it really was time for his guests to go.
Though he was back again in his armchair, regard for time
appeared in his attitude. Justin could not fail to connect
this with the telephone and the smile that had not completely died. It became clear, staringly clear, that throughout the evening his host had been no more than marking
time. This made Justin say "Yes" (in a loud pertinacious
voice), "this evening's been quite an event for us. Your
house has more than its legend, Robinson; it has really
remarkable character. However, all good things—" Stiff
with anger, he stood up.

"Must you?" said Robinson, rising. "I'm so sorry."

Lighting-up time, fixed by Nature, had passed. The
deaf woman, from her place in the window, had been
watching lights of cars bend over the hill. Turning with
the main road, that had passed the foot of the mountains,
each car now drove a shaft of extreme brilliance through
the dark below Robinson's pampas-grass. Slipping, dropping with a rush past the gate, illuminating the dust on
the opposite wall, car after car vanished after its light—
there was suddenly quite a gust of them, as though the
mountain country, before sleeping, had stood up and
shaken them from its folds. The release of movement excited Queenie—that and the beat of light's wings on her
face. She turned round very reluctantly as Justin approached and began to make signs to her.

"Why, does Mr. Robinson want us to go?" she said.

"That's the last thing I want!" shouted Robinson.

("She can't hear you.")

"Christ . . ." said Robinson, rattled. He turned the
lights on—the three, each with a different face of despair,
looked at each other across the exposed room, across the
teatray on the circular table and the superb leather backs
of the chairs. "My brother thinks we've kept you too

long," she said—and as a lady she looked a little shaken, for the first time unsure of herself. Robinson would not for worlds have had this happen; he strode over and took and nursed her elbow, which tensed then relaxed gently inside the muslin sleeve. He saw, outdoors, his window cast on the pampas, saw the whole appearance of shattered night. She looked for reassurance into his face, and he saw the delicate lines in hers.

"And look how late it's got, Mr. Robinson!"

"It's not that," he said in his naturally low voice, "but—"

A car pulled up at the gate. Alarmed by the lit window it cut its lights off and could be felt to crouch there, attentive, docile, cautious, waiting to turn in. "Your friend is arriving," Justin said.

On that last lap of her drive, the eighteen miles of flat road along the base of the mountains, the last tingling phase of darkness had settled down. Grassy sharpness passed from the mountains' outline, the patches of firs, the gleam of watery ditch. The west sky had gradually drunk its yellow and the ridged heights that towered over her right hand became immobile cataracts, sensed not seen. Animals rising out of the ditches turned to Emma's headlamps green lamp-eyes. She felt the shudder of night, the contracting bodies of things. The quick air sang in her ears; she drove very fast. At the crossroads above Robinson's town she pulled round in a wide swerve: she saw the lemon lights of the town strung along under the black trees, the pavements and the pale humble houses below her in a faint, mysterious glare as she slipped down the funnel of hill to Robinson's gate. (The first white gate on the left, you cannot miss it, he'd said.) From the road she peered up the lawn and saw, between pampas-tufts, three people upright in his lit room. So she pulled up and switched her lights and her engine off and sat crouching in her crouching car in the dark—night began to creep up her bare legs. Now the glass porch sprang into prominence like a lantern—she saw people stiffly saying goodbye. Down the drive came a man and woman almost in flight; not addressing each other, not looking back—putting the back of a fist to her mouth quickly Emma checked the uprush of an uncertain laugh. She marked a lag in the steps—turning their heads quickly the man and woman looked with involuntary straightness into the car, while her eyes were glued to their silhouettes. The two turned down to the town and she turned in at the gate.

Farouche, with her tentative little swagger and childish, pleading air of delinquency, Emma came to a halt in Robinson's living-room. He had pulled down the blind. She kept recoiling and blinking and drawing her fingers over her eyes, till Robinson turned off the top light. "Is that that?" There was only the reading-lamp.

She rested her shoulder below his and grappled their enlaced fingers closer together as though trying to draw calmness from him. Standing against him, close up under his height, she held her head up and began to look round the room. "You're whistling something," she said, after a moment or two.

"I only mean, take your time."

"Why, am I nervous?" she said.

"Darling, you're like a bat in out of the night. I told you not to come along too fast."

"I see now, I came too early," she said. "Why didn't you tell me you had a party? Who were they? What were they doing here?"

"Oh, they're just people in this place. He's a bit screwy and she's deaf, but I like them, as a matter of fact."

"They're mackintoshy sort of people," she said. "But I always thought you lived all alone. . . . Is there anyone else in the house now?"

"Not a mouse," said Robinson, without change of expression. "My housekeeper's gone off for the night."

"I see," said Emma. "Will you give me a drink?"

She sat down where Justin had just been sitting, and, bending forward with a tremulous frown, began to brush ash from the arm of the chair. You could feel the whole of her hesitate. Robinson, without hesitation, came and sat easily on the arm of the chair from which she had brushed the ash. "It's sometimes funny," he said, "when people drop in like that. 'My God,' I thought when I saw them, 'what an evening to choose.' " He slipped his hand down between the brown velvet cushion and Emma's spine, then spread the broad of his hand against the small of her back. Looking kindly down at her closed eyelids he went on: "However, it all went off all right. Oh, and there's one thing I'd like to tell you—that chap called me a genius."

"How would he know?" said Emma, opening her eyes.

"We never got that clear. I was rather out of my depth. His sister was deaf . . ." here Robinson paused, bent down and passed his lips absently over Emma's forehead. "Or did I tell you that?"

"Yes, you told me that. . . . Is it true that this house is blue?"

"You'll see tomorrow."

"There'll hardly be time, darling; I shall hardly see this house in the daylight. I must go on to—where I'm supposed to be."

"At any rate, I'm glad that was all O.K. They're not on the telephone, where you're going?"

"No, it's all right; they're not on the telephone. . . . *You'll* have to think of something that went wrong with my car."

"That will all keep," said Robinson. "Here you are."

"Yes, here I am." She added: "The night was lovely," speaking more sadly than she knew. Yes, here she was, being settled down to as calmly as he might settle down to a meal. Her naïvety as a lover . . . She could not have said, for instance, how much the authoritative male room —the electric clock, the sideboard, the unlit grate, the cold of the leather chairs—put, at every moment when he did not touch her, a gulf between her and him. She turned her head to the window. "I smell flowers."

"Yes, I've got three flowerbeds."

"Darling, for a minute could we go out?"

She moved from his touch and picked up Queenie's tea-tray and asked if she could put it somewhere else. Holding the tray (and given countenance by it) she halted

in front of the photographs. "Oh . . ." she said. "Yes.
Why?" "I wish in a way you hadn't got any children." "I
don't see why I shouldn't have: you have."

"Yes, I . . . But Vivie and Di are not so much *like*
children—"

"If they're like you," he said, "those two will be having a high old time, with the cat away—"

"Oh darling, I'm not the cat."

In the kitchen (to put the tray down) she looked
round: it shone with tiling and chromium and there
seemed to be switches in every place. "What a whole lot
of gadgets you have," she said. "Look at all those electric . .." "Yes, I like them." "They must cost a lot of
money. My kitchen's all over blacklead and smoke and
hooks. My cook would hate a kitchen like this."

"I always forget that you have a cook." He picked up
an electric torch and they went out. Going along the side
of the house, Robinson played a mouse of light on the
wall. "Look, really blue." But she only looked absently.
"Yes— But have I been wrong to come?" He led her off
the gravel on to the lawn, till they reached the edge of a
bed of stocks. Then he firmly said: "That's for you to say,
my dear girl."

"I know it's hardly a question—I hardly know you, do
I?"

"We'll be getting to know each other," said Robinson.

After a minute she let go of his hand and knelt down
abruptly beside the flowers: she made movements like
scooping the scent up and laving her face in it—he, meanwhile, lighted a cigarette and stood looking down. "I'm
glad you like my garden," he said. "You feel like getting
fond of the place?"

"You say you forget that I have a cook."

"Look, sweet, if you can't get that off your mind you'd
better get in your car and go straight home . . . But you
will."

"Aunt Fran's so old, too old; it's not nice. And the
Major keeps thinking about the war. And the children
don't think I am good; I regret that."

"You have got a nerve," he said, "but I love that. You're with me. Aren't you with me?—Come out of that flowerbed."

They walked to the brow of the lawn; the soft feather-plumes of the pampas rose up a little over her head as she stood by him overlooking the road. She shivered. "What are all those trees?" "The demesne—I know they burnt down the castle years ago. The demesne's great for couples." "What's in there?" "Nothing, I don't think; just the ruin, a lake . . ."

"I wish—"

"Now, what?"

"I wish we had more time."

"Yes: we don't want to stay out all night."

So taught, she smothered the last of her little wishes for consolation. Her shyness of further words between them became extreme; she was becoming frightened of Robinson's stern, experienced delicacy on the subject of love. Her adventure became the quiet practice with him. The adventure (even, the pilgrimage) died at its root, in the childish part of her mind. When he had headed her off the cytherean terrain—the leaf-drowned castle ruin, the lake—she thought for a minute he had broken her heart, and she knew now he had broken her fairytale. He seemed content—having lit a new cigarette—to wait about in his garden for a few minutes longer: not poetry but a sort of tactile wisdom came from the firmness, lawn, under their feet. The white gateposts, the boles of beeches above the dust-whitened wall were just seen in reflected light from the town. There was no moon, but dry, tense, translucent darkness: no dew fell.

Justin went with his sister to her door in the square. Quickly, and in their necessary silence, they crossed the grass under the limes. Here a dark window reflected one of the few lamps, there a shadow crossed a lit blind, and voices of people moving under the trees made a reverberation in the box of the square. Queenie let herself in; Justin heard the heavy front door drag shut slowly across the mat. She had not expected him to come in, and he did not know if she shared his feeling of dissonance, or if she recoiled from shock, or if she were shocked at all. Quitting the square once, he took the direct way to his hotel in the main street. He went in at the side door, past the bar in which he so often encountered Robinson.

In his small, harsh room he looked first at his bed. He looked, as though out of a pit of sickness, at his stack of books on the mantelpiece. He writhed his head round sharply, threw off his coat and began to unknot his tie. Meanwhile he beat round, in the hot light, for some crack of outlet from his constriction. It was at his dressing table, for he had no other, that he began and ended his letter to Robinson: the mirror screwed to the dressing-table constituted a witness to this task—whenever his look charged up it met his own reared head, the flush heightening on the bridge of the nose and forehead, the neck from which as though for an execution, the collar had been taken away.

"*My dear Robinson,*

"*Our departure from your house (Bellevue, I think?) tonight was so awkwardly late, and at the last so hurried, that I had inadequate time in which to thank you for your hospitality to my sister and to myself. That we exacted this hospitality does not make its merit, on your part, less. Given the inconvenience we so clearly caused you, your forbearance with us was past praise. So much so that (as you may be glad to hear) my sister does not appear to realise how very greatly we were de trop. In my own case—which is just—the same cannot be said. I am conscious that, in spite of her disability, she did at least prove a less wearisome guest than I.*

"*My speculations and queries must, to your mind, equally seem absurd. This evening's fiasco has been definitive: I think it better our acquaintance should close. You will find it in line with my usual awkwardness that I should choose to state this decision of mine at all. Your indifference to the matter I cannot doubt. My own lack of indifference must make its last weak exhibition in this letter—in which, if you have fine enough nostrils (which*

I doubt) every sentence will almost certainly stink. In attempting to know you I have attempted to enter, and to comport myself in, what might be called an area under your jurisdiction. If my inefficacies appeared to you ludicrous, my curiosities (as in one special instance tonight) appeared more—revolting. I could gauge (even before the postscript outside your gate) how profoundly I had offended you. Had we either of us been gentlemen, the incident might have passed off with less harm.

"My attempts to know you I have disposed of already. My wish that you should know me has been, from the first, ill found. You showed yourself party to it in no sense, and the trick I played on myself I need not discuss. I acted and spoke (with regard to you) upon assumptions you were not prepared to warrant. You cannot fail to misunderstand what I mean when I say that a year ago this might not have happened to me. But—the assumptions on which I acted, Robinson, are becoming more general in a driven world than you yet (or may ever) know. The extremity to which we are each driven must be the warrant for what we do and say.

"My extraordinary divagation towards you might be said to be, I suppose, an accident of this summer. But there are no accidents. I have the fine (yes) fine mind's love of the fine plume, and I meet no fine plumes down my own narrow street. Also, in this place (birthplace) you interposed your solidity between me and what might have been the full effects of an exacerbating return. In fact, you had come to constitute for me a very genuine holiday. As things are, my five remaining days here will have to be seen out. I shall hope not to meet you, but must fear much of the trap-like size of this town. (You need not, as I mean to, avoid the hotel bar.) Should I, however, fail to avoid you, I shall again, I suppose, have to owe much, owe any face I keep, to your never-failing imperviousness. Understand that it will be against my wish that I re-open this one-sided account.

"I wish you good night. Delicacy does not deter me from adding that I feel my good wish to be superfluous. I imagine that, incapable of being haunted, you are in-

*capable of being added to. To-morrow (I understand)
you will feel fine, but you will not know any more about
love. If the being outside your gate came with a question,
it is possible that she should have come to me. If I had
even seen her she might not go on rending my heart. As
it is, as you are, I perhaps denounce you as much on her
behalf as my own. Not trying to understand, you at least
cannot misunderstand the mood and hour in which I
write. As regards my sister, please do not discontinue
what has been your even kindness to her: she might be
perplexed. She has nothing to fear, I think.*

"Accept, my dear Robinson (without irony)

"My kind regards,

"J.C."

Justin, trembling, smote a stamp on this letter. Going
down as he was, in the hall he unhooked his mackintosh
and put it over his shirt. It was well past midnight; the
street, empty, lay in dusty reaches under the few lamps.
Between the shutters his step raised an echo; the cold of
the mountains had come down; two cats in his path un-
clinched and shot off into the dark. On his way to the
letterbox he was walking towards Bellevue; on his way
back he still heard the drunken woman sobbing against
the telegraph pole. The box would not be cleared till to-
morrow noon.

Queenie forgot Justin till next day. The house in which
her rooms were was so familiar that she went upstairs
without a pause in the dark. Crossing her sitting-room she
smelled oil from the cooker behind the screen: she went
through an arch to the cubicle where she slept. She was
happy. Inside her sphere of silence that not a word
clouded, the spectacle of the evening at Bellevue reigned.
Contemplative, wishless, almost without an "I," she un-
hooked her muslin dress at the wrists and waist, stepped
from the dress and began to take down her hair. Still in
the dark, with a dreaming sureness of habit, she dropped
hairpins into the heart-shaped tray.

This was the night she knew she would find again. It

had stayed living under a film of time. On just such a summer night, once only, she had walked with a lover in the demesne. His hand, like Robinson's, had been on her elbow, but she had guided him, not he her, because she had better eyes in the dark. They had gone down walks already deadened with moss, under the weight of July trees; they had felt the then fresh aghast ruin totter above them; there was a moonless sky. Beside the lake they sat down, and while her hand brushed the ferns in the cracks of the stone seat emanations of kindness passed from him to her. The subtle deaf girl had made the transposition of this nothing or everything into an everything—the delicate deaf girl that the man could not speak to and was afraid to touch. She who, then so deeply contented, kept in her senses each frond and breath of that night, never saw him again and had soon forgotten his face. That had been twenty years ago, till to-night when it was now. To-night it was Robinson who, guided by Queenie down leaf tunnels, took the place on the stone seat by the lake.

The rusted gates of the castle were at the end of the square. Queenie, in her bed facing the window, lay with her face turned sideways, smiling, one hand lightly against her cheek.

Songs My Father Sang Me

"*WHAT'S* the matter," he asked, "have I said something?"

Not troubling to get him quite into focus, she turned her head and said, "No, why—did you say anything?"

"Or p'r'aps you don't like this place?"

"I don't mind it—why?" she said, looking round the night club, which was not quite as dark as a church, as though for the first time. At some tables you had to look twice, to see who was there; what lights there were were dissolved in a haze of smoke; the walls were rather vault-like, with no mirrors; on the floor dancers drifted like pairs of vertical fish. He, meanwhile, studied her from across their table with neither anxiety nor acute interest, but with a dreamlike caricature of both. Then he raised the bottle between them and said, "Mm-mm?" to which she replied by placing the flat of her hand mutely, mulishly, across the top of her glass. Not annoyed, he shrugged, filled up his own and continued, "Then anything isn't really the matter, then?"

"This tune, this song, is the matter."

"Oh—shall we dance?"

"No." Behind her agelessly girlish face, sleekly framed

by the cut of her fawn-blonde hair, there passed a wave of genuine trouble for which her features had no vocabulary. "It's what they're playing—this tune."

"It's pre-war," he said knowledgeably.

"It's last war."

"Well, last war's pre-war."

"It's the tune my father remembered he used to dance to; it's the tune I remember him always trying to sing."

"Why, is your father dead?"

"No, I don't suppose so; why?"

"Sorry," he said quickly, "I mean, if . . ."

"Sorry, why are you sorry?" she said, raising her eyebrows. "Didn't I ever tell you about my father? I always thought he made me rather a bore. Wasn't it you I was telling about my father?"

"No. I suppose it must have been someone else. One meets so many people."

"Oh, what," she said, "have I hurt your feelings? But you haven't got any feelings about me."

"Only because you haven't got any feelings about me."

"Haven't I?" she said, as though really wanting to know. "Still, it hasn't seemed all the time as though we were quite a flop."

"Look," he said, "don't be awkward. Tell me about your father."

"He was twenty-six."

"When?"

"How do you mean, 'when'? Twenty-six was my father's age. He was tall and lean and leggy, with a casual sort of way of swinging himself about. He was fair, and the shape of his face was a rather long narrow square. Sometimes his eyes faded in until you could hardly see them; sometimes he seemed to be wearing a blank mask. You really only quite got the plan of his face when it was turned halfway between a light and a shadow—*then* his eyebrows and eyehollows, the dints just over his nostrils, the cut of his upper lip and the cleft in his chin, and the broken in-and-out outline down from his temple past his cheekbone into his jaw all came out at you, like a message you had to read in a single flash."

She paused and lighted a cigarette. He said, "You sound as though you had never got used to him."

She went on, "My father was one of the young men who were not killed in the last war. He was a man in the last war until that stopped; then I don't quite know what he was, and I don't think he ever quite knew either. He got his commission and first went out to France about 1915, I think he said. When he got leaves he got back to London and had good times, by which I mean something larky but quite romantic, in the course of one of which, I don't know which one, he fell in love with my mother and they used to go dancing, and got engaged in that leave and got married the next. My mother was a flapper, if you knew about flappers? They were the pin-ups *de ses jours,* and at the same time inspired idealistic feeling. My mother was dark and fluffy and as slim as a wraith; a great *glacé* ribbon bow tied her hair back and stood out like a calyx behind her face, and her hair itself hung down in a plume so long that it tickled my father's hand while he held her while they were dancing and while she sometimes swam up at him with her violet eyes. Each time he had to go back to the front again she was miserable, and had to put her hair up, because her relations said it was high time. But sometimes when he got back again on leave she returned to being a flapper again, to please him. Between his leaves she had to go back to live with her mother and sisters in West Kensington; and her sisters had a whole pack of business friends who had somehow never had to go near the front, and all these combined in an effort to cheer her up, but, as she always wrote to my father, nothing did any good. I suppose everyone felt it was for the best when they knew there was going to be the patter of little feet. I wasn't actually *born* till the summer of 1918. If you remember, I told you my age last night.

"The first thing *I* remember, upon becoming conscious, was living in one of those bungalows on the flats near Staines. The river must have been somewhere, but I don't think I saw it. The only point about that region is that it has no point and that it goes on and on. I think there are floods there sometimes, there would be nothing to stop them; a forest fire would be what is needed really, but that would not be possible as there are no trees. It would have looked better, really, just left as primeval marsh, but someone had once said, 'Let there be bungalows.' If you ever motored anywhere near it you probably asked yourself who lives there, and why. Well, my father and mother and I did, and why?—because it was cheap, and there was no one to criticize how you were getting on. Our bungalow was tucked well away in the middle, got at by a sort of maze of in those days unmade roads. I'm glad to say I've forgotten which one it was. Most of our neighbours kept themselves to themselves for, probably, like ours, the best reasons, but most of them kept hens also; we didn't even do that. All round us, nature ran riot between corrugated iron, clothes-lines and creosoted lean-to sheds.

"I know that our bungalow had been taken furnished; the only things we seemed to have of our own were a number of satin cushions with satin fruits stitched on. In order to dislodge my biscuit crumbs from the satin apples my mother used to shake the cushions out of the window on to the lawn. Except for the prettiness of the dandelions, our lawn got to look and feel rather like a hearth-rug; I mean, it got covered with threads and cinders and shreds; once when I was crawling on it I got a pin in my hand, another time I got sharp glass beads in my knee. The next-door hens used to slip through and pick about; never, apparently, quite in vain. At the far end, some Dorothy Perkins roses tried to climb up a pergola that was always falling down. I remember my father reaching up in his shirt-sleeves, trying to nail it up. Another thing he had to do in our home was apply the whole of his strength to the doors, french window and windows, which warped until they would not open nor shut. I used to come up behind him and push too.

"The war by now, of course, had been over for some years; my father was out of the British Army and was what was called taking his time and looking around. For how long he had been doing so I can't exactly tell you.

He not only read all the "post vacant" advertisements every day but composed and succeeded in getting printed an advertisement of himself, which he read aloud to me: it said he was prepared to go anywhere and try anything. I said, 'But what's an ex-officer?', and he said, 'I am.' Our dining-room table, which was for some reason possibly me, sticky, was always spread with new newspapers he had just brought home, and he used to be leaning over them on his elbows, biting harder and harder on the stem of his pipe. I don't think I discovered for some years later that the principal reason for newspapers is news. My father never looked at them for that reason—just as he always lost interest in any book in which he had lost his place. Or perhaps he was not in the mood for world events. My mother had never cared much for them at the best of times. 'To think of all we expected after the war,' she used to say to my father, from day to day.

"My mother, by this time, had had her hair shingled— in fact, *I* never remember her any other way than with a dark shaved point tapered down the back of her neck. I don't know when she'd begun to be jealous of him and me. Every time he came back from an interview that he hadn't got to or from an interview that hadn't come to anything, he used to bring me back something, to cheer himself up, and the wheels off all the mechanical toys got mixed with the beads and the threads and the cinders into our lawn. What my mother was really most afraid of was that my father would bundle us all off into the great open spaces, in order to start fresh somewhere and grow something. I imagine he knew several chaps who had, or were going to. After one or two starts on the subject he shut up, but I could see she could see he was nursing it. It frustrated her from nagging at him all out about not succeeding in getting a job in England: she was anxious not to provide an opening for him to say, 'Well, there's always one thing we *could* do . . .' The hard glassy look her eyes got made them look like dolls' eyes, which may partly have been what kept me from liking dolls. So they practically never talked about anything. I don't think she even knew he minded about her hair.

"You may be going to ask when my father sang. He often *began* to sing—when he hammered away at the pergola, when something he thought of suddenly struck him as good, when the heave he gave at the warped french window sent it flying open into the garden. He was constantly starting to sing, but he never got very far—you see, he had no place where he could sing unheard. The walls were thin and the lawn was tiny and the air round the bungalow was so silent and heavy that my mother was forced to listen to every note. The lordly way my father would burst out singing, like the lordly way he cocked his hat over one eye, had come to annoy her, in view of everything else. But the still more unfortunate thing was that my father only knew, or else only liked, two tunes, which were two tunes out of the bygone years which made him think of the war and being in love. Yes, they were dance tunes; yes, we have just heard one; yes, they also reminded my mother of war and love. So when he had got to the fourth or fifth bar of either, she would call out to know if he wanted to drive her mad. He would stop and say, 'Sorry,' but if he was in the mood he'd be well away, the next minute, with the alternative tune, and she would be put to the trouble of stopping that.

"Mother did not know what to look like now she was not a flapper. Mostly she looked like nothing—I wonder whether she knew. Perhaps that was what she saw in the satin cushions: they looked like something—at least, to her. The day she and I so suddenly went to London to call on her sister's friend she did certainly manage, however, to look like something. My father, watching us down the garden path, ventured no comment on her or my appearance. However, which ought to have cheered me up, we created quite a furore in the train. We went sailing into the richly-appointed office of mother's sister's friend, who was one of those who, during the war, had felt mother should be cheered up. Can I, need I, describe him? The usual kind of business pudge, in a suit. He looked in a reluctant way at my mother, and reluctantly, slightly morbidly, at me. I don't know how I got the impression mother held all the cards. The conversation, of course, flowed over my head—I just cruised round and round the room, knocking objects over. But the outcome —as I gathered when we got home—was that my mother's sister's friend said he'd give my father a job. He had said he could use an ex-officer, provided it was an ex-officer with charm. What my father would have to do was to interest housewives, not in himself but in vacuum cleaners. If it helped to interest some housewives in vacuum cleaners, he could interest them just a little bit in himself. Mother's sister's friend called this, using judgment of character.

"When my mother, that evening, put all this to my father, he did not say anything but simply stood and stared. *She* said, 'Then I suppose you want us to starve?'

"So my father stopped being a problem and became a travelling salesman. The best part was that the firm allowed him a car.

"I must say for my mother that she did not ask my father how he was getting on. At least she had much less trouble about the singing: sometimes he'd be away for two or three days together; when he was home he simply sprawled in his chair, now and then asking when there'd be something to eat, as unmusical as a gramophone with the spring broken. When I came filtering in he sometimes opened one eye and said, 'And what have *you* been doing?'—as though he'd just finished telling me what he'd been doing himself. He garaged the car some way down the next road, and in the mornings when he was starting off I used to walk with him to the garage. He used to get into the car, start up the engine, back out, then look round at me and say, 'Like to come out on the job?—yes, I bet you would,' then let the clutch in and whizz off. Something about this always made me feel sick.

"I don't of course clearly remember when this began, or how long it went on for; but I know when it stopped. The night before my seventh birthday was a June night, because my birthdays are in June. The people who lived all round us were sitting out, on the verandas or on their lawns, but my mother had sent me to bed early because she was having a party for me next day and did not want

to get me over-excited. My birthday cake which had arrived from the shop was on the dining-room sideboard,
with a teacloth over it to keep the flies off, and my father
and mother were in the lounge with the french window
shut, because she had several things to say to him that
she did not want the people all round to hear. The heat
travelled through the roof into all the rooms, so that I
could not sleep: also, my bed was against the wall of my
room, and the lounge was the other side of the wall. My
mother went on like someone who has been saving up—
just some touch, I suppose, had been needed to set her
off. She said she would like to know why there was not
more money—my father's job, I suppose now, was on a
commission basis. Or, she said, was he keeping another
woman?—a thing she had heard that most travelling sales-
men did. She said she really felt quite ashamed of having
foisted my father on to her sister's friend, and that she
only wondered how long the firm would stand for it. She
said her sisters pitied her, though she had tried to conceal
from them that her life was hell. My father, who had
as usual got home late and as usual had not yet had any
supper, could not be heard saying anything. My mother
then said she wished she knew why she had married him,
and would like still more to know why he had married her.

"My father said, 'You were so lovely—you've no idea.'

"Next morning there was a heat-haze over everything.
I bustled into the dining-room to see if there was anything on my plate. I forget what my mother had given
me, but her richest sister had sent me a manicure-set in a
purple box: all the objects had purple handles and lay in
grooves on white velvet. While I was taking them out and
putting them back again, my father suddenly looked up
from his coffee and said *his* present for me was in the car,
and that I'd have to come out and fetch it. My mother
could hardly say no to this, though of course I saw her
opening her mouth. So out we set, I gripping the manicure-set. I don't think my father seemed odder than usual,
though he was on the point of doing an unexpected thing
—when he had got the car started and backed out he
suddenly held open the other door and said, 'Come on,

nip in, look sharp; my present to you is a day trip.' So then
I nipped in and we drove off, as though this were the
most natural thing in the world.

"The car was a two-seater, with a let-down hood . . .
No, of course I cannot remember what make it was. That
morning, the hood was down. Locked up in the dickie
behind my father kept the specimen vacuum cleaner he
interested women in. He drove fast, and as we hit the
bumps in the road I heard the parts of the cleaner clonk-
ing about. As we drove, the sun began to burn its way
through the haze, making the roses in some of the grander
gardens look almost impossibly large and bright. My bare
knees began to grill on the leather cushion, and the crum-
ples eased out of the front of my cotton frock.

"I had never been with my father when he was driving a car—it felt as though speed and power were streaming out of him, and as if he and I were devouring everything that we passed. I sat slumped round with my cheek
against the hot cushion and sometimes stared at his profile, sometimes stared at his wrists, till he squinted round
and said, 'Anything wrong with *me?*' Later on, he added,
'Why not look at the scenery?' By that time there *was*
some scenery, if that means grass and trees; in fact, these
had been going on for some time, in a green band streaming behind my father's face. When I said, 'Where are we
going?' he said, 'Well, where *are* we going?' At that point
I saw quite a large hill, in fact a whole party of them, lapping into each other as though they would never stop, and
never having seen anything of the kind before I could not
help saying, 'Oh, I say, look!'

"My father gave a nod, without stopping singing—I
told you he had begun to sing? He had not only started
but gone on: when he came to the end of his first tune he
said, 'Pom-*pom*,' like a drum, then started through it
again; after that he worked around to the second, which
he sang two or three times, with me joining in. We both
liked the second still better, and how right we were—and
it's worn well, hasn't it? That's what this band's just
played."

"Oh, what they've just played?" he said, and looked

narrowly at the band; while, reaching round for the bottle on the table between them he lifted it to replenish her glass and his. This time she did not see or did not bother to stop him: she looked at her full glass vaguely, then vaguely drank. After a minute she went on:

"Ginger beer, sausage rolls, chocolate—that was what we bought when we stopped at the village shop. Also my father bought a blue comb off a card of combs, with which he attempted to do my hair, which had blown into tags and ratstails over my eyes and face. He looked at me while he combed in a puzzled way, as though something about me that hadn't struck him became a problem to him for the first time. I said, 'Aren't we going to sell any vacuum cleaners?' and he said, 'We'll try and interest the Berkshire Downs.' I thought that meant, meet a family; but all we did was turn out of the village and start up a rough track, to where there could not be any people at all. The car climbed with a slow but exciting roar: from the heat of the engine and the heat of the sun the chocolate in the paper bag in my hands was melting by the time we came to the top.

"From the top, where we lay on our stomachs in the shade of the car, we could see—oh well, can't you imagine, can't you? It was an outsize June day. The country below us looked all colours, and was washed over in the most reckless way with light; going on and on into the distance the clumps of trees and the roofs of villages and the church towers had quivering glimmers round them; but most of all there was space, sort of moulded space, and the blue of earth ran into the blue of sky.

"My father's face was turned away from me, propped up on his hand. I finally said to him, 'What's that?'

" 'What's what?' he said, startled.

" 'What we're looking at.'

" 'England,' he said, 'that's England. I thought I'd like to see her again.'

" 'But don't we live in England?'

"He took no notice. 'How I loved her,' he said.

" 'Oh, but don't you now?'

" 'I've lost her,' he said, 'or she's lost me; I don't quite know which; I don't understand what's happened.' He rolled round and looked at me and said, 'But *you* like it, don't you? I thought I'd like you to see, if just once, what I once saw.'

"I was well into the third of my sausage rolls: my mouth was full, I could only stare at my father. He said, 'And there's something else down there—see it?' I screwed my eyes up but still only saw the distance. 'Peace,' he said. 'Look hard at it; don't forget it.'

" 'What's peace?' I said.

" 'An idea you have when there's a war on, to make you fight well. An idea that gets lost when there isn't a war.'

"I licked pastry-crumbs off my chin and began on chocolate. By this time my father lay on his back, with his fingers thatched together over his eyes: he talked, but more to the sky than me. None of the things he was saying now went anywhere near my brain—a child's brain, how could they?—his actual words are gone as though I had never heard them, but his meaning lodged itself in some part of my inside, and is still there and has grown up with me. He talked about war and how he had once felt, and about leaves and love and dancing and going back to the war, then the birth of me—'Seven years ago to-day,' he said, 'seven years; I remember how they brought me the telegram.'

"Something else, on top of the sausage and heat and chocolate suddenly made me feel sick and begin to cry. 'Oh please, oh please don't,' I said, 'it's my birthday.'

" 'Don't what?' he said. I, naturally, didn't know. My father again looked at me, with the same expression he had worn when attempting to comb my hair. Something about me—my age?—was a proposition. Then he shut his eyes, like—I saw later, not at the time—somebody finally banishing an idea. 'No; it wouldn't work,' he said. 'It simply couldn't be done. You can wait for me if you want. I can't wait for you.'

"Then he began acting like somebody very sleepy: he yawned and yawned at me till I yawned at him. I didn't feel sick any more, but the heat of the afternoon came down like a grey-blue blanket over my head. 'What you and I want,' my father said, watching me, 'is a good sleep.'

"I wish I could tell you at *which* moment I fell asleep, and stopped blurrily looking at him between my eyelids, because *that* was the moment when I last saw my father.

"When I woke, there was no more shadow on my side of the car; the light had changed and everything looked bright yellow. I called to my father but he did not answer, for the adequate reason that he was not there. He was gone. For some reason I wasn't at all frightened; I thought he must have gone to look for something for us for tea. I remembered that I was not at my birthday party, and I must say I thought twice about that pink cake. I was more bored than anything, till I remembered my manicure-set, which owing to the funniness of the day I had not been able to open a second time. I took the objects out of their velvet bedding and began to prod at my nails, as I'd seen my mother do. Then I got up and walked, once more, all the way round the car. It was then that I noticed what I had missed before: a piece of white paper twisted into the radiator. I couldn't read handwriting very well, but did at last make out what my father had put. *'The car and the vacuum cleaner are the property of Messrs. X and X"* (the firm of my mother's sister's friend), *'the child is the property of Mrs. So-and-so, of Such-and-such'* (I needn't bother to give you my mother's name and the name of our bungalow), *'the manicure-set, the comb and anything still left in the paper bags are the property of the child. Signed——'* It was signed with my father's name.

"The two dots I saw starting zigzag up the side of the down turned out to be two sweating policemen. What happened when they came to where I was was interesting at the moment but is not interesting now. They checked up on the message on the front of the car, then told me my father had telephoned to the police station, and that I was to be a good girl and come with them. When they had checked up on the cleaner, we all drove down. I remember the constable's knobbly, sticky red hands looked queer on the wheel where my father's had lately been

. . . At the police station, someone or other's wife made quite a fuss about me and gave me tea, then we piled into another car and drove on again. I was soon dead asleep; and I only woke when we stopped in the dark at the gate of the bungalow.

"Having tottered down the path, in the light from the front door, my mother clawed me out of the car, sobbing. I noticed her breath smelt unusual. We and the policeman then trooped into the lounge, where the policeman kept nodding and jotting things on a pad. To cheer up my mother he said that England was very small—'And he's not, so far as you know, in possession of a passport?' I sucked blobs of chocolate off the front of my frock while my mother described my father to the policeman. 'But no doubt,' the policeman said, 'he'll be thinking better of this. A man's home is a man's home, I always say.'

"When my mother and I were left alone in the lounge, we stared at each other in the electric light. While she asked if I knew how unnatural my father was, she kept pouring out a little more from the bottle: she said she had to have medicine to settle her nerves, but it seemed to act on her nerves just the opposite way. That I wouldn't say what my father had said and done set her off fairly raving against my father. To put it mildly, she lost all kind of control. She finished up with: 'And such a fool, too—a fool, a fool!'

" 'He is not a fool,' I said, 'he's my father.'

" 'He is not your father,' she screamed, 'and he is a fool.'

"That made me stare at her, and her stare at me.

" 'How do you mean,' I said, 'my father is not my father?'

"My mother's reaction to this was exactly like as if someone had suddenly pitched a pail of cold water over her. She pulled herself up and something jumped in her eyes. She said she had not said anything of the sort, and that if I ever said she had I was a wicked girl. I said I hadn't said she had, but she had said so. She put on a worried look and put a hand on my forehead and said she could feel I'd got a touch of the sun. A touch of the sun,

she said, would make me imagine things—and no wonder, after the day I'd had.

"All next day I was kept in bed; not as a punishment
but as a kind of treat. My mother was ever so nice to me;
she kept coming in to put a hand on my forehead. The
one thing she did not do was get the doctor. And afterwards, when I was let get up, nothing was good enough
for me; until really anyone would have thought that my
mother felt she was in my power. Shortly after, her rich
sister came down, and my mother then had a fine time,
crying, talking and crying; the sister then took us back
with her to London, where my mother talked and cried
even more. Of course I asked my aunt about what my
mother had said, but my aunt said that if I imagined such
wicked things they would have to think there was something wrong with my brain. So I did not re-open the subject, and am not doing so now. In the course of time my
mother succeeded in divorcing my father for desertion;
she was unable to marry her sister's friend because he was
married and apparently always had been, but she did
marry a friend of her sister's friend's, and was soon re-
spectably settled in Bermuda, where as far as I know she
still is."

"But your father?" he said.

"Well, what about my father?"

"You don't mean you never heard anything more of
him?"

"I never said so—he sent me two picture postcards.
The last"—she counted back—"arrived fourteen years
ago. But there probably have been others that went
astray. The way I've always lived, I'm not long at any
address."

He essayed, rashly, "Been a bit of a waif?"

The look he got back for this was halfway between
glass and ice. "A waif's the first thing I learned not to be.
No, more likely my father decided, better leave it at that.
People don't, on the whole, come back, and I've never
blamed them. No, why should he be dead? Why should
not he be—any place?"

"Here, for instance?"

"To-night, you mean?"

"Why not?" he said. "Why not—as you say?"

"Here?" She looked round the tables, as though she hardly knew where she was herself. She looked round the tables, over which smoke thickened, round which khaki melted into the khaki gloom. Then her eyes returned, to fix, with unsparing attention, an addled trio of men round the fifty-five mark. "Here?" she repeated, "my father?—I hope not."

"But I thought," he said, watching her watching the old buffers, "I thought we were looking for someone of twenty-six?"

"Give me a cigarette," she said, "and, also, don't be cruel."

"I wouldn't be," he said, as he lighted the cigarette, "if you had any feeling for me."

The Inherited Clock

"YES I can see you now," said Aunt Addie, "skipping
about the terrace at Sandyhill in your little scarlet high-
wayman coat. I think I had never seen you in such high
spirits. It was such a beautiful March day, hazy, but
warm and sunny, and Cousin Rosanna and your mother
and I were in the winter-garden with the door open. Each
time you came dancing down our end of the terrace you
would toss your curls and go dancing away again. Your
mother feared you were over-excited; I said, 'It's the
spring, perhaps,' but Cousin Rosanna said, 'Not at all: it's
the clock.' We three had come down for the day; Paul
was staying with her. I don't remember where *he* was at
the time: I'm afraid probably sulking somewhere about
the place."

"I remember my coat," said her niece Clara, "but I
don't remember the day. What has made you think of it?"

"As you know, I was at Sandyhill yesterday: they are
taking two more of Cousin Rosanna's servants, so she has
decided to close some more of the house, including that
little ante-room through to the library. She had been hesi-
tating whether to move the clock: before I left, after tea,
she had made up her mind not to—that might have meant
some unnecessary jolt or jar. 'How it is to travel to Clara's

ultimately,' she said, 'is not my affair. I am taking no risks with it during my own lifetime.'"

Clara, surprised, said: "Travel to me?"

"That will have to be thought of, of course, dear."

"But what clock are you talking about?"

Miss Detter began to say something, tripped up, glanced askance at her niece, then turned an unhappy red, as though Clara had said something irreligious. "Why, yours—the one she is leaving to you," she said. "You know she refers to that constantly, in your presence. That skeleton clock that you like so much. How can you look so blank? Cousin Rosanna would be quite hurt if she thought it meant as little as that to you. It was the discussion yesterday, whether or not to move it, that brought back that day when you wore—"

"My scarlet coat. Yes, but why?"

"As we watched you through the door of the winter-garden, Cousin Rosanna turned and said to your mother, 'I have been telling Clara that, ultimately, she is to have the clock.' Your mother, knowing what a part the clock had played in Rosanna's life, was much touched. There was a good deal of bustle, I remember, about getting us off to the train, it being discovered, just before we started, that you had hurt the poor little forefinger of your right hand. It was really rather a shocking sight: black and blue with several small ugly cuts. You were loyally mum about what had happened, but we all suspected that Master Paul had been up to some more cruel tricks. This, naturally, made you a little nervous in the train. So your mother, hoping to cheer you up, said 'So, Clara, when Cousin Rosanna goes to Heaven she is going to send you her lovely skeleton clock.' I don't know whether it was the idea of Cousin Rosanna going away to Heaven, or whether the word 'skeleton' frightened you, but you burst into tears and became almost hysterical. Not liking to see you cry in a railway carriage, I said, 'You know the reason Cousin Rosanna loves it? It has not stopped ticking for more than a hundred years!' But that only seemed to un-settle you still more."

"Well, if you say this happened, Aunt Addie, of course

it did," Clara said—with a somehow encaged and rebellious feeling. "I know I was six the winter I had that coat: I am thirty now—one cannot expect to remember everything."

"Yes, I remember you before you remember yourself," said Aunt Addie, looking at her affectionately. "Of course, I have always taken an interest in you—but then, you have always taken an interest in yourself. I don't mean that unkindly: why shouldn't you? You have an exceptional character."

"Only to you, I think."

"At least," Aunt Addie said, in a brisker tone, "you will make a point, won't you, next time you're at Sandyhill, of saying something enthusiastic about the clock? Let her see how much you are looking forward to it."

"Might that not seem—?"

"Why, Clara? You know Cousin Rosanna likes you and Paul to be perfectly natural about the money, and if about money why not about the clock, when she so much connects it with you in her own mind?"

There was, it was true, a singular lack of nonsense about Rosanna Detter's relations with her two young heirs. She had named them as such early on in their infancy, made a point of having them frequently at her house, and insisted that their expectations should be discussed and defined. The contents of her will had long ago been made known, and she proposed, she said, in ordinary fairness to make no changes in it without warning. Apart from bequests to charities, legacies to old servants and £5000 for Addie Detter (who had declared fervently this was much too much) Rosanna's fortune was to be divided equally between Paul Ardeen and Clara Detter, respectively son and daughter of two of her first cousins, and, thus, second cousins to one another. Clara lived, as a child, with her widowed mother in a small house in Ealing; Paul with his not prosperous doctor father on the outskirts of an industrial town: the two young people's surroundings, as well as their temperaments, could not fail to attach them to their auspicious future.

Meanwhile, Cousin Rosanna made them no allowances and few presents—though there were times when the watchful Clara suspected that Rosanna paid the more pressing of Paul's debts.

It gratified Cousin Rosanna, herself an only child, to watch these two high-spirited only children quarrel. Their co-heirship had not created a happy tie. Dark bullet-headed Paul, at once cool and bragging, and blonde fine-strung Clara, with her fairy-like affectations, seldom relaxed, during visits to Sandyhill, their resourceful campaign against one another. Cousin Rosanna, in packing them off to play (for she could tolerate neither for very long at a time) could assure herself that they were equally tough. The children worked on each other like two inde-structible pieces of sandpaper. It might have been thought that Rosanna, in selecting heirs near in age and of oppo-site sexes, entertained some romantic spinsterish project that they should marry, and that their declared hostility pleased her as being, admittedly, the first phase of love. This cannot have been so, for Paul's marriage, at twenty-two, was, by all showing, not adversely seen. It was Clara, surprisingly, who was piqued. She perceived, if Rosanna chose to ignore, a touch of Paul's usual insolence in the choice. The fortunate Edmée—blonde like Clara, but of how different a type—was to be recognized, at the first glance, as being just one more in the succession of fancies with whom Paul by habit went round town: nor did she show any reason why she should be the last. Sum-moned for the occasion to Sandyhill, Clara stood by at the presentation of the heavy-lidded bride. She was able to watch Paul fold, with expressionless satisfaction, prepar-atory to slipping into his wallet, Rosanna's five-hundred-pound cheque for the honeymoon.

It had been two years later, when she was twenty-one, that Clara met her fate in the person of Henry Harley; who, already a married man, was forced to tell her that he saw little prospect of changing his way of life. He was not well off; his wife had been irreproachable; the pay-ment of alimony would cripple him, and he was not dis-posed to let scandal prejudice his career. She chose to continue obstinate in her feeling, and in her hopes of things taking a better turn. Her poverty, to which one dared set no term, meanwhile made everything more difficult: the circumstances under which their affair was conducted constantly alarmed Henry and oppressed her. This had gone on now for nine years, and provided the reason why Clara at thirty was unmarried. As the years went by, she became increasingly grateful to Cousin Rosanna for either her resolute ignorance or her tolerance, and she had reproached herself, before the war started, for not going down more often to Sandyhill. Since the war, she was tied to exacting work; also, the closing of that coastal area interdicted visits from London—except, of course, on the plea of family business that could from time to time be produced. Cousin Rosanna's influence in her neighbourhood was more considerable than one ought, these days, to admit. The officially dangerous position of Sandyhill disqualified the house as a hospital or a repository for children; but also, so far no soldiers had been billeted there. And she had kept intact, until very lately, her staff of middle-aged servants.

Sandyhill itself was to go to Paul, who did not conceal his intention of selling it. It might do well, he expected, for a private asylum, when peace should bring back happier days. The house *had,* it is true, already in some ways the look of in institution, though of an expensive kind: it stood among pleasure-grounds dark with ilex, girt by a high flint wall. The avenue ran downhill between ramparts of evergreen, to debouch into the main street of an unassuming seaside resort. Sandyhill had been built by Rosanna's great-uncle, from whom (fairly late in her own life) she had inherited it, with substantial wealth: cleverly sheltered by trees from the sea winds, it faced south and enjoyed a good deal of sunshine. From the terrace, from the adjoining winter-garden and from the plate-glass windows upstairs and down, you also enjoyed, if this were your pleasure, a view of the Channel above the ilex groves. Indoors, the rooms were powerfully heated, brocade-papered, and so planned that you looked through an enfilade of pine-framed doorways. They composed a museum of discredited *objets d'art* which, up to now, had been always specklessly kept.

In one of the hollows about the grounds had been placed a small lake, sunless most of the day and over-looked by a kiosk. Into this lake had dropped, since Clara's last visit, what had so far been Sandyhill's only bomb; the blast had wrenched the shutters off the kiosk, and, by a freak of travel, obliterated the glass winter-garden projecting west of the house . . . This day of Clara's return, not long after the conversation with Aunt Addie, was an almost eerie extension of her aunt's mem-ory: it was in March, "hazy, but warm and sunny." Clara and Cousin Rosanna lunched in the morning-room. "As Addie no doubt will have told you, they've taken Preeps and Marchant, so I have closed the dining-room and the library." Nodding towards a door on her left hand, Cousin Rosanna added: "Therefore the house stops there."

"May I look, later?"

Cousin Rosanna stared. "By all means, if you are inter-ested in dust-sheets." Her eyes, always prominent, were to-day more so: about her face and her manner appeared the something you less at the time observe than after-wards recollect—*then,* you say you saw the beginning of the end. At sixty-five, the big woman was to be felt con-tracting, withdrawing from life with the same heavy in-difference with which she withdrew her life from room after room. Clara did notice that her dictatorial "ulti-matelys" were fewer. Though lunch was served with most of its old formality the dried-egg omelette was rubbery: the contempt with which Cousin Rosanna ate it had been, more, a contempt for her own palate, that with impunity one could now insult.

She now, by abruptly turning her chair to the fire, implied she had left the table: her guest could do as she liked. Clara, accordingly, rose and went frankly straight to the door where the house had been forced by war to stop. This led to the ante-room which, in its turn, led to the library. At once, she could hear a clock expectantly ticking. The ante-room french window was shuttered up: only cracks of light from the terrace fell on the shrouded sofa and on the sheet tucked bibwise over the bookcase on which the clock stood. The gleam of the glass of the dome inside which the ticking proceeded was just, but only just, to be seen.

"What are you up to in there?" called out Cousin Rosanna. "Looking at your clock?"

"I can't see it, yet."

"Well, you ought to know what it looks like, goodness knows!"

Clara did not reply. Her cousin, restless, repeated: "What are you doing *now*?"

"Opening a shutter—may I?"

"If you shut it again. You haven't got Preeps and Marchant to dance round clearing up after you now, you know."

The skeleton clock, in daylight, was threatening to a degree its oddness could not explain. Looking through the glass at its wheels, cogs, springs and tensions, and at its upraised striker, awaiting with a sensible quiver the finish of the hour that was in force, Clara tried to tell herself that it was, only, shocking to see the anatomy of time. The clock was without a face, its twelve numerals being welded on to a just visible wire ring. As she watched, the minute hand against its background of nothing made one, then another, spectral advance. This was enough: if she did not yet feel she could anticipate feeling her sanity being demolished, by one degree more, as every sixtieth second brought round this unheard click. Retreating, she looked round the walls of the ante-room: she saw the dark-patterned oblongs where the pictures had hung. She could remember which picture used to hang in each oblong; she remembered the names of the books in the bookcase under the sheet.

But as far as she knew she had not seen the clock before.

"None the worse, you see," vouchsafed Cousin Rosanna, as Clara returned to the morning-room.

"You mean," Clara said with an effort, "the same as ever?"

"No, I don't; I mean none the worse for the bomb. As

it stood up to that, it should see *you* out, we may hope. So you can take it for granted, as I have done, instead of rushing to look for it every time you come here." Cousin Rosanna, however, did not seem wholly displeased.

"Do I really?" said Clara, trying to smile this off.

"Unless you walk in your sleep, and sleep in daytime, in which case you had better go to the doctor.—Have you seen the winter-garden?"

"Not yet; I—"

"It isn't there.—By the way, you will have to see that that clock's attended to. I have had the same man, out from Southstone, to wind it for twenty-four years: he took on when that previous poor fellow—shocking affair that was!—And another thing: keep a careful eye on Paul, or he'll get his hands on it before you can say knife. However, you don't need me to tell you *that!*"

"No, no, of course not, Cousin Rosanna . . . He wants it so much," Clara added, as though musingly.

"For the reason we know," said Rosanna, with a protuberant meaning stare. "You know really, Clara, in view of all, you ought not to begrudge Paul that one bit of fun. Dear me, a cat would have laughed, and I must say I did. I can see you now—"

"I was wearing my scarlet coat?"

"Scarlet? Good heavens no; at least, I should hope not: you were fat to be wearing scarlet at fourteen. Not that, with you standing there with that glass thing over your head, one looked twice at whatever else you had on. However—'Now then, Paul,' I said, 'that's enough. She can't breathe in there: take it off her.'—However," concluded Cousin Rosanna, who for the first time to-day showed genuine pleasure, "easier said than done." Her mood changed; she looked at Clara with moody boredom. "Did you say you wanted to go for a turn?" she said. "Because if that's what you want you had better go."

Clara was fat no longer: that growing phase had been brief. To-day her step on the terrace, if more assertive, was not much heavier than it had been as a child's. Her height and her feverish fair good looks were set off by clothes that showed an expensive taste—taste that she could not fully indulge, yet. She glanced, without shock as without feeling, at the site of the winter-garden—here some exotic creepers had already perished against the exposed wall. Then she slanted downwards across the lawn, into one of the paths that entered the woods of ilex. These sombre pleasure-grounds, unchanging as might have been a photograph of themselves, were charged for her with a past that, though discontinuous, maintained a continuous atmosphere of its own. To these she had sometimes escaped; they had equally been the scene of those unescapable games with Paul. She could have thought she heard what war had suspended—still dead leaves being brushed from hard paths with stiff brooms. To each cut-out of a branch against the diluted sky attached some calculation or fear or unhopeful triumph. Every glade, every seat, every vista at the turn of a path only drew out the story. To be coming, for instance, into view of the lake, and of the kiosk reflected in its apathetic water, was to breathe the original horror of Paul's telling her that "they" kept the headless ladies locked up in there. He had looked in, he told her, between the slats of the shutters, but could not advise her to do the same. Now, with the shutters gone, she saw mildewed inside walls: as she stared at the kiosk, like someone performing an exercise, even lungfuls of horror seemed salutary. No, there was nothing, no single thing, in the history of Clara at Sandyhill that she could not remember.—Yet, was there?

With regard to no place other than Sandyhill could this opening and splitting wider of a crevasse in her memory have alarmed her more. At its deepness, she dared not attempt to guess; its extent, if it ever did stop, must simply wait to be seen.

That, as things turned out, was to be Clara's last visit to Sandyhill, except for the day of Cousin Rosanna's funeral. Neither Clara nor Paul received any deathbed summons: their cousin's loss of interest must have been so entire that she could not be bothered putting them through the last hoop. The funeral was correct but for one detail—Paul failed to be there. Stationed far up north, he had (his telegram told them) missed the necessary train. Clara returned to London that same evening, leaving Aunt Addie at Sandyhill to console the servants and to receive Paul whenever he should arrive. A week later, fairly late in the evening, Aunt Addie came staggering into Clara's St. John's Wood flat with the clock embraced inside her exhausted arms. It was not packed—in a packing-case it might have got knocked about, in which case it might have stopped. As it was, it had gone on ticking, and had struck twice in the train, to the interest of everyone, and once again in the lift, coming up here to Clara's flat.

"I took the precaution of travelling first class," Aunt Addie said. "I knew you would want to have it as soon as possible. Look, I am putting it *here*, for the time being" —(that meant, the only table the size of the room allowed)—"but when I get my breath back, we'll put it where you intend. You must often have seen it here, in your mind's eye.—Not, I hope, on anything it could fall off?"

"In that case, I can only think of the floor."

"Oh," said Aunt Addie, preoccupied, "I seem to have left fingerprints on the dome." She breathed on the glass and began to polish them off. "Naturally, you have had a good deal to think about. In fact, I should not be surprised if this changed the course of your life."

"A clock—how could it?" said Clara wildly.

"No, I was referring to Cousin Rosanna's death, dear. I could already see some little changes in Paul."

". . . By the way, did Paul say anything when you took the clock?"

"Er, no," said Aunt Addie, colouring faintly. "He was not about, as it happened; he was so busy."

Clara's life, ever since she had been told of the will (which was practically as far back as she could remember) had, of course, hinged on the prospect of this immense change. Not unreasonably, she expected everything to go better. She perceived that her nature was of the kind that is only able to flower in clement air: either wealth or reciprocal love, ideally both, was necessary. To begin with, she intended to buy herself surroundings that suited her, that would set her off. But chiefly, as her obsessive love for Henry became, in the course of nine years, the centre of everything, she had quite simply looked to her coming money for the one consummation of this, marriage. The humiliating uncertainties of their relationship, and, still more, the thought of him living there with his wife, were more of a torment than she had dared to allow. Humble about herself with regard to him, and humbly bare of illusions regarding Henry, she believed that her, Clara's, coming into her money would be the one thing needed to make him break with his wife. Should his career show damage from the divorce proceedings, he could afford to abandon it: she could compensate him. She could buy open some other door for his ambition. As for love—so far Henry had only loved her, as you might say, on trust. She had yet to gain him wholly by showing what she could, in the whole, be. Now she could feel the current of her nature stirring strongly under the thinning ice. Had it been the strength of the current that thinned the ice? Or had the ice had to be thinned by the breath of financial summer before the current, however strong, could be felt?

When Aunt Addie had gone, Clara tried again to realize all that was now, since last week, within her reach. She went across to the mirror and stood and stared at herself imperiously. But the current, without warning, ceased to be felt: no kind of exultation was possible. The newly-arrived clock, chopping off each second to fall and perish, recalled how many seconds had gone to make up her years, how many of these had been either null or bitter, how many had been void before the void claimed them. She had been subject to waiting as to an illness; the tissues of her being had been consumed by it. Was it impossible that the past should be able to injure the future irreparably? Turning away from the mirror, she made herself face the clock; she looked through into the nothing behind its hands. Turning away from the clock, she went to the telephone.

Henry's reply, at the same time cautious and social, warned her that, as so often at this hour, he was not alone.

—All the same: "What do you think? My clock has arrived," she said. "Aunt Addie has just brought it, from Sandyhill."

"Indeed. Which is that?"

"Which clock? Surely you know, Henry. The one I must have so often told you about . . . Didn't I? Well, it's with me now, in this room. Can you hear it ticking?"

"No, I'm afraid not."

She got up, pulling the telephone with her as far as the cord would go, then stretched the receiver at arm's length towards the glass dome. After some seconds she went on: "You heard it *that* time? I like to think we are hearing the same thing. They say it has never stopped for more than a hundred years: don't you think it sounds like that? Cousin Rosanna insisted I was to have this clock."

"Thrown in," Henry said, "with the pound of tea." But his voice, besides being ironical, was distrait: all the time, he was thinking up some story that could account for his end of the conversation, and was being careful to make, in his wife's hearing, no remark that would not fit in with that.

"Yes," said Clara, quivering, "with, with my pound of tea. Do you think that could mean she did really care for me? I wish I could think so. There is something frightening about the death of someone who always kept one so near her, without love. Still, there it is: she's dead. And because of that—Henry, tell me again that you're glad?"

"Of course."

"For both our sakes—yours and mine?"

"Of course . . . Well, this has been nice, but I fear I must say good night. We were thinking of listening to the European news."

"Stop, wait, don't go for a minute! I can't bear this clock! I dread it; I can't stay with it in the room! What am I to do this evening? Where can I go?"

"I'm afraid I can't think, really."

"There's no *possible* chance you . . . ?"

"No, I'm afraid not."

"But you do love me?"

"Of course."

So Clara, to stop herself thinking, rang up two or three friends, but not one of them answered: their telephones went on ringing. Therefore she put on her overcoat, found her torch, dropped down in the lift and went for a walk in the black-out. It was late enough for the streets to be almost empty. Clara, walking at high speed into the solid darkness, was surprised all over her body to feel no impact: she seemed to pass like a ghost through an endless wall. No segment of moon peered at her, no stars guided. Brought to a halt for breath, she began to spy with her torch at the things round her—a post-box, a corner with no railing, the white plate of a street-name. Nothing told her anything, except one thing—unless she had lost her memory, she had lost her way. She dived into a wardens' post to ask where this was, or where she was, and in the glare in there they all stared at her. "Where did you want to get back to?" someone said, and for either a second or an eternity she fancied she might be unable to tell him . . . When Clara once again found herself at the portico of the block of flats where she lived, to-morrow had begun to curdle the sky. Having hesitated with her key in her own door she let herself in and went quickly through to her bedroom. But the wall between herself and the clock was thin. Getting up, lying down, getting up, she continued, until her telephone called her, her search for the earplugs that Aunt Addie had given her when first the raids began.

When Aunt Addie rang up, two mornings later, it was to announce that, after a search of London, she *had* succeeded in finding an old man to wind the clock. "I knew you'd be anxious; I know I was! Providentially, however, I am in time."

"In time for what?"

"For the day it is always wound. So you will know when to expect the man," said Aunt Addie.

Therefore Clara, who started for work at cock-crow, not to return till some time on in the evening, told the porter to admit, on whichever day he should come, an old man to wind the clock in her flat. The day must have

been Friday, for that evening she came home to find a
door ajar. There was somebody, besides the clock, in possession—this turned out to be Paul. Having arranged the
black-out and turned the lights on, he was comfortably
sitting on her sofa, smoking one of his superior cigarettes.
He was, of course, in khaki. "Really, what hours you
keep!" he said. "However, I've had my dinner. I trust you
have?" At this point, as though recollecting himself, Paul
sprang up and smote Clara matily on the shoulder. He
then stood back to inspect her. "Radiant—and can one
wonder?" he added. "By the way, I was sorry to miss you
the other day. I hope I wasn't missed?"

"At the funeral? Everyone thought that looked pretty
queer, and Cousin Rosanna, of course, would have been
furious."

"If so, most unfairly. I missed my train that morning
because I had made a night of it, and I made a night of it
because I felt like hell. You might not think so, and I was
surprised myself. After all, she had never wanted anything."

"Never wanted us to love her?"

"Well, if you put it that way—never gave us a chance.
However, I snapped out of that. I feel fine now."

"How nice . . . How is Edmée?"

"I thought her looking wonderfully herself. And how
is Henry? As nice as ever?"

Clara said frigidly: "How did you get in?"

"A civil old burglar, or somebody, let me in. He said
nothing to me, so I said nothing to him. He put the glass
back on the clock and went away quietly, so I decided
to wait."

Paul, whose way of standing about was characteristic,
did not seem disposed to sit down again. Having flicked
ash into a shell not meant for an ashtray, he remained
with his back to the mantelpiece, fixing on nothing particular his tolerant, narrow-eyed, level look. His uniform
fitted and suited him just a degree too well, and gave him
the air of being on excellent terms with war. He had thickened slightly: otherwise, little change appeared in the
dark bullet-head, rather Mongolian features and compact,

tactile hands that had made him by turns agreeably disagreeable and disagreeably agreeable as a little boy. "Tick-
tock, tick-tock," he said, out of the blue. "Sounds louder
than ever, in here; though as nice as ever, of course. You
don't think it's a little large for the room?"

"I shall be moving soon, I expect," said Clara, who had
not only sat down but put her feet up on her sofa, to show
that Paul's presence affected her in no sort of way.

"Oh, shall you really? How right." Paul glanced down
at the toe of one shoe, lifted his eyebrows and went on:
"This isn't, of course, a point I should ever bother to
raise, but you do of course realize that nothing should
have left Sandyhill until the valuation had been made for
probate?"

"I don't suppose Aunt Addie understood that. You
could always have stopped her!"

"On the contrary: the devoted creature nipped off to
the train with the clock while my back was turned. When
I thought of your face at this end, I must say I had to
smile."

"Really," said Clara touchily, "why?"

Paul not only looked at his cousin but, somehow, gave
the impression that only indolence kept him from looking harder. "It is just as well, as we both see now," he
observed, "that the point of that joke *is* known only to
you and me. That you have never enjoyed it seems unfair. Still, I suppose it is partly in view of that that I've
come round this evening to do the handsome thing—"

"Yes, I wondered what you had come about."

"I make you an offer, Clara. I'll buy you out of the
clock. Cash down—as soon as I touch the cash."

Clara, not so much as raising her eyes from her rather
too delicate ringless hands, said: "Cousin Rosanna warned
me this might happen."

"What you mean—and how stupid of me, and how
right you are—is that cash is no longer an object with
you, either? Look, I'll go one better: I'll take the clock
away for nothing. And better still, I'll take it away to-
night."

Clara went rigid immediately: her cheeks flamed and

her voice shot into the particular note for so long familiar to her and Paul.

"Why should you take it simply because you want it?"

"Why should you keep it when you don't want it, simply because I do?" Even Paul's imperturbability showed, as of old, a crack. "Well, we both know why—and better leave it at that. All the same, Clara, have some sense. It's one thing to cut your nose off to spite my face. But is it really worth going crackers?"

"Crackers—what do you mean?"

"Well, look at yourself in the glass."

The mirror being exactly opposite the sofa, Clara had looked before she could stop herself. As quickly, she said: "I don't see anything wrong. And didn't you say I was looking radiant?"

"Because, frankly, my one thought was, 'We must keep her calm.'" Paul, having ground out his cigarette with an air at once resigned and concerned, came to sit down on the sofa beside Clara. He pushed her feet off gently to make room for himself. Leaning a little towards her, he placed one hand, like a hostage, or like an invitation to read his entire motive, palm upwards on the brocade between them. His nearness enveloped Clara in a sense of complicity, frightening because it was acutely familiar, more frightening because she could not guess at its source. While his eyes expressed no more than good-natured fondness, and his manner regretful conciliation, both conveyed a threat for which no memory could account. "I hate," he said, "to see you all shot up. Doesn't Henry?"

"Why should he? I haven't asked him."

Her cousin, at once quickly and darkly, said: "Possibly better not. I'm all, if we can, for keeping this in the family."

"The clock?"

"No, I mean its effect on you. When you think it's only three days since Aunt Addie imported it.—And to think how well she meant, the old dear!"

Rearing up among the cushions at her end of the sofa, Clara exclaimed: "You think that will work? Cousin

Rosanna intended the clock for me. So this is just one thing you must do without. I would sooner drop it out of the window. . . ."

"I am sure you would," said Paul. "In fact, I expect you've tried?"

He was right. Once in the small hours of a sleepless night, once on the occasion of an unnerving return home, that solution had already offered itself. Clara had turned the lights out, opened her eighth-floor window, found her way to the clock by the noise it made in the dark and gone so far as to balance it on the window-sill. In her finger-tips, as they supported it, could be felt its confident vibration—through the dome, through the stand projecting some inches into the night. She had awaited in vain some infinitesimal check, some involuntary metallic shudder with which the clock should anticipate its last second, the first it would not consume for a hundred years. Annihilation waited—the concrete roadway under the block of flats. By the concrete roadway the clock would be struck, not to strike again. Towards the dawn of the coming unthreatened day, some early goer to work would halt, step back and bend his torch on the cogs, uncoiled springs and incomprehensible splinters that had startled him by crunching under his boot.—But, suppose not. Suppose gravity failed? Or suppose the tick stayed up here without the clock, or the nothing that had shown through its skeleton form continued to bear its skeleton shadow? If what she purposed to do could *be* done, how was it it had never been done before? . . . Clara, quailing, hoped that she only did so before the conventionality of her own nature. She was not the woman, it seemed (if there were indeed such a woman) who could drop a clock from the window of a St. John's Wood flat. The chance of somebody passing at the decisive second, the immediate alarm to be raised by what would sound like a bomb, the likelihood of the affair being traced to her, the attention already drawn to the clock by its sentimental arrival with Aunt Addie and her own talk about it with the flats porter—all these Clara, too gladly, let weigh with her.

She reprieved not so much the clock as her own will. She had returned the clock to its place on the table— twice.

"However," Paul said, "if that's how you feel . . . I let you see that I want it—apparently, that's enough." He shrugged his shoulders, and slowly withdrew his hand: the interlude of frankness could be taken as over. Getting up, he strolled across to the clock, and, taking up his stand between it and Clara, could be felt to hold communication with it. Intently stooping, he squinted into its works. "Yes," he said remotely, "I am stuck on this clock. Always have been, and I suppose always shall."

"Why?"

"Why should there be any why?" said Paul, without turning round. "I am simply stuck on this clock. One is bound to be stuck on something: what is wrong with a clock? *Your* trouble seems to be that you are stuck on the past."

Clara, eyes indecisively on Paul's khaki back, licked her lips once or twice before she actually spoke. Then she cried: "Have you *no* idea that I've no idea what you mean? Or Cousin Rosanna, or Aunt Addie either? Unless you three are combining to send me mad, someone had better tell me what this is all about. As far as I know, the first time I saw that clock was the last day I spent with Rosanna at Sandyhill. I detest it, and should be glad if you'd tell me why. Every time I am told I remember something I don't remember, it turns out to be something about that clock; and there's such high feeling about it I don't know which way to turn.—Did you, for instance, once put the clock-glass over my head, and did I get stuck inside it?"

This engaged Paul's attention: he turned round slowly, gained time by soundlessly whistling, then said: "You're not serious?" He considered her. "But what a thing to forget! We damn' nearly chipped your face off. Besides, that came quite late on."

"But, late on in what?"

"In our story. If you'll tell me how much you've for-

gotten, I'll tell you where we begin. If you *have* forgotten, you must have some rather too good reason—in which case, don't I err in bringing the whole thing up?
. . . Very well. Yes, I popped that thing over your head because it was time to stop you, and I thought that might do it. Stop you what? Stop you blackmailing me. We were by then no longer in the Garden of Eden, and I observed Rosanna showing the red light."—At this point, Paul gave Clara a final suspicious look: what he saw appeared to convince him, for he went on: "Since the day we did that with the clock you had almost never let up. It was, 'Oh, Paul, I feel so wicked; we've been so wicked; I have simply got to confess to Cousin Rosanna!' Then, 'Very well, kiss me, then perhaps I'll feel better, then perhaps I won't have to tell Cousin Rosanna *this* time.' And this year in, year out, my sweet, every holiday you and I were at Sandyhill. Castor oil got to be lovely compared to your upturned face. Your particular *mise en scène* was the ante-room: you used to put your ear to the clock glass and say, 'You know, it *still* doesn't sound the same.' That meant you're feeling bad and my having to come across. To make things more interesting, one could never be certain that Rosanna might not pop in at one or the other door, not to speak of her passing the terrace window. You and me on such close terms (she wasn't to know the reason) and, of all places, right there by her precious clock—that *would* have finally torn it, for you and me."

"You don't mean, she'd have cut us out of the will?"

"Well, Clara, ask yourself—would she not? Given, I mean, that peculiar obsession *she* had."

"If Rosanna had an obsession, I don't remember that, either." She attempted a wintry smile, and added: "This seems to be like a whole continent that's submerged, you know."

"Poetic idea," Paul conceded, with a glance to the left of his cousin's ear. "To return to Cousin Rosanna—you know how when you are waiting you have to look back and back again at the clock? Now our friend, as it happened, had been Rosanna's from girlhood, so it was this clock she connected with her particular habit—a habit she'd had every reason to form. There was nothing Rosanna did not know about waiting. Great-uncle, from whom she got Sandyhill and the money, did not quit the stage till she was well on in life. Therefore Rosanna waited, throughout what are called one's best years—not only for money, exactly like you and me, but for a young man, like, if I may say so, you. The young man—not a nice character, unlike Henry—wasn't moving till Rosanna could declare the bank open. Great-uncle, unfriendly to romance, lived just too long: by the time the money came to Rosanna the man had lost heart and married somebody else. And in those days, if you remember, that was considered final. So Rosanna, like the great girl she was, in her way, cut her losses in the romance direction and went all out to make the money her big thing. She felt free, all things considered, to buy what she liked with it; she jingled her new purse and looked around for her fun. You and I were her fun. Can't you see how the thing worked out? The younger the heirs you name, the longer they have to wait, and the more the waiting can do to them. Again, *she'd* expected both love and money, and got money only: can you blame her if she was damned if she'd contemplate you and me, or you or me, having both? So my marriage—than which I'm sure there are many worse—and your, er, stalemate with regard to Henry, suited her book ideally—couldn't have suited better. As for you and me, biting bits out of each other all over Sandyhill—how her dear old good face used to light up! The better we loathed each other, the better she liked us. But then came what looked like our interlude—that *that* was no more than a new and more subtle manifestation of mutual hate was, I suppose unavoidably, lost on her. Therefore that, as I tell you, did damn' nearly cook our goose."

"How ironical," supplied Clara, "that would have been, we well know.—All the same, what made her so set on my having to have the clock?"

"I can only think, because you were a fellow-woman. It was Rosanna's way of saying, 'Over to you!' "

"But, so equally set on the clock never being yours?"

"*That* couldn't be clearer. I'd more than shown that I liked it; I'd asked her for it point-blank. I was a man, so she liked my going without. Yes, I did get those cheques, I know—as you also noted. She liked me to make a fool of myself *qua* man. I wanted the clock, so you were to have it—could the mental process be more straightforward? . . . Yes, I tell you, I asked for it. I was a fool, at nine, and that clock was the only thing in that god-awful house I liked. So I piped up. That was the day our bit of trouble began.

"It was one of those typical headachy Sandyhill March mornings—house heated to bursting-point and a livery sun outdoors. A family gathering was in progress—you and your aunt and your mother had come down for the day. I mouldered off by myself, as I frequently did do, to watch the old clock at its cheering work. Rosanna came in and said, 'You like that, don't you?' to which I said, 'Yes, I should like to have it.' To which she said, 'Yes, I daresay you would.' At which point you came prancing into the room. I suppose you were about six, and your mother had got you up in a perfectly sickening little scarlet coat, like a monkey wears on a barrel-organ. The moment was jam for Rosanna; she turned to you and she said, 'Clara, one day I intend *you* to have that clock. Do you know it has never stopped, and it never will?' You registered pleasure, and I went off down the woods.—*None* of this comes back?"

"Nothing," said Clara firmly—with growing fear.

"So that really you don't remember my catching you, later on, in the ante-room, you having glided back for a private gloat at your clock? Or what I said, or we did, or what happened then?"

"No, *no*. Why? What do you mean? Paul, you're simply making me worse.—And what are you *doing*? Leave that alone: *it's mine!*"

"That's just why I'm asking you to step over here,"

said Paul, who was lifting the dome with becoming care, to place it on the table beside the clock. "Why? To make an experiment. Let's face it. Either this works—which it may not—or I take you by hand to-morrow to a psychiatrist. Blood is thicker than water, after all. Come on—I can't wait all night; I have got a date."

Hooking his arm round Clara's reluctant waist, Paul approached his cousin relentlessly to the clock. After four or five seconds of this enforced staring into the diligent works, Clara began to relax—was she hypnotized? In the absolute nothing behind the clock's anatomy there appeared and began to dilute, like colour dropped into water, the red of the Sandyhill ante-room wallpaper: meanwhile, there crept on another sense the smell of pitched pine exasperated by heating. There could be felt the stare of a draped and open door-window, in which, from moment to moment, somebody might appear. The murmur of voices out of the winter-garden hung on the hazy terrace behind Paul's voice.

"*I'll tell you something, Clara. Have you ever* SEEN *a minute? Have you actually had one wriggling inside your hand? Did you know, if you keep your finger inside a clock for a minute, you can pick out that very minute and take it home for your own?*" So it is Paul who stealthily lifts the dome off. It is Paul who selects the finger of Clara's that is to be guided, shrinking, then forced wincing into the works, to be wedged in them, bruised in them, bitten into and eaten up by the cogs. "*No, you have got to keep it there, or you will lose the minute. I am doing the counting—the counting up to sixty.*" . . . But there is to be no sixty. The ticking stops.

We have stopped the clock.

The hundred years are all angry. "*Stop crying, idiot: that won't start it again!*" . . . But oh, oh but, it won't let my finger go! . . . O-o-h! . . . "*Suck it, be quiet, don't make a noise!*". . . What have you made me do? "*You wanted to.*" You made me want to . . . What shall we, what shall we, what shall we do, do, *do?* . . . "*You go out and skip about on the terrace, make them keep on watching you, then they won't come in."* But what will you do? *"Something."* But it's stopped ticking! . . . *"I tell you, go out and skip about on the terrace."*

For the second time, Paul withdrew Clara's finger, with a painful jerk, from the clock which had stopped ticking. Her finger was bitten, but not so badly: it had grown too big to go in so deep this time. He was, meanwhile, going on smoothly: "We were in luck that Friday —because it *was* a Friday, of course. All I did was put the glass back and walk away. But half an hour later, the regular chap from Southstone turned up to wind it. With a mouth that butter couldn't possibly melt in, I tailed him into the ante-room, just to see. The clock stopped and that half-hour missing made even him turn pale. He sent me to find Rosanna. I was unable to. I came back to watch him put through a long and amazing job. The ladies were upstairs, tying up your finger. By the time he had got the clock set and going, he found he had run things fine for his bus home. He decided, therefore, as Rosanna was missing, not to report the occurrence till the following week. Owing to hurry or worry, the poor brute, he shot out of Sandyhill gate and across the main street in time to be flattened out by a bus coming the other way. Any evidence perished with him: Rosanna was spared the knowledge. In gratitude, you and I subscribed sixpence each towards the funeral wreath. But of course you would never remember *that?*"

"I remember giving the sixpence for the wreath," said Clara slowly, not looking up from her finger.

"But only that?"

"No, *not* only that—thank you, Paul." There ensued an unavoidable pause, at the end of which Clara said: "I expect you would like to go now? I think I heard you say you had got a date?"

"Nothing need stand, my dear, if you'd rather not be alone?"

"Thank you very much; I, I shall sit with my memories. I expect to spend some time getting to know them." Turning away, with all the detachment possible, she occupied herself in emptying Paul's ash from the shell into a more suitable tray. "Oh, by the way, Paul," she added, "do by all means have the clock. Aunt Addie ought to have known that you wanted it. And, apart from any sentiment of Rosanna's, it means nothing to me. Won't you take it along now?"

"Thanks, that is nice of you, Clara," said Paul promptly. "Actually, under the circumstances, I could not very easily take it along this evening; and in fact I have nowhere to put it for the duration. Could you keep it for me, or would it be in your way?"

"There is no reason why it should be in my way; as I say, I expect to move to a larger flat. It is not very useful at present to tell the time by, but apart from that I should never know it was there."

Sunday Afternoon

"*SO HERE* you are!" exclaimed Mrs. Vesey to the new-comer who joined the group on the lawn. She reposed for an instant her light, dry fingers on his. "Henry has come from London," she added. Acquiescent smiles from the others round her showed that the fact was already known —she was no more than indicating to Henry the role that he was to play. "What are your experiences?—Please tell us. But nothing dreadful: we are already feeling a little sad."

"I am sorry to hear that," said Henry Russel, with the air of one not anxious to speak of his own affairs. Draw-ing a cane chair into the circle, he looked from face to face with concern. His look travelled on to the screen of lilac, whose dark purple, pink-silver, and white plumes sprayed out in the brilliance of the afternoon. The late May Sunday blazed, but was not warm: something less than a wind, a breath of coldness, fretted the edge of things. Where the lilac barrier ended, across the sun-polished meadows, the Dublin mountains continued to trace their hazy, to-day almost colourless line. The cold-ness had been admitted by none of the seven or eight people who, in degrees of elderly beauty, sat here full in the sun, at this sheltered edge of the lawn: they con-tinued to master the coldness, or to deny it, as though with each it were some secret *malaise*. An air of fastidious, stylized melancholy, an air of being secluded behind glass, characterized for Henry these old friends in whose shadow he had grown up. To their pleasure at having him back among them was added, he felt, a taboo or warning—he was to tell a little, but not much. He could feel with a shock, as he sat down, how insensibly he had deserted, these last years, the æsthetic of living that he had got from them. As things were, he felt over him their suspended charm. The democratic smell of the Dublin bus, on which he had made the outward journey to join them, had evaporated from his person by the time he was halfway up Mrs. Vesey's chestnut avenue. Her house, with its fanlights and tall windows, was a villa in the Italian sense, just near enough to the city to make the country's sweetness particularly acute. Now, the sensations of wartime, that locked his inside being, began as surely to be dispelled—in the influence of this eternalized Sunday afternoon.

"Sad?" he said, "that is quite wrong."

"These days, our lives seem unreal," said Mrs. Vesey— with eyes that penetrated his point of view. "But, worse than that, this afternoon we discover that we all have friends who have died."

"Lately?" said Henry, tapping his fingers together.

"Yes, in all cases," said Ronald Cuffe—with just enough dryness to show how much the subject had been beginning to tire him. "Come, Henry, we look to you for distraction. To us, these days, you are quite a figure. In fact, from all we have heard of London, it is something that you should be alive. Are things there as shocking as they say—or are they more shocking?" he went on, with distaste.

"Henry's not sure," said someone, "he looks pontifical."

Henry, in fact, was just beginning to twiddle this faroff word "shocking" round in his mind, when a diversion caused some turning of heads. A young girl stepped out of a window and began to come their way across the lawn. She was Maria, Mrs. Vesey's niece. A rug hung over her bare arm: she spread out the rug and sat down at her aunt's feet. With folded arms, and her fingers on her thin pointed elbows, she immediately fixed her eyes on Henry Russel. "Good afternoon," she said to him, in a mocking but somehow intimate tone.

The girl, like some young difficult pet animal, seemed in a way to belong to everyone there. Miss Ria Store, the patroness of the arts, who had restlessly been refolding her fur cape, said: "And where have *you* been, Maria?"

"Indoors."

Someone said, "On this beautiful afternoon?"

"Is it?" said Maria, frowning impatiently at the grass.

"Instinct," said the retired judge, "now tells Maria it's time for tea."

"No, this does," said Maria, nonchalantly showing her wrist with the watch on it. "It keeps good time, thank you, Sir Isaac." She returned her eyes to Henry. "What have you been saying?"

"You interrupted Henry. He had been just going to speak."

"*Is* it so frightening?" Maria said.

"The bombing?" said Henry. "Yes. But as it does not connect with the rest of life, it is difficult, you know, to know what one feels. One's feelings seem to have no language for anything so preposterous. As for thoughts—"

"At that rate," said Maria, with a touch of contempt, "your thoughts would not be interesting."

"Maria," said somebody, "that is no way to persuade Henry to talk."

"About what is important," announced Maria, "it seems that no one can tell one anything. There is really nothing, till one knows it oneself."

"Henry is probably right," said Ronald Cuffe, "in considering that this—this outrage is *not* important. There is no place for it in human experience; it apparently cannot make a place of its own. It will have no literature."

"Literature!" said Maria. "One can see, Mr. Cuffe, that *you* have always been safe!"

"Maria," said Mrs. Vesey, "you're rather pert."

Sir Isaac said, "What does Maria expect to know?"

Maria pulled off a blade of grass and bit it. Something

calculating and passionate appeared in her; she seemed to be crouched up inside herself. She said to Henry sharply: "But you'll go back, of course?"

"To London? Yes—this is only my holiday. Anyhow, one cannot stay long away."

Immediately he had spoken Henry realized how subtly this offended his old friends. Their position was, he saw, more difficult than his own, and he could not have said a more cruel thing. Mrs. Vesey, with her adept smile that was never entirely heartless, said: "Then we must hope your time here will be pleasant. Is it so very short?"

"And be careful, Henry," said Ria Store, "or you will find Maria stowed away in your baggage. And there would be an embarrassment, at an English port! We can feel her planning to leave us at any time."

Henry said, rather flatly: "Why should not Maria travel in the ordinary way?"

"Why should Maria travel at all? There is only one journey now—into danger. We cannot feel that that is necessary for her."

Sir Isaac added: "We fear, however, that that is the journey Maria wishes to make."

Maria, curled on the lawn with the nonchalance of a feline creature, through this kept her eyes cast down. Another cold puff came through the lilac, soundlessly knocking the blooms together. One woman, taken quite unawares, shivered—then changed this into a laugh. There was an aside about love from Miss Store, who spoke with a cold, abstracted knowledge—"Maria has no experience, none whatever; she hopes to meet heroes—she meets none. So now she hopes to find heroes across the sea. Why, Henry, she might make a hero of you."

"It is not that," said Maria, who had heard. Mrs. Vesey bent down and touched her shoulder; she sent the girl into the house to see if tea were ready. Presently they all rose and followed—in twos and threes, heads either erect composedly or else deliberately bowed in thought. Henry knew the idea of summer had been relinquished: they would not return to the lawn again. In the dining-room— where the white walls and the glass of the pictures held the reflections of summers—burned the log fire they were so glad to see. With her shoulder against the mantelpiece stood Maria, watching them take their places at the round table. Everything Henry had heard said had fallen off her —in these few minutes all by herself she had started in again on a fresh phase of living that was intact and pure. So much so, that Henry felt the ruthlessness of her disregard for the past, even the past of a few minutes ago. She came forward and put her hands on two chairs—to show she had been keeping a place for him.

Lady Ottery, leaning across the table, said: "I must ask you—we heard you had lost everything. But that cannot be true?"

Henry said, unwillingly: "It's true that I lost my flat, and everything in my flat."

"*Henry,*" said Mrs. Vesey, "all your beautiful things?"

"Oh dear," said Lady Ottery, overpowered, "I thought that could not be possible. I ought not to have asked."

Ria Store looked at Henry critically. "You take this too calmly. What has happened to you?"

"It was some time ago. And it happens to many people."

"But not to everyone," said Miss Store. "I should see no reason, for instance, why it should happen to me."

"One cannot help looking at you," said Sir Isaac. "You must forgive our amazement. But there was a time, Henry, when I think we all used to feel that we knew you well. If this is not a painful question, at this juncture, why did you not send your valuables out of town? You could have even shipped them over to us."

"I was attached to them. I wanted to live with them."

"And now," said Miss Store, "you live with nothing, for ever. Can you really feel that that is life?"

"I do. I may be easily pleased. It was by chance I was out when the place was hit. You may feel—and I honour your point of view—that I should have preferred, at my age, to go into eternity with some pieces of glass and jade and a dozen pictures. But, in fact, I am very glad to remain. To exist."

"On what level?"

"On any level."

"Come, Henry," said Ronald Cuffe, "that is a cynicism one cannot like in you. You speak of your age: to us, of course that is nothing. You are at your maturity."

"Forty-three."

Maria gave Henry an askance look, as though, after all, he were not a friend. But she then said: "Why should he wish he was dead?" Her gesture upset some tea on the lace cloth, and she idly rubbed it up with her handkerchief. The tug her rubbing gave to the cloth shook a petal from a Chinese peony in the centre bowl on to a plate of cucumber sandwiches. This little bit of destruction was watched by the older people with fascination, with a kind of appeasement, as though it were a guarantee against something worse.

"Henry is not young and savage, like you are. Henry's life is—or was—an affair of attachments," said Ria Store. She turned her eyes, under their lids, on Henry. "I wonder how much of you *has* been blown to blazes."

"I have no way of knowing," he said. "Perhaps you have?"

"Chocolate cake?" said Maria.

"Please."

For chocolate layer cake, the Vesey cook had been famous since Henry was a boy of seven or eight. The look, then the taste, of the brown segment linked him with Sunday afternoons when he had been brought here by his mother; then, with a phase of his adolescence when he had been unable to eat, but only to look round. Mrs. Vesey's beauty, at that time approaching its last lunar quarter, had swum on him when he was about nineteen. In Maria, child of her brother's late marriage, he now saw that beauty, or sort of physical genius, at the start. In Maria, this was without hesitation, without the halting influence that had bound Mrs. Vesey up—yes, and bound Henry up, from his boyhood, with her—in a circle of quizzical half-smiles. In revenge, he accused the young girl who moved him—who seemed framed, by some sort of anticipation, for the new catastrophic *outward* order of life—of brutality, of being without spirit. At his age, between two generations, he felt cast out. He felt Mrs. Vesey might not forgive him for having left her for a world at war.

Mrs. Vesey blew out the blue flame under the kettle, and let the silver trapdoor down with a snap. She then gave exactly one of those smiles—at the same time, it was the smile of his mother's friend. Ronald Cuffe picked the petal from the sandwiches and rolled it between his fingers, waiting for her to speak.

"It is cold, *indoors*," said Mrs. Vesey. "Maria, put another log on the fire.—Ria, you say the most unfortunate things. We must remember Henry has had a shock. —Henry, let us talk about something better. You work in an office, then, since the war?"

"In a Ministry—in an office, yes."

"Very hard?—Maria, that is all you would do if you went to England: work in an office. This is not like a war in history, you know."

Maria said: "It is not in history yet." She licked round her lips for the rest of the chocolate taste, then pushed her chair a little back from the table. She looked secretively at her wrist-watch. Henry wondered what the importance of time could be.

He learned what the importance of time was when, on his way down the avenue to the bus, he found Maria between two chestnut trees. She slanted up to him and put her hand on the inside of his elbow. Faded dark-pink stamen from the flowers above them had moulted down on to her hair. "You have ten minutes more, really," she said. "They sent you off ten minutes before your time. They are frightened someone would miss the bus and come back; then everything would have to begin again. As it is always the same, you would not think it would be so difficult for my aunt."

"Don't talk like that; it's unfeeling; I don't like it," said Henry, stiffening his elbow inside Maria's grasp.

"Very well, then: walk to the gate, then back. I shall be able to hear your bus coming. It's true what they said —I'm intending to go away. They will have to make up something without me."

"Maria, I can't like you. Everything you say is destructive and horrible."

"Destructive?—I thought you didn't mind."

"I still want the past."

"Then how weak you are," said Maria. "At tea I admired you. The past—things done over and over again with more trouble than they were ever worth?—However, there's no time to talk about that. Listen, Henry: I must have your address. I suppose you *have* an address now?" She stopped him, just inside the white gate with the green drippings: here he blew stamen off a page of his notebook, wrote on the page and tore it out for her. "Thank you," said Maria, "I might turn up—if I wanted money, or anything. But there will be plenty to do: I can drive a car."

Henry said: "I want you to understand that I won't be party to this—*in any way.*"

She shrugged and said: "You want *them* to understand" —and sent a look back to the house. Whereupon, on his entire being, the suspended charm of the afternoon worked. He protested against the return to the zone of death, and perhaps never ever seeing all this again. The cruciform lilac flowers, in all their purples, and the colourless mountains behind Mrs. Vesey's face besought him. The moment he had been dreading, returning desire, flooded him in this tunnel of avenue, with motors swishing along the road outside and Maria standing staring at him. He adored the stoicism of the group he had quitted —with their little fears and their great doubts—the grace of the thing done over again. He thought, with nothing left but our brute courage, we shall be nothing but brutes.

"What is the matter?" Maria said. Henry did not answer: they turned and walked to and fro inside the gates. Shadow played over her dress and hair: feeling the disenchantedness of his look at her she asked again, uneasily, "What's the matter?"

"You know," he said, "when you come away from here, no one will care any more that you are Maria. You will no longer be Maria, as a matter of fact. Those looks, those things that are said to you—they make you, you silly little girl. You are you only inside their spell. You may think action is better—but who will care for you when you only act? You will have an identity number, but no identity. Your whole existence has been in contradistinction. You may think you want an ordinary fate—but there is no ordinary fate. And that extraordinariness in the fate of each of us is only recognized by your aunt. I admit that her view of life is too much for me—that is why I was so stiff and touchy to-day. But where shall we be when nobody has a view of life?"

"You don't expect me to understand you, do you?"

"Even your being a savage, even being scornful—yes, even that you have got from them.—Is that my bus?"

"At the other side of the river: it has still got to cross the bridge.—Henry——" She put her face up. He touched it with kisses thoughtful and cold. "Good-bye," he said, "Miranda."

"—Maria—"

"Miranda. This is the end of *you*. Perhaps it is just as well."

"I'll be seeing you—"

"You'll come round my door in London—with your little new number chained to your wrist."

"The trouble with you is, you're half old."

Maria ran out through the gates to stop the bus, and Henry got on to it and was quickly carried away.

The Demon Lover

TOWARDS the end of her day in London Mrs. Drover
went round to her shut-up house to look for several things
she wanted to take away. Some belonged to herself, some
to her family, who were by now used to their country life.
It was late August; it had been a steamy, showery day:
at the moment the trees down the pavement glittered in
an escape of humid yellow afternoon sun. Against the
next batch of clouds, already piling up ink-dark, broken
chimneys and parapets stood out. In her once familiar
street, as in any unused channel, an unfamiliar queerness
had silted up; a cat wove itself in and out of railings, but
no human eye watched Mrs. Drover's return. Shifting
some parcels under her arm, she slowly forced round her
latchkey in an unwilling lock, then gave the door, which
had warped, a push with her knee. Dead air came out to
meet her as she went in.

The staircase window having been boarded up, no light
came down into the hall. But one door, she could just see,
stood ajar, so she went quickly through into the room and
unshuttered the big window in there. Now the prosaic
woman, looking about her, was more perplexed than she
knew by everything that she saw, by traces of her long
former habit of life—the yellow smoke-stain up the white
marble mantelpiece, the ring left by a vase on the top of

the escritoire; the bruise in the wallpaper where, on the door being thrown open widely, the china handle had always hit the wall. The piano, having gone away to be stored, had left what looked like claw-marks on its part of the parquet. Though not much dust had seeped in, each object wore a film of another kind; and, the only ventilation being the chimney, the whole drawing-room smelled of the cold hearth. Mrs. Drover put down her parcels on the escritoire and left the room to proceed upstairs; the things she wanted were in a bedroom chest.

She had been anxious to see how the house was—the part-time caretaker she shared with some neighbours was away this week on his holiday, known to be not yet back. At the best of times he did not look in often, and she was never sure that she trusted him. There were some cracks in the structure, left by the last bombing, on which she was anxious to keep an eye. Not that one could do anything—

A shaft of refracted daylight now lay across the hall. She stopped dead and stared at the hall table—on this lay a letter addressed to her.

She thought first—then the caretaker *must* be back. All the same, who, seeing the house shuttered, would have dropped a letter in at the box? It was not a circular, it was not a bill. And the post office redirected, to the address in the country, everything for her that came through the post. The caretaker (even if he *were* back) did not know she was due in London to-day—her call here had been planned to be a surprise—so his negligence in the manner of this letter, leaving it to wait in the dusk and the dust, annoyed her. Annoyed, she picked up the letter, which bore no stamp. But it cannot be important, or they would know . . . She took the letter rapidly upstairs with her, without a stop to look at the writing till she reached what had been her bedroom, where she let in light. The room looked over the garden and other gardens: the sun had gone in; as the clouds sharpened and lowered, the trees and rank lawns seemed already to smoke with dark. Her reluctance to look again at the letter came from the fact that she felt intruded upon—and by someone contemptuous of her ways. However, in the tenseness preceding the fall of rain she read it: it was a few lines.

DEAR KATHLEEN,

You will not have forgotten that to-day is our anniversary, and the day we said. The years have gone by at once slowly and fast. In view of the fact that nothing has changed, I shall rely upon you to keep your promise. I was sorry to see you leave London, but was satisfied that you would be back in time. You may expect me, therefore, at the hour arranged.

Until then . . .

K.

Mrs. Drover looked for the date: it was to-day's. She dropped the letter on to the bed-springs, then picked it up to see the writing again—her lips, beneath the remains of lipstick, beginning to go white. She felt so much the change in her own face that she went to the mirror, polished a clear patch in it and looked at once urgently and stealthily in. She was confronted by a woman of forty-four, with eyes starting out under a hat-brim that had been rather carelessly pulled down. She had not put on any more powder since she left the shop where she ate her solitary tea. The pearls her husband had given her on their marriage hung loose round her now rather thinner throat, slipping into the V of the pink wool jumper her sister knitted last autumn as they sat round the fire. Mrs. Drover's most normal expression was one of controlled worry, but of assent. Since the birth of the third of her little boys, attended by a quite serious illness, she had had an intermittent muscular flicker to the left of her mouth, but in spite of this she could always sustain a manner that was at once energetic and calm.

Turning from her own face as precipitately as she had gone to meet it, she went to the chest where the things were, unlocked it, threw up the lid and knelt to search. But as rain began to come crashing down she could not keep from looking over her shoulder at the stripped bed on which the letter lay. Behind the blanket of rain the clock of the church that still stood struck six—with rapidly heightening apprehension she counted each of the slow strokes. "The hour arranged . . . My God," she said, "*what* hour? How should I . . . ? After twenty-five years. . . ."

The young girl talking to the soldier in the garden had not ever completely seen his face. It was dark; they were saying good-bye under a tree. Now and then—for it felt, from not seeing him at this intense moment, as though she had never seen him at all—she verified his presence for these few moments longer by putting out a hand, which he each time pressed, without very much kindness, and painfully, on to one of the breast buttons of his uniform. That cut of the button on the palm of her hand was, principally, what she was to carry away. This was so near the end of a leave from France that she could only wish him already gone. It was August 1916. Being not kissed, being drawn away from and looked at intimidated Kathleen till she imagined spectral glitters in the place of his eyes. Turning away and looking back up the lawn she saw, through branches of trees, the drawing-room window alight: she caught a breath for the moment when she could go running back there into the safe arms of her mother and sister, and cry: "What shall I do, what shall I do? He has gone."

Hearing her catch her breath, her fiancé said, without feeling: "Cold?"

"You're going away such a long way."

"Not so far as you think."

"I don't understand?"

"You don't have to," he said. "You will. You know what we said."

"But that was—suppose you—I mean, suppose."

"I shall be with you," he said, "sooner or later. You won't forget that. You need do nothing but wait."

Only a little more than a minute later she was free to run up the silent lawn. Looking in through the window at her mother and sister, who did not for the moment perceive her, she already felt that unnatural promise drive down between her and the rest of all human kind. No other way of having given herself could have made her feel so apart, lost and forsworn. She could not have plighted a more sinister troth.

Kathleen behaved well when, some months later, her fiancé was reported missing, presumed killed. Her family not only supported her but were able to praise her courage without stint because they could not regret, as a husband for her, the man they knew almost nothing about. They hoped she would, in a year or two, console herself—and had it been only a question of consolation things might have gone much straighter ahead. But her trouble, behind just a little grief, was a complete dislocation from everything. She did not reject other lovers, for these failed to appear: for years she failed to attract men —and with the approach of her 'thirties she became natural enough to share her family's anxiousness on this score. She began to put herself out, to wonder; and at thirty-two she was very greatly relieved to find herself being courted by William Drover. She married him, and the two of them settled down in this quiet, arboreal part of Kensington: in this house the years piled up, her children were born and they all lived till they were driven out by the bombs of the next war. Her movements as Mrs. Drover were circumscribed, and she dismissed any idea that they were still watched.

As things were—dead or living the letter-writer sent her only a threat. Unable, for some minutes, to go on kneeling with her back exposed to the empty room, Mrs. Drover rose from the chest to sit on an upright chair whose back was firmly against the wall. The desuetude of her former bedroom, her married London home's whole air of being a cracked cup from which memory, with its reassuring power, had either evaporated or leaked away, made a crisis—and at just this crisis the letter-writer had, knowledgeably, struck. The hollowness of the house this evening cancelled years on years of voices, habits and steps. Through the shut windows she only heard rain fall on the roofs around. To rally herself, she said she was in a mood—and, for two or three seconds shutting her eyes, told herself that she had imagined the letter. But she opened them—there it lay on the bed.

On the supernatural side of the letter's entrance she was not permitting her mind to dwell. Who, in London, knew she meant to call at the house to-day? Evidently, however, this had been known. The caretaker, *had* he come back, had had no cause to expect her: he would have taken the letter in his pocket, to forward it, at his own time, through the post. There was no other sign that the caretaker had been in—but, if not? Letters dropped in at doors of deserted houses do not fly or walk to tables in halls. They do not sit on the dust of empty tables with the air of certainty that they will be found. There is needed some human hand—but nobody but the caretaker had a key. Under circumstances she did not care to consider, a house can be entered without a key. It was possible that she was not alone now. She might be being waited for, downstairs. Waited for—until when? Until "the hour arranged." At least that was not six o'clock: six has struck.

She rose from the chair and went over and locked the door.

The thing was, to get out. To fly? No, not that: she had to catch her train. As a woman whose utter dependability was the keystone of her family life she was not willing to return to the country, to her husband, her little boys and her sister, without the objects she had come up to fetch. Resuming work at the chest she set about making up a number of parcels in a rapid, fumbling-decisive way. These, with her shopping parcels, would be too much to carry; these meant a taxi—at the thought of the taxi her heart went up and her normal breathing resumed. I will ring up the taxi now; the taxi cannot come too soon: I shall hear the taxi out there running its engine, till I walk calmly down to it through the hall. I'll ring up— But no: the telephone is cut off . . . She tugged at a knot she had tied wrong.

The idea of flight . . . He was never kind to me, not really. I don't remember him kind at all. Mother said he never considered me. He was set on me, that was what it was—not love. Not love, not meaning a person well. What did he do, to make me promise like that? I can't remember— But she found that she could.

She remembered with such dreadful acuteness that the twenty-five years since then dissolved like smoke and she instinctively looked for the weal left by the button on the palm of her hand. She remembered not only all that he said and did but the complete suspension of *her* existence during that August week. I was not myself—they all told me so at the time. She remembered—but with one white burning blank as where acid has dropped on a photograph: *under no conditions* could she remember his face.

So, wherever he may be waiting, I shall not know him. You have no time to run from a face you do not expect.

The thing was to get to the taxi before any clock struck what could be the hour. She would slip down the street and round the side of the square to where the square gave on the main road. She would return in the taxi, safe, to her own door, and bring the solid driver into the house with her to pick up the parcels from room to room. The idea of the taxi driver made her decisive, bold: she unlocked her door, went to the top of the staircase and listened down.

She heard nothing—but while she was hearing nothing the *passé* air of the staircase was disturbed by a draught that travelled up to her face. It emanated from the basement: down there a door or window was being opened by someone who chose this moment to leave the house.

The rain had stopped; the pavements steamily shone as Mrs. Drover let herself out by inches from her own front door into the empty street. The unoccupied houses opposite continued to meet her look with their damaged stare. Making towards the thoroughfare and the taxi, she tried not to keep looking behind. Indeed, the silence was so intense—one of those creeks of London silence exaggerated this summer by the damage of war—that no tread could have gained on hers unheard. Where her street debouched on the square where people went on living she grew conscious of and checked her unnatural pace.

Across the open end of the square two buses impassively passed each other; women, a perambulator, cyclists, a man wheeling a barrow signalized, once again, the ordinary flow of life. At the square's most populous corner should be—and was—the short taxi rank. This evening, only one taxi—but this, although it presented its blank rump, appeared already to be alertly waiting for her. Indeed, without looking round the driver started his engine as she panted up from behind and put her hand on the door. As she did so, the clock struck seven. The taxi faced the main road: to make the trip back to her house it would have to turn—she had settled back on the seat and the taxi *had* turned before she, surprised by its knowing movement, recollected that she had not "said where." She leaned forward to scratch at the glass panel that divided the driver's head from her own.

The driver braked to what was almost a stop, turned round and slid the glass panel back: the jolt of this flung Mrs. Drover forward till her face was almost into the glass. Through the aperture driver and passenger, not six inches between them, remained for an eternity eye to eye. Mrs. Drover's mouth hung open for some seconds before she could issue her first scream. After that she continued to scream freely and to beat with her gloved hands on the glass all round as the taxi, accelerating without mercy, made off with her into the hinterland of deserted streets.

Ivy Gripped the Steps

IVY gripped and sucked at the flight of steps, down which with such a deceptive wildness it seemed to be flowing like a cascade. Ivy matted the door at the top and amassed in bushes above and below the porch. More, it had covered, or one might feel consumed, one entire half of the high, double-fronted house, from the basement up to a spiked gable: it had attained about halfway up to the girth and more than the density of a tree, and was sagging outward under its own weight. One was left to guess at the size and the number of windows hidden by looking at those in the other side. But these, though in sight, had been made effectively sightless: sheets of some dark composition that looked like metal were sealed closely into their frames. The house, not old, was of dull red brick with stone trimmings.

To crown all, the ivy was now in fruit, clustered over with fleshy pale green berries. There was something brutal about its fecundity. It was hard to credit that such a harvest could have been nourished only on brick and stone. Had not reason insisted that the lost windows must, like their fellows, have been made fast, so that the suckers for all their seeking voracity could not enter, one could have convinced oneself that the ivy must be feeding on something inside the house.

The process of strangulation could be felt: one wondered how many more years of war would be necessary for this to complete itself. And, the conventionality of the house, the remains, at least, of order in its surroundings made what was happening more and more an anomaly. Mrs. Nicholson's house had always enjoyed distinction—that of being detached, while its neighbours, though equally "good," had been erected in couples or even in blocks of four; that of being the last in the avenue; that of having on one hand as neighbour the theatre, to whose façade its front was at right angles. The theatre, set back behind shallow semicircular gardens, at once crowned and terminated the avenue, which ran from it to the Promenade overhanging the sea. And the house, apart from the prestige of standing just where it stood, had had the air of reserving something quite of its own. It was thus perhaps just, or not unfitting, that it should have been singled out for this gothic fate.

This was, or had been, one of the best residential avenues in Southstone, into which private hotels intruded only with the most breathless, costly discretion: if it was not that now it was nothing else, for there was nothing else for it to be. Lines of chestnut trees had been planted along the pavements, along the railed strip of lawn that divided the avenue down the centre—now, the railings were, with all other ironwork, gone; and where the lawn was very long rusty grass grew up into the tangles of rusty barbed wire. On to this, as on to the concrete pyramids—which, in the course of four years of waiting to be pushed out to obstruct the invader, had sunk some inches into the soil—the chestnuts were now dropping their leaves.

The decline dated from the exodus of the summer of 1940, when Southstone had been declared to be in the front line. The houses at the sea end of the avenue had, like those on the Promenade, been requisitioned; but some of those at the theatre end stayed empty. Here and there, portions of porches or balustrades had fallen into front gardens, crushing their overgrowth; but there were no complete ruins; no bomb or shell had arrived immediately here, and effects of blast, though common to all of

Southstone, were less evident than desuetude and decay. It was now the September of 1944; and, for some reason, the turn of the tide of war, the accumulation of the Invasion victories, gave Southstone its final air of defeat. The withdrawal of most of the soldiers, during the summer, had drained off adventitious vitality. The A.A. batteries, this month, were on the move to another part of the coast. And, within the very last few days, the silencing of the guns across the Channel had ended the tentative love affair with death: Southstone's life, no longer kept to at least a pitch by shelling warnings, now had nothing but an etiolated slowness. In the shuttered shopping streets, along the Promenade, in the intersecting avenues, squares and crescents, vacuum mounted up. The lifting of the ban on the area had, so far, brought few visitors in.

This afternoon, for minutes together, not a soul, not even a soldier, crossed the avenue: Gavin Doddington stood to regard the ivy in what was, virtually, solitude. The sky being clouded, though not dark, a timeless flat light fell on to everything. Outside the theatre a very few soldiers stood grouped about; some moodily, some in no more than apathy. The theatre gardens had been cemented over to make a lorry park; and the engine of one of the lorries was being run.

Mrs. Nicholson could not be blamed for the ivy: *her* absence from Southstone was of long standing, for she had died in 1912—two years before the outbreak of what Gavin still thought of as Admiral Concannon's war. After her death, the house had been put up for auction by her executors: since then, it might well have changed hands two or three times. Probably few of the residents dislodged in 1940 had so much as heard Mrs. Nicholson's name. In its condition, to-day, the house was a paradox: having been closed and sealed up with extreme care, it had been abandoned in a manner no less extreme. It had been nobody's business to check the ivy. Nor, apparently, had there been anybody to authorize a patriotic sacrifice of the railings—Gavin Doddington, prodding between the strands of ivy, confirmed his impression that that iron lacework still topped the parapet of the front garden. He could pursue with his finger, though not see, the pattern that with other details of the house, outside and in, had long ago been branded into his memory. Looking up at the windows in the exposed half he saw, still in position along the sills, miniature reproductions of this pattern, for the support of window boxes. Those, which were gone, had been flowery in her day.

The assumption was that, as lately as 1940, Mrs. Nicholson's house *had* belonged to someone, but that it belonged to nobody now. The late owner's death in some other part of England must have given effect to a will not brought up to date, by which the property passed to an heir who could not be found—to somebody not heard of since Singapore fell or not yet reported anything more than "missing" after a raid on London or a battle abroad. Legal hold-ups dotted the worldwide mess . . . So reasoning, Gavin Doddington gave rein to what had been his infant and was now his infantile passion for explanation. But also he attached himself to the story as to something nothing to do with him; and did so with the intensity of a person who must think lest he should begin to feel.

His passion for explanation had been, when he knew Mrs. Nicholson, raised by her power of silently baulking it into the principal reason for suffering. It had been among the stigmata of his extreme youth—he had been eight when he met her, ten when she died. He had not been back to Southstone since his last stay with her.

Now, the lifting of the official ban on the area had had the effect of bringing him straight back—why? When what one has refused is put out of reach, when what one has avoided becomes forbidden, some lessening of the inhibition may well occur. The ban had so acted on his reluctance that, when the one was removed, the other came away with it—as a scab, adhering, comes off with a wad of lint. The transmutation, due to the fall of France, of his "*I* cannot go back to Southstone" into "*One* cannot go there" must have been salutary, or, at least, exteriorizing. It so happened that when the ban came off he had been due for a few days' leave from the Ministry. He had at once booked a room at one of the few hotels that remained at the visitor's disposition.

Arriving at Southstone yesterday evening, he had confined his stroll in the hazy marine dusk to the cracked, vacant and wire-looped Promenade—from which he returned with little more than the wish that he had, after all, brought somebody down here with him. Amorist since his 'teens, he had not often set off on a holiday uncompanioned. The idea of this as a pilgrimage revolted him: he remained in the bar till the bar closed. This morning he had no more than stalked the house, approaching it in wavering closing circles through the vaguer Southstone areas of association. He had fixed for the actual confrontation that hour, deadline for feeling, immediately after lunch.

The story originated in a friendship between two young girls in their Dresden finishing year. Edith and Lilian had kept in touch throughout later lives that ran very widely apart—their letters, regularly exchanged, were perhaps more confidential than their infrequent meetings. Edith had married a country gentleman, Lilian a business man. Jimmie Nicholson had bought the Southstone house for his wife in 1907, not long before his death, which had been the result of a stroke. He had been senior by about fifteen years: their one child, a daughter, had died at birth.

Edith Doddington, who had never been quite at ease on the subject of Lilian's marriage, came to stay more often now her friend was a widow, but still could not come as often as both would have liked. Edith's own married life was one of contrivance and of anxiety. After money, the most pressing of Edith's worries centred round the health of her second son: Gavin had been from birth a delicate little boy. The damp of his native county, inland and low-lying, did not suit him: there was the constant question of change of air—till his health stabilized, he could not go away to school. It was natural that Lilian, upon discovering this, should write inviting Gavin to stay at Southstone—ideally, of course, let his mother bring him; but if Edith could not be free, let him come alone. Mrs. Nicholson hoped he and she, who had not yet met, would not, or would not for long, be shy of each other. Her maid Rockham was, at any rate, good with children.

Gavin had heard of Southstone as the scene of his mother's only exotic pleasures. The maid Rockham was sent to London to meet him: the two concluded their journey with the absurdly short drive, in an open victoria, from the station to Mrs. Nicholson's house. It was early in what was a blazing June: the awnings over the windows rippled, the marguerites in the window-boxes undulated, in a hot breeze coming down the avenue from the sea. From the awnings the rooms inside took a tense bright dusk. In the sea-blue drawing-room, up whose walls reared mirrors framed in ivory brackets, Gavin was left to await Mrs. Nicholson. He had time to marvel at the variety of the bric-à-brac crowding brackets and tables, the maniness of the cut-crystal vases, the earliness of the purple and white sweet pea—at the Doddingtons', sweet pea did not flower before July. Mrs. Nicholson then entered: to his surprise she did not kiss him.

Instead, she stood looking down at him—she was tall —with a glittering, charming uncertainty. Her head bent a little lower, during consideration not so much of Gavin as of the moment. Her *coiffeur* was like spun sugar: that its crisp upward waves should seem to have been splashed with silvery powder added, only, marquise-like glowing youth to her face.

The summery light-like fullness of her dress was accentuated by the taut belt with coral-inlaid clasp: from that small start the skirts flowed down to dissipate and spread where they touched the floor. Tentatively she extended her right hand, which he, without again raising his eyes, shook. "Well . . . Gavin," she said. "I hope you had a good journey? I am so very glad you could come."

He said: "And my mother sends you her love."

"Does she?" Sitting down, sinking an elbow into the sofa cushions, she added: "How *is* Edith—how is your mother?"

"Oh, she is very well."

She vaguely glanced round her drawing-room, as though seeing it from his angle, and, therefore, herself seeing it for the first time. The alternatives it offered could be distracting: she soon asked him her first intimate question—"Where do you think you would like to sit?"

Not that afternoon, nor, indeed, until some way on into this first visit did Gavin distinguish at all sharply between Mrs. Nicholson and her life. Not till the knife of love gained sufficient edge could he cut out her figure from its surroundings. Southstone was, for the poor landowner's son, the first glimpse of the enchanted existence of the *rentier*. Everything was effortless; and, to him, consequently, seemed stamped with style. This society gained by smallness: it could be comprehended. People here, the company that she kept, commanded everything they desired, were charged with nothing they did not. The expenditure of their incomes—expenditure calculated so long ago and so nicely that it could now seem artless— occupied them. What there was to show for it showed at every turn; though at no turn too much, for it was not too much. Such light, lofty, smooth-running houses were to be found, quite likely, in no capital city. A word to the livery stables brought an imposing carriage to any door: in the afternoons one drove, in a little party, to reflect on a Roman ruin or to admire a village church. In the Promenade's glare, at the end of the shaded avenue, parasols passed and repassed in a rhythm of leisure. Just inland were the attentive shops. There were meetings for good causes in cool drawing-rooms, afternoon concerts in the hotel ballrooms; and there was always the theatre, where applause continued long after Gavin had gone to bed. Best of all, there were no poor to be seen.

The plan of this part of Southstone (a plateau backed by the downs and overhanging the sea) was masterful. Its architecture was ostentatious, fiddling, bulky and mixed. Gavin was happy enough to be at an age to admire the one, to be unaware of the other—he was elated, rather than not, by this exhibition of gimcrack size; and bows, bays, balustrades, glazed-in balconies and French-type

mansardes not slowly took up their parts in the fairy tale.
As strongly was he impressed by the strong raying out,
from such points as station and theatre, of avenues; each
of which crossed, obliquely, just less wide residential
roads. Lavishness appeared in the public flowers, the mu-
nicipal seats with their sofa-like curving backs, the flag-
poles, cliff grottoes, perspectives of lawn. There was a
climate here that change from season to season, the rough-
est Channel gale blowing, could not disturb. This town
without function fascinated him—outside it, down to the
port or into the fishing quarter, "old Southstone," he did
not attempt to stray. Such tameness might have been
found odd in a little boy: Mrs. Nicholson never thought
of it twice.

Gavin's estimation of Southstone—as he understood
much later—coincided with that of a dead man. When
Jimmie Nicholson bought the house for his wife here,
Southstone was the high dream of his particular world.
It was as Lilian's husband he made the choice: alone, he
might not have felt capable of this polished leisure. His
death left it uncertain whether, even *as* Lilian's husband,
he could have made the grade. The golf course had been
his object: failing that he was not, perhaps, so badly
placed in the cemetery, which was also outside the town.
For, for Southstone dividends kept their mystic origin:
they were as punctual as Divine grace, as unmentioned
as children still in wombs. Thickset Jimmie, with his pur-
suant reek of the City, could have been a distasteful re-
minder of money's source.

Gavin, like his dead host, beheld Southstone with all
the ardour of an outsider. His own family had a touch
of the brutishness that comes from any dependence upon
land. Mr. and Mrs. Doddington were constantly in wet
clothes, constantly fatigued, constantly depressed. Nothing new appeared in the squire's home; and what was
old had acquired a sort of fog from being ignored. An austere, religious idea of their own standing not so much inspired as preyed upon Gavin's parents. Caps touched to
them in the village could not console them for the letters
they got from their bank. Money for them was like a

spring in a marsh, feebly thrusting its way up to be absorbed again: any profit forced from the home farm, any rents received for outlying lands went back again into upkeep, rates, gates, hedging, draining, repairs to cottages and renewal of stock. There was nothing, no nothing ever, to show. In the society round them they played no part to which their position did not compel them: they were poor gentry, in fact, at a period when poverty could not be laughed away. Their lot was less enviable than that of any of their employees or tenants, whose faces, naked in their dejection, and voices pitched to complaints they could at least utter, had disconcerted Gavin, since babyhood, at the Hall door. Had the Doddingtons been told that their kind would die out, they would have expressed little more than surprise that such complicated troubles could end so simply.

Always towards the end of a stay at Southstone Gavin's senses began to be haunted by the anticipation of going back. So much so that to tread the heat-softened asphalt was to feel once more the suck of a sticky lane. *Here,* day and night he breathed with ease that was still a subconscious joy: the thought of the Midlands made his lungs contract and deaden—such was the old cold air, sequestered by musty baize doors, of the corridors all the way to his room at home.

His room *here* was on the second floor, in front, looking on to the avenue. It had a frieze of violets knotted along a ribbon: as dusk deepened, these turned gradually black. Later, a lamp from the avenue cast a tree's shifting shadow on to the ceiling above his bed; and the same light pierced the Swiss skirts of the dressing-table. Mrs. Nicholson, on the first occasion when she came as far as his door to say good night, deprecated the "silliness" of this little room. Rockham, it seemed, had thought it suitable for his age—she, Rockham, had her quarters on the same floor—Mrs. Nicholson, though she did not say so, seemed to feel it to be unsuitable for his sex. "Because I don't suppose," she said, "that you really ever *are* lonely in the night?"

Propped upright against his pillows, gripping his glass of milk, he replied: "I am never frightened."

"But, lonely—what makes you lonely, then?"

"I don't know. I suppose, thoughts."

"Oh, but why," she said, "don't you like them?"

"When I am here the night seems a sort of waste, and I don't like to think what a waste it is."

Mrs. Nicholson, who was on her way out to dinner, paused in the act of looping a gauze scarf over her hair and once again round her throat. "Only tell me," she said, "that you're not more lonely, Gavin, because I am going out? Up here, you don't know if I am in the house or not."

"I do know."

"Perhaps," she suggested humbly, "you'll go to sleep? They all say it is right for you, going to bed so early, but I wish it did not make days so short.—I must go."

"The carriage hasn't come round yet."

"No, it won't: it hasn't been ordered. It is so lovely this evening, I thought I would like to walk." She spoke, though, as though the project were spoiled for her: she could not help seeing, as much as he did, the unkindness of leaving him with this picture. She came even further into the room to adjust her scarf at his mirror, for it was not yet dark. "Just once, one evening perhaps, you could stay up late. Do you think it would matter? I'll ask Rockham."

Rockham remained the arbiter: it was she who was left to exercise anything so nearly harsh as authority. In even the affairs of her own house Mrs. Nicholson was not heard giving an order: what could not be thought to be conjured into existence must be part of the clockwork wound up at the start by Jimmie and showing no sign of beginning to run down yet. The dishes that came to table seemed to surprise her as much, and as pleasingly, as they did Gavin. Yet the effect she gave was not of idleness but of preoccupation: what she did with her days Gavin did not ask himself—when he did ask himself, later, it was too late. They continued to take her colour—those days she did nothing with.

It was Rockham who worked out the daily programme,

devised to keep the little boy out of Madam's way. "Because Madam," she said, "is not accustomed to children."
It was by Rockham that, every morning, he was taken
down to play by the sea: the beach, undulations of orange
shingle, was fine-combed with breakwaters, against one
of which sat Rockham, reading a magazine. Now and
then she would look up, now and then she would call.
These relegations to Rockham sent Gavin to angry ex-
tremes of infantilism: he tried to drape seaweed streamers
around her hat; he plagued to have pebbles taken out of
his shoe. There was a literal feeling of degradation about
this descent from the plateau to the cliff's foot. From close
up, the sea, with its heaving mackerel vacancy, bored him
—most of the time he stood with his back to it, shading
his eyes and staring up at the heights. From right down
here, though Southstone could not be seen—any more
than objects set back on a high shelf can be seen by somebody standing immediately underneath it—its illusion, its
magical artificiality, was to be savoured as from nowhere
else. Tiny, the flags of the Promenade's edge, the figures
leaning along the railings, stood out against a dazzle of
sky. And he never looked up at these looking down without an interrupted heartbeat—might she not be among
them?

The rule was that they, Rockham and Gavin, walked
zigzag down by the cliff path, but travelled up in the lift.
But one day fate made Rockham forget her purse. They
had therefore to undertake the ascent. The path's artful
gradients, hand-railed, were broken by flights of steps and
by niched seats, upon every one of which Rockham
plumped herself down to regain breath. The heat of mid-
day, the glare from the flowered cliff beat up Gavin into
a sort of fever. As though a dropped plummet had struck
him between the eyes he looked up, to see Mrs. Nicholson's face above him against the blue. The face, its colour rendered transparent by the transparent silk of a
parasol, was inclined forward: he had the experience of
seeing straight up into eyes that did not see him. Her
look was pitched into space: she was not only not seeing
him, she was seeing nothing. She was listening, but not

attending, while someone talked.

Gavin, gripping the handrail, bracing his spine against it, leaned out backwards over the handrail into the void, in the hopes of intercepting her line of view. But in vain. He tore off clumps of sea pinks and cast the too-light flowers outwards into the air, but her pupils never once flickered down. Despair, the idea that his doom must be never, never to reach her, not only now but ever, gripped him and gripped his limbs as he took the rest of the path—the two more bends and few more steps to the top. He clawed his way up the rail, which shook in its socket.

The path, when it landed Gavin on to the Promenade, did so some yards from where Mrs. Nicholson and her companion stood. Her companion was Admiral Concannon. "Hello, hello!" said the Admiral, stepping back to see clear of the parasol. "Where have *you* sprung from?"

"Oh, but Gavin," exclaimed Mrs. Nicholson, also turning, "why not come up in the lift? I thought you liked it."

"Lift?" said the Admiral. "Lift, at his age? What, has the boy got a dicky heart?"

"No indeed!" she said, and looked at Gavin so proudly that he became the image of health and strength.

"In that case," said the Admiral, "do him good." There was something, in the main, not unflattering about this co-equal masculine brusqueness. Mrs. Nicholson, looking over the railings, perceived the labouring top of her maid's hat. "It's poor Rockham," she said, "that I am thinking about; she hasn't got a heart but she has attacks.—How hazy it is!" she said, indicating the horizon with a gloved hand. "It seems to be days since we saw France. I don't believe Gavin believes it is really there."

"It is there all right," said the Admiral, frowning slightly.

"Why, Rockham," she interposed, "you look hot. Whatever made you walk up on a day like this?"

"Well, I cannot fly, can I, madam; and I overlooked my purse."

"Admiral Concannon says we may all be flying.—What are you waiting for?"

"I was waiting for Master Gavin to come along."

"I don't see why he should, really—which would you rather, Gavin?"

Admiral Concannon's expression did not easily change, and did not change now. His features were severely clear cut; his figure was nervy and spare; and he had an air of eating himself—due, possibly, to his retirement. His manners of walking, talking and standing, though all to be recognized at a distance, were vehemently impersonal. When in anything that could be called repose he usually kept his hands in his pockets—the abrupt extraction of one hand, for the purpose of clicking thumb and finger together, was the nearest thing to a gesture he ever made. His voice and step had become familiar, among the few nocturnal sounds of the avenue, some time before Gavin had seen his face, for he escorted Mrs. Nicholson home from parties to which she had been wilful enough to walk. Looking out one night, after the hall door shut, Gavin had seen the head of a cigarette, immobile, pulsating sharply under the dark trees. The Concannons had settled at Southstone for Mrs. Concannon's health's sake: their two daughters attended one of the schools.

Liberated into this blue height, Gavin could afford to look down in triumph at the sea by whose edge he had lately stood. But the Admiral said: "Another short turn, perhaps?"—since they were to *be* three, they had better be three in motion. Mrs. Nicholson raised her parasol, and the three moved off down the Promenade with the dignified aimlessness of swans. Ahead, the distance dissolved, the asphalt quivered in heat; and she, by walking between her two companions, produced a democracy of masculine trouble into which age did not enter at all. As they passed the bandstand she said to Gavin: "Admiral Concannon has just been saying that there is going to be a war."

Gavin glanced across at the Admiral, who remained in profile. Unassisted and puzzled, he said: "Why?"

"Why indeed?" she agreed.—"There!" she said to the Admiral. "It's no good trying to tease me, because I never believe you." She glanced around her and added: "After all, we live in the present day! History is quite far back;

it is sad, of course, but it does seem silly. I never even cared for history at school; I was glad when we came to the end of it."

"And when, my dear, did you come to the end of history?"

"The year I put up my hair. It had begun to be not so bad from the time we started catching up with the present; and I was glad I had stayed at school long enough to be sure that it had all ended happily. But oh, those unfortunate people in the past! It seems unkind to say so, but can it have been their faults? They can have been no more like us than cats and dogs. I suppose there *is* one reason for learning history—one sees how long it has taken to make the world nice. Who on earth could want to upset things now?—No one could want to," she said to the Admiral. "You forget the way we behave now, and there's no other way. Civilized countries are polite to each other, just as you and I are to the people we know, and uncivilized countries are put down—but, if one thinks, there are beautifully few of those. Even savages really prefer wearing hats and coats. Once people wear hats and coats and can turn on electric light, they would no more want to be silly than you or I do.—Or *do* you want to be silly?" she said to the Admiral.

He said: "I did not mean to upset you."

"You don't," she said. "I should not dream of suspecting *any* civilized country!"

"Which civilized country?" said Gavin. "France?"

"For your information," said the Admiral coldly, "it is Germany we should be preparing to fight, for the reason that she is preparing to fight us."

"I have never been happier anywhere," said Mrs. Nicholson, more nearly definitely than usual. "Why," she added, turning to Gavin, "if it were not for Germany, now I come to think of it, you would not be here!"

The Admiral, meanwhile, had become intent on spearing on the tip of his cane a straying fragment of paper, two inches torn off a letter, that was defiling the Promenade. Lips compressed, he crossed to a litter basket (which had till then stood empty, there being no litter) and knocked the fragment into it off his cane. He burst out: "I should like to know what this place is coming to —we shall have trippers next!"

This concern his beautiful friend *could* share—and did so share that harmony was restored. Gavin, left to stare out to sea, reflected on one point in the conversation: he could never forget that the Admiral had called Mrs. Nicholson, "My dear."

Also, under what provocation had the Admiral threatened Mrs. Nicholson with war? . . . Back at Gavin's home again, once more with his parents, nothing was, after all, so impossible: this was outside the zone of electric light. As late summer wore slowly over the Midlands, the elms in the Doddingtons' park casting lifeless slate-coloured shadows over sorrel, dung, thistles and tufted grass, it was borne in on Gavin that this existence belonged, by its nature, to *any* century. It was unprogressive. It had stayed as it was while, elsewhere, history jerked itself painfully off the spool; it could hardly be more depressed by the fateful passage of armies than by the flooding of tillage or the failure of crops; it was hardly capable, really, of being depressed further. It was an existence mortgaged to necessity; it was an inheritance of uneasiness, tension and suspicion. One could pre-assume the enmity of weather, prices, mankind, cattle. It was this dead weight of existence that had supplied to history not so much the violence or the futility that had been, as she said, apparent to Mrs. Nicholson, but its repetitive harshness and its power to scar. This existence had no volition, but could not stop; and its never stopping, because it could not, made history's ever stopping the less likely. No signs of even an agreeable pause were to be seen round Doddington Hall. Nor could one, at such a distance from Southstone, agree that time had laboured to make the world nice.

Gavin now saw his mother as Mrs. Nicholson's friend. Indeed, the best of the gowns in which Edith went out to dinner, when forced to go out to dinner, had been Lilian's once, and once or twice worn by her. Worn by Edith, they still had the exoticism of gifts, and dispelled from their

folds not only the giver's sachets but the easy pitiful lov-
ingness of the giver's mood. In them, Gavin's mother's
thin figure assumed a grace whose pathos was lost to
him at the time. While the brown-yellow upward light of
the table oil-lamp unkindly sharpened the hollows in Mrs.
Doddington's face and throat, Gavin, thrown sideways out
of his bed, fingered the mousseline or caressed the satin
of the skirts with an adoring absorption that made his
mother uneasy—for fetishism is still to be apprehended
by those for whom it has never had any name. She would
venture: "You like, then, to see me in pretty clothes?"
. . . It was, too, in the first of these intermissions between his visits to Southstone that he, for the first time,
took stock of himself, of his assets—the evident pleasing-
ness of his manner; his looks—he could take in better and
better part his elder brother's jibes at his pretty-prettiness
—his quickness of mind, which at times made even his father smile; and his masculinity, which, now he tried it out,
gave him unexpected command of small situations. At
home, nights were not a waste: he attached himself to his
thoughts, which took him, by seven-league strides, on-
ward to his next visit. He rehearsed, using his mother, all
sorts of little gratuities of behaviour, till she exclaimed:
"Why, Lilian has made quite a little page of you!" At her
heels round the garden or damp extensive offices of the
Hall at her elbow as she peered through her letters or
resignedly settled to her accounts, he reiterated: "Tell
me about Germany."

"Why Germany?"

"I mean, the year you were there."

A gale tore the slates from the Hall stables, brought
one tree down on to a fence and another to block the
drive, the night before Gavin left for Southstone. This
time he travelled alone. At Southstone, dull shingly roar-
ing thumps from the beach travelled as far inland as the
railway station; from the Promenade—on which, someone said, it was all but impossible to stand upright—there
came a whistling strain down the avenues. It was early
January. Rockham was kept to the house by a nasty cold;

so it was Mrs. Nicholson who, with brilliantly heightened colour, holding her muff to the cheek on which the wind blew, was on the station platform to meet Gavin. A porter, tucking the two of them into the waiting carriage, replaced the foot-warmer under the fur rug. She said: "How different this is from when you were with me last. Or do you like winter?"

"I like anything, really."

"I remember one thing you don't like: you said you didn't like thoughts." As they drove past a lighted house from which music came to be torn about by the wind, she remembered: "You've been invited to several parties."

He was wary: "Shall you be going to them?"

"Why, yes; I'm sure I *could* go," she said.

Her house was hermetic against the storm: in the drawing-room, heat drew out the smell of violets. She dropped her muff on the sofa, and Gavin stroked it— "It's like a cat," he said quickly, as she turned round. "Shall I have a cat?" she said. "Would you like me to have a cat?" All the other rooms, as they went upstairs, were tawny with fires that did not smoke.

Next morning, the wind had dropped; the sky reflected on everything its mild brightness; trees, houses and pavements glistened like washed glass. Rockham, puffy and with a glazed upper lip, said: "Baster Gavid, you've brought us better weather." Having blown her nose with what she seemed to hope was exhaustive thoroughness, she concealed her handkerchief in her bosom as guiltily as though it had been a dagger. "Badam," she said, "doesn't like to be to have a cold.—Poor Bisses Codcaddod," she added, "has been laid up agaid."

Mrs. Concannon's recovery must be timed for the little dinner party that they were giving. Her friends agreed that she ought to reserve her strength. On the morning of what was to be the day, it was, therefore, the Admiral whom one met out shopping: Gavin and Mrs. Nicholson came on him moodily selecting flowers and fruit. Delayed late autumn and forced early spring flowers blazed, under artificial light, against the milder daylight outside the florist's plate glass. "For to-night, for the party?" exclaimed

Mrs. Nicholson. "Oh, let us have carnations, scarlet carnations!"

The Admiral hesitated. "I think Constance spoke of chrysanthemums, white chrysanthemums."

"Oh, but these are so washy, so like funerals. They will do poor Constance no good, if she still feels ill."

Gavin, who had examined the prices closely, in parenthesis said: "Carnations are more expensive."

"No, wait!" cried Mrs. Nicholson, gathering from their buckets all the scarlet carnations that were in reach, and gaily shaking the water from their stems, "you must let me send these to Constance, because I am so much looking forward to to-night. It will be delightful."

"I hope so," the Admiral said. "But I'm sorry to say we shall be an uneven number: we have just heard that poor Massingham has dropped out. Influenza."

"Bachelors shouldn't have influenza, should they— But then, why not ask somebody else?"

"So very much at the last moment, that might seem a bit—informal."

"Dear me," she teased, "have you really got *no* old friend?"

"Constance does not feel . . ."

Mrs. Nicholson's eyebrows rose: she looked at the Admiral over the carnations. This was one of the moments when the Admiral could be heard to click his finger and thumb. "What a pity," she said. "I don't care for lopsided parties. *I* have one friend who is not touchy—invite Gavin!"

To a suggestion so completely outrageous, who was to think of any reply? It was a *coup*. She completed, swiftly: "To-night, then? We shall be with you at about eight."

Gavin's squiring Mrs. Nicholson to the Concannons' party symptomized this phase of their intimacy; without being, necessarily, its highest point. Rockham's cold had imperilled Rockham's prestige: as intervener or arbiter she could be counted out. There being no more talk of these odious drops to the beach, Gavin exercised over Mrs. Nicholson's mornings what seemed a conqueror's rights to a terrain; while with regard to her afternoons she showed a flattering indecision as to what might not please him or what he could not share. At her tea-table, his position was made subtly manifest to her guests. His bedtime was becoming later and later; in vain did Rockham stand and cough in the hall; more than once or twice he had dined downstairs. When the curtains were drawn, it was he who lit the piano candles, then stood beside her as she played—ostensibly to turn over the music, but forgetting the score to watch her hands. At the same time, he envisaged their two figures as they would appear to someone —his other self—standing out there in the cold dark of the avenue, looking between the curtains into the glowing room. One evening, she sang 'Two Eyes of Grey that used to be so Bright.'

At the end, he said: "But that's supposed to be a song sung by a man to a woman."

Turning on the piano stool, she said: "Then you must learn it."

He objected: "But your eyes are not grey."

Indeed they were never neutral eyes. Their sapphire darkness, with that of the sapphire pendant she was wearing, was struck into by the Concannons' electric light. That round fitment on pulleys, with a red silk frill, had been so adjusted above the dinner table as to cast down a vivid circle, in which the guests sat. The stare and sheen of the cloth directly under the light appeared supernatural. The centrepiece was a silver or plated pheasant, around whose base the carnations—slightly but strikingly "off" the red of the shade, but pre-eminently flattering in their contrast to Mrs. Nicholson's orchid *glacé* gown— were bunched in four silver cornets. This was a party of eight: if the Concannons had insisted on stressing its "littleness," it was, still, the largest that they could hope to give. The evident choiceness of the guests, the glitter and the mathematical placing of the silver and glass, the prompt, meticulous service of the dishes by maids whose suspended breath could be heard—all, all bespoke art and care. Gavin and Mrs. Nicholson were so placed as to face one another across the table: her glance contained him, from time to time, in its leisurely, not quite attentive play.

He wondered whether she felt, and supposed she must, how great had been the effrontery of their entrance.

For this dinner-party lost all point if it were not *de rigueur*. The Concannon daughters, even (big girls, but with hair still down their backs) had, as not qualified for it, been sent out for the evening. It, the party, had been balanced up and up on itself like a house of cards: built, it remained as precarious. Now the structure trembled, down to its base, from one contemptuous flip at its top story—Mrs. Nicholson's caprice of bringing a little boy. Gavin perceived that night what he was not to forget: the helplessness, in the last resort, of society—which he was never, later, to be able to think of as a force. The pianola-like play of the conversation did not drown the nervousness round the table.

At the head of the table the Admiral leaned just forward, as though pedalling the pianola. At the far end, an irrepressible cough from time to time shook Mrs. Concannon's décolletage and the crystal pince-nez which, balanced high on her face, gave her a sensitive blankness. She had the *dévote* air of some sailors' wives, and was heroic in pale blue without a wrap—arguably, nothing could make her iller. The Admiral's pride in his wife's courage passed a current over the silver pheasant. For Mrs. Concannon, joy in sustaining all this for his sake, and confidence in him, provided a light armour: she possibly did not feel what was felt for her. To Gavin she could not have been kinder; to Mrs. Nicholson she had only and mildly said: "He will not be shy, I hope, if he does not sit beside you?"

Rearrangement of the table at the last moment could not but have disappointed one or other of the two gentlemen who had expected to sit, and were now sitting, at Mrs. Nicholson's right and left hand. More and more, as course followed course, these two showed how highly they rated their good fortune—indeed, the censure around the rest of the table only acted for them, like heat drawing out scent, to heighten the headiness of her immediate aura. Like the quick stuff of her dress her delinquency, even, gave out a sort of shimmer: while she, neither arch nor indolent, turned from one to the other her look—if you like, melting; for it dissolved, her pupils, which had never been so dilated, dark, as to-night. In this look, as dinner proceeded, the two flies, ceasing to struggle, drowned.

The reckoning would be on the way home. Silent between the flies' wives, hypnotized by the rise and fall of Mrs. Nicholson's pendant, Gavin ate on and on. The ladies' move to the drawing-room sucked him along with it in the wake of the last skirt. . . . It was without a word that, at the end of the evening, the Admiral saw Mrs. Nicholson to her carriage—Gavin, like an afterthought or a monkey, nipping in under his host's arm extended to hold open the carriage door. Light from the porch, as they drove off, fell for a moment on that erect form and implacable hatchet face. Mrs. Nicholson seemed to be occupied in gathering up her skirts to make room for Gavin. She then leaned back in her corner, and he in his: not a word broke the tension of the short dark drive home. Not till she had dropped her cloak in front of her drawing-room fire did she remark: "The Admiral's angry with me."

"Because of me?"

"Oh dear no; because of her. If I did not think to be angry was very silly, I could almost be a little angry with him."

"But you meant to make him angry, didn't you?" Gavin said.

"Only because he's silly," said Mrs. Nicholson. "If he were not so silly, that poor unfortunate creature would stop coughing: she would either get better or die." Still standing before her mantelpiece, she studied some freesias in a vase—dispassionately, she pinched off one fading bloom, rolled it into a wax pill between her thumb and finger, then flicked it away to sizzle in the heart of the fire. "If people," she said, "give a party for no other reason but to show off their marriage, what kind of evening can one expect?—However, I quite enjoyed myself. I hope you did?"

Gavin said: "Mrs. Concannon's quite old. But then, so's the Admiral."

"He quite soon will be, at this rate," said Mrs. Nicholson. "That's why he's so anxious to have that war. One would have thought a man could just be a man.—What's the matter, Gavin; what are you staring at?"

"That is your most beautiful dress."

"Yes; that's why I put it on." Mrs. Nicholson sat down on a low blue velvet chair and drew the chair to the fire: she shivered slightly. "You say such sweet things, Gavin: what fun we have!" Then, as though within the seconds of silence ticked off over her head by the little Dresden clock her own words had taken effect with her, she turned and, with an impulsive movement, invited him closer to her side. Her arm stayed round him; her short puffed sleeve, disturbed by the movement, rustled down into silence. In the fire a coal fell apart, releasing a seam of gas from which spurted a pale tense quivering flame. "Aren't you glad we are back?" she said, "that we are only you and me?—Oh, why endure such people when all the time there is the whole world! Why do I stay on and on here; what am I doing? Why don't we go right away somewhere, Gavin; you and I? To Germany, or into the sun? Would that make you happy?"

"That—that flame's so funny," he said, not shifting his eyes from it.

She dropped her arm and cried, in despair: "After all, what a child you are!"

"I am not."

"Anyhow, it's late; you must go to bed."

She transmuted the rise of another shiver into a slight yawn.

Overcharged and trembling, he gripped his way, flight by flight, up the polished banister rail, on which his palms left patches of mist; pulling himself away from her up the staircase as he had pulled himself towards her up the face of the cliff.

After that midwinter visit there were two changes: Mrs. Nicholson went abroad, Gavin went to school. He overheard his mother say to his father that Lilian found Southstone this winter really too cold to stay in. "Or, has made it too hot to stay in?" said Mr. Doddington,

from whose disapproval the story of Gavin and the Concannons' party had not been able to be kept. Edith Doddington coloured, loyal, and said no more. During his first
term, Gavin received at school one bright picture postcard of Mentone. The carefully chosen small preparatory
school confronted him, after all, with fewer trials than his
parents had feared and his brother hoped. His protective
adaptability worked quickly; he took enough colour, or
colourlessness, from where he was to pass among the
others, and along with them—a civil and indifferent little
boy. His improved but never quite certain health got him
out of some things and secured others—rests from time
to time in the sick-room, teas by the matron's fire. This
spectacled woman was not quite unlike Rockham; also,
she was the most approachable edge of the grown-up am-
bience that connected him, however remotely, with Mrs.
Nicholson. At school, his assets of feeling remained, one
would now say, frozen.

His Easter holidays had to be spent at home; his summer holidays exhausted their greater part in the same concession to a supposed attachment. Not until September
was he dispatched to Southstone, for a week, to be set up
before his return to school.

That September was an extension of summer. An ad-
mirable company continued its season of light opera at
the theatre, in whose gardens salvias blazed. The lawns,
shorn to the roots after weeks of mowing, were faintly
blond after weeks of heat. Visitors were still many; and
residents, after the fastidious retreat of August, were returning—along the Promenade, all day long, parasols,
boater hats and light dresses flickered against the dense
blue gauze backdrop that seldom let France be seen. In
the evenings the head of the pier was a lighted musical
box above the not yet cooling sea. Rare was the blade of
chill, the too crystal morning or breathlike blur on the
distance that announced autumn. Down the avenues the
dark green trees hardened but did not change: if a leaf
did fall, it was brushed away before anyone woke.

If Rockham remarked that Gavin was now quite a little man, her mistress made no reference to his schoolboy

state. She did once ask whether the Norfolk jacket that
had succeeded his sailor blouse were not, in this weather,
a little hot; but that he might be expected to be more
gruff, mum, standoffish or awkward than formerly did not
appear to strike her. The change, if any, was in her. He
failed to connect—why should he?—her new languor, her
more marked contrarieties and her odd little periods of
askance musing with the illness that was to be her death.
She only said, the summer had been too long. Until the
evenings she and Gavin were less alone, for she rose late;
and, on their afternoon drives through the country, inland along the coast or towards the downs, they were as
often as not accompanied by, of all persons, Mrs. Concannon. On occasions when Mrs. Concannon returned to
Mrs. Nicholson's house for tea, the Admiral made it his
practice to call for her. The Concannons were very much
occupied with preparations for another social event: a
Southstone branch of the Awaken Britannia League was
to be inaugurated by a drawing-room meeting at their
house. The daughters were busy folding and posting leaflets. Mrs. Nicholson, so far, could be pinned down to nothing more than a promise to send cakes from her own, or
rather her cook's, kitchen.

"But at least," pleaded Mrs. Concannon, at tea one
afternoon, "you should come if only to hear what it is
about."

By five o'clock, in September, Mrs. Nicholson's house
cast its shadow across the avenue on to the houses opposite, which should otherwise have received the descending sun. In revenge, they cast shadow back through her
bow window: everything in the drawing-room seemed to
exist in copper-mauve glass, or as though reflected into a
tarnished mirror. At this hour, Gavin saw the pale
walls, the silver lamp stems, the transparent frills of the
cushions with a prophetic feeling of their impermanence.
At her friend's words, Mrs. Nicholson's hand, extended,
paused for a moment over the cream jug. Turning her
head she said: "But I know what it is about; and I don't
approve."

With so little reference to the Admiral were these words

spoken that he might not have been there. There, however, he was, standing drawn up above the low tea table,
cup and saucer in hand. For a moment, not speaking, he
weighed his cup with a frown that seemed to ponder its
exact weight. He then said: "Then, logically, you should
not be sending cakes."

"Lilian," said Constance Concannon fondly, "is never
logical with regard to her friends."

"Aren't I?" said Mrs. Nicholson.—"But cake, don't
you think, makes everything so much nicer? You can't
offer people nothing but disagreeable ideas."

"You are too naughty, Lilian. All the League wants is
that we should be alert and thoughtful.—Perhaps Gavin
would like to come?"

Mrs. Nicholson turned on Gavin a considering look
from which complicity seemed to be quite absent; she appeared, if anything, to be trying to envisage him as alert
and thoughtful. And the Admiral, at the same moment,
fixed the candidate with a measuring eye. "What may
come," he said, "is bound, before it is done, to be his affair." Gavin made no reply to the proposition—and it was
found, a minute or two later, that the day fixed for the
drawing-room meeting was the day fixed for his return
home. School began again after that. "Well, what a pity,"
Mrs. Concannon said.

The day approached. The evenings were wholly
theirs, for Mrs. Nicholson dined out less. Always, from
after tea, when any guests had gone, he began to reign.
The apartnesses and frustrations of the preceding hours,
and, most of all, the occasional dissonances that those
could but produce between him and her, sent him pitch-
ing towards the twilight in a fever that rose as the week
went on. This fever, every time, was confounded by the
sweet pointlessness of the actual hour when it came. The
warmth that lingered in the exhausted daylight made it
possible for Mrs. Nicholson to extend herself on the *chaise
longue* in the bow window. Seated on a stool at the foot
of the *chaise longue,* leaning back against the frame window, Gavin could see, through the side pane of the glass
projection in which they sat, the salvias smouldering in

the theatre gardens. As it was towards these that her chair faced, in looking at them he was looking away from her. On the other hand, they were looking at the same thing. So they were on the evening that was his last. At the end of a minute or two of silence she exclaimed: "No, I don't care, really, for scarlet flowers.—You do?"

"Except carnations?"

"I don't care for public flowers. And you look and look at them till I feel quite lonely."

"I was only thinking, *they* will be here to-morrow."

"Have you been happy this time, Gavin? I haven't sometimes thought you've been quite so happy. Has it been my fault?"

He turned, but only to finger the fringe of the Kashmir shawl that had been spread by Rockham across her feet. Not looking up, he said: "I have not seen you so much."

"There are times," she said, "when one seems to be at the other side of glass. One sees what is going on, but one cannot help it. It may be what one does not like, but one cannot feel."

"Here, I always feel."

"Always feel what?" she remotely and idly asked.

"I just mean, here, I feel. I don't feel, anywhere else."

"And what is 'here'?" she said, with tender mocking obtuseness. "Southstone? What do you mean by 'here'?"

"Near you."

Mrs. Nicholson's attitude, her repose, had not been come at carelessly. Apparently relaxed, but not supine, she was supported by six or seven cushions—behind her head, at the nape of her neck, between her shoulders, under her elbows and in the small of her back. The slipperiness of this architecture of comfort enjoined stillness —her repose depended on each cushion staying just where it was. Up to now, she had lain with her wrists crossed on her dress: a random turn of the wrist, or flexing of fingers, were the nearest things to gestures she permitted herself—and, indeed, these had been enough. *Now,* her beginning to say, "I wonder if they were right . . ." must, though it sounded nothing more than reflective, have been accompanied by an incautious movement, for a cushion fell with a plump to the ground. Gavin went round, recovered the cushion and stood beside her: they eyed one another with communicative amazement, as though a third person had spoken and they were uncertain if they had heard aright. She arched her waist up and Gavin replaced the cushion. He said: "If who were right?"

"Rockham . . . The Admiral. She's always hinting, he's always saying, that I'm in some way thoughtless and wrong with you."

"Oh, him."

"I know," she said. "But you'll say good-bye to him nicely?"

He shrugged. "I shan't see him again—this time."

She hesitated. She was about to bring out something that, though slight, must be unacceptable. "He *is* coming in," she said, "for a moment, just after dinner, to fetch the cakes."

"Which cakes?"

"The cakes for to-morrow. I had arranged to send them round in the morning, but that would not do; no, that would not be soon enough. Everything is for the Admiral's meeting to make us ready, so everything must be ready in good time."

When, at nine o'clock, the Admiral's ring was heard, Mrs. Nicholson, indecisively, put down her coffee cup. A wood fire, lit while they were at dinner, was blazing languidly in the already warm air: it was necessary to sit at a distance from it. While the bell still rang, Gavin rose, as though he had forgotten something, and left the drawing-room. Passing the maid on her way to open the front door, he made a bolt upstairs. In his bedroom, Rockham was in possession: his trunk waited, open, bottom layer packed; her mending-basket was on the bureau; she was taking a final look through his things—his departure was to be early to-morrow morning. "Time flies," she said. "You're no sooner come than you're gone." She continued to count handkerchiefs, to stack up shirts. "I'd have thought," she said, "you'd have wanted to bring your school cap."

"Why? Anyway, it's a silly beastly old colour."

"You're too old-fashioned," she said sharply. "It was high time somebody went to school.—Now you *have* come up, just run down again, there's a good boy, and ask Madam if there's anything for your mother. If it's books, they ought to go in here among your boots."

"The Admiral's there."

"Well, my goodness, you know the Admiral."

Gavin played for time, on the way down, by looking into the rooms on every floor. Their still only partial familiarity, their fullness with objects that, in the half light coming in from the landing, he could only half perceive and did not yet dare touch, made him feel he was still only at the first chapter of the mystery of the house. He wondered how long it would be before he saw them again. Fear of Rockham's impatience, of her calling down to ask what he was up to, made him tread cautiously on the thickly carpeted stairs: he gained the hall without having made a sound. Here he smelled the fresh-baked cakes, waiting in a hamper on the hall table. The drawing-room door stood ajar, on, for a minute, dead silence. The Admiral must have gone, without the cakes.

But then the Admiral spoke. "You must see, there is nothing more to be said. I am only sorry I came. I did not expect you to be alone."

"For once, that is not my fault," replied Mrs. Nicholson, unsteadily. "I do not even know where the child is." In a voice that hardly seemed to be hers she cried out softly: "Then this is to go on always? What more do you ask? What else am I to be or do?"

"There's nothing more you can do. And all you must be is, happy."

"How easy," Mrs. Nicholson said.

"You have always said that that was easy, for you. For my own part, I have never considered happiness. There you misunderstood me, quite from the first."

"Not quite. Was I wrong in thinking you were a man?"

"I'm a man, yes. But I'm not that sort."

"That is too subtle for me," said Mrs. Nicholson.

"On the contrary, it is too simple for you. You ignore the greater part of my life. You cannot be blamed, perhaps; you have only known me since I was cursed with too much time on my hands. Your—your looks, charm and gaiety, my dear Lilian, I'd have been a fool not to salute at their full worth. Beyond that, I'm not such a fool as I may have seemed. Fool?—all things considered, I could not have been simply that without being something a good deal viler."

"I have been nice to Constance," said Mrs. Nicholson.

"Vile in my own eyes."

"I know, that is all you think of."

"I see, now, where you are in your element. You know as well as I do what your element is; which is why there's nothing more to be said. Flirtation's always been off my beat—so far off my beat, as a matter of fact, that I didn't know what it was when I first saw it. There, no doubt, I was wrong. If you can't live without it, you cannot, and that is that. If you have to be dangled after, you no doubt will be. But don't, my dear girl, go for that to the wrong shop. It would have been enough, where I am concerned, to watch you making a ninnie of that unfortunate boy."

"Who, poor little funny Gavin?" said Mrs. Nicholson. "Must I have nothing?—I have no little dog. You would not like it, even, if I had a real little dog. And you expect me to think that you do not care. . . ."

The two voices, which intensity more than caution kept pitched low, ceased. Gavin pushed open the drawing-room door.

The room, as can happen, had elongated. Like figures at the end of a telescope the Admiral and Mrs. Nicholson were to be seen standing before the fire. Of this, not a glint had room to appear between the figures of the antagonists. Mrs. Nicholson, head bent as though to examine the setting of the diamond, was twisting round a ring on her raised left hand—a lace-edged handkerchief, like an abandoned piece of stage property, had been dropped and lay on the hearth-rug near the hem of her skirts. She gave the impression of having not moved: if they had not, throughout, been speaking from this distance, the Admiral must have taken a step forward. But this, on his part, must have been, and must be, all—his head was averted from her, his shoulders were braced back, and behind his back he imprisoned one of his own wrists in a handcuff grip that shifted only to tighten. The heat from the fire must have made necessary, probably for the Admiral when he came, the opening of a window behind the curtains; for, as Gavin advanced into the drawing-room, a burst of applause entered from the theatre, and continued, drowning the music which had begun again.

Not a tremor recorded the moment when Mrs. Nicholson knew Gavin was in the room. Obliquely and vaguely turning her bowed head she extended to him, in an unchanged look, what might have been no more than an invitation to listen, also, to the music. "Why, Gavin," she said at last, "we were wondering where you were."

Here he was. From outside the theatre, stink still travelled to him from the lorry whose engine was being run. Nothing had changed in the colourless afternoon. Without knowing, he had plucked a leaf of the ivy which now bred and fed upon her house. A soldier, passing behind him to join the others, must have noticed his immobility all the way down the avenue; for the soldier said, out of the side of his mouth: "Annie doesn't live here any more." Gavin Doddington, humiliated, affected to study the ivy leaf, whose veins were like arbitrary vulgar fate-lines. He thought he remembered hearing of metal ivy; he knew he had seen ivy carved round marble monuments to signify fidelity,. regret, or the tomb-defying tenaciousness of memory—what you liked. Watched by the soldiers, he did not care to make the gesture that would be involved by throwing the leaf away: instead, he shut his hand on it, as he turned from the house. Should he go straight to the station, straight back to London? Not while the impression remained so strong. On the other hand, it would be a long time before the bars opened.

Another walk round Southstone, this afternoon, was necessary: there must be a decrescendo. From his tour of annihilation, nothing out of the story was to be missed. He walked as though he were carrying a guide-book.

Once or twice he caught sight of the immune downs, on the ascent to whose contours war had halted the villas. The most open view was, still, from the gates of the cemetery, past which he and she had so often driven without a thought. Through those gates, the extended dulling white marble vista said to him, only, that the multiplicity of the new graves, in thirty years, was enough in itself to make the position of hers indifferent—she might, once more, be lying beside her husband. On the return through the town towards the lip of the plateau overhanging the sea, the voidness and the air of concluded meaning about the plan of Southstone seemed to confirm her theory: history, after this last galvanized movement forward, had come, as she expected, to a full stop. It had only not stopped where or as she foresaw. Crossing the Promenade obliquely, he made, between wire entanglements, for the railings; to become one more of the space-out people who leaned along them, willing to see a convoy or gazing with indifference towards liberated France. The path and steps up the cliff face had been destroyed; the handrail hung out rotting into the air.

Back in the shopping centre, he turned a quickening step, past the shuttered, boarded or concave windows, towards the corner florist's where Mrs. Nicholson had insisted on the carnations. But this had received a direct hit: the entire corner was gone. When time takes our revenges out of our hands it is, usually, to execute them more slowly: her vindictiveness, more thorough than ours, might satisfy us, if, in the course of her slowness, we did not forget. In this case, however, she had worked in the less than a second of detonation. Gavin Doddington paused where there was no florist—was he not, none the less, entitled to draw a line through this?

Not until after some time back in the bar did it strike him—there had been one omission. He had not yet been to the Concannons'. He pushed his way out: it was about seven o'clock, twenty minutes or so before the black-out. They had lived in a crescent set just from a less expensive reach of the Promenade. On his way, he passed houses and former hotels occupied by soldiers or A.T.S. who had not yet gone. These, from top to basement, were in a state of naked, hard, lemon-yellow illumination. Interposing dark hulks gave you the feeling of nothing more than their recent military occupation. The front doors of the Concannons' crescent opened, on the inland side, into a curved street, which, for some military reason now probably out of date, had been blocked at the near end; Gavin had to go round. Along the pavements under the front doorsteps there was so much wire that he was thrust out into the road—opposite only one house was there an inviting gap in the loops. Admiral Concannon, having died in the last war, could not have obtained this as a concession—all the same this *was*, as the number faintly confirmed, his house. Nobody now but Gavin recognized its identity or its importance. Here had dwelled, and here continued to dwell, the genius of the Southstone that now was. Twice over had there been realized the Admiral's alternative to love.

The Concannons' dining-room window, with its high triple sashes, was raised some distance above the street. Gavin, standing opposite it, looked in at an A.T.S. girl seated at a table. She faced the window, the dusk and him. From above her head, a naked electric light bulb, on a flex shortened by being knotted, glared on the stripped, whitish walls of the room and emphasized the fact that she was alone. In her khaki shirt, sleeves rolled up, she sat leaning her bare elbows on the bare table. Her face was abrupt with youth. She turned one wrist, glanced at the watch on it, then resumed her steady stare through the window, downwards at the dusk in which Gavin stood.

It was thus that, for the second time in his life, he saw straight up into eyes that did not see him. The intervening years had given him words for trouble: a phrase, *"l'horreur de mon néant,"* darted across his mind.

At any minute, the girl would have to approach the window to do the black-out—for that, along this coast, was still strictly enforced. It was worth waiting. He lighted a cigarette: she looked at her watch again. When she did rise it was, first, to unhook from a peg beside the dining-room door not only her tunic but her cap. Her being dressed for the street, when she did reach up and, with a succession of movements he liked to watch, begin to twitch the black stuff across the window, made it his object *not* to be seen—just yet. Light staggered, a moment longer, on the desiccated pods of the wallflowers that, seeded from the front garden, had sprung up between the cracks of the pavement, and on the continuous regular loops or hoops of barbed wire, through all of which, by a sufficiently long leap, one *could* have projected oneself head foremost, unhurt. At last she had stopped the last crack of light. She had now nothing to do but to come out.

Coming smartly down the Concannons' steps, she may just have seen the outline of the civilian waiting, smoking a cigarette. She swerved impassively, if at all. He said: "A penny for your thoughts." She might not have heard. He fell into step beside her. Next, appearing to hear what he had not said, she replied: "No, I'm *not* going your way."

"Too bad. But there's only one way out—can't get out, you know, at the other end. What have *I* got to do, then —stay here all night?"

"*I* don't know, I'm sure." Unconcernedly humming, she did not even quicken her light but ringing tramp on the curved street. If he kept abreast with her, it was casually, and at an unpressing distance: this, and the widening sky that announced the open end of the crescent, must have been reassuring. He called across to her: "That house you came out of, I used to know people who lived there. I was just looking round."

She turned, for the first time—she could not help it. "People lived there?" she said. "Just fancy. I know I'd sooner live in a tomb. And that goes for all this place. Imagine anyone coming here on a holiday!"

"I'm on a holiday."

"Goodness. What do you do with yourself?"

"Just look round."

"Well, I wonder how long you stick it out.—Here's where we go different ways. Good night."

"I've got nobody to talk to," Gavin said, suddenly standing still in the dark. A leaf flittered past. She was woman enough to halt, to listen, because this had not been said to her. If her "Oh yes, we girls have heard that before" was automatic, it was, still more, wavering. He cast away the end of one cigarette and started lighting another: the flame of the lighter, cupped inside his hands, jumped for a moment over his features. Her first thought was: yes, he's quite old—that went along with his desperate jauntiness. Civilian, yes: too young for the last war, too old for this. A gentleman—they were the clever ones. But he had, she perceived, forgotten about her thoughts —what she saw, in that moment before he snapped down the lighter, stayed on the darkness, puzzling her somewhere outside the compass of her own youth. She had seen the face of somebody dead who was still there— "old" because of the presence, under an icy screen, of a whole stopped mechanism for feeling. Those features had been framed, long ago, for hope. The dints above the nostrils, the lines extending the eyes, the lips' grimacing grip on the cigarette—all completed the picture of someone wolfish. A preyer. But who had said, preyers are preyed upon?

His lower lip came out, thrusting the cigarette up at a debonair angle towards his eyes. "Not a soul," he added —this time with calculation, and to her.

"Anyway," she said sharply, "I've got a date. Anyway, what made you pick on this dead place? Why not pick on some place where you know someone?"

The Happy Autumn Fields

THE family walking party, though it comprised so many, did not deploy or straggle over the stubble but kept in a procession of threes and twos. Papa, who carried his Alpine stick, led, flanked by Constance and little Arthur. Robert and Cousin Theodore, locked in studious talk, had Emily attached but not quite abreast. Next came Digby and Lucius, taking, to left and right, imaginary aim at rooks. Henrietta and Sarah brought up the rear.

It was Sarah who saw the others ahead on the blond stubble, who knew them, knew what they were to each other, knew their names and knew her own. It was she who felt the stubble under her feet, and who heard it give beneath the tread of the others a continuous different more distant soft stiff scrunch. The field and all these outlying fields in view knew as Sarah knew that they were Papa's. The harvest had been good and was now in: he was satisfied—for this afternoon he had made the instinctive choice of his most womanly daughter, most nearly infant son. Arthur, whose hand Papa was holding, took an anxious hop, a skip and a jump to every stride of the great man's. As for Constance—Sarah could often see the flash of her hat-feather as she turned her head, the curve of her close bodice as she turned her torso. Constance gave Papa her attention but not her thoughts, for she had already been sought in marriage.

The landowners' daughters, from Constance down, walked with their beetle-green, mole or maroon skirts gathered up and carried clear of the ground, but for Henrietta, who was still ankle-free. They walked inside a continuous stuffy sound, but left silence behind them. Behind them, rooks that had risen and circled, sun striking blue from their blue-black wings, planed one by one to the earth and settled to peck again. Papa and the boys were dark-clad as the rooks but with no sheen, but for their white collars.

It was Sarah who located the thoughts of Constance, knew what a twisting prisoner was Arthur's hand, felt to the depths of Emily's pique at Cousin Theodore's inattention, rejoiced with Digby and Lucius at the imaginary fall of so many rooks. She fell back, however, as from a rocky range, from the converse of Robert and Cousin Theodore. Most she knew that she swam with love at the nearness of Henrietta's young and alert face and eyes which shone with the sky and queried the afternoon.

She recognized the colour of valediction, tasted sweet sadness, while from the cottage inside the screen of trees wood-smoke rose melting pungent and blue. This was the eve of the brothers' return to school. It was like a Sunday; Papa had kept the late afternoon free; all (all but one) encircling Robert, Digby and Lucius, they walked the estate the brothers would not see again for so long. Robert, it could be felt, was not unwilling to return to his books; next year he would go to college like Theodore; besides, to all this they saw he was not the heir. But in Digby and Lucius aiming and popping hid a bodily grief, the repugnance of victims, though these two were further from being heirs than Robert.

Sarah said to Henrietta: "To think they will not be here to-morrow!"

"*Is* that what you are thinking about?" Henrietta asked, with her subtle taste for the truth.

"More, I was thinking that you and I will be back again

by one another at table. . . ."

"You know we are always sad when the boys are going, but we are never sad when the boys have gone." The sweet reciprocal guilty smile that started on Henrietta's lips finished on those of Sarah. "Also," the young sister said, "we know this is only something happening again. It happened last year, and it will happen next. But oh how should I feel, and how should you feel, if it were something that had not happened before?"

"For instance, when Constance goes to be married?"

"Oh, I don't mean *Constance!*" said Henrietta.

"So long," said Sarah, considering, "as, whatever it is, it happens to both of us?" She must never have to wake in the early morning except to the birdlike stirrings of Henrietta, or have her cheek brushed in the dark by the frill of another pillow in whose hollow did not repose Henrietta's cheek. Rather than they should cease to lie in the same bed she prayed they might lie in the same grave. "You and I will stay as we are," she said, "then nothing can touch one without touching the other."

"So you say; so I hear you say!" exclaimed Henrietta, who then, lips apart, sent Sarah her most tormenting look. "But I cannot forget that you chose to be born without me; that you would not wait—" But here she broke off, laughed outright and said: "Oh, *see!*"

Ahead of them there had been a dislocation. Emily took advantage of having gained the ridge to kneel down to tie her bootlace so abruptly that Digby all but fell over her, with an exclamation. Cousin Theodore had been civil enough to pause beside Emily, but Robert, lost to all but what he was saying, strode on, head down, only just not colliding into Papa and Constance, who had turned to look back. Papa, astounded, let go of Arthur's hand, whereupon Arthur fell flat on the stubble.

"Dear me," said the affronted Constance to Robert.

Papa said: "What is the matter there? May I ask, Robert, where you are going, sir? Digby, remember that is your sister Emily."

"Cousin Emily is in trouble," said Cousin Theodore.

Poor Emily, telescoped in her skirts and by now scarlet

under her hatbrim, said in a muffled voice: "It is just my bootlace, Papa."

"Your bootlace, Emily?"

"I was just tying it."

"Then you had better tie it.—Am I to think," said Papa, looking round them all, "that you must all go down like a pack of ninepins because Emily has occasion to stoop?"

At this Henrietta uttered a little whoop, flung her arms round Sarah, buried her face in her sister and fairly suffered with laughter. She could contain this no longer; she shook all over. Papa, who found Henrietta so hopelessly out of order that he took no notice of her except at table, took no notice, simply giving the signal for the others to collect themselves and move on. Cousin Theodore, helping Emily to her feet, could be seen to see how her heightened colour became her, but she dispensed with his hand chillily, looked elsewhere, touched the brooch at her throat and said: "Thank you, I have not sustained an accident." Digby apologized to Emily, Robert to Papa and Constance. Constance righted Arthur, flicking his breeches over with her handkerchief. All fell into their different steps and resumed their way.

Sarah, with no idea how to console laughter, coaxed, "Come, come, come," into Henrietta's ear. Between the girls and the others the distance widened; it began to seem that they would be left alone.

"And why not?" said Henrietta, lifting her head in answer to Sarah's thought.

They looked around them with the same eyes. The shorn uplands seemed to float on the distance, which extended dazzling to tiny blue glassy hills. There was no end to the afternoon, whose light went on ripening now they had scythed the corn. Light filled the silence which, now Papa and the others were out of hearing, was complete. Only screens of trees intersected and knolls made islands in the vast fields. The mansion and the home farm had sunk for ever below them in the expanse of woods, so that hardly a ripple showed where the girls dwelled.

The shadow of the same rook circling passed over Sarah

then over Henrietta, who in their turn cast one shadow
across the stubble. "But, Henrietta, we cannot stay here
for ever."

Henrietta immediately turned her eyes to the only
lonely plume of smoke, from the cottage. "Then let us
go and visit the poor old man. He is dying and the others
are happy. One day we shall pass and see no more smoke;
then soon his roof will fall in, and we shall always be
sorry we did not go to-day."

"But he no longer remembers us any longer."

"All the same, he will feel us there in the door."

"But can we forget this is Robert's and Digby's and
Lucius's good-bye walk? It would be heartless of both
of us to neglect them."

"Then how heartless Fitzgeorge is!" smiled Henrietta.

"Fitzgeorge is himself, the eldest and in the Army.
Fitzgeorge I'm afraid is not an excuse for us."

A resigned sigh, or perhaps the pretence of one, heaved
up Henrietta's still narrow bosom. To delay matters for
just a moment more she shaded her eyes with one hand, to
search the distance like a sailor looking for a sail. She
gazed with hope and zeal in every direction but that in
which she and Sarah were bound to go. Then—"Oh, but
Sarah, here *they* are, coming—they are!" she cried. She
brought out her handkerchief and began to fly it, drawing it to and fro through the windless air.

In the glass of the distance, two horsemen came into
view, cantering on a grass track between the fields. When
the track dropped into a hollow they dropped with it,
but by now the drumming of hoofs was heard. The reverberation filled the land, the silence and Sarah's being;
not watching for the riders to reappear she instead fixed
her eyes on her sister's handkerchief which, let hang limp
while its owner intently waited, showed a bitten corner
as well as a damson stain. Again it became a flag, in furious motion.—"Wave too, Sarah, wave too! Make your
bracelet flash!"

"They must have seen us if they will ever see us," said
Sarah, standing still as a stone.

Henrietta's waving at once ceased. Facing her sister she

crunched up her handkerchief, as though to stop it acting a lie. "I can see you are shy," she said in a dead voice.
"So shy you won't even wave to *Fitzgeorge?*"

Her way of not speaking the *other* name had a hundred meanings; she drove them all in by the way she did
not look at Sarah's face. The impulsive breath she had
caught stole silently out again, while her eyes—till now
at their brightest, their most speaking—dulled with un-
comprehending solitary alarm. The ordeal of awaiting
Eugene's approach thus became for Sarah, from moment
to moment, torture.

Fitzgeorge, Papa's heir, and his friend Eugene, the
young neighbouring squire, struck off the track and rode
up at a trot with their hats doffed. Sun striking low turned
Fitzgeorge's flesh to coral and made Eugene blink his
dark eyes. The young men reined in; the girls looked up
the horses. "And my father, Constance, the others?" Fitzgeorge demanded, as though the stubble had swallowed
them.

"Ahead, on the way to the quarry, the other side of
the hill."

"We heard you were all walking together," Fitzgeorge
said, seeming dissatisfied.

"We are following."

"What, alone?" said Eugene, speaking for the first time.

"Forlorn!" glittered Henrietta, raising two mocking
hands.

Fitzgeorge considered, said "Good" severely, and signified to Eugene that they would ride on. But too late:
Eugene had dismounted. Fitzgeorge saw, shrugged and
flicked his horse to a trot; but Eugene led his slowly between the sisters. Or rather, Sarah walked on his left hand,
the horse on his right and Henrietta the other side of the
horse. Henrietta, acting like somebody quite alone, looked
up at the sky, idly holding one of the empty stirrups.
Sarah, however, looked at the ground, with Eugene inclined as though to speak but not speaking. Enfolded, diz-
zied, blinded as though inside a wave, she could feel his
features carved in brightness above her. Alongside the
slender stepping of his horse, Eugene matched his natu-

rally long free step to hers. His elbow was through the reins; with his fingers he brushed back the lock that his bending to her had sent falling over his forehead. She recorded the sublime act and knew what smile shaped his lips. So each without looking trembled before an image, while slow colour burned up the curves of her cheeks. The consummation would be when their eyes met.

At the other side of the horse, Henrietta began to sing. At once her pain, like a scientific ray, passed through the horse and Eugene to penetrate Sarah's heart.

We surmount the skyline: the family come into our view, we into theirs. They are halted, waiting, on the decline to the quarry. The handsome statufied group in strong yellow sunshine, aligned by Papa and crowned by Fitzgeorge, turn their judging eyes on the laggards, waiting to close their ranks round Henrietta and Sarah and Eugene. One more moment and it will be too late; no further communication will be possible. Stop oh stop Henrietta's heartbreaking singing! Embrace her close again! Speak the only possible word! Say—oh, say what? Oh, the word is lost!

"Henrietta . . ."

A shock of striking pain in the knuckles of the outflung hand—Sarah's? The eyes, opening, saw that the hand had struck, not been struck: there was a corner of a table. Dust, whitish and gritty, lay on the top of the table and on the telephone. Dull but piercing white light filled the room and what was left of the ceiling; her first thought was that it must have snowed. If so, it was winter now.

Through the calico stretched and tacked over the window came the sound of a piano: someone was playing Tchaikovsky badly in a room without windows or doors. From somewhere else in the hollowness came a cascade of hammering. Close up, a voice: "Oh, *awake*, Mary?" It came from the other side of the open door, which jutted out between herself and the speaker—he on the threshold, she lying on the uncovered mattress of a bed. The speaker added: "I had been going away."

Summoning words from somewhere she said: "Why?
I didn't know you were here."

"Evidently— Say, who is 'Henrietta'?"

Despairing tears filled her eyes. She drew back her hurt
hand, began to suck at the knuckle and whimpered, "I've
hurt myself."

A man she knew to be "Travis," but failed to focus,
came round the door saying: "Really I don't wonder."
Sitting down on the edge of the mattress he drew her
hand away from her lips and held it: the act, in itself
gentle, was accompanied by an almost hostile stare of
concern. "Do listen, Mary," he said. "While you've slept
I've been all over the house again, and I'm less than ever
satisfied that it's safe. In your normal senses you'd never
attempt to stay here. There've been alerts, and more than
alerts, all day; one more bang anywhere near, which may
happen at any moment, could bring the rest of this down.
You keep telling me that you have things to see to—but
do you know what chaos the rooms are in? Till they've
gone ahead with more clearing, where can you hope to
start? And if there *were* anything you could do, you
couldn't do it. Your own nerves know that, if you don't:
it was almost frightening, when I looked in just now, to
see the way you were sleeping—you've shut up shop."

She lay staring over his shoulder at the calico window.
He went on: "You don't like it here. Your self doesn't
like it. Your will keeps driving your self, but it can't be
driven the whole way—it makes its own get-out: sleep.
Well, I want you to sleep as much as you (really) do.
But *not* here. So I've taken a room for you in a hotel; I'm
going now for a taxi, you can practically make the move
without waking up."

"No, I can't get into a taxi without waking."

"Do you realize you're the last soul left in the terrace?"

"Then who is that playing the piano?"

"Oh, one of the furniture-movers in Number Six. I
didn't count the jaquerie; of course *they're* in possession
—unsupervised, teeming, having a high old time. While
I looked in on you in here ten minutes ago they were
smashing out that conservatory at the other end. Glass

being done in in cold blood—it was brutalizing. You never batted an eyelid; in fact, I thought you smiled." He listened. "Yes, the piano—they are highbrow all right. You know there's a workman downstairs lying on your blue sofa looking for pictures in one of your French books?"

"No," she said, "I've no idea who is there."

"Obviously. With the lock blown off your front door anyone who likes can get in and out."

"Including you."

"Yes. I've had a word with a chap about getting that lock back before to-night. As for you, you don't know what is happening."

"I did," she said, locking her fingers before her eyes.

The unreality of this room and of Travis's presence preyed on her as figments of dreams that one knows to be dreams can do. This environment's being in semi-ruin struck her less than its being some sort of device or trap; and she rejoiced, if anything, in its decrepitude. As for Travis, he had his own part in the conspiracy to keep her from the beloved two. She felt he began to feel he was now unmeaning. She was struggling not to contemn him, scorn him for his ignorance of Henrietta, Eugene, her loss. His possessive angry fondness was part, of course, of the story of him and Mary, which like a book once read she remembered clearly but with indifference. Frantic at being delayed here, while the moment awaited her in the cornfield, she all but afforded a smile at the grotesquerie of being saddled with Mary's body and lover. Rearing up her head from the bare pillow, she looked, as far as the crossed feet, along the form inside which she found herself trapped: the irrelevant body of Mary, weighted down to the bed, wore a short black modern dress, flaked with plaster. The toes of the black suède shoes by their sickly whiteness showed Mary must have climbed over fallen ceilings; dirt engraved the fate-lines in Mary's palms.

This inspired her to say: "But I've made a start; I've been pulling out things of value or things I want."

For answer Travis turned to look down, expressively,

at some object out of her sight, on the floor close by the bed. "*I* see," he said, "a musty old leather box gaping open with God knows what—junk, illegible letters, diaries, yellow photographs, chiefly plaster and dust. Of all things, Mary!—after a missing will?"

"Everything one unburies seems the same age."

"Then what are these, where do they come from—family stuff?"

"No idea," she yawned into Mary's hand. "They may not even be mine. Having a house like this that had empty rooms must have made me store more than I knew, for years. I came on these, so I wondered. Look if you like."

He bent and began to go through the box—it seemed to her, not unsuspiciously. While he blew grit off packets and fumbled with tapes she lay staring at the exposed laths of the ceiling, calculating. She then said: "Sorry if I've been cranky, about the hotel and all. Go away just for two hours, then come back with a taxi, and I'll go quiet. Will that do?"

"Fine—except why not now?"

"*Travis . . .*"

"Sorry. It shall be as you say . . . You've got some good morbid stuff in this box, Mary—so far as I can see at a glance. The photographs seem more your sort of thing. Comic but lyrical. All of one set of people—a beard, a gun and a pot hat, a schoolboy with a moustache, a phaeton drawn up in front of mansion, a group on steps, a *carte de visite* of two young ladies hand-in-hand in front of a painted field—"

"*Give that to me!*"

She instinctively tried, and failed, to unbutton the bosom of Mary's dress: it offered no hospitality to the photograph. So she could only fling herself over on the mattress, away from Travis, covering the two faces with her body. Racked by that oblique look of Henrietta's she recorded, too, a sort of personal shock at having seen Sarah for the first time.

Travis's hand came over her, and she shuddered. Wounded, he said: "Mary . . ."

"Can't you leave *me* alone?"

She did not move or look till he had gone out saying: "Then, in two hours." She did not therefore see him pick up the dangerous box, which he took away under his arm, out of her reach.

They were back. Now the sun was setting behind the trees, but its rays passed dazzling between the branches into the beautiful warm red room. The tips of the ferns in the jardiniere curled gold, and Sarah, standing by the jardiniere, pinched at a leaf of scented geranium. The carpet had a great centre wreath of pomegranates, on which no tables or chairs stood, and its whole circle was between herself and the others.

No fire was lit yet, but where they were grouped was a hearth. Henrietta sat on a low stool, resting her elbow above her head on the arm of Mamma's chair, looking away intently as though into a fire, idle. Mamma embroidered, her needle slowed down by her thoughts; the length of tatting with roses she had already done overflowed stiffly over her supple skirts. Stretched on the rug at Mamma's feet, Arthur looked through an album of Swiss views, not liking them but vowed to be very quiet. Sarah, from where she stood, saw fuming cataracts and null eternal snows as poor Arthur kept turning over the pages, which had tissue paper between.

Against the white marble mantelpiece stood Eugene. The dark red shadows gathering in the drawing-room as the trees drowned more and more of the sun would reach him last, perhaps never: it seemed to Sarah that a lamp was lighted behind his face. He was the only gentleman with the ladies: Fitzgeorge had gone to the stables, Papa to give an order; Cousin Theodore was consulting a dictionary; in the gunroom Robert, Lucius and Digby went through the sad rites, putting away their guns. All this was known to go on but none of it could be heard.

This particular hour of subtle light—not to be fixed by the clock, for it was early in winter and late in summer and in spring and autumn now, about Arthur's bedtime—had always, for Sarah, been Henrietta's. To be with her indoors or out, upstairs or down, was to share the same crepitation. Her spirit ran on past yours with a laughing shiver into an element of its own. Leaves and branches and mirrors in empty rooms became animate. The sisters rustled and scampered and concealed themselves where nobody else was in play that was full of fear, fear that was full of play. Till, by dint of making each other's hearts beat violently, Henrietta so wholly and Sarah so nearly lost all human reason that Mamma had been known to look at them searchingly as she sat instated for evening among the calm amber lamps.

But now Henrietta had locked the hour inside her breast. By spending it seated beside Mamma, in young imitation of Constance the Society daughter, she disclaimed for ever anything else. It had always been she who with one fierce act destroyed any toy that might be outgrown. She sat with straight back, poising her cheek remotely against her finger. Only by never looking at Sarah did she admit their eternal loss.

Eugene, not long returned from a foreign tour, spoke of travel, addressing himself to Mamma, who thought but did not speak of her wedding journey. But every now and then she had to ask Henrietta to pass the scissors or tray of carded wools, and Eugene seized every such moment to look at Sarah. Into eyes always brilliant with melancholy he dared begin to allow no other expression. But this in itself declared the conspiracy of still undeclared love. For her part she looked at him as though he, transfigured by the strange light, were indeed a picture, a picture who could not see her. The wallpaper now flamed scarlet behind his shoulder. Mamma, Henrietta, even unknowing Arthur were in no hurry to raise their heads.

Henrietta said: "If I were a man I should take my bride to Italy."

"There are mules in Switzerland," said Arthur.

"Sarah," said Mamma, who turned in her chair mildly, "where are you, my love; do you never mean to sit down?"

"To Naples," said Henrietta.

"Are you not thinking of Venice?" said Eugene.

"No," returned Henrietta, "why should I be? I should like to climb the volcano. But then I am not a man, and am still less likely ever to be a bride."

"Arthur . . ." Mamma said.

"Mamma?"

"Look at the clock."

Arthur sighed politely, got up and replaced the album on the circular table, balanced upon the rest. He offered his hand to Eugene, his cheek to Henrietta and to Mamma; then he started towards Sarah, who came to meet him. "Tell me, Arthur," she said, embracing him, "what did you do to-day?"

Arthur only stared with his button blue eyes. "You were there too; we went for a walk in the cornfield, with Fitzgeorge on his horse, and I fell down." He pulled out of her arms and said: "I must go back to my beetle." He had difficulty, as always, in turning the handle of the mahogany door. Mamma waited till he had left the room, then said: "Arthur is quite a man now; he no longer comes running to me when he has hurt himself. Why, I did not even know he had fallen down. Before we know, he will be going away to school too." She sighed and lifted her eyes to Eugene. "To-morrow is to be a sad day."

Eugene with a gesture signified his own sorrow. The sentiments of Mamma could have been uttered only here in the drawing-room, which for all its size and formality was lyrical and almost exotic. There was a look like velvet in darker parts of the air; sombre window draperies let out gushes of lace; the music on the pianoforte bore tender titles, and the harp though unplayed gleamed in a corner, beyond sofas, whatnots, arm-chairs, occasional tables that all stood on tottering little feet. At any moment a tinkle might have been struck from the lustres' drops of the brighter day, a vibration from the musical instruments, or a quiver from the fringes and ferns. But the towering vases upon the consoles, the albums piled on the tables, the shells and figurines on the flights of brackets, all had, like the alabaster Leaning Tower of Pisa, an equilibrium of their own. Nothing would fall or change. And everything in the drawing-room was muted, weighted, pivoted by Mamma. When she added: "We shall not feel quite the same," it was to be understood that she would not have spoken thus from her place at the opposite end of Papa's table.

"Sarah," said Henrietta curiously, "what made you ask Arthur what he had been doing? Surely you have not forgotten to-day?"

The sisters were seldom known to address or question one another in public; it was taken that they knew each other's minds. Mamma, though untroubled, looked from one to the other. Henrietta continued: "No day, least of all to-day, is like any other— Surely that must be true?" she said to Eugene. "You will never forget my waving my handkerchief?"

Before Eugene had composed an answer, she turned to Sarah: "Or *you*, them riding across the fields?"

Eugene also slowly turned his eyes on Sarah, as though awaiting with something like dread her answer to the question he had not asked. She drew a light little gold chair into the middle of the wreath of the carpet, where no one ever sat, and sat down. She said: "But since then I think I have been asleep."

"Charles the First walked and talked half an hour after his head was cut off," said Henrietta mockingly. Sarah in anguish pressed the palms of her hands together upon a shred of geranium leaf.

"How else," she said, "could I have had such a bad dream?"

"That must be the explanation!" said Henrietta.

"A trifle fanciful," said Mamma.

However rash it might be to speak at all, Sarah wished she knew how to speak more clearly. The obscurity and loneliness of her trouble was not to be borne. How could she put into words the feeling of dislocation, the formless dread that had been with her since she found herself in the drawing-room? The source of both had been what she must call her dream. How could she tell the others with what vehemence she tried to attach her being to each second, not because each was singular in itself, each a drop condensed from the mist of love in the room, but because she apprehended that the seconds were numbered? Her hope was that the others at least half knew. Were Henrietta and Eugene able to understand how completely, how nearly for ever, she had been swept from them, would they not without fail each grasp one of her hands?—She went so far as to throw her hands out, as though alarmed by a wasp. The shred of geranium fell to the carpet.

Mamma, tracing this behaviour of Sarah's to only one cause, could not but think reproachfully of Eugene. Delightful as his conversation had been, he would have done better had he paid this call with the object of interviewing Papa. Turning to Henrietta she asked her to ring for the lamps, as the sun had set.

Eugene, no longer where he had stood, was able to make no gesture towards the bell-rope. His dark head was under the tide of dusk; for, down on one knee on the edge of the wreath, he was feeling over the carpet for what had fallen from Sarah's hand. In the inevitable silence rooks on the return from the fields could be heard streaming over the house; their sound filled the sky and even the room, and it appeared so useless to ring the bell that Henrietta stayed quivering by Mamma's chair. Eugene rose, brought out his fine white handkerchief and, while they watched, enfolded carefully in it what he had just found, then returned the handkerchief to his breast pocket. This was done so deep in the reverie that accompanies any final act that Mamma instinctively murmured to Henrietta: "But you will be my child when Arthur has gone."

The door opened for Constance to appear on the threshold. Behind her queenly figure globes approached, swimming in their own light: these were the lamps for which Henrietta had not rung, but these first were put on the hall tables. "Why, Mamma," exclaimed Constance, "I cannot see who is with you!"

"Eugene is with us," said Henrietta, "but on the point of asking if he may send for his horse."

"Indeed?" said Constance to Eugene. "Fitzgeorge has been asking for you, but I cannot tell where he is now."

The figures of Emily, Lucius and Cousin Theodore crisscrossed the lamplight there in the hall, to mass behind Constance's in the drawing-room door. Emily, over her sister's shoulder, said: "Mamma, Lucius wishes to ask you whether for once he may take his guitar to school."—"One objection, however," said Cousin Theodore, "is that Lucius's trunk is already locked and strapped." "Since Robert is taking his box of inks," said Lucius, "I do not see why I should not take my guitar."—"But Robert," said Constance, "will soon be going to college."

Lucius squeezed past the others into the drawing-room in order to look anxiously at Mamma, who said: "You have thought of this late; we must go and see." The others parted to let Mamma, followed by Lucius, out. Then Constance, Emily and Cousin Theodore deployed and sat down in different parts of the drawing-room, to await the lamps.

"I am glad the rooks have done passing over," said Emily, "they make me nervous."—"Why," yawned Constance haughtily, "what do you think could happen?" Robert and Digby silently came in.

Eugene said to Sarah: "I shall be back to-morrow."

"But, oh—" she began. She turned to cry: "Henrietta!"

"Why, what is the matter?" said Henrietta, unseen at the back of the gold chair. "What could be sooner than to-morrow?"

"But something terrible may be going to happen."

"There cannot fail to be to-morrow," said Eugene gravely.

"*I* will see that there is to-morrow," said Henrietta.

"You will never let me out of your sight?"

Eugene, addressing himself to Henrietta, said: "Yes, promise her what she asks."

Henrietta cried: "She *is* never out of my sight. Who are you to ask me that, you Eugene? Whatever tries to come between me and Sarah becomes nothing. Yes, come to-morrow, come sooner, come—when you like, but no one will ever be quite alone with Sarah. You do not even know what you are trying to do. It is *you* who are making something terrible happen.—Sarah, tell him that that is true! Sarah—"

The others, in the dark on the chairs and sofas, could be felt to turn their judging eyes upon Sarah, who, as once before, could not speak—

—The house rocked; simultaneously the calico window split and more ceiling fell, though not on the bed. The enormous dull sound of the explosion died, leaving a minor trickle of dissolution still to be heard in parts of the house. Until the choking stinging plaster dust had had time to settle, she lay with lips pressed close, nostrils not breathing and eyes shut. Remembering the box, Mary wondered if it had been again buried. No, she found, looking over the edge of the bed: that had been unable to happen because the box was missing. Travis, who must have taken it, would when he came back no doubt explain why. She looked at her watch, which had stopped, which was not surprising; she did not remember winding it for the last two days, but then she could not remember much. Through the torn window appeared the timelessness of an impermeably clouded late summer afternoon.

There being nothing left, she wished he would come to take her to the hotel. The one way back to the fields was barred by Mary's surviving the fall of ceiling. Sarah was right in doubting that there would be to-morrow: Eugene, Henrietta were lost in time to the woman weeping there on the bed, no longer reckoning who she was.

At last she heard the taxi, then Travis hurrying up the littered stairs. "Mary, you're all right, Mary—*another?*" Such a helpless white face came round the door that she could only hold out her arms and say: "Yes, but where have *you* been?"

"You said two hours. But I wish—"

"I have missed you."

"Have you? Do you know you are crying?"

"Yes. How are we to live without natures? We only know inconvenience now, not sorrow. Everything pulverizes so easily because it is rot-dry; one can only wonder that it makes so much noise. The source, the sap must have dried up, or the pulse must have stopped, before you and I were conceived. So much flowed through people; so little flows through us. All we can do is imitate love or sorrow.—Why did you take away my box?"

He only said: "It is in my office."

She continued: "What has happened is cruel: I am left with a fragment torn out of a day, a day I don't even know where or when; and now how am I to help laying that like a pattern against the poor stuff of everything else?—Alternatively, I am a person drained by a dream. I cannot forget the climate of those hours. Or life at that pitch, eventful—not happy, no, but strung like a harp. I have had a sister called Henrietta."

"And I have been looking inside your box. What else can you expect?—I have had to write off this day, from the work point of view, thanks to you. So could I sit and do nothing for the last two hours? I just glanced through this and that—still, I know the family."

"You said it was morbid stuff."

"Did I? I still say it gives off something."

She said: "And then there was Eugene."

"Probably. I don't think I came on much of his except some notes he must have made for Fitzgeorge from some book on scientific farming. Well, there it is: I have sorted everything out and put it back again, all but a lock of hair that tumbled out of a letter I could not trace. So I've got the hair in my pocket."

"What colour is it?"

"Ash-brown. Of course, it is a bit—desiccated. Do you want it?"

"No," she said with a shudder. "Really, Travis, what revenges you take!"

"I didn't look at it that way," he said puzzled.

"Is the taxi waiting?" Mary got off the bed and, picking her way across the room, began to look about for things she ought to take with her, now and then stopping to brush her dress. She took the mirror out of her bag to see how dirty her face was. "Travis—" she said suddenly.

"Mary?"

"Only, I—"

"That's all right. Don't let us imitate anything just at present."

In the taxi, looking out of the window, she said: "I suppose, then, that I am descended from Sarah?"

"No," he said, "that would be impossible. There must be some reason why you should have those papers, but that is not the one. From all negative evidence Sarah, like Henrietta, remained unmarried. I found no mention of either, after a certain date, in the letters of Constance, Robert or Emily, which makes it seem likely both died young. Fitzgeorge refers, in a letter to Robert written in his old age, to some friend of their youth who was thrown from his horse and killed, riding back after a visit to their home. The young man, whose name doesn't appear, was alone; and the evening, which was in autumn, was fine though late. Fitzgeorge wonders, and says he will always wonder, what made the horse shy in those empty fields."

Mysterious Kôr

FULL moonlight drenched the city and searched it; there was not a niche left to stand in. The effect was remorseless: London looked like the moon's capital—shallow, cratered, extinct. It was late, but not yet midnight; now the buses had stopped the polished roads and streets in this region sent for minutes together a ghostly unbroken reflection up. The soaring new flats and the crouching old shops and houses looked equally brittle under the moon, which blazed in windows that looked its way. The futility of the black-out became laughable: from the sky, presumably, you could see every slate in the roofs, every whited kerb, every contour of the naked winter flowerbeds in the park; and the lake, with its shining twists and tree-darkened islands would be a landmark for miles, yes, miles, overhead.

However, the sky, in whose glassiness floated no clouds but only opaque balloons, remained glassy-silent. The Germans no longer came by the full moon. Something more immaterial seemed to threaten, and to be keeping people at home. This day between days, this extra tax, was perhaps more than senses and nerves could bear. People stayed indoors with a fervour that could be felt: the buildings strained with battened-down human life, but not a beam, not a voice, not a note from a radio escaped. Now and then under streets and buildings the earth rumbled: the Underground sounded loudest at this time.

Outside the now gateless gates of the park, the road coming downhill from the north-west turned south and became a street, down whose perspective the traffic lights went through their unmeaning performance of changing colour. From the promontory of pavement outside the gates you saw at once up the road and down the street: from behind where you stood, between the gateposts, appeared the lesser strangeness of grass and water and trees. At this point, at this moment, three French soldiers, directed to a hostel they could not find, stopped singing to listen derisively to the waterbirds wakened up by the moon. Next, two wardens coming off duty emerged from their post and crossed the road diagonally, each with an elbow cupped inside a slung-on tin hat. The wardens turned their faces, mauve in the moonlight, towards the Frenchmen with no expression at all. The two sets of steps died in opposite directions, and, the birds subsiding, nothing was heard or seen until, a little way down the street, a trickle of people came out of the Underground, around the anti-panic brick wall. These all disappeared quickly, in an abashed way, or as though dissolved in the street by some white acid, but for a girl and a soldier who, by their way of walking, seemed to have no destination but each other and to be not quite certain even of that. Blotted into one shadow, he tall, she little, these two proceeded towards the park. They looked in, but did not go in; they stood there debating without speaking. Then, as though a command from the street behind them had been received by their synchronized bodies, they faced round to look back the way they had come.

His look up the height of a building made his head drop back, and she saw his eyeballs glitter. She slid her hand from his sleeve, stepped to the edge of the pavement and said: "Mysterious Kôr."

"What is?" he said, not quite collecting himself.

"This is—

> '*Mysterious Kôr thy walls forsaken stand,*
> *Thy lonely towers beneath a lonely moon—*'

—this is Kôr."

"Why," he said, "it's years since I've thought of that."

She said: "I think of it all the time—

> '*Not in the waste beyond the swamps and sand,*
> *The fever-haunted forest and lagoon,*
> *Mysterious Kôr thy walls——*'

—a completely forsaken city, as high as cliffs and as white as bones, with no history—"

"But something must once have happened: why had it been forsaken?"

"How could anyone tell you when there's nobody there?"

"Nobody there since how long?"

"Thousands of years."

"In that case, it would have fallen down."

"No, not Kôr," she said with immediate authority. "Kôr's altogether different; it's very strong; there is not a crack in it anywhere for a weed to grow in; the corners of stones and the monuments might have been cut yesterday, and the stairs and arches are built to support themselves."

"You know all about it," he said, looking at her.

"I know, I know all about it."

"What, since you read that book?"

"Oh, I didn't get much from that; I just got the name. I knew that must be the right name; it's like a cry."

"Most like the cry of a crow to me." He reflected, then said: "But the poem begins with 'Not'—'*Not in the waste beyond the swamps and sand—*' And it goes on, as I remember, to prove Kôr's not really anywhere. When a poem says there's no such place—"

"What it tries to say doesn't matter: I see what it makes me see. Anyhow, that was written some time ago, at that time when they thought they had got everything taped, because the whole world had been explored, even the middle of Africa. Every thing and place had been found and marked on some map; so what wasn't marked on any map couldn't be there at all. So *they* thought: that was why he wrote the poem. '*The world is disenchanted.*' it goes on. That was what set me off hating civilization."

"Well, cheer up," he said; "there isn't much of it left."

"Oh, yes, I cheered up some time ago. This war shows we've by no means come to the end. If you can blow whole places out of existence, you can blow whole places into it. I don't see why not. They say we can't say what's come out since the bombing started. By the time we've come to the end, Kôr may be the one city left: the abiding city. I should laugh."

"No, you wouldn't," he said sharply. "*You* wouldn't —at least, I hope not. I hope you don't know what you're saying—does the moon make you funny?"

"Don't be cross about Kôr; please don't, Arthur," she said.

"I thought girls thought about people."

"What, these days?" she said. "Think about people? How can anyone think about people if they've got any heart? I don't know how other girls manage: I always think about Kôr."

"Not about me?" he said. When she did not at once answer, he turned her hand over, in anguish, inside his grasp. "Because I'm not there when you want me—is that my fault?"

"But to think about Kôr *is* to think about you and me."

"In that dead place?"

"No, ours—we'd be alone there."

Tightening his thumb on her palm while he thought this over, he looked behind them, around them, above them—even up at the sky. He said finally: "But we're alone here."

"That was why I said 'Mysterious Kôr.'"

"What, you mean we're there now, that here's there, that now's then? . . . *I* don't mind," he added, letting out as a laugh the sigh he had been holding in for some time. "You ought to know the place, and for all I could tell you we might be anywhere: I often do have it, this funny feeling, the first minute or two when I've come up out of the Underground. Well, well: join the Army and see the world." He nodded towards the perspective of traffic lights and said, a shade craftily: "What are those, then?"

Having caught the quickest possible breath, she replied: "Inexhaustible gases; they bored through to them and lit them as they came up; by changing colour they show the changing of minutes; in Kôr there is no sort of other time."

"You've got the moon, though: that can't help making months."

"Oh, and the sun, of course; but those two could do what they liked; we should not have to calculate when they'd come or go."

"We might not have to," he said, "but I bet I should."

"I should not mind what you did, so long as you never said, 'What next?' "

"I don't know about 'next,' but I do know what we'd do first."

"What, Arthur?"

"Populate Kôr."

She said: "I suppose it would be all right if our children were to marry each other?"

But her voice faded out; she had been reminded that they were homeless on this his first night of leave. They were, that was to say, in London without any hope of any place of their own. Pepita shared a two-roomed flatlet with a girl friend, in a by-street off the Regent's Park Road, and towards this they must make their half-hearted way. Arthur was to have the sitting-room divan, usually occupied by Pepita, while she herself had half of her girl friend's bed. There was really no room for a third, and least of all for a man, in those small rooms packed with furniture and the two girls' belongings: Pepita tried to be grateful for her friend Callie's forbearance—but how could she be, when it had not occurred to Callie that she would do better to be away to-night? She was more slow-witted than narrow-minded—but Pepita felt she owed a kind of ruin to her. Callie, not yet known to be home later than ten, would be now waiting up, in her house-coat, to welcome Arthur. That would mean three-sided chat, drinking cocoa, then turning in: that would be that, and that would be all. That was London, this war—they were lucky to have a roof—London, full enough before the Americans came. Not a place: they would even grudge you sharing a grave—that was what even married couples complained. Whereas in Kôr . . .

In Kôr . . . Like glass, the illusion shattered: a car hummed like a hornet towards them, veered, showed its scarlet tail-light, streaked away up the road. A woman edged round a front door and along the area railings timidly called her cat; meanwhile a clock near, then another set further back in the dazzling distance, set about striking midnight. Pepita, feeling Arthur release her arm with an abruptness that was the inverse of passion, shivered; whereat he asked brusquely: "Cold? Well, which way?—we'd better be getting on."

Callie was no longer waiting up. Hours ago she had set out the three cups and saucers, the tins of cocoa and household milk and, on the gas-ring, brought the kettle to just short of the boil. She had turned open Arthur's bed, the living-room divan, in the neat inviting way she had learnt at home—then, with a modest impulse, replaced the cover. She had, as Pepita foresaw, been wearing her cretonne house-coat, the nearest thing to a hostess gown that she had; she had already brushed her hair for the night, rebraided it, bound the braids in a coronet round her head. Both lights and the wireless had been on, to make the room both look and sound gay: all alone, she had come to that peak moment at which company should arrive—but so seldom does. From then on she felt welcome beginning to wither in her, a flower of the heart that had bloomed too early. There she had sat like an image, facing the three cold cups, on the edge of the bed to be occupied by an unknown man.

Callie's innocence and her still unsought-out state had brought her to take a proprietary pride in Arthur; this was all the stronger, perhaps, because they had not yet met. Sharing the flat with Pepita, this last year, she had been content with reflecting heat of love. It was not, surprisingly, that Pepita seemed very happy—there were times when she was palpably on the rack, and this was not what Callie could understand. "Surely you owe it to Arthur," she would then say, "to keep cheerful? So long as you love each other——" Callie's calm brow glowed— one might say that it glowed in place of her friend's; she became the guardian of that ideality which for Pepita was constantly lost to view. It was true, with the sudden prospect of Arthur's leave, things had come nearer to earth: he became a proposition, and she would have been as glad if he could have slept somewhere else. Physically shy, a brotherless virgin, Callie shrank from sharing this flat with a young man. In this flat you could hear everything: what was once a three-windowed Victorian drawing-room had been partitioned, by very thin walls, into kitchenette, living-room, Callie's bedroom. The living-room was in the centre; the two others opened off it. What was once the conservatory, half a flight down, was now converted into a draughty bathroom, shared with somebody else on the girls' floor. The flat, for these days, was cheap—even so, it was Callie, earning more than Pepita, who paid the greater part of the rent: it thus became up to her, more or less, to express goodwill as to Arthur's making a third. "Why, it will be lovely to have him here," Callie said. Pepita accepted the goodwill without much grace—but then, had she ever much grace to spare?—she was as restlessly secretive, as self-centred, as a little half-grown black cat. Next came a puzzling moment: Pepita seemed to be hinting that Callie should fix herself up somewhere else. "But where would I go?" Callie marvelled when this was at last borne in on her. "You know what London's like now. And, anyway"—here she laughed, but hers was a forehead that coloured as easily as it glowed—"it wouldn't be proper, would it, me going off and leaving just you and Arthur; I don't know what your mother would say to me. No, we may be a little squashed, but we'll make things ever so homey. I shall not mind playing gooseberry, really, dear."

But the hominess by now was evaporating, as Pepita and Arthur still and still did not come. At half-past ten, in obedience to the rule of the house, Callie was obliged to turn off the wireless, whereupon silence out of the stepless street began seeping into the slighted room. Callie recollected the fuel target and turned off her dear little table lamp, gaily painted with spots to make it look like a toadstool, thereby leaving only the hanging light. She laid her hand on the kettle, to find it gone cold again and sighed for the wasted gas if not for her wasted thought. Where are they? Cold crept up her out of the kettle; she went to bed.

Callie's bed lay along the wall under the window: she did not like sleeping so close up under glass, but the clearance that must be left for the opening of door and cupboards made this the only possible place. Now she got in and lay rigidly on the bed's inner side, under the hanging hems of the window curtains, training her limbs not to stray to what would be Pepita's half. This sharing of her bed with another body would not be the least of her sacrifice to the lovers' love; to-night would be the first night—or at least, since she was an infant—that Callie had slept with anyone. Child of a sheltered middle-class household, she had kept physical distances all her life. Already repugnance and shyness ran through her limbs; she was preyed upon by some more obscure trouble than the expectation that she might not sleep. As to *that*, Pepita was restless; her tossings on the divan, her broken-off exclamations and blurred pleas had been to be heard, most nights, through the dividing wall.

Callie knew, as though from a vision, that Arthur would sleep soundly, with assurance and majesty. Did they not all say, too, that a soldier sleeps like a log? With awe she pictured, asleep, the face that she had not yet, awake, seen—Arthur's man's eyelids, cheek-bones and set mouth turned up to the darkened ceiling. Wanting to savour darkness herself, Callie reached out and put off her bedside lamp.

At once she knew that something was happening— outdoors, in the street, the whole of London, the world.

An advance, an extraordinary movement was silently taking place; blue-white beams overflowed from it, silting, dropping round the edges of the muffling black-out curtains. When, starting up, she knocked a fold of the curtain, a beam like a mouse ran across her bed. A searchlight, the most powerful of all time, might have been turned full and steady upon her defended window; finding flaws in the black-out stuff, it made veins and stars. Once gained by this idea of pressure she could not lie down again; she sat tautly, drawn-up knees touching her breasts, and asked herself if there were anything she should do. She parted the curtains, opened them slowly wider, looked out—and was face to face with the moon.

Below the moon, the houses opposite her window blazed black in transparent shadow; and something—was it a coin or a ring?—glittered half-way across the chalk-white street. Light marched in past her face, and she turned to see where it went: out stood the curves and garlands of the great white marble Victorian mantelpiece of that lost drawing-room; out stood, in the photographs turned her way, the thoughts with which her parents had faced the camera, and the humble puzzlement of her two dogs at home. Of silver brocade, just faintly purpled with roses, became her house-coat hanging over the chair. And the moon did more: it exonerated and beautified the lateness of the lovers' return. No wonder, she said to herself, no wonder—if this was the world they walked in, if this was whom they were with. Having drunk in the white explanation, Callie lay down again. Her half of the bed was in shadow, but she allowed one hand to lie, blanched, in what would be Pepita's place. She lay and looked at the hand until it was no longer her own.

Callie woke to the sound of Pepita's key in the latch. But no voices? What had happened? Then she heard Arthur's step. She heard his unslung equipment dropped with a weary, dull sound, and the plonk of his tin hat on a wooden chair. "Sssh-sssh!" Pepita exclaimed, "she *might* be asleep!"

Then at last Arthur's voice: "But I thought you said——"

"I'm not asleep; I'm just coming!" Callie called out with rapture, leaping out from her form in shadow into the moonlight, zipping on her enchanted house-coat over her night-dress, kicking her shoes on, and pinning in place, with a trembling firmness, her plaits in their coronet round her head. Between these movements of hers she heard not another sound. Had she only dreamed they were there? Her heart beat: she stepped through the living-room, shutting her door behind her.

Pepita and Arthur stood the other side of the table; they gave the impression of being lined up. Their faces, at different levels—for Pepita's rough, dark head came only an inch above Arthur's khaki shoulder—were alike in abstention from any kind of expression; as though, spiritually, they both still refused to be here. Their features looked faint, weathered—was this the work of the moon? Pepita said at once: "I suppose we are very late?"

"I don't wonder," Callie said, "on this lovely night."

Arthur had not raised his eyes; he was looking at the three cups. Pepita now suddenly jogged his elbow, saying, "Arthur, wake up; say something; this is Callie—well, Callie, this is Arthur, of course."

"Why, yes, of course this is Arthur," returned Callie, whose candid eyes since she entered had not left Arthur's face. Perceiving that Arthur did not know what to do, she advanced round the table to shake hands with him. He looked up, she looked down, for the first time: she rather beheld than felt his red-brown grip on what still seemed her glove of moonlight. "Welcome, Arthur," she said. "I'm so glad to meet you at last. I hope you will be comfortable in the flat."

"It's been kind of you," he said after consideration.

"Please do not feel that," said Callie. "This is Pepita's home, too, and we both hope—don't we, Pepita?—that you'll regard it as yours. Please feel free to do just as you like. I am sorry it is so small."

"Oh, I don't know," Arthur said, as though hypnotized; "it seems a nice little place."

Pepita, meanwhile, glowered and turned away.

Arthur continued to wonder, though he had once been

told, how these two unalike girls had come to set up together—Pepita so small, except for her too-big head, compact of childish brusqueness and of unchildish passion,
and Callie, so sedate, waxy and tall—an unlit candle. Yes,
she was like one of those candles on sale outside a church;
there could be something votive even in her demeanour.
She was unconscious that her good manners, those of an
old-fashioned country doctor's daughter, were putting
the other two at a disadvantage. He found himself touched
by the grave good faith with which Callie was wearing
that tartish house-coat, above which her face kept the
glaze of sleep; and, as she knelt to relight the gas-ring
under the kettle, he marked the strong, delicate arch of
one bare foot, disappearing into the arty green shoe.
Pepita was now too near him ever again to be seen as he
now saw Callie—in a sense, he never *had* seen Pepita for
the first time: she had not been, and still sometimes was
not, his type. No, he had not thought of her twice; he had
not remembered her until he began to remember her with
passion. You might say he had not seen Pepita coming:
their love had been a collision in the dark.

Callie, determined to get this over, knelt back and said:
"Would Arthur like to wash his hands?" When they had
heard him stumble down the half-flight of stairs, she said
to Pepita: "Yes, I was so glad you had the moon."

"Why?" said Pepita. She added: "There was too
much of it."

"You're tired. Arthur looks tired, too."

"How would you know? He's used to marching about.
But it's all this having no place to go."

"But, Pepita, you—"

But at this point Arthur came back: from the door he
noticed the wireless, and went direct to it. "Nothing much
on now, I suppose?" he doubtfully said.

"No; you see it's past midnight; we're off the air. And,
anyway, in this house they don't like the wireless late.
By the same token," went on Callie, friendlily smiling,
"I'm afraid I must ask you, Arthur, to take your boots
off, unless, of course, you mean to stay sitting down. The
people below us—"

Pepita flung off, saying something under her breath, but Arthur, remarking, "No, I don't mind," both sat down and began to take off his boots. Pausing, glancing to left and right at the divan's fresh cotton spread, he said: "It's all right is it, for me to sit on this?"

"That's my bed," said Pepita. "You are to sleep in it."

Callie then made the cocoa, after which they turned in. Preliminary trips to the bathroom having been worked out, Callie was first to retire, shutting the door behind her so that Pepita and Arthur might kiss each other good night. When Pepita joined her, it was without knocking: Pepita stood still in the moon and began to tug off her clothes. Glancing with hate at the bed, she asked: "Which side?"

"I expected you'd like the outside."

"What are you standing about for?"

"I don't really know: as I'm inside I'd better get in first."

"Then why not get in?"

When they had settled rigidly, side by side, Callie asked: "Do you think Arthur's got all he wants?"

Pepita jerked her head up. "We can't sleep in all this moon."

"Why, you don't believe the moon does things, actually?"

"Well, it couldn't hope to make some of us *much* more screwy."

Callie closed the curtains, then said: "What do you mean? And—didn't you hear?—I asked if Arthur's got all he wants."

"That's what I meant—have you got a screw loose, really?"

"Pepita, I won't stay here if you're going to be like this."

"In that case, you had better go in with Arthur."

"What about me?" Arthur loudly said through the wall. "I can hear practically all you girls are saying."

They were both startled—rather that than abashed. Arthur, alone in there, had thrown off the ligatures of his social manner: his voice held the whole authority of his sex—he was impatient, sleepy, and he belonged to no one.

"Sorry," the girls said in unison. Then Pepita laughed soundlessly, making their bed shake, till to stop herself she bit the back of her hand, and this movement made her elbow strike Callie's cheek. "Sorry," she had to whisper. No answer: Pepita fingered her elbow and found, yes, it was quite true, it was wet. "Look, shut up crying, Callie: what have I done?"

Callie rolled right round, in order to press her forehead closely under the window, into the curtains, against the wall. Her weeping continued to be soundless: now and then, unable to reach her handkerchief, she staunched her eyes with a curtain, disturbing slivers of moon. Pepita gave up marvelling, and soon slept: at least there is something in being dog-tired.

A clock struck four as Callie woke up again—but something else had made her open her swollen eyelids. Arthur, stumbling about on his padded feet, could be heard next door attempting to make no noise. Inevitably, he bumped the edge of the table. Callie sat up: by her side Pepita lay like a mummy rolled half over, in forbidding, tenacious sleep. Arthur groaned. Callie caught a breath, climbed lightly over Pepita, felt for her torch on the mantelpiece, stopped to listen again. Arthur groaned again: Callie, with movements soundless as they were certain, opened the door and slipped through to the living-room. "What's the matter?" she whispered. "Are you ill?"

"No; I just got a cigarette. Did I wake you up?"

"But you groaned."

"I'm sorry; I'd no idea."

"But do you often?"

"I've no idea, really, I tell you," Arthur repeated. The air of the room was dense with his presence, overhung by tobacco. He must be sitting on the edge of his bed, wrapped up in his overcoat—she could smell the coat, and each time he pulled on the cigarette his features appeared down there, in the fleeting, dull reddish glow. "Where are you?" he said. "Show a light."

Her nervous touch on her torch, like a reflex to what

he said, made it flicker up for a second. "I am just by the door; Pepita's asleep; I'd better go back to bed."

"Listen. Do you two get on each other's nerves?"

"Not till to-night," said Callie, watching the uncertain swoops of the cigarette as he reached across to the ash-tray on the edge of the table. Shifting her bare feet patiently, she added: "You don't see us as we usually are."

"She's a girl who shows things in funny ways—I expect she feels bad at our putting you out like this—I know I do. But then we'd got no choice, had we?"

"It is really I who am putting you out," said Callie.

"Well, that can't be helped either, can it? You had the right to stay in your own place. If there'd been more time, we might have gone to the country, though I still don't see where we'd have gone there. It's one harder when you're not married, unless you've got the money. Smoke?"

"No, thank you. Well, if you're all right, I'll go back to bed."

"I'm glad she's asleep—funny the way she sleeps, isn't it? You can't help wondering where she is. You haven't got a boy, have you, just at present?"

"No. I've never had one."

"I'm not sure in one way that you're not better off. I can see there's not so much in it for a girl these days. It makes me feel cruel the way I unsettle her: I don't know how much it's me myself or how much it's something the matter that I can't help. How are any of us to know how things could have been? They forget war's not just only war; it's years out of people's lives that they've never had before and won't have again. Do you think she's fanci-ful?"

"Who, Pepita?"

"It's enough to make her—to-night was the pay-off. We couldn't get near any movie or any place for sitting; you had to fight into the bars, and she hates the staring in bars, and with all that milling about, every street we went, they kept on knocking her even off my arm. So then we took the tube to that park down there, but the place was as bad as daylight, let alone it was cold. We hadn't the nerve—well, that's nothing to do with you."

"I don't mind."

"Or else you don't understand. So we began to play—
we were off in Kôr."

"Core of what?"

"Mysterious Kôr—ghost city."

"Where?"

"You may ask. But I could have sworn she saw it, and
from the way she saw it I saw it, too. A game's a game,
but what's a hallucination? You begin by laughing, then
it gets in you and you can't laugh it off. I tell you, I woke
up just now not knowing where I'd been; and I had to
get up and feel round this table before I even knew where
I was. It wasn't till then that I thought of a cigarette.
Now I see why she sleeps like that, if that's where she
goes."

"But she is just as often restless; I often hear her."

"Then she doesn't always make it. Perhaps it takes me,
in some way—— Well, I can't see any harm: when two
people have got no place, why not want Kôr, as a start?
There are no restrictions on wanting, at any rate."

"But, oh, Arthur, can't wanting want what's human?"

He yawned. "To be human's to be at a dead loss." Stopping yawning, he ground out his cigarette: the china tray
skidded at the edge of the table. "Bring that light here a
moment—that is, will you? I think I've messed ash all over
these sheets of hers."

Callie advanced with the torch alight, but at arm's
length: now and then her thumb made the beam wobble.
She watched the lit-up inside of Arthur's hand as he
brushed the sheet; and once he looked up to see her
white-nightgowned figure curving above and away from
him, behind the arc of light. "What's that swinging?"

"One of my plaits of hair. Shall I open the window
wider?"

"What, to let the smoke out? Go on. And how's your
moon?"

"Mine?" Marvelling over this, as the first sign that
Arthur remembered that she was Callie, she uncovered
the window, pushed up the sash, then after a minute said:
"Not so strong."

Indeed, the moon's power over London and the im-

agination had now declined. The siege of light had relaxed; the search was over; the street had a look of sur-
vival and no more. Whatever had glittered there, coin or
ring, was now invisible or had gone. To Callie it seemed
likely that there would never be such a moon again; and
on the whole she felt this was for the best. Feeling air
reach in like a tired arm round her body, she dropped
the curtains against it and returned to her own room.

Back by her bed, she listened: Pepita's breathing still
had the regular sound of sleep. At the other side of the
wall the divan creaked as Arthur stretched himself out
again. Having felt ahead of her lightly, to make sure her
half was empty, Callie climbed over Pepita and got in.
A certain amount of warmth had travelled between the
sheets from Pepita's flank, and in this Callie extended her
sword-cold body: she tried to compose her limbs; even
they quivered after Arthur's words in the dark, words
to the dark. The loss of her own mysterious expectation,
of her love for love, was a small thing beside the war's
total of unlived lives. Suddenly Pepita flung out one hand:
its back knocked Callie lightly across the face.

Pepita had now turned over and lay with her face up.
The hand that had struck Callie must have lain over the
other, which grasped the pyjama collar. Her eyes, in the
dark, might have been either shut or open, but nothing
made her frown more or less steadily: it became certain,
after another moment, that Pepita's act of justice had
been unconscious. She still lay, as she had lain, in an avid
dream, of which Arthur had been the source, of which
Arthur was not the end. With him she looked this way,
that way, down the wide, void, pure streets, between
statues, pillars and shadows, through archways and col-
onnades. With him she went up the stairs down which
nothing but moon came; with him trod the ermine dust
of the endless halls, stood on terraces, mounted the extreme tower, looked down on the statued squares, the
wide, void, pure streets. He was the password, but not
the answer: it was to Kôr's finality that she turned.

ELIZABETH BOWEN, *Anglo-Irish novelist and short-story writer, was born in Dublin in 1898. A lasting attachment to her native Ireland and County Cork inspired two works of nonfiction,* The Shelbourne Hotel *(1951) and* Bowen's Court *(1942). Among her novels are* The House in Paris *(1936),* The Death of the Heart *(1939),* The Heat of the Day *(1949), and* A World of Love *(1955). Her books of short stories include* Look at All Those Roses *(1941) and* Ivy Gripped the Steps *(1946).*

The text of this book is set in Caledonia, a Linotype face designed by W. A. Dwiggins. Caledonia belongs to the family of printing types called "modern face" by printers—a term used to mark the change in style of type-letters that occurred about 1800. Caledonia borders on the general design of Scotch Modern, but is more freely drawn than that letter. Composed, printed, and bound by THE COLONIAL PRESS INC., Clinton, Massachusetts. Paper manufactured by S. D. WARREN COMPANY, Boston, Massachusetts. Cover design by ALFRED ZALON.

Vintage Books